The Siege of Shadow

Quinton A. Foote

Explore the world of Litore on all social media platforms and wherever you get your Podcasts.

PRODUCTIONS

To my parents and sisters, who never failed to encourage my dreams.

To my friends who helped blossom my love of story telling.

And to my very own Queen Em, the love of my life.

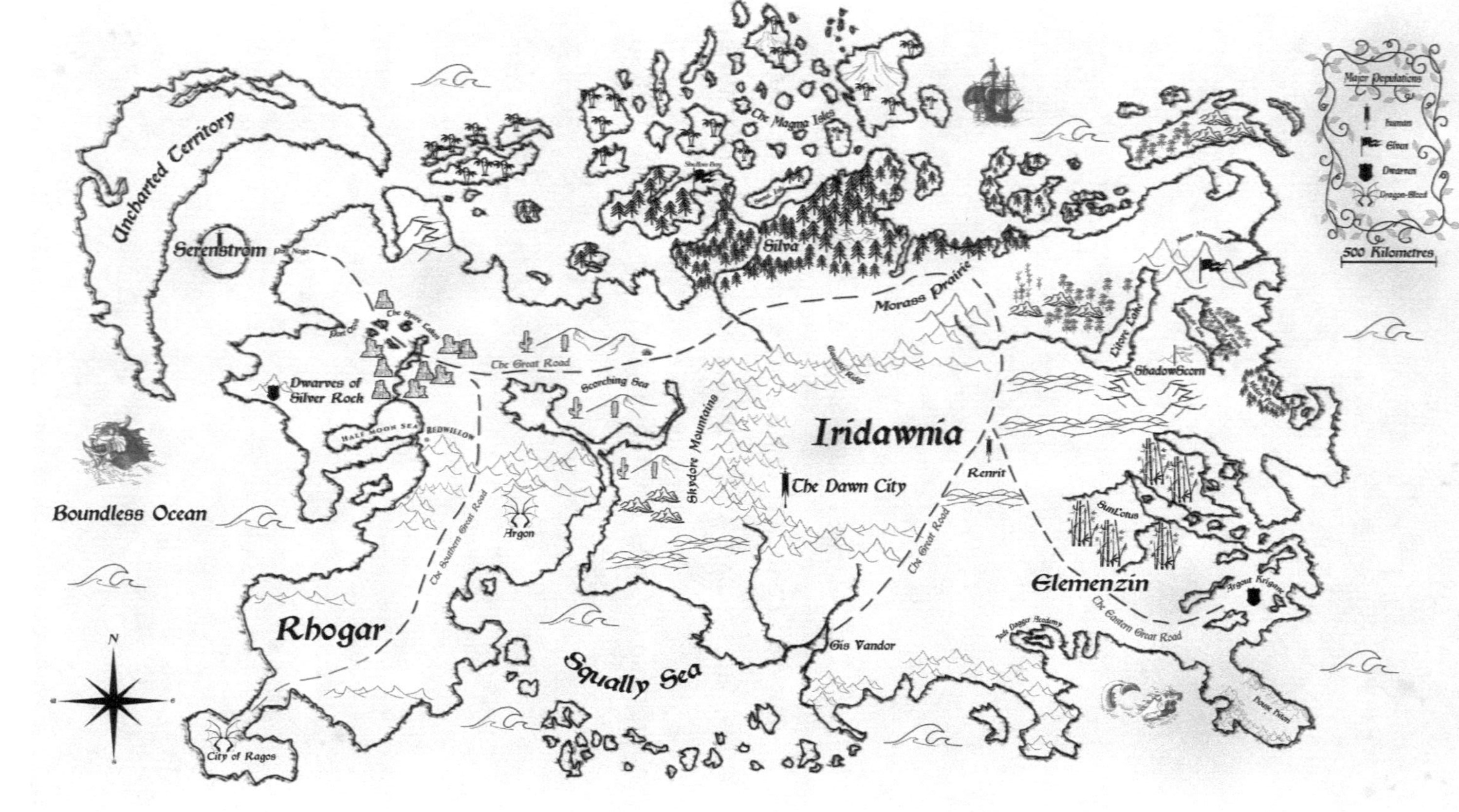

Uncharted Territory
Serenstrom
Boundless Ocean
Rhogar
City of Rages
Dwarves of Silver Rock
The Spire Lakes
Half Moon Sea
Redwillow
The Southern Great Road
Argon
The Great Road
Scorching Sea
Skydore Mountains
Iridawnia
The Dawn City
Silva
The Magma Isles
Morass Prairie
Litore Lake
Shadowthorn
Renrit
The Great Road
SunLotus
Elemenzin
The Eastern Great Road
Gis Vandor
Squally Sea
N
Major Populations
Human
Elven
Dwarven
Dragon-Blood
500 Kilometres

Map of Litore

Table of Contents

"Open the gate!" A Scorn Guard captain shouted from atop the high walls protecting the City of Shadow. Below, two other Scorn Guard began cranking a huge winch that would raise the iradinium portcullis as four other guards swung the massive stone gates inward. Before this was even accomplished, Scorn soldiers by the hundreds were attempting to retreat back into their city. A rainfall of arrows coated the retreating warriors as the largest army of Sesaran soldiers ever brought to ShadowScorn mercilessly slaughtered them.

"My King! You must retreat!" Commander Brenis Andula of the Scorn Guard screamed at King Arwr. The king, in his physical prime was cutting down the besiegers with a fervour he had only known a handful of times in his life. Roiling storm clouds hung low above them, turning the highlands surrounding ShadowScorn into a soggy mess. The blood of fallen humans and Scorn dyed the fields of green and yellow moss, red and black. In a second that felt eternal, King Arwr, third king of ShadowScorn saw his penultimate foe leading this army, and knew it to be Ivan the Revered. Gleaming white and gold plate mail, wielding a sword that delivered pulses of devastating blue energy with every swing meant another innocent Scorn had met their end. King Arwr moved a step forward, determined to end this now, no matter the odds stacked against him. He was struck in the back of the head, by none other than his son, Prince Scarnin.

"Brenis, help me!" Scarnin shouted, and soon the two burly Scorn elves were dragging their king away. An elite female force known as the 'Ghosts of Aceia' shadow-walked in front of their leaders to cover their retreat.

Ivan the Revered, Arch Paladin of Sesara, was in his early thirties and was known throughout their faith as their greatest warrior. He had never lost a campaign and watched now, from horseback as his greatest enemy to date was retreating back behind their walls with defeat nipping at their heels.

"Longbows!" Ivan shouted over his army. In expert rehearsal, the short-bow archers who had been laying down heavy fire on the retreating soldiers, swapped positions with the long-bow archers, who proceeded to aim their volleys over the high walls to now rain down on the Scorn scrambling for shelter. No sooner did the bell atop the royal palace ring, signifying all residents to retreat into its great halls. Ivan watched on with the smugness of a youth too cunning and powerful to understand his own detriment.

Arch Priest Torvic Gloom was on the city streets, tending to wounded soldiers and helping panicked citizens to the palace, when the arrows began soaring over the walls. He watched as Scorn by the dozens fell to the ground with one or more arrows protruding from their flesh. He was the most proficient arcane master in the city and rallied his other priests to conjure a barrier of smoky magic that shielded many of those retreating, yet he was left to curse himself for not being able to save more.

Inside the palace, the citizens were met with a youthful Princess Scáth and their outspoken Queen Katia. They both worked tirelessly to assure the Scorn flooding inside that everything would be okay, and offered various items of comfort. Eventually, they were relieved of that role as they saw Arwr being carried in by Prince Scarnin and Commander Brenis. They were escorted by Brenis' daughter and Scáth's dearest friend, Aelis. She was her fathers equal in almost every respect, save a century of battle experience. Scáth and Aelis embraced tightly; the princess was elated to see her closest friend in this life unscathed from another battle.

"Aelis, enact a full lock down," Brenis commanded his daughter. She nodded firmly and sprinted off to organize the remaining Scorn Guard.

"What happened to him?" Katia asked with a demeanour akin to scolding.

"You know father," Scarnin answered out of breath. "He was going to get himself killed"

Katia rolled her eyes at her son's rash actions but conceded the point.

"Get him to our chamber," she instructed. "Find Torvic," she demanded rather harshly of Scáth who proceeded to do so without question.

Within half an hour they were all inside the royal bedchamber and Torvic was healing the head wound Arwr had received from his son, including the many cuts and gashes from the hours long battle before. Scáth and her brother were on a veranda attached to the bedchamber as Brenis and Katia watched Torvic's good work.

The royal siblings observed as the Sesaran soldiers rolled what looked like two giant crossbows fastened together, near the city wall. There were over a dozen of the strange contraptions and as they launched the first one, it soared over the wall and the metal head sprung apart acting like a huge grapple. From there, spiked wheels were turned, causing the wood linked rope to go taught, forming a sort of ramp to ascend the wall on. Thanks to the quick thinking of Brenis, the main gate and portcullis could not be opened after he ordered his guards to sabotage the winches. However, their enemies flooded up the ramps and over the wall by the hundreds.

"There it is, the first time our walls are breached," Scarnin voiced in disbelief. Scáth unconsciously dug her finger nails into the smooth stone handrail in horror. The pair were ripped from their shock as Scarnin was gripped firmly by the collar, spun around, and struck in the face by his father.

Brenis, Torvic and Katia were surprisingly cowed by their kings vulgar behaviour. Scarnin was struck twice more as Arwr berated him before the prince hit the ground.

"Look at what you've done!" He shouted. "I could have prevented this!" Arwr lifted his son back up and forced him to watch their enemies marching through ShadowScorn streets. Scáth saw the tears streaming Scarnin's face but he dare not whimper.

"Da!" She yelled at her father, matching his level of voice. "It's not his fault." When this did nothing to stop the king, she did the unthinkable, and slapped her father. He flicked his fiery gaze upon his daughter, upon his 'little shadow.' Scáth did not back down, for their bond was stronger than most. She knew her father was better than this, and expected him to act like it. Arwr released his son, and looked away from Scáth, utterly ashamed but too proud or perhaps angry to show it. He left the room, summoning his commander to follow. Torvic remained with his eyes to the floor as Queen Katia strolled up to her children and helped Scarnin up.

"Ever strike your father again, and I will teach you a real lesson, girl." She threatened her daughter with an air of coldheartedness which Scáth was somewhat accustomed to from her mother. Their relationship had always been contentious and the two often butt-heads. The princess understood emotions were flying high but felt her mother had just crossed a line; or revealed true feelings.

"Tend to the wounded, Arch Priest, and take my insolent daughter with you," Katia demanded, and Torvic was all too glad to be dismissed.

"Get these doors open," Ivan directed to one of his finest engineers and a team of dwarves, who appeared pleased by the challenge. Ivan Fjell stood atop the City of Shadow for a long while, basking in his achievement. He understood now that victory was only a matter of time. He was the Arch Paladin of his faith and would go down in history as the one to fulfill Sesara's edicts. Long ago, a Macer Erik in Serenstrom declared that Sesara came to him in a vision, decreeing that the ShadowScorn were a mockery, placed on Litore by Aceia to spite the goddess of life. 900 years later, he stood where none had before. He brushed his thick blood soaked brown hair back from his face and walked down into the city. He entered an ornate home that had been somewhat converted into a base of operations for him. Maps, letters, and updates on his troops were scattered across a large blackglass table. A steaming bowl of water had been placed on a hutch, and Ivan quickly cleaned his face and hair. Taking a deep breath he looked up as bloody water dripped from his beard. He saw a humble oil painting of two Scorn humans and their baby, hanging above his vat of water. He removed it from the wall and stared into the life-like portrait for a significant length of time.

"Ivan," A feminine voice beckoned behind him. He swiftly spun himself around but no one was there. The veteran paladin skeptically scanned the room before unceremoniously dropping the small portrait into the soiled water. Ivan left the home when the skin on his neck crawled as if being spied on. In fact, a great sense of discomfort had consumed him since entering that Scorn home, and he now itched to be done with this campaign. As he walked through the smooth stone streets, scores of soldiers moved out of his way and bowed in respect to him. Nearing the palace, he heard a commotion down one alley. He paused at the precipice of it, and peered in. Three figures were standing around a fourth smaller one, pushing them around and acting loudly. Ivan immediately recognized the situation and approached.

"What is the meaning of this?" Ivan asked, rather jovially. His men looked at their fearless leader with awe as they stood around a helpless, weeping Scorn lad.

'We found ourselves one of them," one man replied.

"We're just thinking about having ourselves a little fun with the welp," A second soldier piped up, rather lewdly. The other two laughed in merriment at that comment.

Ivan's demeanour changed like the flick of a ravens head. "You will stand at attention when addressing your superior." The soldiers laughed at that, too caught up in the elation of their victory, and most likely dreaming up what awful things they could do to their captive. Ivan clocked the nearest soldier in the temple, dropping him to the ground, cold. Unconscious.

They immediately stomped one foot, stood up straight in attention with their hands firmly at their sides.

"You will pick up this weakling, and submit yourselves to the nearest C.O for 30 lashings each. Do you understand me?" Ivan spat vehemently at them.

"Yes, Sir!" They both answered in unison, before swiftly picking up their still-limp comrade, exiting the alley. Ivan stood over the Scorn who remained on his knees, shaking with fear.

"Your age?" he demanded, but the Scorn did not answer. Ivan got down to one knee and spoke with more empathy. "Your age, lad?"

"Nine, sir," the Scorn answered, speaking formally as he had heard the soldiers do. Ivan put his gauntleted hand under the child's chin and lifted it to meet his own piercing brown eyes. The boys pupils appeared as swirling orbs of shadow, almost like the eye of a hurricane.

"I'm giving you a chance. Do not get caught again," Ivan asserted, as if giving advice, which of course he was. The life of a Scorn outside these walls was one on the run, rarely accepted or able to settle and build a life. The price of a single ShadowScorn on the slaver market was enough to live the rest of your days in opulence and never have to lift a finger again. The Arch Paladin stood up and left the alley. As he walked closer to the palace, he noted the men he had reprimanded getting their lashes. Ivan's reputation was one of sheer respect in his world. Soldiers and citizens revered the very air Ivan breathed, solely based on their respect for him. He was kind but brutal, cunning yet empathetic, and the type of leader all looked up too.

"I woke up with Torvic over me and felt the din of battle still. I would never hurt Scarnin; I do not know what came over me." King Arwr confessed to his closest friend and wisest adviser, Brenis Andula. The pair stood in the council hall where great floor to ceiling windows overlooked the city. Brenis considered his friends' words as he watched the Sesaran soldiers roam his streets: the very streets he grew up on and knew like the lines of his palm.

"There is a first for everything," his voice strained. "Including the fact that I am for once without counsel to offer."

That bothered Arwr more than he wanted to express. He leaned heavily on his friend Brenis during war times, for there was no greater strategist in ShadowScorn. Even though Arwr was capable of, and excelled at, creating a plan of attack, few could do it with Commander Andula's spontaneity and effectiveness.

"Any attempts to reach out to Aceia have been met with eerie silence," Arwr said as if he were an abandoned child. Brenis nodded, expecting such bad luck. "Perhaps we should have met our end on the highlands. Our cage has never been smaller," Arwr added, in a rare moment of defeat.

"If your subjects were to hear such-"

"-I am not speaking to one of my subjects." Arwr cut his friend short. "I am speaking to an equal. A brother." The king finished by putting one hand on Brenis' shoulder and firmly gripped him. Brenis looked at him, his eyes brimming with pride.

"If it is to be our end, then know my heart-"

"My king!" The voice of a panicked Torvic Gloom rang out as his feet could barely keep up with his hurried momentum. Arwr and Brenis both turned to glare at Torvic for interrupting them, but quickly washed any anger away when they saw the stoic Scorn in a frenzied state.

"What is it Arch Priest?" Arwr asked.

"You must see for yourself." Torvic did not even wait for a response before he turned tail and ran back out.

Back in the grand foyer, the royal family, remaining troops, and many citizens watched a bright blue light creating massive sparks as it cut through the iradinium locks holding the two great doors together. It was in the top quarter of the door but was making quick progress.

"It's as if they have a small continual bolt of lighting cutting through the locks my king," Torvic explained. Though he was not sure what device or magic was doing it.

"It's now or never for one of your schemes," Arwr told his trusty companion. Brenis looked from the base of the door all the way up, tilting his head till he could no more.

"You're not going to like this one. Aelis, grab 10 stone smithies, and five of our largest guard," he demanded from his daughter who was all too happy to oblige. "Gather your forces, and be ready for the signal," he said to Arwr before rushing up a particular staircase. Arwr grinned, having a small inclination as to what his commander was devising.

Brenis crested the top of the spiral stairs and emerged inside the bell tower. He looked over the western side and it was a sheer drop to the palace entrance. The bell was supported by a small dome connected by four pillars. Aelis and her assembled folk joined her father moments later.

"I want this to land on their troops. You all know the time limit you have," he spoke encouragingly.

"Consider it done commander," one of the smithies said, before instructing his colleagues to begin their work. Brenis immediately began back down the stairs but stopped as Aelis started to follow. "Wait here until it does, daughter," he instructed.

"I will fight beside you as I always have," Aelis shot back. "Not this time." He lifted a gloved hand to her bruised cheek. "So much like your mother." Those words cracked the hard exterior and persona Aelis was known for. "When you're done here, protect Scáth and the Queen."

"I won't lose you too, pa." Aelis lifted her hand to grasp her fathers.

He moved to embrace her tightly.

"Wherever darkness reigns, know I am there." He quickly tore himself away and rushed down the stairs, for another second in that embrace, may have broken his heart entirely.

"The Macer will be most pleased to hear of your invention's efficiency." Ivan praised a wizard who stood at his side, with some wretched form of bone disease that left him crooked and hunched over.

"Thank you Ivan, it is all in the name of Sesara." The wizard snickered gleefully. By now they were more than halfway down the main gates of the palace as the cutting torch illuminated the whole entry with its blinding light. Shortly thereafter, several retracting thuds echoed out from the doors and the torch stopped.

"They've unlocked the doors!" A soldier shouted to the rear ranks. Ivan's face screwed up in immediate worry. Looking all about, he tried to consider every possibility. Then, the doors swung inward revealing a pitch black foyer. Without giving a command, Ivan's army moved forward with excitement.

"Halt, damn you, halt!" He roared, then came a single ring from the castle bell and the sound of rumbling stone. He shot his gaze upwards as a 4,000 kilogram bell and hundreds of stone chunks fell from the castle. "Get back!" His command echoed out but it was too late. The bell and stone landed on hundreds of the Sesaran soldiers, splattering those just out of range in blood and chunks of human remains. A great cloud of debris washed out in all directions, leaving those unharmed stunned and choking on fine particulates.

Ivan was far enough back to remain unharmed but felt his stomach drop at the devastation of it all. As the dust had barely settled, the remaining Scorn army poured out from the castle gates. The forward assault shadow-walking to the soldiers left unharmed while the rear quickly and efficiently put an end to any remaining stragglers near the entry. At the front of them all was King Arwr, Prince Scarnin, and Commander Brenis, cutting a devastating line straight for Ivan.

The Arch Paladin called upon his two fiercest warriors, a red Dragon-Blood known as Ragow and human female battle sorcerer called Ivy. "Keep the king and commander busy. I will crush their spirits by removing their prince from this equation." His renowned warriors nodded in delightful devilry. Ragow sprouted his huge draconic wings and soared for the commander while Ivy vanished in a cloud of green mist. Ivan watched for his perfect moment to catch the prince off-balance. The Arch Paladin admitted that Scarnin was a blessed combatant but none had been able to match his own skill with a blade thus far.

Ragow hovered above Brenis as his throat burned brightly with fire before spewing a line of flame at the commander. Brenis suffered greatly as he turned and his back lit ablaze. However, he shadow stepped above the red dragon-blood and landed on him, bringing the two down to the ground in a frenzied fall. They landed hard but Ragow was quick to recover, letting out a truly terrifying roar and slashing Brenis across the face with his sharp claws.

Ivy appeared in front of Arwr with a sly grin on her face, the Scorn King was confused by this but quickly took a step forward, ready to strike. She blew a heavy breath at him and so came a cloud of green spores. They breached against his face like a breaking wave and Arwr quickly dropped to one knee, overcome by a sense of pain as the veins on his neck bulged. Several Scorn Guard noticed this and rushed to their king's aid, but it only bought Arwr a brief period of time as Ivy made quick work of them.

"Father!" Scarnin yelled just as he cut one stubborn foe down. As he was about to make his way to the king, the prince was struck with a pulse of blue energy. He hit the ground so hard that he tumbled end over end twice before regaining control. Ivan slowly approached the off balance Scorn.

"You! You're responsible for all of this!" Scarnin screamed at Ivan. "This has been going for centuries longer than either of us. But I will be the one to end it." Ivan swung his great sword with devastating strength. Scarnin parried and spun out of the way, striking his blackglass and iradinium sword across Ivan's breastplate. It did little but scratch the white and gold paint, however. Ivan responded by ramming his armoured elbow into Scarnin's nose, spurting black blood everywhere. Scarnin gave a fierce defiant battle cry and shadow-stepped behind Ivan, sword raised. Ivan, without even looking, raised his arm behind him and gripped the princes throat tightly. Ivan swung his sword arm over his extended one, to cleanly chop off the princes head, but Scarnin raised his gauntlet made of the strongest material on Litore, iradinium. It blocked the blade and he jumped up, wrapping both legs around Ivan, throwing them to the ground. Scarnin expertly manoeuvred on top, proceeded to jab a dagger in the back of Ivan's knee where the armour did not protect the paladin. Ivan grunted in pain and summoned every ounce of divine arcane might he could muster, conjuring a bolt of lightning from the sky that struck them both. It blew them apart and left them convulsing on the ground from the residual energy coursing through their muscles.

A peel of thunder rumbled across the sky as Scáth, Aelis and Katia watched the battle from the veranda of the royal chambers. "I should be down there," Aelis voiced with anger.

"Your father is among the greatest of us, have faith in him." Katia spoke in that way only a confident and doubtless person could. Scáth envied her mothers ability to do so but wondered why she rarely showed such compassion to her.

Arwr was of strong constitution and when he saw his own people dying to protect him, he stood up resolutely. He brandished his scimitar and attacked Ivy with a flurry of strikes she could barely perceive. Locked in a series of attacks and parries, she eventually dug a dagger deep into his knee. Arwr dropped to one knee; his free hand clasped the dagger that she was twisting deep into his flesh, whilst his sword hand held her other weapon at bay. She took another deep breath to release some foul magic. Not willing to let her accomplish that, he let go of her dagger in his leg and covered her mouth, digging his fingers into her jaw. He forced their swords down, to break the lock and twirled it back around to run it along the back of his forearm as he cut a clean line across her throat. He wasted no time in springing back up on his good leg to survey the battle. He could not spot his son in the tumult but saw Brenis locked in fierce combat with a larger than normal dragon-blood. They were dozens of metres apart and separated by bloody shoulder to shoulder warfare. Yet, the king was determined to reach his friend.

Brenis was starting to wear from the relentless attacks of the dragon-blood. Each parry of his great axe felt like his arms were being bashed against stone. The commander understood his time was limited against this opponent and he simply had no energy left to shadow-walk.

"Brenis!" Arwr shouted, and the commander flinched in dire

understanding. He didn't want this creature anywhere near his king and dear friend. So, Brenis spent the last of his stamina to jump at the dragon-blood and swing his weapon for his face. Ragow caught the Scorn by the collar, and in one last moment of effort, Brenis plunged the dagger deep into Ragow's neck. He roared in pain but it was not enough to kill the huge draconic warrior. Ragow lowered Brenis Andula closer with a single arm, and bit his head off in a single chomp. He threw the headless corpse to the ground and retreated to the sky. Arwr simply stopped where he stood, overtaken with grief, stunned by his reality.

Ivan was quicker to his feet than Scarnin for he was expecting the bolt, and suffered lesser by his well placed shot. He made eye contact with King Arwr and saw the fury in his eyes. Ivan was quick to find the prince as the king rushed towards them. Scarnin was trying to regain control of his body but felt numb and disillusioned. The Arch Paladin hoisted the prince to his feet and stood him upright, facing his father. Ivan remained behind the prince with the sword resting on the back of his neck. Arwr halted just a few paces from his boy.

"Son."

"Da?" Scarnin voiced still unsure of what was going on or where he even was.

"You're gonna be okay."

"Where's ma, and little sister?" He questioned his father like a boy waking from a bad dream.

"You can have me, just let him go, Ivan," Arwr demanded. Ivan remained steadfast though.

"You seem to forget Arwr ShadowScorn, I don't want any of you alive." He gripped the hilt of his sword, releasing that devastating pulse of blue magic. Scarnin's head viscerally popped, spraying Arwr with the remains of his son. The Scorn King let out a scream so powerful all in the city heard his pain. From his body emitted a preternatural black orb of writhing and shrieking darkness that consumed both Ivan and Arwr. As it did so, all in the City of Shadow stopped mid-movement, frozen in time.

"Look at what your children do in your name." Aceia, god of shadow spoke resonantly, having replaced Arwr.

"They are lost, twisted by lesser's who've gained power," Sesara, goddess of life and sustenance answered, in replacement of Ivan. "I bore this race on the opposite side of the world from your zealots, yet here they are. Destroying all that is peaceful and good. We both know what is coming, so why don't I simply do away with you now, Sesara?" The dark deity's eyes poured with shadow.

"Nothing that wouldn't eventually come to pass. Perhaps, time to mend the wrong doings I've let go unpunished. Yet, those of us who ascended before the first age know each other all the same. Which is safe to say, my argument is not strong enough to stay your decision."

"You are among the last of us to put your final chip on the table. Why?" Aceia asked the question that had been burning in his mind for centuries.

"I have faith that those who inherit this world will be enough. Worry not, for now even I have played a final move." "Send the invaders away. I offer this to you out of respect, Sesara. If you do not, I will kill you and every single one of your followers here." "What you ask of me is not within my power. But know this, Aceia, to kill me will result in your own demise." Sesara in all her infinite radiance and resplendence bowed her head to Aceia. The shadow that poured from Aceia's eyes now raised like writhing flame. "Would you not sacrifice yourself for your children?" Aceia answered plainly.

The orb that had encapsulated Arwr and Ivan burst into thousands of pieces of shrapnel, striking more Sesaran soldiers than not. Those who were hit, made no sound, though their actions would dictate otherwise as they slowly disintegrated into lingering shadow and drawn into Glass Mountain.

Ivan and Arwr had not moved a muscle, completely aware of the conversation that transpired and that they themselves had been avatars for the gods. With that experience, came all the knowledge and wisdom from ultimate ascension for even a moment.

"Do you understand?" Ivan asked, hoping, praying Arwr knew the feeling he was experiencing.

"I do," the Scorn King replied, as he knelt beside his dead son. "It's over."

Ivan looked on with tears streaming from his brown eyes. He lifted those watery eyes up and saw the approaching Scorn Guard. Ivan took an unsteady step back before calling for a retreat to the few of those left in his army.

Ch1 - The Days Before

It was with great pain that Scáth did not spend her first night back in
ShadowScorn by Ven's side. She wanted more than anything to be
there when he first awoke after being rescued off the mountain side.
Torvic Gloom, the Arch Priest of Aceia, assured her that he would be
fine and would be sleeping for several days. Scáth was denied to go
along with the rescue party that retrieved the two Kyst elves. Within
the first hour back, the fact she was already being told 'no' did not set
well with the returned princess. She had instructed Commander Aelis
Andula, her dearest and oldest friend, to give her some time before
being reunited with her parents. And so, the commander bought
Scáth all the time she might need to gather her thoughts.

The princess walked wearily across the palace hall's blackglass
floor. Her entire body ached, and her heart felt as though it could bear
no more stress lest it suddenly stop altogether. She had been a
prisoner for months mostly locked in a rod iron cage, concealed by
canvas, stuck to a wagon bound west. Only upon the horrible events
during one dark and dreary evening, when her captors were struck
upon by a hoard of Siphons, was she able to free herself. Her journey
for many days after was what now most of her nightmares forced her
to relive. A foreign land, lost and alone with brutal mercenaries and
horrid monsters on her trail. She did not stop running for two days.
Every time she fell, bashing or cutting a limb, she would rise and
continue to flee; running blindly with some small glint of hope that
whatever was before her could not be as bad as what was behind. As
her end seemed nigh and a pack of wolves were nipping at her toes, a

stranger had emerged from the darkness.

"Ven," wistfully and unconsciously escaped her lips. She was forever grateful for his actions and strong moral belief in doing what was right. She was forced to shake those thoughts from her mind as she passed the last great stained glass window and approached her parent's private chambers. Scáth paused for a long moment outside the smooth single door. She truly did not want to step inside that room, for it would mean stepping back into her old life. She had grown so much since her abduction; she had learned to trust in her instincts and believe in one's self. Taking a collection of deep breaths, the fierce Scorn elf opened the door.

Sitting at a small table next to a brightly burning hearth sat Commander Aelis Andula and Scáth's mother, Queen Katia. Yet, what her eyes instantly fell upon was her father King Arwr, bent sickly over in his chair wrapped tightly in a fur blanket. Scáth would never forget the two distinct looks that appeared on the faces of her parents. Her mother was clearly caught by surprise at her daughter's return, and Scáth easily saw through Katia's predictable attempt to cover her disappointment up with exaggerated tears of joy. Even though her father looked so much worse than she could have imagined, she had never seen such a smile cross his face. Her own eyes filled to the brim with tears after noticing his had already done so. The moment was roughly switched as Katia threw her arms around Scáth, holding her daughter tightly. She didn't reciprocate the hug at first but did succumb to what was once such a world-securing embrace between mother and daughter. Katia was taken aback by her daughter's strength as she pushed her away to step towards Arwr. The king stood from his chair to stand proudly and welcome his beloved child back home with open arms. She launched herself against him and rested her face against his bony chest. They held each other for several soul-nourishing minutes before he slightly pulled her back by the shoulders to lock eyes.

"How is my little shadow?" He asked, with the worry only a father could have for his little girl. That pulled at her heart and she involuntarily gave a deep frown before a cracked chuckle and a wide smile reappeared.

"Missing her Pa," she answered softly, responding to her lifelong nickname. They hugged each other once more. It was no secret that the king and his princess were model examples of love among family. Yet, when Aelis looked upon Katia, hesitant to join in on that hug which by all means should have been one of the happiest days in the queen's life, a great many questions took root in the commander's mind. Aelis and Scáth grew up as sisters, given that the former Commander of ShadowScorn and closest friend to King Arwr was Brenis Andula, her father. They learned early on in their childhood, that they would go further in life if they supported each other, as their fathers did. After the sudden disappearance of Scáth, Aelis begged the king and queen to let her go after the abducted princess. Perhaps, Arwr would have agreed if there was even a single shred of evidence as to her disappearance. But she had simply vanished without a trace to be followed. Many whispers among the palace were that Scáth had chosen to leave. Yet, those who knew her best understood Scáth would have never considered the abandonment of her people. She was an important figure to the city and loved by all of its citizens. Even so, it was decided with a heavy-heart that no party would be sent after the princess. For surely a band of roaming ShadowScorn would be hunted down, to be murdered or captured and sold into a horrible fate.

So instead, the king declared that every night, every Scorn citizen would meet in the town's historic square and mine entrance. As dusk fell to eve, the Priests of Aceia, deity of shadow and the one responsible for their transformation, was called upon. It truly was a sight worthy of the gods. Every night for two months, they gathered, prayed, and asked for the safe return of their beloved Scáth. It was a testament to the love she had for her people; every single one of the ten thousand citizens attended each night's prayer.

It was an indisputable fact in the eyes of Aelis, that Katia could barely look at her beaten and worn down child. But why? Katia had known the loss of her first born, Scarnin. Surely knowing a child that was thought to be lost but now returned would be all Katia could desire. Her thought was, however, interrupted by her dismissal from the king. Aelis bowed low and gave Scáth a warm smile before exiting the chamber. Scáth reciprocated, watching her friend take leave, before finally taking a seat. It had been months since she had taken a proper seat around a proper table.

"Tell us everything," Arwr begged as Katia sat down to join them. "If it's not too difficult, my dear?" Her mother said with genuine warmth, clearly offering Scáth an opportunity to rest and collect herself first. However, almost immediately, Scáth began to recount the first half of her journey. Although being a heavily guarded prisoner offered little in the way of tales to recount. She then spent a significant portion of the night explaining everything she could about meeting Ven and Athvar, insisting it was Ven's bravery and Athvar's experience that brought her home. She told them of the arduous journey; the story she had mostly got second hand about the bog witch and their chance encounter with Agan. She mentioned the girl she had saved from captors much like her own, then the training in combat and survival she received, and finally their trek along Glass Mountain.

"Now I sit here before you, a different Scorn than the one you raised." She ended with a heavy gaze set upon her mother. She did not need an answer as to why a party had never been sent for her, that was obvious to the princess and she approved of that decision. She did suspect her mother of having a strange behaviour the few days prior to her disappearance. Katia had become rather cold-hearted when Scarnin died during the siege of Ivan the Revered. When Arwr had fallen sick, some six months ago, Katia had hit a new depth of heartlessness. As memories fluttered throughout her mind, Scáth suddenly remembered an argument she had gotten into with her mother a few cycles before she was taken from her room. They had been arguing over a topic that had grown in frequency as of late, regarding the increasing number of Scorn citizens succumbing to an infectious illness. Katia took the stance that the people were growing weak and lazy. Scáth refused to believe that her mother, who was ever cunning, could have such short sightedness on the matter. Unfortunately, the fights had begun to meld together and she couldn't recall what exactly was said.

Katia looked back with tears brimming but quickly threw herself into another hug with Scáth. Arwr gave his daughter a curious stare. He was all too aware of the relationship his dearest women shared: one with the presence of love but a fundamental aversion for each other. It had always been that way, Arwr leaving most arguments the two had to blow away like any storm. Yet, the contempt he heard in Scáth's voice was more than alarming for the ever devoted father. However, it was late and Scáth still had not found rest since her return.

"Let us all find dreams of peace. Surely I'll sleep the deepest now my little shadow is home." Arwr kissed Scáth's forehead and stood up with the assistance of Katia.

"Goodnight, love." Katia blew Scáth a kiss as she helped Arwr enter an archway that led into their bed chambers. Scáth remained next to the hearth for a long while. Completely motionless, and utterly defeated. The same fear played over and over in her mind, wondering if she had erred in coming back.

The next morning was spent with her companions in Ven's recovery room.

"How long they sayin' he'll be like this?" The burly half-orc, half-elf, Agan Dusk bellowed, his large frame hanging over the fur lined arm chair. His red to green gradient skin tone, which he was named 'Dusk' for, appeared softened by the dancing flame of a warm hearth.

"A half-cycle," answered Athvar's upbeat and chipper voice. The remarkably dusty gnome lay with his fingers locked on his chest, head resting on the foot board of Ven's bed. A half-cycle was known as four days in Litore, a full-cycle being eight. It was a common way of keeping track of time in Litore as it followed the rotation of the Caelestis, the largest of the three moons that blotted the sky. Scholars of every civilization had spent millennia trying to better understand those planets that were so close you felt as though you could touch them, but remained so impossibly far away.

Scáth was quiet, sitting next to the Kyst's bed and rubbing Faenla between the ears. Athvar and Agan looked to each other, both acknowledging the difficult state of mind Scáth was in.

"Ya know, Lady Scáth, I was told by one of yar Clerics that goes by thee name of Torvic Gloom, that Ven is to receive some special treatment today." Athvar offered the good news in hopes that it might relax her. Scáth didn't look away from Ven, but nodded in response. The gnome looked back to Agan with wide eyes, obviously instructing the brute to chime in. Agan rolled his eyes at the filthy gnome before asking.

"Perhaps, during that time, you could give us a proper tour? We could attend any meetings you might have, to ensure your comfort in these uncertain times." Agan finished with a full smile that cracked

Scáth's heart. She wasn't sure if she had ever seen Agan actually smile before, so it became clear to her how hard he was trying. She got up from the chair that her legs were curled on, flicking her ever misting black hair behind her shoulders.

"That would be nice, Agan. A tour is the least I could do, considering all you did to get me here." She was happy to have allies such as these on her already unsteady return home. She planted a kiss on the forehead of Ven and Faenla before exiting with Agan and Athvar. Faenla got up and paced the room a few times before laying back down on the smooth worked stone, curling tightly into a ball at Ven's right.

The great wolf was exhausted from the journey like all of the companions. Yet, this beast of the wild had found little comfort in the city thus far. He did, however, look forward to the plate upon plate of raw meat being delivered to him, just as instructed by Scáth. After finally getting comfortable, the wolf felt the stone door shifting the air in the room as it opened. His ears shot up in an attempt to identify who had entered. After failing to recognize the footfalls, the giant wolf sprang up and planted his front paws on Ven's bed, making Faenla well over two metres tall. He snarled down on a truly terrified ShadowScorn. It was a scrawny Scorn man with tightly kept facial hair and a bald pate that looked like a glossy globe of onyx. He wore tight but stiff black robes, that nearly swept the floor. A faint whimper escaped his trembling lips as he peered up at the malevolent-looking animal. Faenla effortlessly leaped over the bed, forcing the Scorn back a series of strides. His hackles taught, fangs bared, and a low growl threatening every move the Scorn made. Faenla forced the intruder out the door and watched him fumble backwards across the hall to trip over a blackglass bench and collide roughly with the floor.

"What is the meaning of this, Oren?" Came a shout that further disturbed the intruder. A tall and graceful Scorn human wearing the sigil of ShadowScorn on his ornate robes and the gleaming icon of Aceia around his neck. The priest had thick layers of white and black robes that added a great deal of size to an otherwise slim-built man.

"This beast just attacked me as I was walking by!" Oren argued while trying to regain some measure of composure.

"I've been assured this particular wolf would not threaten anyone unless he felt his master was in danger." Torvic walked over to Faenla who was still threatening the intruder.

"I want him gone, Torvic! As the administrator I demand it!" Oren more confidently insisted as he fumbled back to his feet and smoothed out his attire.

"Please Faenla, return to his side," Torvic asked in a calm but firm tone. Faenla eventually backed down, giving a derisive snort before lumbering back into the room. The wolf on all fours was 190 centimetres and far taller than most humanoids on Litore. Torvic closed the door and returned to Oren.

"Begone from here, Oren. You have no business being near the Kyst in the first place." He felt as though he was scolding Oren like a child. "I'll be going where ever I damn please, Torvic. You are the Cleric, I'm the Administrator. Don't forget it." Oren attempted to storm off with what minimal dignity he had left.

"This isn't a good look for you," Torvic shouted at his indignant colleague. Torvic Gloom was the Arch Priest of Aceia in ShadowScorn. Which meant his position had constant dealings with the Administrator of ShadowScorn. The title of 'Administrator' meant Oren had been elected by the citizens to sit in on every meeting the king and queen had, to ensure the interests of the commoners were never forgotten. The two Scorn men had been serving their stations together for nearly 200 years. In that time, they had seen each other's every moral tested, broken and weathered through countless trials. Torvic, in his fifth century of life was as keen as ever. Oren on the other hand was only in his third century and seemed off as of late. Regardless, he shook the thoughts from his head and entered the chamber of Ven Devar, ready to deliver his divine healing touch. He immediately saw Faenla sitting rump down at his full height, watching everything Torvic did.

"They weren't exaggerating, you really do look like the night sky," Torvic said to Faenla as the priest walked up beside Ven. The wolf simply starred at the Scorn man, which Torvic found strangely comforting.

That night, Athvar and Faenla watched over Ven's rest as Scáth had taken Agan to an important meeting. The pair moved stoically through the magnificent palace halls as many ShadowScorn went about their evening. It utterly unnerved Agan as he counted a dozen

Scorn in this hallway alone, and not a single one of them made the slightest sound in their actions. Even the ruffling of their clothes was not to be heard. His memory of the more recent past was still a blur but his skills as a fighter remained razor sharp. Much to the relief of Agan's discomfort, Scáth suddenly turned right through a small open archway. Quickly following behind her, he was bewildered at the great hall presented before him. A huge slab of blackglass was fastened upon a slightly raised dais. Many elegantly carved thrones surrounded the slab, worked into thin but strong interweaving spirals of blackglass, giving the impression of the chair being made from hundreds of shadowy tendrils. Blackglass was a substance found only in Glass mountain, glossy and slightly translucent, somehow seeming to trap light within it. The Scorn people had perfected the art of strengthening it, and used it to create many wonderful and beautiful objects. The Council Hall had strong pillars surrounding it, supporting an upper balcony where onlookers could observe. Often, ranking members of their army would gather here prior to a battle to be briefed. Agan was still in the archway, standing in awe, when he noticed Scáth beckoning for him to sit beside her. The fighter noticed only Scorn sitting around the table. Nevertheless, he walked up and sat at Scáth's left with confidence. The half orc-elf had served as a close adviser to the King of Rhogar in the war with the Silver Rock Dwarves, so this process was not entirely foreign to him.

To Scáth's right was the king, at the head of the table. Across from the Princess sat the Queen, beside her sat Oren the Administrator. On Agan's left was Torvic Gloom and at the other end of the table was an Aelis Andula, plated in intricately embossed heavy armour.

"Let us all thank you once more Agan Dusk, for the aid in seeing my daughter returned home," Arwr stated proudly before giving a slight seated bow. In turn, everyone, including Scath, bowed their heads out of respect.

"It was my honour, Your Highness. Though I believe she helped me more than I can say I aided her." Agan then turned to Scáth, reciprocating the bow he had just received. Scáth smirked, for though she knew he was being honest. She also knew he never complimented without somewhat jesting.

"Scáth has informed us you served as an advisor to King Dusanith of Rhogar in the 'War of a Thousand Dragons.'" Arwr stated. Everyone looked to Agan in disbelief, except Aelis, who truthfully appeared unimpressed.

"I did. I found myself in their kingdom when the borderland skirmishes first broke out." Agan left it there for he spoke little of those years. Too much pain was associated with that period in his life. No one else at the table seemed bothered though, as they were not here to trade stories.

"Commander, update." Arwr finished with an especially harsh and wet cough.

"I sent three scouts, two days past. Only one returned and with minimal information. They are from Renrit but bolstered by Serenstrom as we expected. They had several bands of roaming scouts, which is how our other two perished. Our survivor could not get a full count before he too was hunted." Aelis was a proud Scorn elf and she was not afraid to show she was wounded by the loss of her two scouts.

"We couldn't precisely count them on the last part of the journey but they have brought a formidable army," Scáth added, alluding to their trek up and along the Glass Mountain.

"What would you know of war, sweetheart?" Katia added in a tone meant to undercut the value of Scáth's words. She shot her mother a disgruntled look.

"I know a great deal about these things. From what I saw, their forces will easily outnumber you three to one," Agan boomed in support of Scáth. "If however, my guess of your ranks is correct?" He asked, looking to Aelis with his illuminating yellow eyes and a smirk staining his face. She returned a stare that was stern but all too telling.

"Perhaps I shall scale the mountain soon and see if I can gather a number from there," Aelis said aloud, happily avoiding the half-orcs comment.

"I will join you," Agan said to the commander before looking to the king, hopeful of his support, which he knew he wouldn't receive after noticing Arwr already shaking his head.

Aelis laughed mockingly. "You are too, orcish. The path is only a dozen centimetres wide at its easiest."

Torvic seemed entertained and thought it refreshing to have an extra voice on the council. He could easily see that Oren was grinding his teeth in frustration. Why was his collegue so irritable of late? That question had been feverishly nagging at Torvic.

"So then what?" Oren cried out. All turned their collective attention to the administrator. "It's just, surely there is more that can be done?" He said, trying to mend his unprofessional outburst. Arwr lay a heavy stare upon Oren, causing the scrawny Scorn to uncomfortably adjust in his chair.

"Of course, as we all know, the proper protocols for a siege are in place." His voice carried great confidence and power. Agan more than once caught himself swept up in the Scorn King's words. "This city has withstood hundreds of sieges in its brief existence. We will weather and survive this one as all the others before it." His tone left little room for debate.

"When will the Kyst awake?" Katia asked Torvic. Scáth noticed, as was her mother's intent, that she refused to use Ven's name. "He has rested nearly three days now. I predict another two or three before he regains consciousness. But he will need a great deal more time to heal."

"He doesn't belong here," Oren said, first looking to Katia then Torvic.

"He's welcome here as long as Scáth permits," Aelis declared evenly.

"Scáth has been gone for months. In lieu of what you have seemingly forgotten, need I remind you she is not your king?" Oren shot Aelis a hateful stare. Scáth simply rolled her eyes at the miserable Scorn. Yet it was true, Scáth rarely, if ever, attended these meetings, for the title of 'princess' really offered nothing in the way of decision making. After the death of Scarnin, her father did counsel and teach Scáth how to be ruler so that one day she could, but it had rarely happened in the Council Hall. She was here now with Agan only due to the given circumstances.

"Ven Devar is a welcomed and a most honoured guest in the City of Shadow. As the administrator to its citizens, I suggest you make my word known to all throughout," Arwr stated calmly, but with a palpable threat directed at Oren. "That goes for everyone," the king boomed while ending his scowling gaze upon his wife. Agan, all too enthused at the level of intrigue here, watched as Katia dropped eye contact from her husband to the floor. The fighter didn't miss the look in the queen's eyes as she stared at Arwr from the corner of her vision.

He had seen that look in the eyes of so many before; a look of scorn. "Perhaps, we could send a messenger to a nearby ally? If we choose wisely, we could easily withstand a siege by the time help arrives." Scáth offered her idea with some hesitance, mostly looking to Aelis for whether it had potential or not. Aelis immediately looked to King Arwr with enthusiasm.

"What ally would possess the army capable, let alone willing, to go against the forces of Sesara?" Oren criticized with obvious skepticism. Scáth looked deterred but was deep in thought, searching for that answer.

"Perhaps, Elemenzin. Many families from the SunLotus region are loyal traders with us-"

"- Too far." Oren snapped. Agan raised a brow in Oren's direction. It was clear to the worldly mercenary, he would break this paltry Scorns face the first chance he got. Scáth looked to her mother who was wearing a grin that boiled her blood. Just then, the princess' eyes shot wide with an idea.

"Then the Snow Elves," She looked from Aelis to Arwr with hope. "From Moon Mountain. Pa, they will help us."

Oren offered a typical scoff but Scáth knew she was onto something when he did not, and probably could not, find a reason to shoot it down. Arwr slumped in his throne. In the months prior to his mysterious illness his powerful torso and strong frame would protrude over the sides of his impressive throne. Now, however, so very emaciated as he was, he appeared no stronger than a withered husk.

"Grand Master Zenair has always been a faithful ally in the past, Your Highness," Torvic added encouragingly. "The Frozen Fist Monks are warriors second to none in the region," Aelis added. Agan coughed slightly under his breath at that, for he had dealings with the elves of Moon Mountain in the past; and knew they were some of the greatest warriors in all the world. "Who could or would be willing to travel the distance? Previous attempts to call for aid have only met more with death for our people." Oren pointed out the failings of similar attempts in past sieges. Agan shot Oren a menacing glare with his luminescent yellow eyes. "I would go," His timbre resonating with courage.

"And I," Both said Torvic and Aelis, giving each other nods and a smile.

"No," Arwr defiantly interjected. "It's two cycles there and back, without trouble. I fear we do not have that time."

"What choice do we have, Pa? We barely survived the last siege from Sesara, and now you are too weak to fight," Scáth asked pleadingly.

"No. I will not willingly send more of my people out to slaughter. We need each and everyone of you here." Scáth dropped her eyes to her lap in defeat.

"With all due respect, I am not your citizen. These types of scenarios are precisely why kings and queens across the many countries of Litore hire me."

"Your willingness does not go unnoticed, Agan. I thank you for it. Yet, a single fighter of even your calibre would not make it, let alone convince the noble Snow Elves to join us." Arwr finished with a slight nod to Agan which he reciprocated, understanding to leave it at that.

"Perhaps, my king we leave it at the protocols set in place for now. I will continue to reach out to Aceia for guidance in the interim," Torvic said with his usual religious optimism.

Everyone, save Scáth, exchanged agreeing nods and began to respectfully depart; except the royal family.

"Wait for me outside," Scáth quietly prompted Agan. He said nothing but replied in kind with a warm smile and a hand on her shoulder before departing. The princess then watched with her own smile as her companion briskly headed in the direction of Aelis. The three of them sat in silence for some time before Katia broke it.

"Never do I wish to see the likes of that green and red-skinned Agora in this hall again." The hatred in her voice profoundly stung Scáth.

"He acted most admirably, Katia. And deserves our infinite respect," Arwr said as if he had already said it to her a score or more times since his arrival.

"No!" The queen roared in defiance. "He is a disgrace to these very walls." She stood with a fury, sending her chair soaring behind her off the raised platform to shatter against the blackglass floor. "Too long have I gone unheard and I say no more of him." Katia's body heaved with anger, she stared her daughter and husband down before storming out of the hall. Scáth watched as her father placed his face into the palm of his hands.

"What have I done wrong, my little shadow?" Came the muffled voice of the king. Scáth went and knelt beside him.

"Everything you have ever done was done because you thought it to be right. Ever have I looked up to you for that." Scáth grabbed her fathers' hand firmly and gently kissed his cheek.

Katia walked through the palace with steely determination. Everyone she passed drew their gaze to the floor and bowed in respect. She descended a wide spiral staircase in the pitch black without a sound. The only distinguishable feature on the queen was the whites of her eyes. Reaching the bottom of the stairs she did not enter the obvious doorway to her left. Which would have taken her to the dungeons beneath the palace. Glancing around quickly she went to the enormous pillar that ran from the base to the very top of the palace. She ran her hand up the smooth stone pillar until she finally felt a slight crease. Pushing on the pillar, a small doorway slid inwards. Upon entering the hollow of the pillar, it turned into more spiralling stairs. The air was far colder down here and a heavy dampness lingered. So thick was it, that by the time the queen reached the bottom and saw torchlight, she appeared sprinkled by rain. The relatively small room was dimly lit with torches, and the smell of spice, exotic plants, and chemicals assailed her nostrils. A scrawny and bald-headed Scorn man was hunched over a poorly planked-together table rushing to accomplish his tincture.

"Are you done yet?" Katia asked rather seductively as she took a step toward the male.

"That wasn't very much time, my love."

"Don't call me that!" She snapped. "I am your queen first and forever." The Scrawny man's shoulders visibly shrunk at her reminder. He took a small brewing pot off an open flame, poured it into a crystalline vial, swirled it five times to the right then five time to the left before pouring it back into a separate vial and corking it.

"Another dose, my queen." Oren turned around, offering the poison with both hands raised out and head held low.

"Well done, Oren." She grabbed the vial and watched the final transformation of the neon red liquid become completely translucent. "Yet, the deed should have been done by now." She looked at him accusingly. Oren's eyes sprang wide.

"Blame Torvic for that. His healing is strong, but the poison will win out in the end." The administrator spoke with an apparent hesitance but was confident his words would prove true.

"Good." Katia slowly placed a kiss on Oren's lips before whispering. "If you're wrong, you may find the next batch you brew, ends up in your own wine."

Oren shivered at the cold words. He had known the queen for two human lifetimes already and understood without a doubt that she would make good on her threat.

The next day brought a heavy blanket of snow across the city but it strangely did not accumulate in the surrounding region. A large and rather bland building located at the rear of the castle was used by the Scorn Guard as an armoury and mess hall. The interior of the building was as refined and ornate as the rest of the palace, however. Proudly displaying great stained glass murals and intricately woven tapestries depicting the great hero's of the Guard, past and present.

One particular tapestry located in the armoury hung above a rack of warpicks. Within the threads weaved a tale of a Scorn Captain wearing a T-visor helmet with a single black feather protruding from its crown. He stood among a battlefield of dead Orcs, Giants, and battered Scorn Guard. The heroic man standing up against unbeatable odds wore a small buckler on his left forearm and held a warpick high in triumph. The Scorn man in the tapestry stood near to it now, dawning the same armour, buckler and weapon.

"Do you believe it?" Asked a Scorn Guard, who was removing his armour after another shift, to a Scorn Dwarf just suiting up for his day.

"Aye, lookin like thee King Arwr draggin us out er night for prayin actually worked," the Dwarf half-heartedly weighed in. "It's truly a miracle, no? Our dear princess returned to us!" The excited Scorn man declared after just unbuckling his greaves. "I wouldn't be callin it a miracle. Her return'l cause greater waves in our city than yer knowin."

"What a ridiculous falsification of -"

"- No," interrupted the now fully-armoured Captain. "Her return will ignite this cities greatest upheaval."

The dwarf laid a condescending look on the man and neither spoke another word. Both of them knew that their Captain, Sindrum Silver, would not tolerate such debates while on duty or on palace grounds.

Ch2 - The Siege

It's been nearly a week since we arrived in what I now know to be the awe distilling City that is ShadowScorn. A truly artistic and humble collection of unique architectures and citizens. The very heart and centre of this great city remains exactly how it was that fateful night Aceia crossed from his realm into ours to gift the folk with his touch. The ShadownScorn people built their great structures and impressive buildings around the original mining settlement. I know since being among the Scorn that they are a grateful, generous, and skilled race that boasts a proud melting pot of cultures. It has left little doubt in my mind that if the armies of Sesara are here to cleanse Litore of all ShadowScorn, then they have indeed lost their way. As of now, the Renrit army that outnumbers the ShadowScorn three to one, has made camp just over a hill from the city. It would appear they intend on keeping us locked behind our walls to succumb to food shortage and disease before attacking. This afternoon, I shall meet with the Commander of the Scorn Guard to scale the face of Glass Mountain in an effort to collect info on the exact numbers of religious zealots we face. I fear the most for Scáth's sick father. It is clear that some of his closest advisors cluster like vultures, as they attempt to seize power after his passing. This concerns me to no end for the safety of Scáth, the woman I yearn to protect now not out of just honour, but a flourishing instinct catalyzed by our increased understanding of each other. Athvar 'The Undusted', is as smitten as ever with Lady Scáth and has barely left her side since arriving. He explained to me in his travels long ago, he sat on the court of House Kazini, of the elemental humans in the Kingdom of Elemenzin. The treachery among politicians, generals, and even family was utterly appalling and for that reason, Athvar trusts no one around Scáth. That gnome never fails to put a smile on our faces. As for Agan, it became clear he was a mixed-blood who loved the fanciful things in life, such as long hours spent in the magnificent limestone bath houses and personal stores of the Royal Family's fine liqueurs. We all encouraged this behaviour as Agan truly had suffered greatly when I found him in that dreaded and claustrophobic fog of the foul bog witch. Little memory has returned to him, but perhaps the much-needed rest and relaxation will be his cure. Still, if he was this comfortable during a siege, we all wondered what level of comfort he could attain when imminent war wasn't looming over us. Faenla, my dearest companion, had found a level of fame and desire inside the walls of ShadowScorn. For the hulking wolf was seen a sign to the citizens, sent by none other than Aceia. It was true that Faenla's fur was as dark as night, sprinkled with white that resembled a star-scattered sky. However, it quickly became clear to me through our shared senses that the wolf hated the attention but moreover, a growing ball of angst was gripping at the wild animal. I understood from the start that Faenla was not meant to exist in a city, he was used to the bountiful expanses that the Great Northern Rainforest offered. It is my wish to discern a great many things from the commander today. I am not a creature of stillness and do not think we should so willingly wait out a siege like animals in a cage. I'm not sure how accurate of an estimation we will get of the enemy forces when we are halfway up the mountain, but doing something is better than doing nothing at all.

- Ven Devar

Ven sat cross-legged with his palms rested firmly on his knees, grounding his senses. He rested atop a thick blanket on the smooth stone floor of his new quarters inside the palace. In front of him was a crackling fire creating waves of dancing yellow behind his closed eyelids. He had only awoken two days ago but had been committing extensive hours to meditation, willing his body through the recovery process. The stitches that ran across his right eye, pulled uncomfortably at skin. His broken bones and wounds were nearly healed, thanks to Torvic, save from the gash on his chest from Rexous' expertly thrown dagger. Faenla was laying on his back with all four paws shot into the air, contorted and wrapped around his dearest companion. Ven slowly opened his green opalescent eyes. The world always appeared fuzzy for a few moments after emerging from a deep mediation. When he opened his heavy lids to look directly into the roaring fireplace, he gasped horrifically, throwing himself into a backwards roll and jumping into his defensive stance. Or at least that was his intention, until he rolled over Faenla, headlong into the footboard of his wooden bed frame. For a second too long, his heart sprang and began reacting to that night of horror when Silva burned with the hottest fires of the underworld. Hitting his head and slumping back down to the cold stone floor, Ven rubbed the welt already forming with a great sigh. A brief sense of embarrassment washed over him before it inevitably transformed into hot rage. The hunter balled his fist and punched the floor, hearing and feeling a distinct crack in his forefinger. He gave a small growl and was about to do it again before Faenla dragged his massive tongue across the Kyst's face. The majestic wolf laid his nearly 40 kilogram head on Ven's legs, nuzzling and pinning him down. The Kyst slowly felt his anguish subside and could do nothing but smile and give his best friend some rubs. Running his slender fingers through Faenla's impossibly thick and soft fur never failed to calm this coastal elf.

"Okay Faen, I can't feel my legs," he groaned, prompting his companion to get off after fully succumbing to a tingling numbness. Ven got up and for the first time since arriving, approached his armour. It was sitting on an armour rack in the corner of the room, looking as exquisite as ever. Ven had found sleep for only three days out of the five that Torvic and the other priests had assumed he would need. In that time, Scáth had the finest Blacksmiths in the city repair the damage that the armour had suffered along the journey. The dagger he had taken to the chest had all but destroyed the upper scale mail of his chest piece. It was now a solid matte-black leather piece with iradinium and silver intricately woven throughout. As with everything here, it was a piece of art in and of itself. Yet, they had assured Scáth that it would offer equal flexibility and significantly enhanced durability; iradinium was the strongest substance known in Litore and only found in a few locations. His short-sword was neatly tied to the armour-stand and was sharpened to an impressive edge. His quiver too was there, including a full bundle of blackglass arrow heads. His trident, as always, hadn't left his side. Even when in his commoner clothes, it was essential for any Kyst Hunter to be equipped with their weapon of choice. Most chose their traditional tridents for its versatility. With the press of a button, its handle could elongate from close-combat to a length of two meters. The nearly ten sheaths that were strategically placed across the full set of armour were now filled with black throwing knives, all showing a silvered edge. Upon retrieving one, Ven found that it slid apart into two thinner knives. A smile crossed the hunters face but he soon replaced them and began dawning his armour. Once fully fitted, he noticed a familiar comfort settle over him. He swept his thick, dark forest green hair back and pulled up his hood, exiting his chamber with Faenla following close at his side.

Ven walked across the Royal Palace. The floor was made of a thick blackglass that the ShadowScorn had harvested from the Mountains core. The impressive light-absorbing crystal was only known to be found in Glass Mountain. Great stained glass windows lined several of the bigger halls, each depicting an important event from their brief but impressive history. Lengthy black tapestries with silver inlay adorned the smaller halls, all of which illustrated a more in-depth look at the culture of the ShadowScorn people. Ven was distracted from the captivating stories that hung from the wall as he passed a large training gymnasium. The sound of ringing steel and intense physical exertion filled him with nostalgia for the former Hunter's Hall of Silva. He looked to Faenla who was intently watching what was happening inside.

The Kyst had nowhere in particular to be in a hurry, given life during a siege seemed unnaturally slow. He entered the great stone room where he saw rows of wooden dummy targets covered in thick canvas. Three separate archery lanes, each a different distance to their respective hay-bale target. A massive and peculiar structure designed for what he surmised would test ones dexterity, lest a long fall to the stone floor below. A handful of Scorn Guard were training and paid him a small sign of respect before continuing with their chosen activity. Ven watched in awe for several moments at a band of five exclusively Scorn women leaping and disappearing into nothing before reappearing somewhere else on the large platform. He was astounded by the unified coordination and acrobatic grace of these women. Not to mention stunned by the fact that they were using the lingering darkness to teleport themselves. Many of the manoeuvres being pulled off by these Scorn would have been otherwise impossible without their unique skill of shadow-walking.

Ven dropped his cloak and quiver, taking up his shortened trident and short-sword in each hand. Faenla however, remained watching the group of women effortlessly train on the dexterity platform. After stretching out the stiffness in his torso, and entire body for that matter, Ven fell into a slow routine of thrusts, slices and dodges with one of the dummies. As he dropped and spun on one leg, he fell back as a sharp pain pulsed from his recently dislocated knee. He quietly grunted away the pain and stood back up, starting his routine from the beginning. He was disappointed with the laziness that had already settled into his muscles and pushed himself to move even quicker. The pain drove him to train harder as a sheer act of defiance to what his body was screaming.

Soon, Ven's consciousness was fighting off a dozen Kintar, all burning Silva to the ground. His heart-rate soared and muscles tightened to a reflexive apex. Moving now between several of the dummies, the hunter dipped and weaved, delivering a death blow with each weapon in his hand before dodging imaginary strikes from the savage Kintar. Faenla immediately sensed this and went over to check on his elf. The wolf felt his animosity but also the good it was doing Ven to release it, so he plopped his rump down and watched. Eventually, Ven felt his strikes separating the arms and heads of the dummies and the subsequent thuds against the floor. In short order, all in the gym were watching the Kyst Hunter dance between the dummies, severing pieces of them with ease, which all had thought to be impossible. Each one of them was in awe at his ability to turn training into something so visually remarkable.

After nearly an hour of Ven never breaking his routine, a thick sweat made his stormy-ocean coloured skin glisten with resolve. Everything ached and though he thought it only to be sweat, many of his stitches had torn, soaking his under garments in blood. When he opened his eyes, he saw only the torso's of the dummies remaining upright and everyone in the gym watching him, including a single new occupant.

"Most impressive," a frail and hunched over Scorn elf said, seated on a bench to Ven's right. The hunter quickly dropped to one knee and lowered his head, after seeing the family resemblance to Scáth and the ornate blackglass crown. Everyone else in the gym proceeded to the exit.

"Forgive me, I did not know you were here, Your Grace," the Kyst offered apologetically.

"No need for that, my boy. Those dummies are as old as I am. How in the gods did you cut them down?" King Arwr asked not in slight but fascination.

"My mentor once said 'it's not about how hard you strike, its about knowing when and where to focus your attack.' Finding one's weakness and exploiting it. That lesson has saved my life a number of times."

"Indeed. Similar thinking is how we Scorn have survived so many wars. I am eternally in your debt, as a king and father, Mighty Ven Devar."

"With all due respect, I cannot accept a debt in which the only deed I did was as any good hearted folk would do. Letting me experience your culture and saving me on the mountain side, is payment enough," Ven said, now rising to stand, only to realize he was in fact bleeding quite harshly. King Arwr simply cracked a smile before patting the bench, inviting the hunter closer. Ven accepted graciously, sheathing his weapons as he approached.

"My grandfather, Risastor Riston was gifted this mountain from dwarves in the Kermon Range. Are you familiar with it?" Arwr asked. Ven knew of the region but only from maps and shrugged as much. "It's the same range Moon Mountain sprouts from. Risastor was a Snow Elf before that fateful night, where all who found themselves there were touched by Aceia. He was sent here by the Grand Master at the time." Ven nodded with keen interest. "Under strict guidance, my grandfather assembled a small mining population and an adventuring party to see the area made safe. That group of collective people, were all transformed into the very first Shadow Scorn"

"Why do you speak to me of this?" Ven asked with a level of confusion and an undercurrent of concern.

"I tell you this now because I need all in Shadow Scorn fighting for the same cause. I pray you never know the feeling of losing a child. It is an experience many of my citizens are familiar with. We are the purest example of a peaceful nation, continuously attacked for no other reason than fear and ignorance. We are a symbol of perseverance, a promise we will not become what they claim us to be. We fight for justice and equality, for the endless and needless loss of our people, past, present and future."

"Thank you for sharing those words with me. I swear to fight for what your people believe in, for what is just. I have been shown nothing that would suggest otherwise." Ven chuckled to himself. "I see now too where Scáth gets her persuasiveness."

Arwr shot the honourable Kyst a warm nod before turning his attention to the entrance where Faenla was greeting Athvar and a Shadow Scorn, who Ven thought at first to be Scáth. As they neared, he felt silly when he saw it to be someone else. However, she was of elven blood like Scáth, and her infusion with shadow did great things to enhance her beauty. Her hair was cut short just below her jawline, and one side was shaved down to reveal a tattoo of black swirling clouds sprouting from her neck. Her hair appeared like vapours misting away from a lake's surface, and given the length, it obscured one half of her face as she moved.

Ven was still awkwardly staring at the Scorn when Athvar introduced her as "Commander Aelis Andula, allow me to introduce Ven Devar of the Great Northern Rainforest." Athvar elbowed Ven in the knee, instinctively forcing the Kyst into the appropriate bow. He didn't see it, but Aelis gave an amused smirk.

"It's an honour to meet you, Ven Devar. Let me thank you personally for bringing back our princess. To you, I may finally find rest again, or at least once this siege has been thwarted."

"The honour is mine, commander," Ven replied, coming out of his bow. "I look forward to learning from you, and offering any assistance I can to bring a swift end to this wrongful attack." Athvar smiled at that and was proud to see Ven's aptitude for diplomacy.

"Treat him with the highest rank, Aelis. Ven is an honoured and esteemed ally," Arwr said, rising from the bench. He walked a short distance and was met by two heavily plated Scorn Guard who escorted the king away.

The commander's armour certainly bolstered her image as a force to be reckoned with. The armour she wore was of the finest Ven had ever laid his eyes on. Two elegant pauldrons sat on her shoulders, a slightly raised fin on each protruded from the top so as to add extra protection to her seemingly delicate neck. A well-formed breastplate had intricate silver embossed across the black and grey palate. Chain mail tightly clung to her form across her belly and elbows, filling gaps where added flexibility was required. The gauntlets distinctly reminded Ven of his new upper chest piece. The greaves were of similar design and the only shred of colour on her whole person came in the form of a deep purple sash around her neck that hung halfway down the breastplate.

"I fear he may not survive this siege," Aelis said with a clearly heartfelt sorrow to her voice. Ven truthfully wasn't all too concerned about the king. His fears, as always, laid with Scáth's safety, and now future. He felt a great comfort knowing Athvar was of the same mind on that.

"Then let us not put any more time between us and our scouting mission," Ven exclaimed confidently. She nodded and began leading them away, Ven first dropped to one knee and whispered something into Athvar's ear. Athvar gave a reassuring nod and Ven followed after the commander. The gnome and wolf sauntered out of the palace in search of a particular half-orc.

Aelis and Ven walked through the city for nearly fifteen minutes before the commander turned into a dead-end alley way. She proceeded to the back where the mountain naturally abutted the city. Ven wasn't sure as to where they were going but followed along patiently. Aelis placed her hand on the cold but smoothed over mountain stone. Ven noticed she held four fingers against the rock. Then one finger, then three, then five. As she rested her palm, a doorway-sized hole dissipated like heat waves on a summer's horizon. She led them out of the secret entrance into the city that Scáth had used upon arriving. It was so well hidden he wondered if the citizens of the city even knew of this route's existence. Upon walking through the now doorway, Ven spotted a pair of Scorn Guard lazily seated around a fire. They instantly recognized their commander and jumped to their feet, saluting their superior. She barely acknowledged them and went to open the stone door before immediately exiting. Ven looked to the Scorn Guard, in their uniformed armour. It was of a similar design to Aelis but was less ornate and overall spectacular.

"Good luck," the oldest of the two guards said to Ven with a reassuring nod. Ven didn't give it much thought, offering a nod and proceeding after the commander once more. As the two walked out onto the mountainside, she directed them to a path separate from the one they had originally walked in on. This immediately required a climb of nearly twenty-metres before levelling off. It turned back into a thin winding path with a steep gradient. Ven had a long moment of panic as the memories of him slipping off the edge played over and over in his mind.

"So tell me, Mighty Devar, why stay and help? Surely this is not your battle," Aelis prodded before pausing briefly to look him up and down with intent. Ven was taken aback by her abruptness and hostile tone. He looked down to see that they were a hundred or so meters above the city, already.

"Honour," he answered simply. She smiled, disbelievingly. "Your gnome companion has told me you are a king in your own right. Surely honour would dictate you return to your people." Ven was beginning to understand the commander's reason for asking him along. He placed his hand over the chest wound he had suffered, as if trying to grab at the pain shooting throughout his torso. "I told Princess Scáth, I would not leave her side until she was safely home. Upon reaching our goal, we see that home, is currently the furthest thing from a safe space. Surely you cannot attempt to convince me otherwise?" Ven offered every word with honesty which in turn came off slightly disrespectfully. Aelis smiled wide and turned to continue up the gruelling path. Ven exhaled deeply as he forced himself through the difficult task that lay before him. The view, however, was never a disappointment. To his right, he saw the southern half of Litore lake. In front of him was the jaggedly beautiful and seemingly infinite Highlands that rolled from here to Renrit, to the Sun Lotus Academy. To his left was the astonishingly wide Twinkle River that drew from Starlight Lake.

"I assure you the view is far more pleasant without the Renrit soldiers tainting our doorstep." Aelis scowled in the direction of the camp. Ven looked down on the army; a sight that severely unnerved him. He had been in more skirmishes and small battles then he could remember, but nothing like this. They had settled behind a low rising hill and therefore couldn't be seen from the city. From up high, it appeared as though they were well dug in with trenches covering their front line and palisades covering their flanks. Nearly thirty minutes went by before either the hunter or commander spoke again. They were busy intently staring and calculating the possible numbers of their enemy. They both peered through a spyglass and studied their adversaries well.

"What's your estimation?" She asked absent minded while still maintaining her line of sight on the army. Ven wasn't totally sure. Truth be told, he was distracted. His brush with death and the murder of Rexous still weighed heavily on the Kyst's mind. His relationship with Rex was something Ven was never truly sure of. Equal respect was known between them and they had spent much of their childhood in each other's company. Yet, Rexous saw the kindred spirits that Ven and the now passed Queen Trilara were, and therefore often acted out of jealousy for his own mothers' attention. It was one of the biggest emotional factors for Ven Devar's estrangement in Silva. And despite him in fact leaving Silva, Rexous travelled nearly halfway across the continent just for a chance to kill him. And despite all that confusion, Ven Devar had never actually fought in a war before. Nevertheless, he had spent most of his time up there working on their numbers.

"12,000 total."

"Good. Cavalry?" She asked before Ven drew his first breath after answering. He did some quick calculations in his head. "One thousand." Answering confidently.

"Estimated time for an attack?" Ven wasn't entirely sure what she meant but answered with what he presumed.

"Five minutes for the cavalry, Fifteen for the rest."

"That doesn't leave us with much time when that time does indeed come. Good work, Devar." She ended by finally turning her commanding gaze upon the Kyst's opalescent eyes that seemed to shine every shade of green.

"How many soldiers do you have, Aelis?" He asked in a rather suspecting tone. She looked back down on her home. The only place she had ever known.

"4,114 expertly trained Scorn Guard. 27 Ghosts of Aceia. 4,145 in all, if we're counting you and your unique companions. Which I am." The news of being outnumbered three to one had Ven's heart in his stomach.

"Then what is your kingdom's plan? Surely you cannot hope to win with these numbers." Before she could respond, the bell in a large tower connected to the palace began to ring. Aelis almost went over the edge as she lurched forward in shock.

"No," she whispered in despair. Ven didn't know what was going on and the next thing he knew, Aelis nimbly darted by him and began making her way back down the mountain as quickly as she dared. Which as it turned out was far quicker than Ven could manage. He couldn't believe her dexterity, and he grew up in the trees. He had been balancing on branches thinner than a finger for as long as he could remember. As he was trying his best to keep pace with the ever determined commander, his left foot rolled on a pebble, off-balancing the Kyst. Overcompensating as his heart skipped a beat, knowing all too well what it meant to fall, his ankle rolled badly. Ven threw his right shoulder against the rock face to ensure he would not fall.

"Damn, this mountain," he cursed under his breath, clearly frustrated by failing what he knew he could do, and do better than most. Unfortunately, his confidence had diminished since his encounter with Rexous. Ven saw Aelis far down the mountain and knew there would be no catching her. So he paused a moment, recollecting the shaken parts of his crumbling self. It was only minutes after the first ring of the palace bell when he tripped and subsequently gazed out on the horizon. A single rider aggressively crested the hill on horseback before rearing the horse to a halt. His armour glinted magnificently against the beaming sun, making him appear as a radiant dot of light against the sparse patches of spongy green grass covering the red rock.

Ch3 - Shifting Tides

Ven was nearly an hour in getting off the mountain and back to the palace. The folk were in a dire panic, fleeing to the safety of their homes. A sense of dread set in the Kyst as memories of his own home up in flames and under attack flooded his mind. He found himself more than once pushing through a congested and fleeing crowd of Scorn. It wasn't until he was within reach of the palace stairs that he was utterly halted by the Scorn Guard forming a tight line around its entire perimeter. Soon, the hunter was confronted by a huge guard with ghostly white skin and piercing black orbs. He easily stood 30 centimetres above the hunter.

"Be gone, freak," the burly guard ordered, sending spittle flying into the face of Ven.

"I'm expected, let me through," Ven pushed his way through but was shoved back several steps by the large Scorn, who did so with absolute ease.

"Are you deaf? I am expected."

The guard didn't appreciate the elf's tone, so he spat on the elf's boots, which was crossing a line in Ven's eyes.

"Fine," the hunter growled while closing the distance back to the guard with slow and assured steps. He relaxed his fist and after standing in front of the ShadowScorn for several heartbeats, Ven snapped his hand up with blinding speed to deliver a devastating punch to his throat. The guard fell to the ground, unaware of what had even just laid him low. Ven took a large step over him and several more paces before being completely encircled with blackglass spears.

He rolled his eyes and gave an exasperated sigh before locking his fingers behind his neck in surrender. As was the customary posture, when indeed, surrendering in Litore.

"State your intent, elf!" Yelled one of the guards at the other end of one spear.

"I'm expected," he growled, clearly tired of having to repeat himself. "My name is -"

"- Ven Devar, you imbeciles!" An approaching guard hollered who was differentiated by a single black feather protruding his matte black helm. It fitted him remarkably well and left a slim but ample t-visor for him to peer through. He batted aside the guards who had surrounded their guest. "I helped him off the mountain side myself."

Ven looked curiously at the man, for no one had made any mention of him in their recounting of the events that transpired in retrieving Ven and Rexous off the precarious cliff. He was well at Ven's side now though, after ordering his guards back into their primary formation.

"And you are?" The Kyst asked, dropping his hands back to his side. "You see, I place Azeni, at the entrance because normally people think twice before throat punching him. Did you think twice, Ven Devar?" The Captain of the Scorn Guard asked while pointing to the large Scorn still gasping for air. Ven looked at the wheezing guard and then back to the captain.

"You know, I even gave it a third thought for good measure," Ven stated with no lack of sarcasm. The captain stared blankly at Ven for a while; too long he thought.

"Captain Sindrum Silver at your service."

"What's happening here?" The Kyst voiced with well founded frustration and confusion.

"I myself am not yet aware. This formation is the first perimeter I set up if the bell has been rung. Do you know your way from here, good elf?" The captain asked with quick haste as he saw another brawl forming down the line.

"I do. Thank you, Captain Sindrum," Ven nodded and made a straight line back to the Council Hall.

Inside was utter silence. He found that the emptiness of the magnificent achromatic halls drained him of what little hope he had for the coming revelation. He had assumed from the ringing bell it was for an impending attack; a thought which had been bolstered when he saw the rider crest the hill. However, it was far too calm for that. It made sense that the rider had been from a nearby scouting party and had come for a look, when they too heard the city bell. After several more frustrating minutes the hunter more or less stumbled upon the entrance to the Council Hall. Upon entering one of the many archways, he stopped dead in his tracks as if he had collided with an invisible barrier. The ornate blackglass table in the centre of the room, acted now as the funeral bed for King Arwr.

Agan Dusk, as so often of late, was in the company of several Scorn women located in a particular establishment that boasted a fine bath house. One of the beautiful Scorn dressed in loose hanging silk was massaging his shoulders and occasionally lifted a glass of expensive Rhogarian liquor to his lips. The other Scorn, who Agan instantly recognized as having elven heritage, with her pointed ears and delicate features, sat atop his lap. From her lips came a hauntingly melodic hymn that reverberated across the water, skipping off the limestone walls to echo like a choir. She gently dragged her index finger along the fighters' many and varied scars found across his torso and limbs. Agan truly relished these moments in life, for they had seemed so rare to him in his turbulent past. There was nothing truly remarkable about his level of happiness or physical stimulation, though both were inflated. It was about the sense of peace that washed over the battle hardened 'Agora', meaning 'outsider' in his Orcish tongue. That word had haunted Agan his entire life, and more importantly the years during his adolescence. His mother had been sacrificed by the tribe for her weakness in being forced upon by an elf; she was of course offered to their God of Battle, Lokor. Agan was then raised as a tribeling, to roam the clan alone and survive by any means possible. Needless to say, growing up as an Orc was rough under typical circumstances, which Agan was not afforded. He grew up mean, strong, and able to defend himself from most by a very young age. Truly, that portion of his past weighed heavily on his mind like an inescapable migraine. It did, however, allow him the life he had now, the life he had always wanted. A sell-sword, adventurer, mercenary, it didn't matter what they called him, for freedom of action was all he craved. So when this particular fighter found himself flanked by arguably the most beautiful females in Litore, gently massaging his worn out muscles and serenading him with their angelic voices, he found peace.

Then they all heard it, the city bells. Agan's head shot up from the Scorn women's arms. He hadn't the slightest idea what it meant, but it wasn't hard to guess. They all jumped from the pool and Agan headed for the room that held his gear. He just about yelled 'stop' as the two Scorn ran full speed into a limestone wall, but they vanished into the lingering shadow. He smirked before spending little time getting back into his fresh gear, provided by Scáth. It had reinforced spaulders with a chest piece that covered his pectoral muscles, wrapping around to his back that offered strong protection for his ribs. The fine iradinium chain was weaved throughout the rest of the leather armour, trimmed with the iconic silver embossment of the ShadowScorn. A single double bearded axe with a sizable blackglass handle hung from his weapon belt. The faces of the axe were a matte black iradinium, except for razor-sharp edges, which Agan had been told was lined with silver.

He quickly exited the bath house to see a surprising amount of panic amongst the citizens as everyone rushed for the safety of their homes. Agan was heading towards the palace with haste but he hadn't made it very far when he spotted four rough-looking Scorn men heading his way. He didn't think much of it past their irregularly rough exteriors, until they were clearly staring his way and putting hand to hilt. A confused Agan looked behind him to only see more rushing civilians. He looked back and noticed two of them had vanished, yet the other two were only a few strides away. The leading Scorn human was now uttering curses at the fighter. Agan made one last-ditch effort to seek out the city guard but to no luck, so he planted his feet and pulled out his axe. The two approaching Scorn did likewise. After a still moment between the three, surrounded by rushing and frightened citizens, Agan shrugged in a manner as to invite them to make the first move. They did so, generating some distance between each other so that they could flank the burly Agora. Agan slid one foot back and defensively took his axe up in both hands. The leading Scorn man came in with a great sweep of his long sword across the chest, however, the half-orc simply leaned back almost 90 degrees as the blade swept over him. The other Scorn man, now in reach, cleaved down with his long sword so Agan let his momentum go and fell back into a roll.

Distinctly hearing the sword connect with the stone, Agan kicked his feet out forcing the lead Scorn off his balance to stumble a few strides back. He flexed his core and shot back up with a great swing of his axe, completely over powering the smaller Scorn man and bashing the long sword from his grasp. The man, now sword-less, looked as though he had just seen a ghost, and reflexively sent a jab into the face of Agan. The half-orc's head barely moved from the blow and he returned the gesture by fully charging his feeble attacker. Agan slammed his spaudler into the Scorn and carried him four-metres, slamming his back into the wall of a dark and putrid ally. A jarring crack was heard and the Scorn let out a sick wheeze. Agan dropped him, fairly confident he wouldn't be getting up for a long while, if ever.

He noticed the leader recovered and blocking the exit of the alley. Agan could only see the silhouette of the Scorn holding a long sword, with two glowing grey eyes glaring back at him. The half-orc, looked no less intimidating, with his yellow eyes giving a slight glow to his gradient green and red skin. He growled with a ferocity that would make Faenla proud, noting the Scorn man actually take a step back in response. Agan was about to rush his enemy when he felt the cold bite of steel penetrate his lower back and the hilt of a dagger press firmly against his skin. The feeling of steel sinking into his flesh was almost nostalgic at this point. He grasped it and instinctively swung around with one hand high on the handle of his axe. Agan spun and felt his weapon cleanly lop the head off a Scorn ruffian who disappeared shortly before the skirmish began. In front of him was a charging Scorn dwarf, who roared with anger at the sight of his decapitated comrade, body slamming Agan. The seasoned fighter stood firm but was slipping backwards under the immense sturdiness of the dwarf. Before Agan could break the stalemate, his legs were swept out from under him as his metal greaves squealed from the leader's long sword. He hit the ground with a thud and the two remaining Scorn wasted no time in mercilessly beating and kicking the downed fighter. Agan reflexively covered his head as the Scorn dwarf made sure each cudgel strike counted. The fighter growled in defiance and tried to rise but felt the slice of steel again as the leader cut the back of his legs. Agan roared in pain, laying bloody, beaten, and making his peace before surely meeting his end. After a particularly nasty blow to the hip, Agan heard a familiar upbeat voice.

"Excuse me, stop that, or my companion here will eat ya for his mid-day meal." Agan couldn't roll over to see but heard the unmistakable sound of Faenla's throat crackling growl, giving great snorts of warning and nipping at the air with his razor-sharp fangs. The two Scorn seeing the approaching wolf quickly ran further down the alley before becoming one with the shadow and disappearing altogether. Athvar quickly jumped off the back of Faenla and rushed over to his friend.

"Oh, Agan," Athvar said more to himself than the fighter. "We'll get ya back and fixed up, I promise."

Agan wasn't sure if it was something Athvar gave him or the loss of blood, either way, he quickly and quietly faded into unconsciousness.

Ven took a hesitant step forward, completely unsure of what to do next. He noted that the upper balcony was filled with Scorn, standing shoulder to shoulder looking down upon their deceased king. Scáth, Katia, Aelis, and Torvic stood around the table, with Torvic at the king's feet leading the room in prayer. Ven was caught off guard, which instantly annoyed him as he heard, and then spotted, a scrawny and bald Scorn man.

"You should leave now, Kyst elf," Oren said in a hushed voice, standing just behind and to Ven's left. The Kyst half peered over his shoulder.

"Your king lies dead, your city crumbles before you, yet you push away valuable allies?" Ven retorted with some level of condescension. "The only ally to the Scorn are the Scorn. Certainly not in the likes of elves who have forsaken Litore millennia ago," Oren said with equal disrespect.

"Spare me the outdated prejudice. My kin left these petty and feeble wars for the solitude of the coast. We do not value ourselves above others and therefore care not to be involved in your squabbles." Ven finished, crossing his arms defiantly.

"All the more reason to leave."

Ven looked back over his shoulder to find empty space. He rolled his eyes at the absurdity of it all, yet he would be lying to himself if he said he wasn't at least a bit worried that he had made a mistake in staying here longer than anticipated. He did after all have his own people to return to, back on Sanctuary Island. By now, he assumed

Vakar would have regrown the forest that burned along with Silva, in preparation for its reconstruction. The Kyst felt a wave of anxiety wash over him at that moment, which increased tenfold as he saw Scáth silently crying beside her still father. To say things were bad in ShadowScorn would be a severe understatement. He feared now more than ever for the safety of Scáth with the loss of her father. Arwr had been described to Ven as a truly admirable king and from the brief conversation they shared, he believed it. Scáth had also told Ven of the rocky relationship with her mother, especially making a point of her strange behaviour before she disappeared, and since her return. It tore at his very heart to see Scáth standing up there holding the hand of Aelis, tears freely flowing. These past months had been filled with so much pain and loss. Ven had barely come to terms with the fall of Silva before running from his fears to escort Scáth home; which he would do again in a heartbeat as he knew it was the right thing to do. However, he also knew sooner or later that he would have to face what awaited him in the Great Northern Rainforest.

Scáth looked up, easily spotting Ven's multitude of colours against the achromatic halls and peoples of her race, albeit a little blurry from the tears. She felt a small level of comfort fill her heart as they shared a brief moment of eye contact, outside of time and space, in their own place. She immediately felt a sense of loneliness again as a pair of Scorn Guard and a priest requested Ven's attention. Under different circumstances the priests walking him away might have been concerning, but she was torn from that thought as she was handed one end of a long silken black sheet. Woven on it was the circular crest of the City of Shadow. Two silhouetted and mirror images of the city skyline; the top coloured a dark purple sky with silver stars whilst the bottom reflected a soft gold, as if bathed by sunlight. Katia held the other side, and together they covered Arwr, the third King of ShadowScorn.

Ven Devar was being rushed down many of the winding corridors of the palace proper to the infirmary. Upon reaching a stark room, save for a single statue of Aceia and many priests rushing about, the two Scorn Guard broke off and stood watch at the door as Ven was escorted inside. There, the hunter stared in disbelief at the sight before him. Agan was stripped down naked, save a wrapping around his waist. His eyes were almost fully swollen shut. Several gashes were currently being stitched up and much of the fighters body had already turned black and blue from bruising. Athvar sat in the corner on a chair propped up next to Agan's bed.

"Faen and I found him, seconds away from his end." Athvars voice was weak with sorrow.

"Where are those responsible?" Ven muttered through gritted teeth as he stood beside Agan.

"A couple of Scorn, man and dwarf I think. Agan severed one's head while another died from a crushed rib cage. 'Twas Faenla scared the survivors off." Ven looked to Faenla who was in a customary position, rump down on the cobblestone floor overlooking the half-orc. The magnificent wolf gave his dearest companion a look of reassurance.

"We will find those responsible." Ven looked to the dusty gnome with fire in his eyes. He felt a bit like a monster after seeing Athvar's surprised reaction, but remained steadfast in his anger. This was unforgivable and he burned for vengeance.

"We will. It's another task on an already lengthy list, I'm afraid," Athvar said with a self-deprecating chuckle.

"Why are we not welcome here, Athvar?" The Kyst asked with palpable despair. Athvar looked to his elven companion and saw the trouble in his heart. The gnome gave the only priest left in the room a knowing glance. The Priest of Aceia bowed and made his exit. Athvar hopped off his chair and walked to the wooden door, peering out to make sure no one was lingering then he quietly closed it.

"I have walked this palace many times. And though I'm sure there is much I have not seen, I'm left with little doubt that the people who stole Princess Scáth away walk within these very halls." Athvar was quiet and careful with words.

"I was asked personally by the administrator to leave with haste," Ven said under his breath, still not looking away from his beaten friend. Athvar crossed his arms and rested his small chin atop one hand, in deep contemplation.

"I will uncover the meaning of it all, I assure ya." When Athvar elicited no response from the Kyst, he asked. "Why'd they ring thee bell?"

"The king is dead."

* * *

Several hours had gone by of Athvar and Ven staring into the flickering flames that burned in the hearth of Agan Dusk's recovery room. They both, including Faenla, turned their gaze to the door when it slowly creaked open. In walked Torvic, Aelis, then Scáth; each with their own predictable faces of defeat and melancholy. Ven sprang up and rushed to Scáth's side, throwing his arms around her in a desperate attempt to smother her sadness with affection. She stood there with arms at her side for what felt like a long moment, before she squeezed the Kyst so hard he thought she might crack his rib.

"I'm sorry," he whispered into her ear through a face full of her stark black and ever billowing hair.

"I should never have come back," her voice squeaked. Ven knew Scáth had not realized Agan was laying in the bed mortally wounded, and he feared what this revelation might bring on.

"Did they tell you of Agan?" He softly asked. He felt her head nod against his chest. Ven pulled Scáth to arm's length and moved slightly to reveal their battered companion behind him. It was then the Kyst realized he would have preferred to see Scáth sob, for a cold and detached look consumed her. She slowly walked over to Agan's right, as Torvic stood on the left casting a divine healing spell. She looked at Agan's beaten face and swollen eyes before gently stroking his usually braided hair off his face. Scáth did not react how anyone expected, rather the distance in her eyes overruled any reactionary emotion.

"He will survive, princess. He has a strength unlike I've ever known," Torvic said with a small smile. Ven noted Athvar and Aelis turn from the hearth to regard him. A sense of intrigue struck Ven as he recognized the look in the gnome's eyes. He then noted Scáth and Torvic holding their gaze on him as well, a slight smirk crossed the Kyst's mouth.

"What?" He asked as if not understanding some inside joke. "We need you to go to Moon Mountain," Aelis said dryly, ending any levity the Kyst had.

His face screwed up in confusion. "Why?" He asked, anyone willing to answer. Scáth seemed distant to Ven because, in truth, this was the last thing she wanted to ask of him.

"They are strong allies to our people," Torvic answered. "They can easily thwart the Renrit besiegers and can help us keep the transition of power, over to Princess Scáth, a peaceful one," Aelis added. Ven's eyes widened, for he had never considered Scáth would so soon become the Queen of ShadowScorn.

"Why would it not be peaceful to begin with?" Ven asked trying to work through a flurry of questions and emotions. Aelis waved her hand over Agan to prove her point.

"Queen Katia is not a direct descendant of King Risastor, the first King of ShadowScorn, therefore the duty of ruling now falls upon Scáth. We believe that Lady Katia will not so easily give up her position of power, however." Torvic never wavered in his confidence and spoke sternly to the coastal elf. Ven looked to Scáth who still sat on the edge of Agan's bed. Ven dropped his face into both palms and shook his head in denial, and in doing so he was reminded of the sharp pain he still felt from his chest wound.

"I can't leave before ensuring Agan's attackers are brought to justice," the hunter said defiantly.

"That's why I'll be stayin," Athvar added quietly, considering his usual disposition.

"You have to protect Scáth," Ven shot back at the gnome. It was then that Faenla rose from near the fire, as he had been watching this whole interaction with significant interest. The huge and nimble wolf sauntered over to Scáth, drawing in everyone's gaze as he went. On all fours, he was already taller than Scáth when she was standing, but now as she sat on the bed, he stood above Scáth protectively, and stared back at Ven. Scáth wrapped her arms around Faen's thick furry neck in response. The Kyst gave a small exhale of disbelief and a smile crossed his face, yet he found no humour.

"I am to go by myself then? Will the people of Moon Mountain trust me?" Ven asked the Scorn.

Aelis approached Ven with a scroll tube. "Inside is a letter with our signatures. Yourself and one of the five Captain's of the Scorn Guard, will deliver this to Grand Master Zenair in the Crescent City atop Moon Mountain."

Ven looked to Scáth before taking it, to see that she was still hugging the wolf tightly.

"Make it Captain Sindrum. I met him earlier," Ven demanded softly. She nodded in agreement. "May Scáth and I have a moment of privacy," Ven said, not leaving any room for debate in his tone. With slight looks of agreement, the room soon cleared out, save for Faenla of course. Ven still sat near the hearth, nervously spinning the scroll tube in his right hand.

"I miss you," Ven whispered.

"I know." She barely replied, for her heart simply hurt in too many ways to begin to understand any of it. "I didn't want to ask you but everyone insisted that 'The Mighty Ven Devar' is our best hope."

Ven recoiled at the title for, as always, it brought to him a sense of shame and discomfort. "Do you believe that?"

"I fear I've forgotten what to believe in," she answered absently. Ven tucked the scroll tube into one of the many pockets inside his PumaSheep cloak and approached Scáth. He grabbed her hand and she stood to meet him. Her gaze was on the floor so he gently placed his hand under her chin and lifted it so they could look into one another's eyes. His heart fluttered as it always did when she looked at him, and on instinct he kissed her with every ounce of passion in his heart. After the briefest moment, she pulled away from the Kyst. "Why would you do that?" She scolded before quickly ripping her hands from his. She stared at him in anger and astonishment before quickly leaving the room. Ven stood there where she had left him, feeling like an idiot. He looked to Faenla who had his head resting on his front paws, holding his piercing blue eyes on the hunter. The Kyst walked over to the wolf and sat in front of him. Ven placed his forehead on Faen's, heaving a great sigh and remained in that position for a long time.

"I will return soon, stay with Scáth until my return," Ven said in his native tongue of Kystin, while making direct eye contact with the one creature he felt understood him. Faenla gave a low growl in agreement, licked the Kyst's face and briskly padded off after the princess. Ven watched his animal companion depart and felt the all too familiar pang of loneliness.

Ch4 - A New Quest

Sindrum was standing in the falling snow under a stormy twilight sky, warming his hands and armour next to a large brazier meant for heating the guard while on watch along the cities great wall. He looked down the nearly 60-metre drop and felt that familiar tingle in his stomach. Closing his eyes he teetered back and forth, envisioning what the fall would feel like. Perhaps he could become one with the shadow before splatting against the loose gravel and large jagged rocks strategically placed below. He opened his eyes and removed his helmet to better feel the winter air against his starkly white skin. As the world continued to darken, Sindrum's skin changed to an onyx black. Many Scorn, if well practised in the art of Shadow-Phasing, changed the achromatic hue of their skin at will. Looking out onto the horizon he hoped, nay, he prayed that the Renrit army would march on their city so they could just be done with it. This Scorn man hated the time before war, never able to find a moment of peace. The screams and stench of death from past battles, never failed to flood his memory with relentless detail. He sighed deeply and turned to look over the palace, where he saw several hundred Scorn Guard still encircling it. He also saw a scrawny, bald-headed Scorn moving in his direction down below. Sindrum lost sight of him in the heavy shadow of the city wall onset by the glow of the moons. As the Captain expected, Oren emerged from the darkness right next to him.

"Administrator," Sindrum said with a purposeful lack of enthusiasm.

"Evening, Captain," Oren replied with paralleled excitement. "How do you fair?"

"Do not waste my time with pleasantries you so covet with the others." Sindrum turned back to look over the rolling highlands where the glow of the enemy camp could be seen. After a moment, Oren stood beside the captain again and leaned on the walls parapet.

"How did she return?" Oren asked accusingly.

"Everyone in ShadowScorn knows it to be the Kyst and her friends. How should I know anything different?"

"This reflects poorly on you."

Sindrum stood tall and indignantly turned to face the 'voice of the people.' The captain was well known throughout the city to be one of its finest fighters, but Oren did not cower.

"I did everything you said," Sindrum stated sternly, poking Oren in his soft chest as he uttered each word.

"And yet the girl has returned."

"I care not anymore. Do what you will with what has been dealt to you." The captain turned back to face the horizon.

Oren scoffed heartily. "You've been summoned by your own commander. Why I bothered to tell you this is beyond my recollection."

Sindrum raised a brow at the administrator.

"On what business?"

"You're going on a quest." Oren turned to walk away. "Best of luck," He offered sarcastically, leaving the captain with the echoes of his laughter.

"I do not know," Scáth said with a true air of confusion. "It does not matter. My father has..." her words silenced by the own realization of having to speak them.

"We've known each other our entire lives. Even if you do not see it, I know when your heart has found what it wants." Aelis wrapped a comforting arm around her oldest and dearest friend. The two powerful Scorn elves looked out and over the city from the balcony of Scáth's private chambers. "Your father was more than just a good Scorn, he was a great Scorn. But believe me when I say, you will be far greater." Aelis planted a kiss on her friends temple before fading away.

She stood there overlooking her beloved city and it unnerved her to see the streets so empty. Everyone would wait in their homes after the bell until instructed otherwise. It was still too soon to discount the possibility of the Renrit army taking advantage and forming a strike. She looked down at the sound of laughter to notice the Scorn Guard, still shoulder to shoulder encircling the entire palace. Suddenly she felt the presence of her mother shadow-walking into her room. Becoming one with darkness was something that the princess could never manage, in fact she was one of the very few in her race who could not in some capacity meld with it. There had been a handful of occasions on her journey back where she thought perhaps she had done so, but to her frustration, never on command. She remained to overlook the cloudy night as her mother wrapped her arms around her daughters shoulders.

"I'm so sorry," Katia whispered with too much hope in her voice for Scáth's liking.

"You once told me to never waste a breath with lies," Scáth replied bluntly while shrugging off her mother and spinning to face her. "I don't know what you've done or how you did it, but I will find out," Scáth threatened with frightening hatred and stern resolve.

Katia took a menacing step towards her daughter. Many years of Scáth's life were spent afraid of her own mother, which instinctively had her maintaining the gap and stepping out into the sparse moonlight. "You were such a determined child," Katia said with intense malice. "I should have just dealt with you myself. I suppose it's never to late," Katia added, while looking over the balcony rail. "The fall from here would end with any in our race but the most skilled of shadow-walkers painting the cobblestone black. Perhaps you threw yourself off out of despair."

Scáth wanted to scream at Katia's open admission to it all, but she held her ground, denying her twisted mother any satisfaction. Katia took another step forward, moving into the moonlight, revealing a sick smirk on her lips. Just then, a pair of glowing eyes popped open in the darkness behind them. Now it was Scáth who gave a wicked smile which put a halt to Katia. The queen jumped up straight and gave a shriek as she heard the threatening snarls of Faenla. She spun on her heel, in utter disbelief that she was caught unaware of the great wolf's presence. Faenla took several slow steps towards Katia, hackles taught, snout snarling to reveal his flesh shredding fangs. She took several panicked steps back until she fully bumped into Scáth.

"Faenla and I would die protecting each other; an instinct that bloomed from love. Who can you say that about, mother? With a husband and son both dead, and a daughter you so veraciously disown."

Katia ran back into the room, avoiding the wolf as best she could, and faded away, quickly becoming one with the darkness. "Suddenly I have lost both my parents." She said weakly under her breath. Faenla however was beside her in a heartbeat, nuzzling his soft snout against Scáth's cheek. She placed a hand on his enormous shoulders for she felt as though she may topple over. She had wisely prevented herself from considering what life would be like if she returned home, for she really didn't believe her eyes would ever see it again. Now she was here, she felt herself longing for those amazing nights by the camp fire with her companions. The way the open wind and cold rain made her skin tingle with life, the exhilaration of battling foe and monsters for their very lives. She held Faenla's fur tightly, almost in disbelief that their relationship started with the wolf attempting to feed her to his pack. But now, she vividly remembered their several months together as some of the greatest of her life. She found herself looking on those moments of closeness with Ven as the fondest of all. She had stolen small kisses on the forehead or cheek of the handsome Kyst before, each one sending her own spirits fluttering. But, she had felt robbed when he had just kissed her so passionately; she had thought about how that first kiss would go more often than she wanted to admit. She even dreamed of it which made her feel all the more silly, reminding her of her younger years, for Scáth was nearing her sixth decade. She wanted their first kiss to be world-shaking, and yet she only felt the numbness. She went to her bed and curled up with Faenla, feeling lost and suddenly orphaned.

Torvic was now leading Ven through a large descending spiral staircase. He held an unlit torch that struck the Kyst as curious considering both of their eyes could function exceptionally well in the dark. Soon, they were in the dungeons of the castle. Ven was assaulted by the blinding light spells that hung in each cell, designed to prevent any Scorn from shadow-walking out of their prison. The hunter noticed a few rather disgruntled and vicious-looking inmates turn a weary glance their way as they proceeded to the end of the dungeon.

"Is all this necessary?" Ven questioned the Arch Priest. When he received no answer, the Kyst considered it a redundant question. The next door required a special enchantment to open, much like the secret passages in Silva. With a few words muttered under his breath, Torvic waved his hand and the sound of stone sliding across stone rumbled through the dungeon. As Ven peered through the small doorway he understood why a torch was needed, for even his advanced Kyst night vision could not penetrate the utter blackness ahead. Torvic then snapped his fingers above the torch and a black fire erupted, white flames licking upwards. The Arch Priest proceeded inwards, while the black flame forced the impenetrable darkness away. Ven kept close to the Scorn as he noticed the torch only roughly illuminated a square metre.

"Why the magical darkness?" Ven asked, catching himself whispering for some reason.

"We've had trouble with wild magic reanimating those in the morgue. Not even the undead could stumble through this," Torvic answered in an equal whisper. After a few moments, the Scorn Cleric whispered the same enchantment to open another door and snuffed out his torch. The air inside bit at their skin with an unrelenting chill yet still managed to smell foul. Ven saw a low ceiling with a room that spanned nearly 100 meters in each direction, his sight interrupted by the occasional load-bearing pillar. Frost clung to every surface and the air escaping his lungs became as clear as smoke. Ven couldn't help but be reminded of time spent around the demon, Hoarfrost, nearly a decade ago. Torvic pointed to a particular blackglass slab that supported a familiar body.

"I'll be right here if you need anything," he offered kindly. Ven nodded in appreciation before slowly striding over to the body. He noted only a few other corpses in the room but paid them no heed. He saw the now blue and frosted remains of Rexous, still dressed in the almost identical armour of Ven. He gently grasped the stiff hand of the former Prince of Silva and stood for a long time, lost in deep reflection. Perhaps it was just a coincidence but he felt a serious pulse of pain in his still healing chest wound. Ven Devar really had not wanted to come down here to see his old counterpart but it was the unrelenting

Athvar that convinced him that it was a necessary part of the grieving process. Now he was down here, he was glad of it. The hunter did not think of their most recent history, but of their time as children. It was never a friendly relationship but one that truly forced both to grow in an effort to outdo each other. Ven truly understood now, that the presence Rex had in his life, shaped him significantly. A wide smile appeared on Ven's face thinking back on the many competitions and petty arguments these two had shared, understanding, now, it to be nothing more than the blustering smoke of youth.

"I'm sorry things ended the way they did," he whispered solemnly. "Never have I known a more skilled hunter, my ol'friend." Ven took a deep breath and one last look at Rexous before walking back to Torvic. "Last requests?"

Ven had to consider that for a moment. "Prepare his body for my return journey. He should be laid to rest with his family." Torvic nodded and lead them back out into the main palace. Ven Devar wasted little time in finding Aelis, Captain Sindrum, and Athvar in a common room just outside the Palace Armoury. They stood around a small wooden table with several dozen lit and half melted candles. They did not turn to regard the Kyst so Ven found some space around the table and listened in. Splayed before them was a canvas map of the region between ShadowScorn and Moon Mountain. Ven even noticed there was detailed navigational charts of Starlight Lake.

"I know the journey by land. I insist if we go by boat we'll find nothing but trouble, or flounder to our watery graves and leave you all without the aid required to survive," Sindrum said almost erratically.

"Not with thee Kyst at yar side," Athvar said, giving a wink to the newly arrived Ven. Captain Sindrum gave Ven a skeptical look. "Then this is the route?" The Kyst asked.

"One of two," replied Sindrum without hiding his cynicism. "The water will shorten your trip there, Sindrum. If Grand Master Zenair is to offer us support, you will surely be walking back," Aelis said sternly, reminding her subordinate of his place. Sindrum's posture eased and he gave a nod of respect. Ven eyed Sindrum, curiously. He didn't much care for the detailed planning of this mission. He had a destination set and knew all too well how even the most thorough of plans could and often would change as quickly as the wind did blow.

"Then a boat will await us?" Ven asked Aelis specifically. A doubtful glance was shared between them before she dropped a hefty sack of coin on the table.

"Buy one."

Ven and Sindrum looked at each other with rye grins. "That simplifies things," Sindrum said, lightly amused before pushing the coin Ven's way. That surprised him but he quickly remembered how hunted the Scorn were beyond their walls and thought it to be a smart move. Ven tucked the coin into a deep pouch on his belt.

"Then we leave with the cover of night?" Ven asked and the two Scorn were quick to agree. The elf looked down to Athvar, and the gnome returned the kind gaze. Although they didn't notice, Sindrum and Aelis walked off to one side of the room to have their own brief conversation.

"What has ya most worried?" Athvar asked with genuine care. "Afraid I can't settle on one," Ven exhaled while kneeling to meet his companions' height.

"It's the same as always. One foot in front of the other," Athvar answered confidently. When that did little to boost the elf's demeanour he added, "Faenla and I will take good care of Scáth and Agan while yar gone." The gnome put a hand on Ven's shoulder, offering a warm smile. Ven reciprocated the gesture, feeling slightly relieved. He was so grateful to have Athvar in his life since the destruction of Silva. The gnome had been a stern hand of experience that Ven needed, as well as a constant source of hope and optimism. Suddenly, hitting him like a ton of bricks, he realised that Athvar was in fact very clean and actually quite fragrant.

"Mark it as a day to remember, for Athvar is dusty no more," Ven said with hardy sarcasm. Athvar gave a belly rumbling chuckle. "In the company of those esteemed enough, I may tolerate a bath now and again," Athvar said with a wink.

"I will return soon."

"Ya will, Ven Devar." Athvar threw his little arms around the elf and the two shared a comforting embrace. Ven stood again and went to check on Sindrum and Aelis while Athvar left to oversee Agan. Aelis and Sindrum shook hands before turning to regard the hunter.

"Ready?" Ven asked of the Scorn Captain.

"As I'll ever be."

Ven looked to Aelis. "Tell Scáth I will return soon, with everything she needs." A curious stare came from the commander. "She should hear it from you."

Ven looked away doubtfully, truly unsure if he believed that statement. He felt as though he had changed since his battle with Rexous. Not physically, as he could already feel his full agility returning; in large thanks to Torvic's powerful healing. Perhaps he had overestimated Scáth's feelings for him. And most of all, he felt very uncomfortable with the idea of death; most notably, how quick he once was to deliver it. He looked to Sindrum and with no more ceremony, the captain led them out of the castle and to a similar stone wall Ven and Aelis had used that morning. This one however, was on the east side of the city. Captain Sindrum, still wearing his full armour was now covered from boot to helm in a long and tattered travelling cloak. He wore his helmet at all times in the wild, so you would have to come face to face with the Scorn to actually see what race he belonged to.

They stepped into a thin crevasse of the mountain that was no more than a metre wide and 20 high before breaking into open sky. Ven looked up and could see only the largest moon of Litore's sky, Caelestis; a bright orb of mostly cherry red dirt, orange clouds, and vast splotches of blue and green. Within a half-hour they were free of the long winding crevasse and out on the northeastern face of Glass Mountain. They walked several hours through the night and stopped at first light to view their destination. Moon Mountain was as far away as the eye could see but loomed like a beacon against the sun's easterly ascent. Starlight Lake was visible in the dark with its natural glimmer, but glowed a different kind of beauty with dawns light. Ven felt a sense of assurance overcome him as he breathed fresh air, overlooking a ruggedly beautiful and dangerous landscape. The ground between Litore Lake and Starlight Lake was now a mosaic of crusted and cracked earth. The land had dried up after a great quake from the war between the Silver Dwarves and Rhogarians had shaken most of Litore, forming Starlight in the process.

The eastern shore of the lake is where they intended on sailing, and boasted the infamous Bayownin Forest. A realm of all things abnormal, Bayownin Forest had hawks with 20-metre wingspan, dire-elk ten metres tall with 100 point antlers, and insects large enough to carry away a fully armoured shield dwarf. The southern tip of the lake boasted a small trade-town with the largest dock on the whole lake.

"We shall find our boat in Rushwater," Sindrum said while pointing to a specific section of the lake. Ven raised a brow the captain's way.

"When Scáth and I travelled, she remained outside of any towns." The Kyst explained, clearly assuming the captain wouldn't risk it either.

"She was smart to do so. The docks of Rushwater never sleep but in the darkness of night, we will secure our vessel." Sindrum looked over at Ven with a disconcertingly excited grin. Ven nodded with a slight smirk of his own and raised his arm, inviting Sindrum to continue leading.

They hit the mountain base by mid-day and were on track to reach Rushwater by morrow's dusk. They walked side by side through tall green grass in a sparse woodland forest of autumn-coloured bark. The red bark and yellow lichen covering most surfaces struck Ven as unusually stunning. It also dawned on him as peculiar for they should have been knee deep in snow.

"It's mid-winter, where is the snow?" Ven asked, finally frustrated by the lack of answers he could think of. Sindrum looked to Ven as if the answer was obvious.

"Surely you remember the Quake of Harazune? Wrought by the dwarves to topple the Kingdom of Rhogar?" Sindrum asked almost rhetorically.

"No...well, yes. But we in the tree tops felt nothing and the thousands of islands in the Northern Archipelago prevented the tsunami's that the rest of Litore suffered. Some would say Kaia kept our waters calm and Āina held the land firm for all Kyst, though I would not."

Sindrum scoffed at that. "Don't be so quick to dismiss the gods. As for the snow, the ground is too hot now. You've seen it on the mountains around us, and even though it snows on us now, it does not accumulate."

Ven spent several moments attempting to wrap his head around that. The proof seemed abundant but how was the ground gaining temperature? Nevertheless, the hunter accepted it for what it was and focused on the task at hand. Like Captain Sindrum, Ven knew that they would be spending much time together and yet, he was not sure if he could trust this Scorn. There was little proof in the city of anyone truly trusting anyone.

"You seem unbothered by the passing of your king," Ven stated flatly. Sindrum didn't skip a beat and kept his eyes forward. "Some have not been thrilled of late with Arwr. Perhaps Aceia took him to the Realm of Eternal Night because he too agrees." Sindrum sounded dispassionate about it, which Ven instantly took as a failed attempt to hide his true feelings. The hunter was nothing if not someone who pushed people.

"Yet, Scáth is the one to rule now. How do you think she will fair?" "It does not matter what I think." The Scorn answered with haste. "If it did not matter I would not ask," the Kyst replied, as he truly was not one to waste one's time.

"As I said, some of late have been unhappy."

That was not what Ven wanted to hear. He felt like stopping right there and turning back for Scáth, yet the words of Athvar echoed in his mind and he was confident that the gnome and wolf would be vigilant in protecting her and Agan. So he left the conversation at that, knowing there were many devious subversion's going on in the darkened halls of that palace. The coastal elf reminded himself that his thoughts needed to be on the road ahead and perhaps no insignificant amount of watchfulness over Sindrum.

"I was surprised to hear you asked for me, specifically I mean, to join on this quest. I am honoured, as any Scorn Guard would have volunteered to do this most important thing for our people," Sindrum explained. Ven wasn't sure what his point was and remained quiet. "So why me?" The captain finally asked, almost as if he had to.

Ven chuckled to himself, there wasn't anything in particular, other than the Kyst had seen his competence and the respect his men had for him.

"This is a new land to me and I needed to be sure I would have 61 someone as competent with the blade as they are with their intellect." "Our encounter lasted but a moment, how could you assume I was either?"

"You are a Captain, aren't you?" Ven said as if that should be enough to answer the Scorn.

"I see why at least your social reputation precedes you. As much as I wish not to find battle on this journey, I am eager to see if your skill as a warrior holds up to the many whispers of the 'Mighty Ven Devar," the captain quipped and before Ven could digest his words, Sindrum threw an arm out, halting them.

Ven shot his glance ahead to a clearing in the sparse wood, a herd of wild bisonbear could be seen running and bellowing as the ground suddenly began to shake.

"Earthquake?" Ven asked clearly concerned, but he was answered as a trio of Mountain Giants came after the fleeing creatures. Ven was awe-struck with the gaps between their strides and the cold grey stone hue to their cracked skin. He guessed the tallest Giant to be 15 metres tall with stitched together leathers and a crude blood-stained club, chiselled from a boulder. He was pulled away from his wonderment as Sindrum shoved him to the ground.

"Are you mad?" Sindrum whispered to the Kyst, anger evident in his voice. Ven did not heed the Scorn's words as he watched one of the giants scoop up no less than three fully grown bisonbear in a single hand. Then he heard a series of deep shouts emanate from the Giants, which he could only assume was in their native tongue; a language that could be easily mistaken for the rumbles of a rock slide. The Kyst watched in awe and before Sindrum could do anything, he was already halfway up a tree so as to get a better view of the colossal creatures. Upon climbing to the very top and peeking his head through the crown of the canopy, he saw the behemoths from eye level. Two of them had shaved heads and sky blue braided beards that swept against their bellies. Their eyes a pale grey and as big as Ven's torso, blinked slowly. The hunter didn't think these Giants did anything quickly on the account of their enormity. The third Giant had long white hair and similar eyes but was clearly female. With a sudden gust of wind, the hunters hood was pulled off and the white haired Giant turned his way. The Kyst's heart skipped several beats and he instinctively froze. The Giant carried a pickaxe with an entire tree-trunk for a handle, she stuck it in the dirt which shook the earth and took an impossibly large step towards the tree line. Sindrum gulped and attempted to hide himself better among the foliage. Ven had noted the colour of the leaves and trusted in his natural ability to camouflage in such environments. The Giant looked at the tree and the entire surrounding area. Ven could see none of this and found little use in listening, for the sound of the other two Giants was all that could be heard. She sniffed the air, took another step forward and paused again. Ven felt the wave of air hit the tree canopy from her shifting momentum. He shifted with the leaves and remained just as he was. Sindrum watched on his side as one of the Giants threw the head of a particularly unfortunate creature at the backside of the white-haired one. With that, the three Mountain Giants kept on moving northwest to Litore Lake. Ven opened his eyes and watched the Giants leave before descending down to the forest floor.

"Unbelievable," was all the flustered Scorn Captain could say. Ven smirked and shrugged in response before crossing the field, leaving Sindrum to doubtfully shake his head. He was, at that time, wondering how the Kyst had survived the journey from the Great Northern Rainforest to ShadowScorn if this was how he acted around such formidable creatures.

Ch5 - Cross a Scorn

A group of Kyst Sages sat on their knees with their palms planted firmly against the forest floor, all murmuring in perfect synchronization. Around them stood a wider circle of Kyst Hunters watching the process with reverence. The hunters were not merely there to watch the ritual but protect it from any creature that could prevent the raising of the great carved bridge to the treetops.

The chanting was steady and rhythmic, barely louder than a soft breeze puppeteering dancing leaves. The hunters looked up in disbelief as the massive wooden walkway floated nearly a kilometre skywards, before locking into joints protruding from the connecting cedar trees. A collective exhale was sounded as the sages all let go of the spell, all but one sage remained distant from exhaustion. Vakar stood with strength, ordained in magnificent green robes and the artifact necklace of Silva displayed proudly around his collar. He too, having just performed the spell of levitation, effortlessly walked over to each sage, offering a steady hand to help them back up to their feet.

"That is enough for today," Vakar declared proudly. Many of the hunters aided the exhausted sages back to their nearby camp. With night fallen, the glowing pools of water and luminescent flora guided their steps back. Vakar quickly found solace in his extra-dimensional tent. Upon walking through the green-canvased flaps, a much larger space than what the exterior of the tent could offer was found; complete with a sleeping chamber, a small library, a large alchemy lab and a quaint fireplace with a fur-lined arm chair. The library and bed-chamber were on a level separated from the rest by three short stairs. At the top and very centre of those three stairs was something that stopped the Kyst King quicker than a heart attack. A single red rose lay at the bottom of a small red-granite pillar, holding a glossy and translucent orb. For some reason he did not question why it was there, he was simply mesmerized by its presence. As the briefest flickers of an image showed inside the orb, Vakar took a few stunted steps forward.

"Excuse us, Your Grace," came two familiar and trusted voices that broke his otherworldly trance.

"Do you see it?" He asked, pointing to the orb.

"See what, my king?" A kind and feminine voice echoed out. Vakar turned to face his trusted generals and pointed to the space occupied by the pillar. The female hunter and male sage both raised a curious brow to each other, truly not seeing anything. Vakar rubbed his eyes.

"It has been a strenuous day, forgive me," he explained. The hunter had beautiful amber-coloured skin and dark oaken hair, pulled back neatly with intricately weaved braids. Her eyes were wide and glistened with a hue of hazelnut, much like her blood-brother, Qiri, was known for having.

"No forgiveness needed." She wrapped her arms around Vakar and embraced him tightly. Vakar couldn't resist smiling at her warmth; a warmth kindred to the one that his former love in life used to offer in these strenuous times.

"Thank you, Eevie. He would have been proud of the formidable Kyst you have become." He gave her a sweet smile before unlocking their arms and slumping into the chair beside the fire. "Have preparations been made?"

The sage stepped forward, wearing a cowl and scarf that obscured much of his face. He was adorned in A-typical loose hanging robes, held firm by a tight and stiff tabard. He was set apart from the other sages by a single caramel-coloured sash tied around his waist that fell to ankle height on his left side. "They have, your Highness. However, I do urge that no harm befall any of the Kyst in ShallowBay, or else the foundations you've laid for a unified rainforest will crack."

"They are the last of the Northern Kyst to refute us. I fear strength may be our only tact left. What do you suggest, Eevie?" Vakar asked of his lead hunter. She pondered it for several moments, even going so far to as pour herself a small glass of wine, drink it, and think on its taste, making the males wait as she did so.

"Pine is right. Physical harm will spark only rebellion. Send as many of us as you dare by land and sea, and show the Kyst of Shallow Bay the force they find themselves up against."

"And if that is not enough?" Vakar insisted.

"It will be," Eevie assured her brother-in-law and king. "Good. Very good. Pine, remain here with the party you already have and complete the raising of the bridges. Eevie and I will depart with 6,000 of our warriors, divided by ship and land, to Shallow Bay."

Pine and Eevie both gave enthusiastic bows before departing. Vakar held his hand up to stay Eevie's exit.

"Yes?" She asked curiously.

"You have shown time and time again the skill and dedication you offer as a Hunter of Silva's people. Furthermore, you have been instrumental in the unification of the north these past months." Eevie was fighting back a smirk. She knew the Vakar of old would have ended this with a jest or some feigned insult. "I have something for you. Reforged after the original Armour of Silva was stolen by Ven."

Eevie scowled at the mention of the traitor Ven Devar. She was his own age, and had heard nothing but brilliant stories from her older but now deceased brother, Qiri, who was often Ven's hunting partner. Yet, it was accepted by all in the Great Northern Rainforest that Ven Devar had gone rogue after the fall of Silva, taking up arms with the hated Kintar and slaughtering his own kind. Vakar was the only person who knew the truth, for he had confirmed after capturing a Kintar, that it was in fact Rexous, impersonating as the 'Mighty Hunter.'

Vakar pointed to a trunk in the corner of the tent and watched her reaction. The hunter looked in that direction, seeing an intricately carved chest. After several hesitant steps forward she lifted the lid and saw extraordinary leather armour, a silvered trident, and her weapon of choice, twin Sai daggers; a formidable weapon with a long thin centre blade and two smaller blades acting as the crossguard. Pulling the armour out revealed a faint glitter from the candlelight surrounding her.

"The Armour and Sai's are infused with diamond dust. The trident is pure iradinium. Not even the famous Silvan Armour of old could boast this level of magnificence."

"I know not what to say."

Vakar chuckled softly. "Say nothing. You and I are all that remains of our two families. I should see my sister adorned with everything she needs to survive. We leave with the first favourable tide." The king proclaimed, turning and walking up the steps to pour himself a glass of wine. Eevie gave a gracious bow and departed the tent with her new equipment.

Vakar sat down and sighed heavily. He dropped one cheek onto his supporting fist as he slowly swirled the wine in his glass. "Surrounded by souls, yet so alone without you my love," He muttered weakly, whilst staring into a small portrait of his true-love, Qiri. He and Vakar were set to marry before he fell in the destruction of Silva, brought on by the raiding Kintar and Uthul the Betrayer. Vakar knew many truths thats most did not, most importantly being that the destruction of Silva only occurred because Ven Devar had Scáth ShadowScorn and offered her protection. Then, despite being anointed king by their queen's dying wish, the mighty hunter left them in their time of need and ran away into the east to see the Scorn safely home. The first King of Kyst drained his glass in one gulp before settling his gaze back on the pillar, holding the mysterious Orb.

"I will find you Ven, I will have my revenge." Barely a second after he spoke the words, the Orb began to fill with what appeared as a miniature storm. Dark roiling clouds blustered within and shots of lightning ricocheted off the glass. Soon, a frosty edge formed from the constant snow seen throughout. The image of two heavily cloaked figures appeared in the Orb. Vakar, mesmerized by the whole sight, slowly crept closer to it. As he did, so too did the image of the figures. Their cloaks fluttered madly as if they had a mind of their own.

Both figures held their arms out in front of their faces as the blizzard assaulted them with snow that felt like razor blades against their skin. Vakar instinctively waved his hand left to right around the Orb and the image within moved. His wine glass slipped between his fingers in shock to shatter against the floor.

"Ven."

Athvar sat at the great blackglass table that had served as the deathbed of King Arwr the previous morning. He was seated between Scáth and Torvic and across from Aelis, Oren, and Katia. The experienced gnome understood that emotions were frayed and tensions were taught. No one had even dared speak since seating themselves. Athvar had vast experience as a travelling Curia Regis and he could confidently say he had never been so uncomfortable in a royal court before.

"If I may have the honour of speaking first, what now?" The finely dressed and spicy smelling gnome asked the table with sincere respect.

"Control your pet, dear," Katia said slyly to Scáth, completely disregarding Athvars' presence. Scáth glowered darkly at her mother. "Excuse my mothers childlike behaviour. She is on edge for what comes next. Athvar is deciding who will be the Queen of ShadowScorn." Scáth tried her best to underline Katia's petty attitude. "Rarely a smooth transition in other Kingdoms. However, I wonder if the Scorn are not above the rest?" Athvar was clearly trying to play on Katia and Oren's ego; a ploy Scáth saw little use in it, yet Aelis took the opportunity to chime in.

"Every transition of royalty has passed down to the child after the death of the leading monarch. As it passed from Scáth's Great Grandfather Risastor to her Grandfather to her Father, it should pass from Arwr to Scáth." Aelis looked directly at Katia and Oren before continuing. "Thus, Scáth will be appointed Queen. As Commander, I assure you all the Scorn Guard will be faithful to our traditions."

"Do not forget the people, Commander. Are their wishes to be ignored?" Oren quickly retorted.

"Please enlighten us on how the people will want anyone but their returned princess as queen?" Aelis shot back with a brutal level of condescension. Oren, looking smug as ever, did not hesitate.

"If you have not figured it for yourselves then yes, let me enlighten you. Many of our people have lost faith in the princess. She simply vanished for months, and unfortunately her return coincides perfectly with the largest siege our great city has ever witnessed." Oren finished by laying a heavy gaze on the Scorn Princess. Scáth dropped her eyes to the floor, feeling a sudden wave of guilt rush over her. Athvar was quick to sneakily rest his little hand atop of hers.

"Is it not your duty to explain to the people the real goings-on so misinformation is not spread, Administrator?" Athvar ever confidently questioned the bald and miserable Scorn. Oren simply curled his lip in frustration at the gnome.

"His duty is to the ruling monarchs," Katia stated, resting her heavy gaze on Torvic and Aelis. "Which is currently, me," Katia said, with a level of superiority and blatant mistrust that rubbed most in the room the wrong way.

Before anyone could continue the argument, a large booming sound was heard and the palace shuddered. Two more thunderous crashes were felt and the floors shook so violently that Oren and Torvic's chairs fell backwards off the raised dais. They both went tumbling down as their blackglass chairs shattered into thousands of pieces. Aelis jumped out of her seat and ran to one of the many large windows in the hall. Katia was quick to Oren's side, helping him to his feet. Scáth seeing this felt a level of disgust overwhelm her but Athvar tugged on her sleeve and they were quickly standing beside Aelis. They watched as one, two, and three more boulders flew over the great city wall devastating the buildings below. The shock wave from one building that lay demolished, shot hundreds of stone bricks like shrapnel into several adjacent homes.

"Sound the alarm," Scáth cried aloud. When no response came she noticed Torvic standing next to them, watching the horror unfold. "Sound the alarm!" She screamed at her mother and Oren. The Scorn man nearly lost his footing, attempting to run out of the hall with such haste. Torvic gasped and threw his hand to the glass as he watched a boulder land on a group of scattering citizens.

That evening, the boulders of Renrit ceased their barrage. Aelis came off the top of the outer parapets where she had just finished directing her soldiers to focus their efforts. Nearly a third of all structures in ShadowScorn had collapsed or suffered extensive damage. The very heart that kept Aelis alive felt as though it would give out from the pain she felt at seeing her beloved city in such ruin. Cries of the Scorn mourning lost ones and the screams of those in physical agony echoed like moaning-wind whipping throughout the stone streets. After walking through the city to assess the extent of the damage, she was met in the old square by Scáth, Athvar, Agan, and Faenla.

Scáth approached Aelis and embraced her tightly.

"This will not go unpunished," Aelis declared, overflowing with anger. Scáth just hugged her dearest friend tighter. Athvar and the now awake and well-recovering Agan shared looks of worry, for the words of Aelis made their skin crawl.

"We will survive. We always do." Scáth whispered, attempting to comfort her sister.

"I am going to make sure of it." Aelis pulled away from her and regarded her companions. "It does my heart well to see you walking again, Agan." The half-orc couldn't suppress a smirk but he did bow out of respect which shocked Athvar to his core.

"May we be of service, Commander?" Agan asked confidently while rolling one shoulder in a stretch. Aelis remained quiet for a moment before locking stares with Faenla. The wolf set his coastal blue eyes on the Scorn elf, peering deep into her soul.

"I am to strike at their base tonight," the commander stated, never breaking the stare with the magnificent beast.

"What?" Scáth spun on her heel. "You can't be serious." Aelis finally broke the stare with Faen to regard her princess and gave her an incredulous look.

"You think I jest?" The Commander turned back to the others. "We will help," Athvar offered optimistically.

"No. Too much blood will run free for likes of you." Aelis finished by walking past the gnome, half-orc, and wolf. Agan dared to grab her wrist as she went by. The proud and powerful Scorn responded with a growl and a dagger-tip poking the neck of the brash fighter.

"Let the wolf and I join you," Agan said rather solemnly. "You are too injured."

"That's not for you to say."

Aelis looked back to Scáth and saw a distant look of loneliness and disappointment on her face. Yet, the commander was determined to prove that the ShadowScorn were not a people easily thwarted.

"Fine." Aelis aggressively threw her arm back out of Agan's relatively soft grip. Faenla gave Scáth a lick and began following Aelis. Agan looked back to Athvar who was now standing with Scáth.

"Stay in the palace until our return, please." Agan did not demand this of Scáth and Athvar as he so often did but instead asked with a clear air of care in his voice. Athvar simply nodded in response and Agan left to catch up.

"Thank you for being here." Scáth dropped a hand to tousle

Athvar's curly hair.

"Ya owe me Lady Scáth," Athvar said jokingly as he began to walk away. "I was a prominent citizen back home mind ya! Put all this nonsense adventuring behind me, like any self-respecting gnome." Scáth chuckled to herself before catching up to the little one.

Several hours past sundown, Agan found himself walking across the rugged highlands outside the city walls with a troop of 50 Scorn Guard, all led by their fearless Commander, Aelis Andula. Everyone wore dark black cloth over their faces and armour. Agan was at a severe disadvantage for, unlike himself, everyone there including Faenla were experts in the art of stealth. However, on his right hand was a ring given to him by Aelis. She called it a 'Night Ring.' It would, on Agan's command, help shift the lingering darkness around him to his call. The half-orc had noticed a single Scorn Priestess deep in prayer from the time they left the city to now. As they neared the hill the army was camped behind, the glow from thousands of torches grew brighter. Agan and Aelis crawled up to the apex and peered over to see a single torch for what must have been every soldier, and a thick line of patrolling guards encircling the perimeter.

"And now?" Agan asked doubtfully.

"Shh," Aelis answered quickly. She motioned for Faenla and the priestess to join them. The Commander whispered something into the ear of the wolf that was missing its tip from a nasty fight with a Feral. He sprinted off and around the camp with a preternatural speed.

Agan, confused as to where his companion just ran off too, looked at the priestess who was clearly concentrating on a ball of writhing shadow that was growing and hovering between her palms.

"When you are ready Lira." Aelis instructed with a hushed tone. The priestess stood tall and as if on cue, a great and long melodic howl was heard from the far side of the base. Then a singular human scream, abruptly silenced. Several more howls sounded and many of the patrolling guards rushed to check it out. The priestess took several long strides down the hill towards the camp, appearing like a midnight ghost haunting the highlands, lost and wandering. A pair of Renrit guards looked at each other in confusion, unsure what they were seeing. Lira got to the base of the hill and to the edge of the camp when the two guards holding torches approached her. "A ghost?" One guard shakily asked the other.

At this comment, Lira opened her eyes to reveal purely black orbs. She threw her arms outwards, leaving the black ball of writhing shadow hovering there. She quickly brought her hands back together and a loud clap echoed through the valley as a single wave of black and purple energy sprung forth. It washed over the entire camp like a tidal wave, extinguishing every torch and source of visible light. Suddenly, the entire camp was left in pitch black.

The two guards stepped back in horror, drawing their swords in reaction. Before either weapon left their scabbards, Aelis shadow walked behind them and struck them low. Within the blink of an eye, all 50 of the Scorn Guard were deep into the camp, killing the unprepared Renrit soldiers without mercy. They started with the guard on watch, soon ending the breath of any soldier who did not go to Faenla's distraction.

Agan was momentarily stunned at the uncanny coordination of the Scorn and their ability to so quickly and quietly dispose of an enemy. The half-orc wondered to himself why anyone would willingly put themselves in a confrontation with such a powerful race. Still on the hilltop, he leaped forward as a Renrit zealot was about to stick a Scorn Guard with a pike. Agan almost vomited at the sudden change of his surroundings as he felt the ring pinch his finger; then he was face to face with the Renrit zealot holding the pike. Agan's eyes shot wide and he heaved his double-bearded axe at the pole-arm, splitting it in two and burying his weapon deep into the guards' sternum. From there the Scorn Guard, under the direct command of Aelis, began entering the tents. Soon, however, not every Renrit soldier could be hushed with a hand over their mouths as they slept, and a Scorn drove a dagger or sword under their chins. The screams of the men that were travelling to the realm of death eventually stirred the rest of the camp awake.

After several minutes of devastating battle, that left well over 200 dead Renrit soldiers strewn across their camp, the Scorn found themselves to be on the back foot. Agan was further ahead than the rest of Scorn Guard and was effortlessly leaving his own trail of dead or dying humans in his wake. Aelis, who was surrounded by her 48 remaining Scorn Guard in a tight defensive formation, watched in true awe as the half-orc with his unparalleled strength and speed could not be seemingly matched by a Renrit soldier. From further in the camp came a large and imposing Dragon-Blood, adorned in glistening gold and white plate mail, sporting the sigil of Sesara. The pommel of his great sword glowed with a divine light and he shoved several of his own soldiers out of his way to get closer to Agan.

Aelis heard herself curse and shouted, "Keep the formation!" Before any of her Guard could question her, she shadow-walked behind Agan, grabbed his arm that was raised to take the head off another soldier and melted into the night back to her troop. Agan nearly continued the down-stroke to accidentally fell a Scorn Guard but instead felt the unwelcome wave of nausea that followed the abrupt teleportation magic.

"Remember, draw them back out," Aelis commanded only loud enough for her troop to hear.

The remaining Guard were in five lines of ten, each line would take a wave of furious attacking Renrit's before the whole troop took two steps back. The front line would then shadow-step to the back, allowing a fresh line to take over and make good distance back towards the city. As the troop of defending Scorn crested the hill, one guard lost his footing and was met by an arrow to the throat. This allowed the opportunity for several more Renrit soldiers to take advantage of the broken line, including the nasty-looking Red Dragon Blood. Just as Agan's line was up, three Scorn were cut down by a single swipe of the Dragon-Blood's great sword, forcing the remainder of his line to shadow-walk to the back. Agan however, extremely familiar with Dragon-Bloods, parried the swing with his axe. Immediately, the two combatants looked at each other, slightly stunned in their own way as they both recognized one another.

Agan was played for the fool when he caught a dagger in the leg by an approaching soldier, falling to his knees in front of the Dragon Blood. The half-orc who was still healing from his wounds was tired and battle weary. As the Dragon-Blood inhaled deeply and fire began whirling in this throat, Agan thought this to be an honourable way to die in battle. The flame had barely left the razor-sharp craw of the Paladin when Faenla came soaring overhead to body slam him. The nearly 250 kilogram wolf knocked one soldier unconscious and sent the Paladin hurling to the ground. Faenla didn't give Agan a choice and scooped him up to re-join the now fully retreating Scorn.

Aelis wore a large smile when she looked over her shoulder to see the over-excited humans from Renrit, charge after them by the hundreds. The Scorn never shadow-walked the entire distance back to the city which would have been simple for them to do. They stayed just far ahead enough to keep the Renrit's on their tail. They were no more than 300-metres away from the city when she gave a signal by holding up a small light with a mirror on the backside. Little did the Renrit soldiers know, as they could not see, that nearly a thousand archers were lining the city walls awaiting them. With that signal given, the parapets erupted in light as the braziers were set aflame. The Scorn Guard shadow-walked the remaining distance and Faenla carrying Agan was already safely let inside. The night sky erupted in a shower of flaming arrows. The Paladin had been shouting for his forces to retreat but had failed in his attempts, for the hundreds upon hundreds of soldiers who already flooded towards the fleeing troop could not hear. Aelis shadow-walked to the top of the wall to watch her war tactics successfully play out. The burning arrows illuminated the low-hanging storm clouds for what felt like an eternity as they swept over the Renrit soldiers with flawless efficiency. Several minutes of free-volleys later, Aelis estimated nearly a thousand soldiers dead, and several hundred wounded.

"A good night," she whispered to herself as a gust of wind blew across the burning corpses of her attackers.

Ch6 - Why Do I Do This

The duo en route to the greatest mountain in Litore was unfortunately caught in the open plains before Starlight Lake, when an unrelenting blizzard struck. Ven wore a thick cowl over most of his face while his cloak offered little warmth as it billowed widely behind him. Soon, he felt a hot sweat dripping down his forehead and when he thought that to be an unusually welcomed sensation he rubbed his brow to reveal extensive blood on his fingers.

"We need shelter!" Ven yelled at the very top of his lungs, wondering if Sindrum would even hear him.

"There won't be any! Keep moving!" Sindrum shouted in response. It sounded distant to Ven and he put his arms up to shield his forehead from the piercing cold and whirling ice that was shredding any exposed skin. Suddenly, he felt a lingering shudder trickle down his spine. It felt as though he was being watched, but then again, maybe he was simply dying of frostbite he thought.

"How much further?" Ven hollered. After no response, he dropped his arm a little and could not see Sindrum in the white-out. "Sindrum!" The Kyst called out over and over. No matter how hard he looked or searched for tracks, Ven could not find his companion. "Typical," the hunter muttered in frustration. He pressed on through the blizzard in the direction he was confident of, taking faith that Sindrum would manage on his own. Ven, on any given day, could walk across a branch no thicker than a twig without breaking it, so he could certainly walk atop snow without sinking. This was achieved only by absolute balance and perfect weight distribution, however, the blizzard was so intense it was burying his legs with every gruelling step. He walked for what felt like another half-hour and if the Kyst had not been mostly frozen, he would have felt the snow beneath his feet start to give way. He didn't notice until his stomach hit his chest and he fell through a sinkhole.

Ven yelped as his back collided with the mass of dirt that had fallen to create the sinkhole. He looked up to see a stone ceiling 15 metres above and an empty dark chamber before him.

"You've got to be-" The hunter was hit by a large mass of falling snow that nearly buried him. He popped his head out of the fluffy stuff and audibly shivered. With his teeth chattering he climbed down from the snowy dirt mound and fumbled to the smooth stone-laid floor. The firmness under his boots caught him off guard as his eyes adjusted from the blinding white of snow to the light-less room before him. He noted right away that everything behind him had been filled with the excess soil and a short but wide room in front of him was void of anything other than tall empty shelving. A wooden door laden with steel studs was shut tight, closing the room off to whatever was beyond. Ven gave a curious sigh before trying to open the door. The Kyst predictably found it to be locked from the other side. With a push of frustration, his entire arm broke through the middle of the door for it was so old and rotten.

"Oh," he remarked gleefully. Wiggling his arm around on the other side, he lifted a large wooden lock upwards, retracted his arm, and gave another small push. The door creaked open and Ven took a step forward to see a long corridor running left and right.

"Hmm, when in doubt, right is right." Ven turned to the right and walked down the hallway. Several doors on either side of the hallway were ajar and upon a brief inspection of a few, he found dusty abandoned bed chambers. Many were still filled with the oddities of everyday life such as bowls, blankets, tables and the sort. Most, if not all, had a single bed that appeared moth-eaten centuries ago. After continuing down the dark cobweb infested corridor for some time, it eventually opened up into a large study. A single grand hearth that took up nearly an entire wall lay dormant. A spiral staircase that ascended three more levels offered access to bookshelves inlaid in every wall on each floor. The sheer size of the library took Ven's breath away.

"What is this place?" The Kyst murmured to himself as he walked further into the study. When he stopped looking up, he noticed several tables with alchemy bottles, books, diagrams, and several metallic items he couldn't begin to decipher. Stepping closer to inspect the curious items, he grabbed a single piece of paper. In doing so, he accidentally knocked over a glass vial, that dumped its contents onto the table, eating its way through the wood planks in seconds. Ven stepped back to ensure he was not splashed by the acid, now dissolving through the floor. Upon studying the parchment in his hand, he shockingly understood it to be a recipe for poison written in his native tongue of Kystin.

"Who are you?" Reverberated throughout the entire library, but the hunter understood it had originated from the second floor. Ven felt his skin crawl as he quickly gazed upwards. He could see only two glowing red eyes peering through a dark doorway above him. He knew that this creature or whatever it was, was concealing itself from his night vision.

"I am Ven Devar, of the Great Northern Rainforest," he echoed authoritatively while slowly dropping his free hand to the short sword strapped on his lower back.

"How did you get in here?" The voice was clearly agitated and the hunter thought he detected a lingering hiss after it spoke. "Sinkhole, believe it or not."

Another defiant hiss echoed through the room. "I do not.." The eye's disappeared from the darkness.

Ven heard the voice this time from the entrance whence he came. He rolled his eyes with grandeur before turning around. Within a single breath, the creature levitated itself and flew at the elf with blinding speed; too fast for Ven to comprehend as he was gripped by the neck and hoisted up by a single arm.

"Oh," the hunter voiced with a wheeze.

"You adventurers break in here for the same reasons, to slay a monster..." The creature wasn't much taller than Ven but had sickly pale skin, unnatural strength, and two fangs protruding from its mouth. "... and steal." The whites of the vampire's eyes turned blood red before throwing Ven with all his might. He went soaring upwards to break through the wooden railing on the second floor. That still was not enough to halt his momentum as he continued to soar through the doorway he had originally spotted the creature in. He came to a skidding halt in the centre of the room and before he had gotten back to his feet the vampire was already in front of him.

"Look, you bloodsucking bastard. I didn't ask to drop in here like this. But since you don't take kindly to visitors, you'll have to try harder than that to kill me," Ven said, spitting blood onto the floor, as if inviting the vampire. It gave another menacing hiss, showing its long pointed fangs. The vampire gave a flick of his wrist, connecting his palm against Ven's chest. A small shock wave emanated and the hunter went flying again, nearly 10 metres, to crash against a rack of spears and pole-arms. A large clatter was heard through the heavy footsteps approaching him. Ven ended up sitting on his arse with his back against the wall. He looked up to see two large statues on either side of the doorway he had just been thrown through. They struck him as oddly familiar in their design, chiselling, and stance. Two lightly armoured, hooded, and heavily armed Elven Hunters looking down on all those who entered. Ven coughed up more blood as the palm strike had his chest wound throbbing.

"A native? So this is no accident but a return." The imposing and resonant sounding vampire slowly approached. Ven dragged one knee to his chest as though he was about to stand. Instead, he drew a throwing knife, slid them apart between his fingers and sent them into the chest of the vampire. The creature recoiled in shocking pain as a steady swirl of steam burned from his skin.

"I sincerely hope that silver stings," Ven said, feigning more exhaustion and pain than he was in. The vampire shot forth, but he rolled out of the way as the creature slashed its powerful claws into the wall, leaving deep gashes in the stone.

"You should slow down or you might hurt yourself," the coastal elf mocked, goading his enemy on. The vampire slowly stepped toward the hunter. Ven threw multiple more silvered knives but the creature either caught them or deftly avoided each one. He gave a disparaging look at the effectiveness of his best weapon. The vampire held its hand out and an elegant rapier that had fallen from the weapon rack flew into his palm. In one swift motion, the undead monster caught the rapier and plunged it toward the hunter's chest. Ven had his trident up and ready in equal speed, catching the rapier and twisting it from the monster's grasp. He followed up by plunging another silver dagger into the thigh of his adversary. It kneed him in the chin, forcing his head to crack against the wall. The Kyst gave a sickening grunt and he was hoisted up once more and hurled across the room into one of the statues. His body rag-dolled off the statue, landing roughly on the floor. Ven caressed the back of his head and gave a low moan. His heart began to race for never had he faced a foe with such strength and speed as this vampire. His warrior instincts were a lifetime of training to stay focused and in-tune with the battle, yet he was struggling to do that now. The elf looked up to see the vampire grabbing a weapon from the hands of the statue he had just collided against.

"Wanna give me a minute?" Ven said while feebly staggering to his feet.

The vampire hissed and as soon as Ven saw him disappear with blinding speed, the hunter turned around, short-sword out, and parried the undead creature. Another shock wave emitted from the weapons colliding. Ven was sent back several metres, the soles of his boots skidding on the floor, only to stop as he plunged his broken sword into the ground. He had a look of disbelief at the realization that his famed short-sword of Silva had just shattered like glass against the weapon from the statue. He looked up to see a smirk on the vampire's face.

Ven felt that sudden unbridled rage consume him and before he knew it he was sprinting towards his foe. He threw his shattered sword at the wrist of the creature, slicing a clean line across it. It hissed and dropped what Ven only noticed now to be another short-sword, this one with a slightly wider and curved blade to it. The Kyst was already sliding towards his foe, dragging another silvered knife across the heel of the vampire and catching the sword. Ven felt a sudden wave of energy coarse through his arm holding the new weapon. He drove the dagger down to turn out of the slide and face his enemy.

"I got your sword," Ven said as if he were a child teasing another. The vampire lunged at him but Ven rolled onto his side before leaping through the door back into the library. He grabbed the ledge of the second-floor walkway and swung himself down to the first floor with the table of acidic vials. Nimbly landing on the table that was still corroding, he grabbed three bottles. Completely accepting he had no idea what any of them would do, Ven awaited the vampire's arrival.

"Why do I do this," he mumbled to himself in great doubt.

With a poof of writhing smoke, the creature suddenly appeared in the centre of the first floor. Ven threw a bottle but before it shattered the vampire spun and caught it. Offering another hiss. Ven responded by throwing the last two bottles in succession. The vampire caught the second one but the third shattered against the creature's hand. Spewing acid all over the monster, it screamed in pain as the second vial slipped from its grasp to shatter, spraying liquid-fire at its feet. The vampire sprang at Ven with blurring speed but the Kyst stood his ground. Feeling strangely invigorated by the new short-sword in his hand. He felt a sudden pressure as the sword skewered the vampire, however it brought the two uncomfortably close together. He saw in his enemies eyes that it knew it was defeated and would do anything to make sure Ven perished with him. The elf was pressed up against the bookshelf now, his sword hilt deep in the chest of the vampire. It gave a horrifying hiss and Ven watched as it elongated its fangs into an impossible length. The hunter was stretching and squirming as best he could to get away, but he felt the cold breath of the creature tickling his neck, then the violating feeling of fangs on skin. He pushed back with all his strength, but too late as Ven gave a desperate scream of pain, fangs plunging into flesh. Ven kept the pressure up with his sword, dropped his hand to a silver knife and plunged it into the crown of the Vampire's skull. He shoved the now limp body to the floor and fell with it in a panic. The hunter aggressively fingered around his neck for the bite marks, the fear of an eternity cursed with hellish vampirism screaming in his mind.

He recoiled as he felt the fang marks but was shocked to feel them heal almost instantly. He felt the sword pulsing energy through his arm but slowly wain. After regaining a level of calm, he went to inspect the now withered and disfigured corpse of possibly his greatest foe to date. It confused the hunter to see two fang marks on the vampire in the identical spot that Ven had been bitten. It was the first time he could take a closer look at the short-sword that had been resting in the statue's hand. The hilt and pommel looked like a thick clump of weaving vines and leaves, while the cross-guard was a wolf head on either side. The blade was of a metal that Ven had never seen, and the forging from a technique he suspected long-forgotten. It had intricate vines embossed along its diamond edge with Kyst runes on either blade face that read 'The Sword of Hunters Protection.' Lost in a whirlwind of confusion, the Kyst gave an involuntary shiver. He looked to the large hearth promising so much warmth, then back to the vampire husk when a small and well-earned smile crossed his face.

Before long, the elf was sitting in front of a warm fire in deep meditation. Around him was a pile of scattered books and papers. It hadn't taken very much time to discern that this underground palace belonged to the Kyst of the First Age. So old, it had once stood proudly among the nature above before sinking, buried by time. He wasn't sure how he was going to get out but he was determined to learn everything he could. After an adequate rest considering the beating he had received, he re-entered the armoury. He studied the two statues closely. The other wore a long bow, made of stone, but also a quiver filled with peculiar arrows. Ven removed one to inspect it further and noticed that the very last few centimetres of the arrow tip was translucent. With a shrug, he replaced his standard quiver with the one on the statue. The quiver did not appear any more or less ornate than the one he carried, save for a single pocket on the side. He unclipped a button holding it closed, and found an iridescent bow-string. He thought it felt warm to the touch and perhaps thicker than was usual. Tucking it back away for later, he went and retrieved his trident thrown to the corner of the room during the fight.

Ven's left ear twitched as he caught the last echo of a distant water droplet. Following it, he exited through a passage from the armoury that led towards the sound. Soon, he found himself in what he assumed was a throne room, and also where the vampire had set up his belongings. He inspected a truly gaudy coffin with a red velvet interior. Hanging above the coffin on the wall was a massive oil painting of a family standing in front of an austere back drop. He saw two parents standing above three children. Ven instantly recognized the only male child, as the vampire he had just slain and burned. He stared into the painted red eyes of the father, as several minutes slipped by. Although he had not mentioned it to anyone, since his awakening after the fight with Rexous, Ven had been struggling with his, at times, often swift delivery of death. Seeing this portrait of a full family, and knowing he had just slain someone's child, made his heart ache. Surely he was confident in his actions this time, but what of all the others?

"My Son?" Ven felt his heart jump, and no sooner did he spin, shortsword drawn with lightning speed. He expected to see someone, yet, the room remained empty of anyone else. "Are you there?" He heard the same voice, deep and harsh in its years. He spotted a wide but shallow bowl floating half a metre off a tall dais. He quickly pinpointed the voice to be emanating from within, and saw too that faint rays of light were reflecting upwards. He slowly placed one foot in front of the other and soon, Ven was looking over the bowl. A thin layer of water was visible, and he saw a reflection that was not his own. The face staring back at him was the same father in the painting.

"Who are you?" The reflection demanded with a lingering hiss. Ven remained still, almost stunned. "Where is my son?"

"I'm sorry," Ven whispered as a tear fell from his eye to hit the liquid, sending ripples out. He was then struck with a torrent of water that reached the high ceilings. It was powerful enough to lift him off his feet and throw him back. Now laying on the ground, the Kyst looked up to see the impossible amount of water, as a face formed from the swirling mass.

"I will find you Kyst Elf!" The booming voice was warbled as if they were drowning and crashed harmlessly into Ven. He got back to his feet and shivered, now drenched.

"I need to get out of here," he mumbled dejectedly. Closing off his other senses he found the distinct dripping sound once more.

Striding towards the noise that promised escape, he found himself in a great hall. As he walked in, he noticed five pillars on the left and the right, all baring torches that immediately ignited upon his entrance. The majority of the floor space was filled with overturned and strewn about benches, chairs, and tables. Judging by the number of skeletons he spotted, Ven thought back to the vampire mentioning adventurers. Looking around the massive hall he noticed that the entire far wall was a stone-carved mural. Its detailed craftsmanship had the hunter walking toward it in awe. A dozen or so metres in front of the wall was a throne that Ven paid little attention too. The Kyst started at what he considered to be the beginning, taking his time to fully understand what the carvings told in its intricate design. It spoke of the great and impressive origins of the Kyst, and how many of the other Elves in Litore made their beginnings. It showed the relentless attacks, battles, and deaths the Kyst suffered for millennia past. In the centre, the carving directly behind the throne was a huge sunrise; Āina and Kaia standing watch. Below was etched an inscription that read: "From the sea, a saviour will arrive. A Kyst bred to fight, born to mend. Grown alone to be never owned."

Ven gently dragged his fingers across the inscription before continuing down the mural. What he saw next shook him to his core, as it displayed the entirety of this Kyst enclave spreading out across Litore's coastline. From there, it told of a babe being raised to reunite the scattered Kyst. He cursed aloud when he noticed the entire last metre had been blown completely off the wall and now lay in a pile of stone rubble. Inspecting the surface around the explosion, Ven guessed a lightning bolt from a powerful spell had inadvertently done the damage. This revelation left Ven at a loss. Had this saviour already come and gone? Surely as far as he was aware, the Kyst did not find themselves shattered or lost. For one of the first times in his life, he didn't know what to do. It was times like these that his mind and heart went back to Vakar. How he missed his oldest friend; the only Kyst or person he truly considered family, before meeting his new companions that is. He had left the Village of Hearth understanding that his and Vakar's relationship had changed, yet a part of Ven still clung to hope that perhaps things could be the way they once were. His heart swelled when he thought of Scáth. What an absolute idiot he had been to leave without saying goodbye to her, to the one he had travelled halfway across the continent for. All because he wouldn't stop kicking himself over the ill-timed kiss they shared. Ven balled up his fists and before he knew it, punched the stone wall. In what he took as karma, another chunk of the carving fell away. He let the pain in his knuckles and wrist wash away the unwanted emotions.

The same drip that caught his ear in the armoury, echoed out again but this time much closer. Ven cocked his head but saw no water. Calming his breath from the outburst of rage, he closed his eyes and awaited the next droplet. When he heard that it came from behind the wall to his right, Ven furrowed a single brow most curiously. He approached the wall and began looking for any sign of water. After another drip, he narrowed it down to a smaller area when he noticed a thin but long crack. He grabbed a bench that had half burned away and begun bashing around the crack in the wall. Soon, he felt a sudden wave of cold, fresh, air rush past him. The dripping sound filled his ears as a carved-out tunnel revealed itself to him, leaking water from the roots and soil above. After crawling for nearly an hour, Ven spotted the end and thought it to lead nowhere. He dragged himself along the now frozen dirt as far as he could, until he spotted a simple wooden hatch leading out. He pushed with one arm but couldn't get it to budge. He laid his back flush against the hutch in a push-up position. After several straining minutes he got his legs under him and finally opened the hatch. Nearly a metre of snow lay on the ground, which was the cause of Ven's struggle. The hunter climbed out, closed the hatch and swept a ton of snow over top to hide it best he could again. Looking around, he took special caution to remember his surroundings in case he ever wished to return. The blizzard had ceased and after emerging through a small cops of trees, he spotted the Town of Rushwater.

Ven approached the settlement a few hours past dusk and entered without trouble. It was comprised of mostly humble homes made of timber and mortar, each with a semi decrepit thatched roof. The town was split in two by Twinkle River as it flowed south. Ven stopped at the crest of a small wooden bridge that connected either side of the town to admire the natural fluorescent rushing water. It reminded him of the river that ran through Silva, albeit the twinkling blue water reflecting against his skin seemed the more impressive. Here the snow was equally as thick yet neither the lake nor river was frozen. It seemed to Ven the more time he spent out in the world, the less he understood. He gave a slight shake of his green mane and walked toward the harbour. The docks were clearly the staple of Rushwater for Ven counted nearly 100, boats, ships, and vessels of the like. Every hull of every ship glowed a brilliant dance of reflecting light from the lake. He stood in the harbour and felt a welcomed sense of familiarity. Sailing was something he was extraordinary at, even by Kyst standards and his heart yearned to control a helm once more. He heard a sharp whistle from a fast looking sloop near the right end of the crescent-shaped harbour. It took him a few moments to arrive but it was Sindrum as he had expected.

"By the gloomy touch of Aceia, what happened to you?" Sindrum exclaimed in shock as Ven climbed aboard, offering the Scorn a view of the Kyst's battered face.

"Tousled with my first vampire," Ven replied rather dryly.
"Tousled?" Sindrum asked in sheer disbelief.

"Well, I sent him to the underworld, scarred by acid and fire," Ven
answered dispassionately, already untying the mooring line. Sindrum
didn't reply but went to unfurling the sail, clearly baffled by Ven's
claim of single handily defeating a Vampire. With little effort, the pair
sailed out of Rushwater towards the ever-looming Moon Mountain.

Ch7 - Corrupt

Vakar walked alongside his sister-in-law and most formidable hunter, Eevie. Behind them was a troop of 3,000 Kyst Hunters and powerful Sages. To their left was the rugged coastline of Litore's Great Northern Rainforest. Nearly 100 longships carrying another 3,000 hunters sailed the waters directly beside the land force. Never in the history of Kyst had there ever been such a large force assembled. Vakar had orchestrated this show of might and didn't even plan to go to war. No, Vakar the Cunning would use his newly acquired power to simply terrify anyone who might oppose his rule as King of Kyst. So far it had worked; after the attacks orchestrated by Uthul and Rexous, masquerading as Ven Devar, Vakar found the unifying struggle he needed. Much like other kingdoms, sage and hunter troops could now be placed at each and every settlement for ultimate protection. Of course, Vakar knew the attacks had not really been Ven Devar, but he still blamed the elf who was once like a brother for the destruction of Silva and the death of his beloved Qiri. Vakar had been up for nearly three days, most of that time had been devoted to watching his mortal nemesis through the crystal ball that had appeared in his quarters. He had witnessed the battle with the vampire and the discovery of the prophecy.

"Are you ready?" Eevie asked, tearing Vakar from his thoughts. He regarded his sister-in-law curiously before they rounded a bend in the trees to reveal Shallow Bay below.

"Let us be done with it," Vakar voiced without tact as he quickened his pace. Eevie shot him a dismissive glare before giving a large wave, motioning for the hunters behind to get into formation. She led the army a respectable distance behind its king. The ships surrounded the mouth of the bay, preventing vessels from entering or leaving.

ShallowBay was built around a kilometre wide cove with a single large bridge extended into the centre. At the end of the bridge stood a magnificent four-story building constructed from great trees that had been washed ashore or found in the forest, roots up. It was entirely adorned with carvings of creatures from both land and sea. The massive structure was supported by trees that through the use of magic, grew from the salty depths, weaving throughout the entire palace. The bay was not that shallow but got its name from the crystal clear water, revealing the abundance of thriving coral below. Vakar could not help but be utterly impressed by this settlements design and its perfect symbiosis with nature, that which all Kyst strive to achieve. He walked past two hunters standing guard at the entrance to the bridge. Upon reaching the same spot, Eevie held up her fist and all 3,000 troops stopped in unison. The two guards looked at the army with obvious fright, Eevie shot them a wink as she walked by to join Vakar. The king confidently strode up to the main entrance with the Artifact of Silva displayed around his neck. He was halted at the grand entrance by two Kyst Hunters wearing the traditional teal and sandy colours of ShallowBay.

"Cease at once," demanded one guard.

"Your armies are not welcome here," added the other.

Vakar stared them down with a sense of disinterest and superiority.

"I could kill you both before my next breath. Decide now if you want your blood painting these fine doors."

Both the hunters cleared their throats awkwardly before giving each other worried looks and moving aside. Vakar wasted no-time in throwing the doors open and striding into the main hall. He saw the walls were lined with ShallowBay Hunters, including a large score of Sages on the upper balconies. Seated in the far side of the room atop a throne of vibrant coral was Queen Saphier. Her beauty was so divine, for it was fabled throughout the Northern Rainforest, that in an act of jealousy, Āina blessed Saphier with unparalleled beauty to spite his lover, Kaia. Even Vakar, whose heart still belonged to a male Kyst, was caught off-guard for the tales of all her resplendence simply could not do her justice. She was adorned in a long blue and sandy-white dress, bedecked in glistening pearls. Her face however, was one of sheer boredom and tedium.

"You disappoint me, Vakar," Saphier said while actively stifling a yawn. "I assure you, that is not my aim."

"No?" Saphier asked in a higher octave, jolting to attention before slowly slumping back into her previous posture. "Well, I hope that the reason for being here is far more impressive than the force I am looking at."

Vakar didn't miss her double connotation and stopped nearly 12 paces from the throne, close enough to let Saphier notice the artifact around his neck, as he studied the Queen's beauty up close.

"You know why I've come. There is no option but to accept the terms I have

laid out for you, and your people."

"My people wouldn't see their leader whispered to by a poison dripper like yourself. Especially one who wields fear to control others. We wish not to be drafted into your Kingdom like the other Kyst. We remain as all elves do, self-thinking and free." Saphier remained devoted to the ideals and traditions of Shallow Bay. Vakar took a step forward, a flare of anger in his eye.

"You would remain as you said. What I offer is peace and security throughout all the Great Northern Rainforest."

"And yet, we did not ask," Saphier said with a tone of finality, waving her hand dismissively.

"I will not be dismissed as some messenger!" Vakar snapped in response. After taking another step towards the queen, she stood up in rage. A sudden bolt of energy shot from the balcony to strike the ground three paces in front of Vakar. Saphier shot her hand up to stay her protectors. She stepped off her raised throne to confront the self-declared King of Kyst.

"You are a sickness to this forest," Saphier muttered threateningly to Vakar quietly, but loud enough for all to hear as it echoed through the hall. "You come to our home, uninvited with a hoard licking your heel, and demand my undying fealty. They say you are cunning, yet, I see only a broken boy spewing lies of peace to camouflage his malice." Saphier gave Vakar a look no one had ever given him before. She was so assured of herself, so confident in her decision that no matter what he did, Shallow Bay would not bend.

The Queen turned away to sit back on her throne, but Vakar grabbed her wrist and spun her back to face him.

"We are not done here," he said with an equal threat. She threw her arm back out of his grasp with a look of sheer rage and slapped him hard across the cheek.

"You dare grab me in my own palace?" Saphier roared. "I could have killed you with the flick of my wrist."

"No," Vakar said while looking around to the nearly 100 or so hunters and sages occupying the room. "You really couldn't." A disturbing grin crossed his face. Saphier threw her hand up, signalling for her people to strike this Kyst down. Within the blink of an eye, the entire hall erupted with the whistle of 70 arrows let loose. Two dozen beams of flame, ice, and pure arcane energy lashed out at the self-proclaimed king. And yet, in the time it took Vakar to raise both hands out to his side, every single projectile, each one surely capable of killing him, stopped as if held by time.

Saphier looked at him with horror; the sheer ease of it was written all over Vakar's face. His necklace began to glow a soft green, he moved one hand up and over towards Saphier. Before she could react, she started to float, uncontrollably. It was as if her entire body but her head was grabbed by the fist of a Mountain Giant and hoisted. She squirmed in agony and before long she was screaming in pain, just as the entrance doors swung open. Revealing the two Kyst who had been guarding the door, now sprawled out on the floor, utterly dazed as Eevie rushed in.

"My King!" She screamed, running closer. "No!" Before Eevie could get any closer, she collided with the energy field holding the projectiles in place. Looking around, she saw scores of hunters attempting to get closer to their queen. Doing anything and everything to save her. Eevie sat on the ground where she had landed, watching in disbelief at this display of Vakar's sheer power, and most notably, the fear he so easily withdrew. Soon, the wall began nipping at her feet. She watched as the arrows and arcane missiles were seemingly reversed and pushed back onto their owners. Several of the hunters threw down their weapons as they saw this and continued to listen in horror as Saphier was slowly crushed. All of them began shouting.

"We surrender!" One cried.

"Just let her go, we'll do what you say!" Another screamed.

"Please spare our queen!" Cried everyone in the room at least once. When Eevie saw the mass murder about to be committed, she leaped up and pushed back against the barrier.

"Qiri would be ashamed," Eevie said evenly, just loud enough for Vakar to hear.

As quickly as it reverberated in the room, the queen hit the ground most awkwardly. All the arrows clattered to the ground and the bursts of fire, ice, and magic evaporated. Several Kyst rushed to the queen's aid but most were too frightened to move.

Vakar turned his blood-thirsty glare upon his commander, his chosen sister, and friend. He slowly approached before stopping face to face with her. His breath was heavy and the pain in his eyes rang loud. He vibrated slightly as the anger had all but consumed him, and he turned his sight to his army marching across the bridge. Without a word more and completely alone, Vakar left ShallowBay, retreating into the forest.

A private burial was held for the fallen King of ShadowScorn beneath the palace in the catacombs of the royal family. Albeit as massive as they were, the catacombs were relatively new and therefore only occupied by few others. The first King of ShadowScorn, Risastor. The second king, Armin and their respective queens, each buried beside them. The former Prince Scarnin, who met his untimely end, and now, King Arwr, Katia and Scáth, stood side by side and closest to the tomb. Behind them stood Torvic, Aelis, and Oren, shoulder to shoulder. Several more rows of important figures to the city, and many close friends of Arwr, were also in attendance. Normally, the entire city would be permitted into the main palace to pay their respects to fallen royalty, but siege times didn't offer such luxury. When Katia gave the word, they watched as Torvic waved his hand and the stone slab-lid, with a detailed statue of the recently deceased, was hoisted atop his tomb. Scraping stone echoed through the catacombs before ending in a resounding thud. Katia and Scáth gave each other distasteful looks before turning and ending the proceedings, allowing everyone gathered proper time to pay their respects to the late king and lost friend. Katia remained behind to greet everyone and receive condolences. Aelis threw her arm around her dearest and oldest friend before they exited the catacombs together.

"Your Agora has the ferocity and skill I may never have seen in a fighter before," Aelis remarked to Scáth, speaking of the night raid where Agan had them all in awe. Scáth smiled at that for it was no secret that other races were seldom let into the city. As it stood currently, aside from a few citizens of ShadowScorn who were not Scorn, Athvar, Agan and Faenla were the only outsiders in the city. So it did Scáth good to hear something genuinely positive said about them being there.

"I thank Aceia for his presence. He has turned out to be a dear friend," Scáth replied solemnly.

"Well, I thank Lokor for those bulging arms of his," Aelis said with a sly grin and wink to her friend. The two shared a sweet blithe laugh in the face of all that had, and continued to transpire, determined to persevere.

"Whilst on the road, I saw him wrestle bodily with a Feral brown bear, before quickly killing and tossing it aside." Scáth recounted the battle the companions had faced against a pack of Ferals outside the shore of Litore Lake. Aelis threw a hand to her forehead, fainting a swoon before they both shared another laugh. Scáth leaned her head against Aelis's shoulder.

"How do you think he fairs?" Scáth asked sheepishly. Aelis knew of course that she was referring to the Kyst.

"They call him 'mighty' for a reason, no? From everything you described to me, there is little he can't overcome." When Scáth said nothing back, Aelis continued. "Captain Sindrum has made many expeditions to Moon Mountain in the past and as you know, is among our greatest Scorn Guard. Fear not, my love. Soon, we will all watch the sunset on our peaceful land once more," Aelis said as reassuringly as possible, as she nuzzled her head against Scáth.

Agan Dusk walked down the streets of ShadowScorn with his two companions. Athvar was on the back of Faenla, now seated in a leather saddle that Scáth had made for them.

"You can't kill any of them," Athvar stated to a rather grumpy Agan.

"Don't tell me what I can and can't do, little man," Agan grumbled back. Athvar gave a great roll of his eyes, ensuring the half-orc noticed now that the two were of equal eye-level.

"We are guests here, Agan. Torvic Gloom entrusted us to bring them back alive. This is city justice. The axe will not solve our problems here," Athvar calmly explained to his ill-tempered friend.

"I'm familiar with city justice, and yet I have still to meet a problem the axe can't solve."

"I do not doubt," the gnome replied with a soft chuckle. The two discussed no more of the topic as they approached the shipping district. Located near the main gate of the city, several large warehouses, wooden cranes, and wagons occupied this section. Prior to this, Torvic Gloom had gone to the companions with word of Agan's attackers. This information and opportunity were offered under the pretense of the attackers being brought back for interrogation. The priests of Aecia, god of Shadow and Assassins, had entire tomes devoted to divining the truth through magical and some non-magical means.

"And besides, this could just be another false tip or dead end," Athvar added, reminding the Orc-Elf of the few leads they had already investigated. The trio stopped in the centre of the warehouses to find it deserted. Since the siege, of course, there had been no trade or farming, in or out of the city.

Athvar jumped off Faenla's back and the colossal wolf went to sniffing about the grounds. He soon found a scent to track, into a warehouse directly in front of him. Athvar and Agan saw this and decided to individually check the remaining two warehouses on either side. Agan found the many entrances all to be locked. Looking around to make sure Athvar was out of sight, he lined himself up with the lock of the door and kicked it open with a thunderous crash. He entered, closing his eyes for a moment. After opening them, they glowed a brighter yellow having adjusted to the darkness within. He saw many more caravan wagons, bales upon bales of hay, and a surprising amount of horse manure. Fresh horse manure he thought to himself. He noted the warehouse had two levels as he suddenly shot his head up when he heard something thud and shuffle above. Slowly and quietly he made his way to the ladder.

Athvar was similarly met with nothing but locked barn doors. He was, however, a gnome of no small skill. He nimbly climbed atop a stack of barrels before hoisting himself through a window on the second floor. He landed quietly on the wooden balcony and quickly surveyed his surroundings. Immediately, he caught the whinnying of five saddled and fully provisioned horses. They currently had free reign over this warehouse but were thoroughly distracted by a fresh pile of hay. Athvar continued to creep above as he circled around the balcony. After ensuring there was no one about, he jumped down into a large stack of burlap sacks. One of the horses paused from his lunch to regard the gnome. Suddenly, the horses' eye's shot wide, for it found the gnome was communicating with him.

Faenla had sniffed himself to the barn door. He swiped his large paw at the door but found it only jostled slightly, locked from the other side. The wolf looked around before circling the whole warehouse. Much to his delight, Faenla found a regular doorway fully opened. The wolf slowly and ever so cautiously proceeded inside. Sniffing intently, he caught the scent once more and followed it into the centre of the warehouse. He stopped when the scent faded, his ears popping up as he heard the disruption of air above him. He sprinted forward with amazing speed. Just as a weighted net fell to the ground and a Scorn man jumped from the ceiling. Faenla growled menacingly but the ruffian just smiled back at the wolf. The Scorn man took a step forward. Faenla pounced to rip his throat out but instead jumped straight into another descending net, giving a great growl as he found himself to be uncontrollably pinned to the ground. The wolf couldn't discern for all its extraordinary intelligence why he was unable to move a muscle. No matter how hard Faen pushed against the net, it was simply too much weight. Although the wolf couldn't know, it was enchanted with a devious spell. Nothing short of Giant kin could break free. Two other Scorn appeared from the shadows in the warehouse, it took all three of them to drag the massive animal away.

Agan had just reached the top of the ladder when a Scorn man shadow-walked to the summit and kicked the fighter squarely in the head. Agan flew off the four-metre ladder and thudded hard against the ground. The air burst from his lungs and he wheezed heartily to fill them again. The Scorn human above pulled a long-knife off his back and leaped down to kill the Agora. Agan's ring finger let out a small pulse of energy, calling upon the Night Ring Aelis had given him. Just as the long-knife plunged toward the filthy warehouse floor, Agan shadow-stepped behind the Scorn. He grabbed the back of his head and shoved the man's face into the ground as hard as he could. Agan bashed the man's head into the wood planks twice more before letting go at the sound of a familiar howl, cut short by a pain-filled whimper.

The gnome and Agora sprinted back into the shipping yard at the same time and rushed for the centre warehouse. The brutish fighter wasted no time in kicking the main door open. They both spotted Faenla being dragged around a corner and two familiar Scorn men waiting for them.

"Get Faen," Agan said through gritted teeth. Athvar knew this look and understood Agan would not lose the fight again, so the gnome shot back outside to go for the captured wolf. Agan instantly recognized these two Scorn as the ones who had beaten him within an inch of his life.

"Torvic said I had to bring you in alive. That doesn't mean you won't wish you were dead," Agan snarled and used his ring to shadow-step behind them, hacking with devastating aggression. Much to his dismay the two Scorn had also shadow-stepped a safe distance away, drawing their weapons, and charging back toward him. Over the next several minutes, not one of them landed a solid blow. Every time Agan thought he had one of them with a great chop, they simply blinked from one place to another. He was harnessing the power of the ring far too much, and found it started to take a toll on his physical energy. Yet, these Scorn were doing it innately and could continue to do so for far longer than Agan could hope. The half-orc looked at them, seeing confidence in their ability to win this fight; not something he was used to seeing in the eyes of his enemies.

"Enough!" The fighter roared while throwing his axe into the manure-caked floor. Agan shadow-stepped forward to the smaller of the two Scorn men, grabbing him by the throat, and throwing him into the second Scorn. He, however, also blinked out of sight before being hit by the flying ruffian. That ruffian continued to crash into, and through, a large support beam. The other appeared right behind Agan and swung with his long sword. Sensing this, Agan dropped low, spinning on his heel to deliver a vomit-inducing gut-punch. The ruffian let out a puking sound before Agan grabbed his crotch and squeezed. The Scorn howled with a high pitch. The fighter heard a pop and laughed heartily. He then punched the forearm holding the long sword and it clattered to the floor. He stood to his full height, staring menacingly down at the Scorn whose eyes bulged in pain.

"I warned you," Agan said, before smashing his forehead on the ruffian's nose, splattering both their faces with matte-black blood. Agan let go of the Scorn who dropped not unlike a sack of potatoes. The ruffian who had been thrown through a solid wood-beam shadow-walked behind the half-orc and almost struck him in the lower back with a dagger. Agan quickly spun and grabbed the wrist that held the weapon.

"Not again," he said with a smile. Agan Dusk squeezed with all the might of his one hand, the Scorn let out an agonizing scream as he felt his wrist snap into shards of bone and his hand hung limply. He then similarly knocked the Scorn unconscious with a head butt that broke the ruffian's nose. Once tying them back to back against each other, Agan rushed after Athvar and Faenla.

By the time Athvar got to the far side of the warehouse, he had lost sight of them. Unsure of where to look he heard another howl that was then cut short by another pained whimper. Faenla's pain was not in vain as Athvar heard it come from the warehouse with the horses in it. The gnome wasted no time in rushing back there, climbing through the window as he had previously done and quietly landing on the second floor. When he peered over the balcony rail he saw three Scorn doing everything they could to tie Faenla's net to the back of one horse. Athvar pulled out his blowgun and the darts laced with a sleep potion. He blew a single dart into the neck of one Scorn and watched with glee. He loved the initial confusion that always followed the first dart. The Scorn pulled it from his neck and regarded it closely, before falling over backwards to collide firmly with the floor. The other two watched in panic as their comrade snored loudly. Athvar shot another one and it too found its mark. The third and apparently most clever took cover behind a wagon. Athvar rolled his eyes impatiently before leaping down. He regarded Faenla who was stuck in a strange contorted position.

"Come on Faen, tear yourself free," Athvar prompted quietly, but Faenla just responded with a series of whines. He threw his belly to the ground when a hand-axe went twirling over his head. The gnome crawled underneath the wagon where the Scorn ruffian was hiding. He popped out with his back to the floor right between the ruffian's legs.

"Hi," Athvar said before blowing a dart that stuck right under the Scorn's chin. The ruffian looked down at the sneaky gnome before batting his eyes lazily and falling asleep. He found it to be quite a novelty when this Scorn fell asleep still standing upright. He rolled his head over to see the hulking Agan burst through another door and body tackle the sleeping ruffian. Athvar watched on with amusement as the two landed on the floor and Agan spotted the dart in the prone man's chin.

"Well done, little man," Agan said with a great laugh. Athvar crawled out from under the wagon as Agan stood up and rushed to Faen. He struggled for some time to remove the net.

"Why can Faenla not move?" He asked while fighting to untangle the wolf. Once Faenla was free, he jumped out and went to profusely licking Athvar's face.

"Of course, I did. You're a part of the family," Athvar said as if in response to the wolf. Agan and Athvar went about inspecting the net.

"It's tainted red on one side. Blood?" Agan asked curiously. Upon inspecting Faenla they saw no obvious wounds which was a relief to them both.

"Put one hand underneath," Athvar instructed Agan, who shrugged and tried it out. Much to his shock, no matter how hard he wiggled and moved his hand, the net did not budge. With his free hand and great care, Agan was able to lift the blue side.

"Impressive," the half-orc bellowed. "I have an idea," Agan said to his companions with a large grin.

An hour or so later, Agan, Athvar, and a proud Faenla were walking through the streets of ShadowScorn with six men tangled and wrapped up in the enchanted net. The Ruffians were being dragged across the rough cobblestone by none other than the horse Athvar had communicated with.

Ch8 - Bitter Realities

"Why is the lake not frozen?" Ven was looking over the taffrail as he asked Sindrum. It was night time and he saw first hand where this lake got its name. Billions of bio-luminescent bubbles floated from the lake floor to settle on the surface before popping and releasing a wisp of vibrant mist. It truly was like looking into star-light.

"Those who live on the lake's floor prevent the freezing," Sindrum replied evenly. Ven stood straight to fully regard the captain with a curious stare.

"Who lives on the lake floor?"

"A great many things. The Aquon hold the greatest presence mind you, and are responsible for keeping the lake temperate," Sindrum explained while at the helm, gliding their sailboat through glassy waters. Ven thought about the 'Aquon' and remembered tales of them living in the oceans, but rarely coming to the surface. Sindrum went on to explain that the fresh water Aquon are much more territorial and prefer to make their presence known.

Shortly after setting sail and completing the necessary rigging, Ven walked to the helm, ready to take over. "Find some rest. We're in my realm now."

Sindrum wasn't about to argue for he truly was drained. He had not slept since the night before they were caught in the blizzard. So the Scorn Captain went and curled up on a coil of rope at the bow. Ven let out a sigh of relief as he leaned back with the tiller tucked under his arm, maintaining a direct course to the northern end of the lake. The hunter looked to his left and saw only open water with no shoreline in sight. On his right, roughly half a kilometre away was the infamous Bayownin Forest. As if to prove the stories he had grown up reading of the world's most imposing forest, an eagle with a 20-metre wingspan soared out from the forest and dive-bombed the water. In its talons came up a trout, the likes Ven had never imagined. It let out a screech of victory that sent shivers down the Kyst Hunter's spine as its echo skipped across the lake.

They expected to be at the far end of Starlight Lake in three days and from there another two-day walk to Moon Mountain, not including the climb which was said to take a half-cycle with good weather. The mountain which was the tallest in all Litore still loomed in the distance like a beacon. With that earth-defying mountain peak, it left Ven with a whirlwind of emotions. His guilt grew for there wasn't an ounce of feeling homesick for Silva or his people. The only real pang of heartache was for the lack of Scáth at his side.

Yet, that was quickly overtaken by a sense of embarrassment at his unexpected kiss replaying in his mind. Furthermore, there was the regret of leaving without saying goodbye to her. That naivety had bitten hard at his ego after his encounter with the Vampire. Ven was still very young, even by human years. He was hardly an adult by Elven standards, his skill and creativity offering him the status he had. But an elf of a century or more would have recognized the slim chance of survival in going to Moon Mountain. That realization didn't strike Ven Devar until right now, which left the Kyst feeling vulnerable and plain stupid.

I often find myself thinking back on the days before Silva was destroyed when I yearned for what I could not have. A life filled with adventure and intrigue. By the time I was 15 years of age, still a mere babe in the life of my people; I had already met and broke every challenge the Great Northern Rainforest could throw at me. Those whose years and experiences vastly outnumbered my own paled in comparison to my skill and wit. Yet, I found myself to be one of the few who did not act from a feeling of superiority. I did not boast the talent I have or attempt to make others feel lesser to bolster my own ego. It stings at my conscience to know all those who acted that way met their end that fiery night. For they never ceased the lies they told themselves and embraced who they truly were. The Scorn I travel with now reeks of that narcissism much like the dead Kyst of Silva did and due to that fact, I fear for the success of our mission. The same cannot be said for

Agan Dusk, a warrior unlike I've ever known. Though we often butt heads, sometimes literally, I truly hope it does not come to real blows as I never wish to cross swords with such a Master Fighter. His ferocity and power make him an adversary that would have any sane humanoid cowering. He is humbled by his abilities and never acts out of superiority or grandiosity. It is that ability that makes him so admirable in my eyes and a dear friend.

-Ven Devar

"Have you met other Kyst?" The hunter asked loudly as Sindrum was in a deep sleep.

The guard captain slowly opened his eyes to regard the elf.

"What?"

"It's a simple question," Ven replied sternly. Sindrum unlocked his fingers from resting on his belly and got up from the furled rope. He went to lean on the taffrail and watched the first rays of dawn peeking through the canopy of Bayownin.

"When I was a child, yes," the Scorn elf answered distantly, clearly lost in the reflection of memories past. Ven, however, pressed his line of questions.

"A visitor to your city?"

Sindrum took a long while to respond, perhaps in search of details forgotten.

"No. There is a prominent Kyst settlement in the Midori Forest, perhaps a full-cycle or more southeast from ShadowScorn."

"What was a young Scorn doing outside the safety of your city?" Ven continued to press but the captain was not so easily interrogated.

"Not until you tell me why you're asking."

Ven answered without hesitation. "I believe it is relevant to our collective goal."

Sindrum scoffed in protest. "Please, our goals here are not aligned. I aim to protect my very culture and prevent the extinction of my people. You simply wish to impress a princess."

Ven laughed at the absurdity of his words. "Now, continue your tale," the hunter requested politely. Sindrum was surprised and somewhat irritated by Ven's ability to avoid verbal conflict.

"I, like many Scorn, had found myself being trafficked. My captors had a ship waiting on the coast to sail me south. One of the most prominent houses in Elemenzin, Hitori by name, planned to purchase me. My captors often reminded me of the pleasure the Hitori Family took in studying Scorn children. Eventually, the experiments would claim your life, but if you were unfortunate enough to endure it, then a show piece for visitors to gossip about or gawk at. The vile and wicked even mixed our skin and flesh into potions and elixirs." Sindrum never missed a beat, so numb to the pain and reality of his past and the world around him. "Shortly after entering the Midori Forest, the convoy came under attack. Like rain from a storm cloud, arrows poured from the tree line. Soon all was silent, and a single Kyst Hunter emerged to unlock my cage. He gave me a horse from a dead captor, a long dagger, and enough rations to make the trip back thrice over."

"They did not see you home?" Ven interrupted with a sense of surprise.

"No, but they did save my life. For that, I will never forget." Sindrum ended with a nod of respect to Ven Devar, which he reciprocated in full.

The early morning turned into violent, choppy waters, forcing Ven to take their vessel closer to shore, closer to Bayownin Forest.

"Watch your distance, I assure you many of the unnaturally huge predators can swim faster than our ship might sail. And most in that forest wouldn't find it difficult to pluck us from our deck," Sindrum warned Ven and to the Kyst, it sounded like he was talking from experience.

"What is it, exactly, that makes these animals so large?"

"Many speculate it is something in the water that the forest produces. But no one really knows, could be a mad old druid having a laugh for all we know."

Fortunate as it was, but to Ven's dismay, they saw no more of the spectacular beasts emerge from the infamous tree line. By mid-day the water continued to roil with rage. The hull of the ship took many great hits from the white-capped waves. One shook the vessel so hard that Sindrum lost his footing and Ven heard the one thing every sailor dreads, the splash of someone overboard.

"Sindrum!" Ven sprang into action, securing a rope to the rail and tossing it at the Scorn. The captain was seriously struggling to tread water in his heavy armour and the upturned waves only hindered him. The Kyst's aim was true though and Sindrum grabbed hold of the lifeline. Ven began reeling Sindrum in before a great opposition was met and the captain was pulled under. Ven pulled back even harder but was thrown off balance by the sudden lack of any resistance. The mighty hunter dropped his cloak, threw the anchor overboard hoping it would catch and jumped in the water with a graceful dive. He elongated his trident and pumped his powerful legs, descending deeper and deeper. He quickly spotted two Aquon dragging a thrashing Sindrum down by his ankles. Both of the pale-blue creatures spotted the Kyst and gave a high-pitched screech in his direction. Ven feared for the time his Scorn companion had before his lungs would fill up. He hurled his trident into the back of one Aquon, the bright bubbles created by all the disruption made the throw difficult but the weapon still found its mark. The fishy humanoid gave a last jolt of life before limply sinking out of sight. The last Aquon screamed so powerfully, circular pockets of bubbles fired at Ven, and as result he felt as though his head would pop from the pressure. Pulling the trident from his dead comrade, the Aquon threw it back at the Kyst. Ven barely recovered in time to catch it with both hands just centimetres from his face. Before he had a chance to react, Sindrum gave a garbled yelp of pain as the Aquon bit down on his throat and quickly vanished. Ven hooked the trident on his belt and swam quickly to his thrashing ally. By the time the Kyst got there, a large cloud of blood obscured the Scorn. Sindrum was clutching at his throat, not likely in an attempt to stem the bleeding but because his lungs were screaming for air. Ven had to swim for them both and it took far longer than the Kyst had wished to breach the surface.

He had the Scorn around his shoulders and used the rope still hanging overboard to hoist them back up. He laid the captain down and inspected the bite marks on his neck. Wrapping a cloth around them, he began compressions in an attempt to force the water out of his lungs. The blood pouring from the Scorns neck was not insignificant and with each compression of his chest, more spurted out the deep wound. After a panic-inducing moment of trying to save his companion, Sindrum vomited up a disturbing amount of water and quickly passed out again.

The Kyst ran to the things he had left on the deck and pulled out a wooden jar of herbal salve from his satchel. He firmly pressed the gooey substance into the neck wounds the captain had suffered and tightly wrapped a fresh cloth around them. He then dragged the captain back to the furled pile of rope and left him to rest on his side. The Mighty Ven Devar slumped back in exhaustion, shivering from his soaked clothes and brutal winter winds. He pulled the golden locket from around his neck, and flicked it open with trembling fingers. He stared at the image of Renic Devar, his former mentor, and the most admirable Kyst he had ever known. That image always filled him with the courage to keep going, for he could never forget how Renic gave his life to save Ven.

The princess, commander, and Arch Priest of ShadowScorn stood atop the city wall watching the Renrit army march for an attack. The Scorn Guard were still outnumbered nearly three to one. Much to the relief of Aelis, she did not spot any of the war machines that had first laid waste to the city. From the very back ranks of the approaching army, the onlookers spotted a small glowing ball of light. It was created by a squadron of wizards. The ball slowly but surely grew, rising into the sky before making the late sun hue over the land bright as mid-day. Aelis commended them by taking away the Scorn's greatest advantage but the commander also learned the Renrits were expecting a long night. Aelis shouted below for barrels of sticky gelatinous oil to be brought up to the top of the wall.

Scáth turned back to her city where the entire Scorn army stood, awaiting orders. She also noticed her three companions travelling back to the palace with a most curious package in tow. Scáth motioned for Torvic to follow her and as they approached to intercept the trio, the Arch Priest couldn't help but laugh to himself.

"Your friends are most unusual, albeit very effective."

A smile sprung across Scáth's face. "They are unique and I have never given my trust so confidently as I do them."

Torvic was in his fifth century of life, a long life considering his human heritage. He was proud and fortunate enough to say he had served the last two Monarchs of ShadowScorn. He was given the mantle of Arch Priest of the city by King Armin. So hearing Scáth speak with such assurance did his heart good. It even occurred to him that perhaps the princess he had always known, was replaced by a queen upon her improbable return.

"I do hope you are confident of their crimes," Torvic said wearily to Athvar and Agan.

"We are," the gnome answered matter-of-factly.

"Why is the army in formation?" Interjected Agan, before Torvic had a chance to continue.

"The Renrit army marches on our gates as we speak," Replied a solemn Scáth. Agan moved for the city gates to join the fight but was halted by the out raised arm of Torvic.

"No. I need you with us," the Arch Priest stated with a resolve to match his actions. Agan towered over the ornately robed man, his yellow eyes glowering down suddenly shot to the side as a soft hand rested on his shoulder.

"Let Aelis do what she knows best, Agan. You're needed elsewhere," Scáth gently pleaded. Agan gave a reluctant growl in agreement. By then, Torvic was inspecting the contents of the net. He only recognized one Scorn ruffian which was a surprise but they were all contorted and bent inside the net, which made it difficult to discern faces

"Were they a trouble to collect?" The Scorn priest asked. Faenla and Athvar slowly met eyes before Athvar coolly replied.

"Nope!"

To which Faenla chortled.

"Good. Let's escort them back to the palace for interrogation."

With the help of a few remaining Scorn Guard, Agan managed to chain each of their prisoners to individual cells. Scáth then proceeded to take a long while in studying each of the ruffians. The only one she could identify as being connected with her disappearance was Snik, the same Scorn that Torvic recognized. So it was decided; Torvic, Scáth, Agan, and Athvar would take part in the interrogation. Athvar was stopped by a crying Faenla. Torvic was shocked, as all were when they first saw Athvar and the colossal wolf appear to be locked in full conversation.

"I don't know buddy. I doubt Ven would approve," Athvar said sympathetically. Faenla responded with a series of snorts and stomps of his paws. Athvar sighed heavily but stood up to his full 83 centimetres and addressed the room.

"Faenla is desperate to join the front gates."

Torvic shrugged with indifference to what the wolf did, however, Scáth appeared as if in some distress. The princess walked over and placed a hand on her fury companion's thick neck.

"Ven would never stop you from doing what is right. But I cannot lose you," she whispered in his ear. Faenla placed a large paw on her hand and licked the side of her face. His intellect and stunning visage never ceased to amaze Scáth. His jet-black fur and white spots always reminded her of the night's most breathtaking star-filled sky. Without any more ceremony, the wolf bounded out of the dungeon for the fight.

"Sure, the wolf can go but I can't," Agan mumbled to himself. Not quietly enough for Athvar to miss though and the gnome chuckled at the half-orcs petulant attitude. Athvar, noting the dart still stuck under the prisoner's chin, quickly removed it.

"Wake him," Torvic instructed the half-orc.

"Gladly," Agan replied before winding up a resounding backhand to the chained-up Scorns face. When that did nothing but rock his head from one side to the other, Agan pinched the Ruffian's nose and clutched his jaw. Within a few heartbeats, Snik violently jerked awake. Everyone remained staring blankly at him as he took a few panicked seconds to grasp his surroundings before his surprise quickly faded into a grimace.

"We need only know one thing for your release. Who do you work for, Snik?" Torvic asked with a clear offering of reason. Snik, however, responded with a pensive stare. "I believe you remember our half-orc friend? Surely you can guess why he is here." Torvic taunted dryly.

"To warm your bed?" Snik insulted and instantly received a slap to the back of the head from Agan.

"We've known each other for a long time. You used to be a dedicated follower at the church. You once had valuable morals. Yet, you have never had nor appreciated the art of planning. So I ask you again, who do you work for?" Torvic demanded the information be shared at once.

"It's too late for that," was all the Scorn ruffian had to say. "Because?" The Arch Priest alluded. Snik only laughed in the face of the question before taking another slap to the head. The ruffian quickly whipped his head at Agan and gnashed his teeth with fury.

"Ooh," Agan mocked before slapping him again.

"She's why," Snik motioned to Scáth. "You shouldn't have come back, princess."

Everyone but Torvic turned to look at Scáth, but she did not shake under his threat.

"My mother hired you?" Scáth asked as if she already knew the answer. Her words surprised everyone, including Snik, which Scáth took to mean her mother was using one or more layers of pawns to keep her away from the blame. At that point, and not being the only one suspecting the queen, the gnome hopped off his chair and walked towards the prisoner.

"The princess' return means that the struggle for power has now increased. But whom bears the loss is the question," Athvar hypothesized confidently, made even more confident by the uncomfortable body signs that Snik was giving off; a skill he learned while on the Court of Lords in Irdawnia.

"I know nothing of the Queen," Snik said in defiance of the gnome's accusation.

"So you admit there is someone above you?" Athvar responded with the quickness of a sharp mind. Snik only looked away in anger but Athvar pursued his line of questioning.

"Aelis perhaps? Someone close to the princess would make sense." Athvar could tell everyone's mood had changed at the mentioning of someone so trusted. Yet, Snik remained pensive. "Perhaps Torvic, himself? That would be most cunning," Athvar said with seriousness, but Snik only smirked in response.

"I think that is quite enough-"

"-Oren," Athvar shouted over an already unimpressed Arch Priest. Snik very slightly recoiled at the name of the City Administrator. Athvar noted too Snik's chest heaved slightly faster.

"Enough! You will not slander the names of good Scorn in this city." Torvic boomed with an echo of divine magic behind it. Athvar bowed to Snik before Torvic, a gesture that the gnome knew the Arch Priest would take offence too. Athvar confidently strode out of the cell but not before giving Scáth a wink and a smile.

"You've lived long enough in the city to know what happens to those who don't cooperate during war times." Torvic said taking the interrogation back over.

"I know you do not have the stomach for torture, Arch Priest," Snik replied with a level of disgust.

"True, but our ally here does." The Scorn motioned to Agan. Before the fighter could respond, Scáth interjected in horror.

"Torture?" Her tone was clearly unimpressed. "Might we speak outside," she demanded, exiting the prison cell. Agan slapped Snik on the back of the head once more and left the cell with Torvic. A furious Scáth turned to face the two.

"So our Arch Priest condones torture now?"

Torvic was actually quite unsettled by Scáth's fury and chose his next words carefully.

"My Princess, the world as you know is unforgiving and out to get us, specifically. In the all too often times of war we face, your grandfather and father have both employed such methods when it stands to make a difference," Torvic explained as carefully as possible, pleading for his princess to understand.

"And that just makes it okay?" She scolded before looking to Agan for support. Much to her disappointment, the fighter had a look of shame written all over his face.

"The information would bring justice to your kidnapping. To every ShadowScorn who has died in this siege," Agan said with a heavy heart and sombre voice.

"You're going to do it no matter what I say, aren't you?" She asked defiantly.

"Respectfully princess, yes," Torvic answered while regaining a small measure of his confidence. The Arch Priest bowed and returned to the cell.

"Then I will be in there when it happens," Scáth answered, determined to suffer the consequences of allowing this to happen. As she walked past Agan back into the cell, he grabbed her bicep, firmly.

"No."

She ripped her arm from him, "Yes."

Agan shook his head. "When you are queen, you will make sure these things never happen in your city again. What comes next is not for the strong of heart or resilient minded. It is the work of the corrupt, or those dead enough inside to do what needs to be done. I will not let your spirit be tainted by this deed." Agan looked down in shame as he entered the cell and slammed the door in Scáth's face.

Scáth slumped her shoulders in defeat. Again, she was being treated like a child and not next in line for the throne. Her contemplation was interrupted by Athvar's whistle down the hall. The gnome was standing at the base of the spiral staircase motioning for Scáth to catch up.

"Did ya get kicked out too?" Athvar teasingly asked Scáth.

"Why are you and Ven the only ones to treat me equally? My whole life I've been told what to do and how to do it. I have so much to offer and am capable of much more," She answered with a life-time of resentment.

"They're just protecting ya."

"I don't want protection, Athvar. I want a life." All ShadowScorn were forced to an existence that didn't go much beyond their walls. In Scáth's case as royalty, that was barely beyond the palace. And even after nearly six decades of constant supervision and supreme caution, she was stolen from her very bed.

"I wish I could say I understand Lady Scáth, I hope my empathy brings ya so

comfort," Athvar said, disappointed in himself that he could not offer better. "What if I don't want to be Queen?"

That question Athvar had been asked before, and he was prepared with an answer.

"That is a question I have heard a number of times. My answer is always the same, sweet Scáth. Will ya be someone who follows the road laid before ya or someone who carves their own?"

The two companions walked side by side and said nothing further as they walked back up to the main palace.

Ch9 - Far side of the World

Aunna Morningthorne sat in the northeastern turret of the magnificent cathedral that was positioned in the centre of Serenstrom. The tower was her own, as each of the ruling members was appointed a spire to show their respective position of power within the church. Her long raven-coloured hair swept past her waist and blew in the humid salty air as she overlooked the city from her balcony. Her rich sapphire eyes glistened in the sun, which bathed her skin in its invigorating warmth. In her hands was the brief but well-documented history of the ShadowScorn. Her study was interrupted by a familiar and friendly voice.

"You know that book wasn't written by the Scorn people," Ivan the Revered said, emerging from her study to join her on the balcony.

"Of course, I do," she replied without lifting her eyes from the horizon. "Then why waste your time?"

"The Macer instructed me to read it, again," Aunna replied with no lack of boredom.

"When you were my student, I never wasted your talents."

Aunna thought about that for a minute. She had been inducted into the church as a babe when her family left her on the grand stoop. Ivan was her first instructor until the age of 17 when she had graduated her training as a Paladin. It did not take long for the girl to begin her training as a healer and travel Litore under the tutelage of a noble Cleric now passed. In the past five years, Macer O'Donnell elevated her status to sit among the ruling council. She was once filled with so much passion to do the right thing and help the people of Litore. Yet, since her elevation to the council, that passion had waned when she understood that men only ever followed the route of power, often misleading others in pursuit of their own gain.

"Do you think Ifan would be proud of the work you have done as a Cleric?" Ivan asked softly as he leaned against the balcony rail.

"He was your brother, you tell me," Aunna answered firmly, and confidently as always, but Ivan detected a crack of weakness in her voice. The remark left him in a familiar state of lament. His brother had died beside Aunna on her last journey out of Serenstrom nearly 10 years ago; a mission that had separated the council strongly in the final days of the 'War of a Thousand Dragons.' The Macer had sent Ifan and Aunna along with a legion of soldiers to the Silver Dwarves, offering aid as they struggled with the near defeat against the Rhogarians. As Ivan and his brother Ifan had advised against going, the Macer demanded they extend a hand. Ivan knew the entire event was a ploy to remove his brother from the council and replace him with someone more impressionable.

Aunna and Ifan found easy passage to Silver Mountain and were greeted with open arms by the dwarves. Unfortunately, they were besieged by the Rhogarians and slaughtered almost to a one. Aunna made her desperate escape from the Dragon-Bloods after witnessing Ifan be tortured to death for information about why the Church of Sesara had joined the fight so late in a war. Little did they know, the only reason was a political move to further the Macers' ultimate sway over the counsel's decisions.

"He was a difficult man to read, but you have made me proud. So yes, I think he too would be."

"I miss him," she voiced, with barely a whisper. Ivan put a gentle hand on her shoulder and she reciprocated by leaning her head against his.

'Me too, Aunna. Me too." The pair looked out over their beloved home for a long while in peaceful silence.

"I don't know what to think about ShadowScorn. It all seems a cruel joke that the solitary action of a god should ripple through our lives like disturbed water for centuries unknown. There must be a greater reason for the Scorn than a simple slight against Sesara." Aunna didn't hide her bitterness or confusion.

"Since the beginning of the ShadowScorn race, how often has the church of Sesara declared war on them?" Ivan asked, knowing the answer, as did his former apprentice.

"Every 15 or 20 years, like clockwork.".

"About the same time, we get a new Macer, no? A simple fact all Macer's seem to ignore is that it was Aceia who put these people on Litore for a reason. Not Sesara. We do not hunt deer because they frighten us, we do it to survive. We travel to the far side of the world to war with a peaceful nation, simply because our Macer's believe it is a matter of survival. Not because a half-cracked Macer some 900 years ago spoke of a vision."

"You taught me that belief is the most dangerous thing in the world," Aunna added, beginning to figure out Ivan's line of thought. Ivan gently slipped out of their embrace and left his former student to reach a conclusion he knew she would find.

The Cathedral of Sesara was the jewel of their faith. It hosted nearly 2,000 servants in its great towering halls and chambers. Ivan walked nearly 30 minutes from the northeastern tower of Aunna to the centre spire that belonged to Macer O'Donnell. It took another fifteen minutes to merely climb the tower's stairs to the Macer's chambers. Ivan did not request entry from the two soldiers standing guard outside his doors, before throwing them open. Inside the great hall and meeting room for the Council, the Macer sat next to a large desk, sipping wine and admiring the view. Beside him with his back facing Ivan, sat Igon, reading over some pertinent information. Neither acknowledged his presence.

"Might I have a private word, Charles?" Ivan requested impatiently. Igon stopped reading aloud mid-sentence. The Macer did not turn his gaze and merely waved Igon off. The moment the doors swung shut, he spun in his chair and stared incredulously at Ivan. The Revered Paladin simply took a seat and stared back.

"Call me by my first name again and I will have you keelhauled on the very next ship leaving port."

Ivan did not appreciate the threat in which such a brutal form of murder would be used, but he knew even the Macer of Serenstrom could not kill him without an uprising; Ivan the Revered was named so by the Lords, Ladies, and commoners of Serenstrom for having fought and won countless crusades. In many regards, Ivan was a threat to the Macer because of the popularity and respect Serenstrom offered him, which was often more than what Charles received.

"How does the Siege of Shadow fair thus far?" Ivan changed the subject without missing a beat.

"It will be reported on at the next council meeting, as always," O'Donnell replied sharply.

"I'm asking you now. Just the two of us."

The Macer groaned in annoyance, he knew Ivan would not give up until he had heard something. "Two attacks have been launched. The first to soften the city, the second to test their improved wall defences."

"And?" Ivan asked, knowing there had to be more by now.

"They launched one counterattack. It proved to be a rather devastating one but much was learned," He answered with confidence, almost ignorant to the true situation.

"Seldom do we find any positives in a 'devastating' loss," Ivan answered dryly.

"Failure is our greatest teacher, you should know. Besides, we still outnumber the wretched creatures nearly three to one." The Macer's response didn't persuade the seasoned Paladin though.

"So?" Ivan prodded, clearly expecting to hear what knowledge they had gained from the defeat. However, Charles remained unyielding with his silence. "Then what of the death of Uthul and the wizard? Clearly dealt by the former prince of Silva." Ivan meant to surprise the Macer with the secret knowledge he had.

"All three of them are dead now. I watched the Scorns pull his corpse off the mountain, along with the other Kyst. They killed each other in a rather poetic fashion," he answered, using the knowledge about the dead Prince of Silva as leverage in their verbal combat.

"You used outlaw magic? To scry on them?" Ivan asked in genuine shock. There were certain rules that held Litore together. The continent and its lengthy history dated back across many failed civilizations, marked by today's scholars as the First and Second Ages. This 'Second Age' of Litore was enforced by a league of extra-dimensional beings. Or so the people thought, for their true origin remained a mystery. It was for good reason that the people of Litore followed their few rules of existence, as the members of The Keepers were individuals who knew Litore's history throughout both Ages. It was said the magics they outlawed were directly linked to the last catastrophic event that had most life wiped from the face of Litore. In accordance with their own edict, they do not use magic to spy on people. However, if one mortal is found guilty of having used 'outlawed magic' by The Keepers, then members known as 'Negators' would be dispatched to erase that person from all existence. Not even the Macer of Serenstrom and his armies could stop The Keepers from enacting their justice.

Charles O'Donnell did not give Ivan the satisfaction of affirmation but merely shrugged, hardly in denial. Ivan quickly got over the shock, now accepting that the Macer of Serenstrom was using dark, forbidden magic on such insignificant events.

"Why have you not sent one of us to oversee the siege? Any one of your council members would be a great asset to its success," Ivan said, deflecting any attention he might have brought to the fact he was aware of the Macer's secret.

"Aunna would all but refute me I'm afraid. Berek cannot leave his duties as Arch Priest to Serenstrom. Igon is of too much importance to my daily operations. Which leaves you. Considering your previous and total defeat in attacking the City of Shadow, I thought it best to leave this siege in the capable hands of our generals," Macer said, in a way clearly meant to jab at Ivan's ego in mentioning his only-ever defeat on the battlefield. In truth, Ivan's only defeat was not totally coincidental. He held his faith in Sesara as she was meant to be worshipped; treat others with kinship, and generosity. His loss to the ShadowScorn was one of the toughest but ultimately thankful moments of his life. The campaign that he had led there was directed by a former Macer nearly 20 years prior, when Ivan's young and enthusiastic heart was easily manipulated.

"Why do you really think this will be any different than all the previous attacks? For you forget that although I lost, I remain the only one to ever breach the city walls." Ivan inquired and pointed out in one last attempt to understand this insanity. The Macer couldn't help but suppress a devilish smile.

"This time, we have someone on the inside," he answered. Ivan's face screwed up in confusion.

"Who?"

"It does not concern you. A bargain has been struck. And so the ever defiant ShadowScorn people will bow not to Aceia the god of

Shadow, but to our Sesara." An utter look of supreme superiority washed over his wrinkled face

which left Ivan in genuine disgust. The shimmering, levitating crown on his head pulsed with energy to match his excitement.

"I hope to hear everything you just told me in the next council meeting." Ivan stood, bowed graciously and left the centre spire of the cathedral. He returned to the southeastern turret of the cathedral, the tower that was under his domain. In the spiral stairwell, he lined the cobblestone wall between each ascending window with an oil painting of every battle he had ever fought. It forced Ivan the Revered to re-live each nightmare-ridden war as he walked to the top of his tower. Upon reaching the summit, he entered into a large dojo-styled training room where a score of paladins in training ran through detailed drills and exercises.

He walked through the room as if surrounded by ghosts, heeding no call of respect, or salute, as he went. Through the smallest and most discreet door in the extravagant room was an impressive library, complete with a ladder track for the floor to ceiling bookshelves. From there, he went through another set of doors that led him to a staircase with a landing in the middle before turning back towards and above the previous two rooms. Here Ivan entered his private chambers. Silk curtains danced softly in the breeze next to the completely open and circular balconies on either side of the room. Soft blue braziers lined the pillars that supported the open structure. He walked to the far side of the room, between two black curtains, to his bed-chamber. There, he pulled down his great sword and shield off the wall above his headboard. Holding the sword in his hand again and wearing the shield on his arm, Ivan paused a moment to let the long-ago sensation take over.

He took the shield and slammed its pointed end into the stone floor. The flashing memory of committing similar actions into the throats and spines of countless enemies barraged him. He steeled his grip though and did this three more times until it had four distinct cracks running through the tile. He then put the tip of his gold-hilted great sword where the cracks met and squeezed his fist. A blue light ignited from the pommel down to the hilt, through the etched blade and out. A small pulse of energy exploded, clearing the tile and rubble away. Inside was a hole designed specifically for a chest. Within the chest was his white plate armour with golden embossing. Next to it was a packed satchel for travelling, filled with enough gems and coin to last the rest of his life if need be.

Ivan laid eyes on the main port that took up most of Serenstrom's eastern shore. The masts of the great galleons and sea-faring vessels could be seen vividly from his balcony. After strapping on his armour and gear, the paladin dawned a matte-brown cloak of extraordinary material. Within the blink of an eye, however, Ivan transformed its appearance into that of tattered grey rags. He pulled the hood forward, walked out onto his balcony and jumped into the night.

Ivan, although far past his physical prime, was at the height of his divine magic. The paladin summoned a great gust of impossibly dense wind that threw him far out over the city. As he neared a clay shingle roof he cast another spell of near weightlessness on himself and gently touched down on the surface. He expertly climbed down a back alley and began his short walk to the dockyard. The sound of waves bumping against hulls and creaking masts filled his ears with a nostalgic comfort. He made his way to a weathered barque and climbed aboard where the crew was enjoying a night of merriment and music. Ivan noticed quickly that all of the sailors were female and very drunk. Three of them played various instruments that sounded sweet but melancholic, while a fourth sang a song of haunting beauty. It was one Ivan was familiar with, the tale of a simple merchant sailor turned pirate who some years later unwittingly killed her true love while plundering a cargo ship. That singer wore a wide-brimmed hat and had thick flowing red hair that swayed with her movement like the sea itself. A tight waistcoat and thigh-high cuffed boots showed off her shapely figure. A dashing rapier was belted to her waist and by the looks of her, Ivan guessed she knew how to use it. They had not noticed him and so he did not want to disturb the song.

As it neared its crescendo Ivan did alarm the crew of 21 to his presence by clapping most graciously. Everyone on deck quickly spun and turned their gaze on Ivan, except for one lass for whom the drink proved too much as she fell off the crate she was seated on.

"Get off my ship," the singer demanded, who Ivan rightfully suspected to be the captain.

"If you can take me to Port Ozos," Ivan threw a purple ruby the size of his fist at the Captain, who caught it with expert reflexes, "There are two more just like it for your troubles."

The Captain looked at him with her almond shaped eyes, the flicker of torchlight illuminating her ship reflected wildly in her pupils.

"I'm guessing ye be wanting a quick departure?" She asked rather rhetorically. To which Ivan just kindly nodded in reply. The captain tossed the ruby into the air and let it fall back into her palm before tossing it to one of her crew.

"We're settin' sail gals!" She yelled and as if a cannonball whizzed past them, every sailor leapt into action, grabbing mooring lines and unfurling the foresail. The Captain walked up to Ivan, intently looking him up and down without a word. They were already pushing off the dock by the time she had finished with a huff. It amused the seasoned veteran as he truthfully couldn't discern her intent.

"I'm Captain Tsuni Tal. Welcome aboard The Horizons Edge." She held out her forearm and Ivan did likewise, clasping each other near the elbow.

"Ifan Fjell," Ivan responded, taking his deceased brother's name for this journey as an alias, as he did so often when venturing on his own.

"Is Port Ozos the final destination or will ye be travelling further?" Tsuni asked out of manners more than interest.

"The western edge of the 'Spire Lakes'," Ivan answered and Tsuni's eyes widened at that. The Lakes of Sen were controlled by a crime syndicate known for their unrelenting brutality and held a toll for all those travelling along that section of Litore's Great Road. The land to either side of the lakes was completely unnavigable and it was the 'Fires of Fel' that built the bridges across the lakes and so aptly controlled them.

"So a one-way trip." She laughed to herself, doubting anyone willing to travel to the western Spire Lakes of all places would be one to survive. "Well follow me, we have a cabin for guests willing to pay such a high price on our ship."

Ch10 - The Frozen Fist

Ven Devar beached their boat at the north end of Starlight Lake. He had sailed their vessel right onto the sandy shore not expecting to use the ship again, and needing easy access for a barely conscious Sindrum to get off. With his adrenaline gone, he barely managed to leap over the rail with the captain around his shoulders. The hunter hit the soft sand and fell to his knees from the excess weight. Bayownin Forest curved and turned east several kilometres prior to the lakes end, so Ven was hoping they'd be safely away from any abnormalities looking to make a meal out of them. Before him lay the beginning of their final trek, traversing the base of the Kermon Mountain Range and up the highest summit in Litore. Ven dropped his shoulder into the sand to gently roll the Scorn down.

"What are we going to do with you," he mumbled disparagingly. Sindrum attempted to respond through closed eyes, but his voice was completely inaudible and came in short wheezes more than any dialog. Ven only had enough clean wrappings to replace them daily, which was far too insufficient for the scale of wound Sindrum had suffered. The cloth was soaked black already and was catching bugs and earthly debris like honey. They would not make the base of Moon Mountain before Sindrum succumbed to an infection in his throat. Ven walked a short distance to the tree line where he grabbed a fist full of snow and placed it on Sindrum's forehead in an effort to stave off his rising body temperature. Eventually, the Kyst hung his head, accepting he was too far removed from his element and experience. He was a hunter of the Great Northern Rainforest, and a damn good one at that. But Ven was still reeling from his brush with death on the side of Glass Mountain. His confidence had been shaken to its core and things had only progressively gotten worse. He had been faced with certain adversity before, but never in such consistent succession and threat.

Torn from his self-deprecating thoughts, his ear twitched at the sound of a high-pitched twig snapping some distance away. Ven rolled to the side, pulling his bow and knocking an arrow as he went. He slowly stood up and inched his way closer to the sound. Soon, his feet were leaving tracks in the snow instead of the sand which caused the hunter to turn his aim upwards. Nothing else could be heard except for the heavy wind blowing through the grove of sparse trees. He eventually dropped his bow to the side and walked back to the shore. When he saw Sindrum, the Scorn was surrounded by five tiny snow creatures covered in little icicles. They all stopped dead in their movements to regard the elf who had spotted them. Ven had never seen such creatures and stood there dumbfounded, wondering if they be friend or foe. They were bipedal and had purely white eyes that seemed to grow or shrink with their reactions. They barely stood the height of Ven's shin. One of them slowly lifted its tiny arm to offer an emphatic wave. Ven furrowed a brow, and slowly returned the gesture. The creatures dematerialized with a gust of wind, turning into snow and floating away as they did. He took a step forward into the soggy sand before stopping again and slowly turning around. There, all five of the creatures stopped where they stood as if just being caught again, watching him most curiously. Ven slowly slung his bow over his shoulder.

"Hi?" He asked in the common tongue. One of the more curious creatures shook his head before pointing to Sindrum. Ven looked to his companion before turning back to the snowy creature. It proceeded to grab its own neck before drooping its head to one side and sticking its tongue out as if it had just died. The others made a sound that Ven took as laughter, for they were all genuinely silly creatures.

"He has little time left," Ven answered while pointing to the Scorn. Another gust of wind kicked up and four out of five of the tiny snow creatures vanished. The one remaining tugged at Ven's greave before he regarded the other four, futilely trying to drag Sindrum into the forest.

"You can help?" He questioned them suspiciously. The one tugging at his leg armour nodded enthusiastically. With a shrug and a sigh, Ven walked over to Sindrum and pulled him up over his shoulders. The tiny band of creatures wasted no time in running off into the sparse snow-blanketed woodlands.

Several hours of heavy snowfall had passed and Ven felt as though he would collapse with each step. He was an elf of slim weight, evolution designing him for dexterity and nimbleness. It was a remarkable feat he had managed to garner the strength required to carry this fully plated Scorn man as far as he had. Just as Ven hit the ground from losing his footing, he heard the unmistakable screech of a mountain lion in mid-pounce.

Ven scrambled forward in the snow, dropping Sindrum and turning with his newly acquired sword in hand. Too late. The Mountain Lion connected with him squarely and the two rolled several times before a fallen tree broke the grapple. Ven had several scratch marks across his face but noticed that so too did the huge feline. The hunter had never encountered a cougar of this size before, for the PumaSheep in the north were far smaller. Its muscles appeared as though they would pop right out of its skin, and its powerful jaw and teeth would have little problem in biting his hand clean off. Before either of the apex predators could make the next move, Ven's new tiny ice-covered allies began appearing all over the beast. Their little bodies working hard to punch and kick with all they could muster. Every time it looked like one might get bit or pawed they would simply dematerialize and appear somewhere else on the mountain lion. Before long, they were chasing the beast off into the bushes, like kids running after a house cat.

Ven sheathed his new sword with a smile on his lips. He recoiled at the stinging sensation of the gashes on his left cheek and jaw, yet somehow, it felt no more than a scratch. With his hand still subconsciously on his new sword hilt, it occurred to him that a magical property of this sword may be damage transference. A moment later his snowy friends appeared from little swirls of wind. The curious one, who earlier pretended to die, shot a single thumb upwards at Ven. The Kyst picked up his companion again and continued for another gruelling hour before reaching a curiously shaped set of trees. Ven watched the five little creatures run between an arch of two crossed branches hanging from those trees. The hunter went around the branches, thinking they wouldn't fit. But when he came around the other side to see no creatures, a sense of frustrated confusion consumed him. He remained freezing, exhausted, his face was soaked with cold blood, and he was now officially lost. After standing there for a few heartbeats utterly defeated, the same curious snow creature stuck its head out on the outside of the branches. Ven's eyes widened when he saw only the smiling creature's head, then the tiny arm waving him back. Ven walked back around the branch to see the creature walk between them once more and disappear with a lingering ripple in space.

"This will be the dumbest or smartest thing we've ever done," Ven grumbled aloud, thinking it was appropriate to include the Scorn. He got down on his belly and crawled through the branches with Sindrum on his back. Before he knew it he was dragging himself through thick luscious grass where the air warmed his lungs and the landscape tickled his skin. An eternal springtime glade filled with boastfully fragrant flowers, fruit, and blooming flower trees lined a small turquoise pond. Butterflies added fluttering bursts of colour to the sky while songbirds filled the air with heartwarming melodies. The cadence, however, was set by another the hunter knew, for far on the other side of the glade came a divine feminine voice; her song reverberating across the glade and inviting the birds to join in. Ven instantly recognized it as Old Elvish, a rather forgotten tongue throughout Litore.

'Drawn by Ammins known to fade.
Heroes appear in Evar Spring Glade.
First and last breath, weep not for it joins our precious life and death.
Drawn by fate seemed left to fade.
Heroes remain in Evar Spring Glade.
Eternal bloom has never known gloom.
For death does not promise doom.
Drawn through to fade in warriors spirit.
For Heroes rejoice in visit to Evar Spring Glade'

The poem soothed the very pain in Ven's body and the emotional anguish he had felt since that fiery night in Silva. He looked down almost euphorically at what he instinctively knew now to be Ammins, the snowy creatures that helped him here, who were now not snowy but covered in green grass. They were all running towards a small cabin on the opposite side of the pond. It too was covered in thick grass and blooming flora. As they approached, Ven finally caught sight of the Singer as she was picking berries and dropping them into a vine weaved basket. The Kyst took several steps closer to the Woman and was about to say something before she beat him to it.

"Fear not, Mighty Ven Devar. The ShadowScorn is safe now." Her voice was so soft but still resonate. Ven only saw the back of her as she continued to gather berries. Her hair was long and brown, held together by a neat crown of braids that fell past her shoulders. Her gown fluttered in the warm breeze, sown together from vines, leaves, and flowers so as to make her an extension of her surroundings. Ven found himself literally fighting to maintain his line of thought. To remember what he was actually doing before entering this soul-soothing place.

"He cannot die, they need him," Ven said while lowering Sindrum into the thick grass. The tall blades of green laid flat in a wide fan against his weight. The eerily calm and graceful Woman was seemingly kneeling beside them in the blink of an eye.

"He has already been tended to, young one," she said while caressing the Kyst's firm jawline with her delicate fingers. Ven slowly looked down from this otherworldly creature to notice that the wrappings around Sindrum's neck were gone, and so too were the vicious bite marks left by the Aquon. She then dragged her fingers across the cougar scratches on his face. He winced but felt nothing. "As have you." The Woman then bent down, planting a kiss on Sindrum's forehead, before standing up and walking into her cabin.

"Where are you going?" Ven ask longingly. For some reason he didn't want to be away from her presence.

"Wait here." Her voice sounded in his head but nowhere else. Ven was disrupted from his lustful gaze by Sindrum lifting his body and stretching his neck. Ven looked as though he was seeing a ghost rise from Sindrum's corpse.

"Where are we?" he asked with understandable confusion. Ven just sat there, chuckling in disbelief.

"The Evar Spring Glade, apparently."

"That's not funny," Sindrum replied, fully knowing that was impossible. However, his entire expression and attitude changed when he saw the Woman returning from her hut. "Quick, how did we get in?" Sindrum slid beside Ven and asked with fearful aggression. Ven was so caught off guard by this he found himself a little flustered and looked around trying to find the entrance.

"I... I don't know." He looked back to Sindrum. What was stranger to Ven, is that he didn't care about that fact. Sindrum rolled his eyes in anger and the two were confronted by the enchanting Woman who seemed to fill every moment she wasn't in conversation, singing that poem.

"Here," she said, offering a vile of clear liquid that clung to the glass like wine before dripping back down. Ven hesitantly took it, looking back to Sindrum hoping for reassurance, he only saw the Scorn profusely shaking his head.

"The chest wound you received will require more time to heal, but this will complete the recovery before you leave," she offered kindly and with reassurance to the Kyst. Ven hoped the decision to down the bottle was his own and not the power of the glade, but he drank the entire vile in one gulp. He quickly grabbed his sternum in writhing pain but it subsided as quickly as it began. It was followed by a hot sensation, then the Kyst felt nimble again, relaxed and without tension from the grievous wound.

"Great, show us the way out," Sindrum demanded with no sign of respect. The Care Taker looked at him with a welcoming smile.

"I did not say you could leave, you know this place?" She asked the Scorn, who groaned in acknowledgement. "Then you should know, you are dead. Ven Devar failed to gain you aid in time. Which means you'll be moving on, not back." She finished speaking with a tone akin to celebration and not fear.

"What?" Ven interjected incredulously. "What is this place?"

She looked at him with tranquility in her eyes, which appeared as orbs of swirling galaxies. "A nexus in the circle of life. The last destination before ascension or descension."

"An entire race depends on our success. They need him. I need him."

Sindrum was caught off-guard by Ven sticking his neck out for him to such an obvious power as this Woman.

"Do you?" She asked the Kyst before staring down Sindrum all-knowingly. "Sindrum Silver has relinquished his right to live. However, if Sindrum Silver thinks himself capable of telling Ven Devar the one thing that Ven Devar needs to know to be successful with Sindrum Silver at his side, the one thing that Sindrum did to end up here, then I will grant your leave from this place. One time."

"Why am I free to go?" Ven queried.

"Your time is not yet up," she responded, never taking her eyes off Sindrum.

The Scorn Captain regarded Ven with an unprecedented look of shame in his eyes. The inner level of self-disgust was visible on the man. He unbuckled his weapon belt and let it fall to the ground before he too fell to his knees in abject horror.

"I am the one, who stole Princess Scáth from her bed," Sindrum said the words with an unmistakable amount of regret. The words took several heartbeats to actually register with the coastal elf. Ven was overwhelmed by his blinding rage once more and threw his knee into Sindrum's nose. The Scorn went reeling back into the grass. Ven aggressively stepped over him. The hunter grabbed Sindrum by the throat with all the force he could muster, drew his short-sword from his lower back and held the diamond-edged blade to his jugular.

"Why?" Ven growled through gnashing teeth.

"No answer will justify the means, Ven. I'm sorry, I was wrong, I know that. Why do you think I agreed to this suicide quest?"

"No answer?" Ven asked with rage, "My whole world burned because of what you did. Thousands dead." The hunter pressed his sword deeper into the Scorn's neck. "I risked a millennium of life to save you." After seeing the true terror in Sindrum's eyes, Ven was struck with that guilt when considering how swift he had been to deal out death. He promised himself that after killing Rexous he would never kill unless it was the last resort. Ven sheathed his sword and shoved Sindrum to the ground before walking back to the Woman.

"Forgive me," Ven said apologetically with a bow.

"You have a mountain of sadness within. Sadness sows the seeds of anger and anger is the ancestor of despair, young Kyst."

Ven simply did not know what to say to that and focused on his next step, with or without Sindrum. "I need to get to the Crescent City atop Moon Mountain. Can you help me?"

The Woman stared deep into the Kyst's opalescent green eyes. She waved her hand over a section of the Glades border to reveal a frosty exit. Ven bowed again most graciously before heading towards the exit.

"Forget not your purpose, Mighty Ven Devar." The words rattled around in Ven's head. He was growing awfully tired of cryptic messages. After stunting his movement to quickly regard the Woman over his shoulder, he walked through the portal.

Sindrum who still lay prone in the grass watched Ven Devar leave then looked up to the Woman.

"You are free to roam once more. Few are gifted this second chance. Remember, all will renew the Glade, as the Glade renews all."

Sindrum found her calm tone disturbing for she was clearly referencing the circle of life and death. Yet, at the same time, she was reminding him to use his second chance more wisely. Sindrum stood, nodded, and made his exit with great haste.

He appeared on the other side and was met with freezing wind and thin air. His feet sunk to his knees in the fresh powdery snow. Several dozen metres ahead was Ven, effortlessly walking atop the snow towards the great curved gates. The Scorn buckled, planting his hands in the snow as an intense wave of nausea plagued him. It was night time and a heavy layer of cloud hung just above them, so many minutes later he found the strength to simply shadow-step ahead of the Kyst. Ven scoffed at the Scorn's appearance just ahead of him.

"We still have a quest to accomplish, can you find the maturity to finish what-"

"-Shut your mouth," Ven interrupted, stopping beside Sindrum and looking down on him as he still had his hands planted in the snow. "Any trust I had for you is gone. Speak not to me of maturity, traitor. We finish what we started and upon our return to ShadowScorn, those responsible for you will decide your fate." Ven remained unyielding in his fury as he stared down the Scorn.

"Good," was all he replied. The two strode the last short distance to the gates of the Crescent City, where they were halted by guards atop a low hanging parapet.

"Halt! State your business," one guard yelled, Ven could barely make out the image as they were enshrouded by the cloud cover.

"I am Ven Devar of the Great Nothern Rainforest, I travel with

Captain Sindrum Silver of Shadow Scorn."

"My people require your immediate assistance. I've been sent here by the Royal family to request council with Grand Master Zenair." Sindrum added, taking a large step forward. A long silence was accompanied by whipping winds. Their concerns were answered when the two gates depicting a glowing crescent moon split inwards, permitting passage inside the city.

The pair walked confidently inside the walls and were greeted by tropical smells and a single Snow Elf. Her eyes were icy grey, her skin starkly white with short, light blue hair. She was adorned not in heavy armour but rather colourful robes, much akin to something Ven knew that was worn by monks. She bowed gracefully before embracing Captain Sindrum who had removed his helm. The duration of their embrace caught Ven off-guard and even had to move up beside them and clear his throat to break it off.

"Thank you for the warm welcome," the Kyst said reverently as he pulled back his hood. He looked around to see vibrant streams flowing throughout the whole city with small stone bridges crossing them. Blossom trees filled the streets with petals instead of snow blanketing the ground. In fact, there was no snow whatsoever in this city atop Litore's highest mountain. Ven rubbed his eyes in confusion before letting it go, thinking his answer would arrive sooner or later.

"Ven Devar, this is Master Zaskee of the Frozen Fist." Sindrum introduced the Snow Elf and Kyst to which both bowed to each other.

"It is an honour to meet a cousin from the famed north. My soldiers have informed me this is a time precious endeavour."

"It is Master," Sindrum answered eagerly. Ven shot the Scorn a side-eye for the captain was almost acting bashful. The Kyst did privately admit Zaskee was stunning to behold. Her soft blue and white robes clung desirably to her muscled and toned form. He noted from the scar tissue on her knuckles that she had seen her fair share of battle.

"Then follow me," The Snow Elf Monk instructed. Ven followed a few paces behind as Sindrum and Zaskee chatted about something he didn't understand. He was told that the Shadow Scorn and Snow Elves had strong relations so it did not surprise him to hear this inside conversation. He followed quietly behind, absorbing the culture and architecture around him. Clearly, some impressive magic was set upon the city as it had impossibly warm weather and springtime flora growing with abundance. The structures were mostly made from wood, all intricately carved in their own unique style. Many of the entry ways were large and circular, appearing to have paper doors. The buildings were painted in bright earth tones and every corner of every roof came out in a curved pointed end; often protected by crescent tiles. Ven noted that each structure proudly displayed some sort of sculpted jade creature, pausing at one to admire its impossible detail of a great white dragon.

After rushing to catch back up, they walked through a small forest of bamboo and came out the other side to see a great palace. It was now that Ven understood why it was called the 'Crescent City', as a cliff ran the entire length of the city it was built around, giving it a distinct crescent shape. The palace itself was nearly six stories tall, each level growing smaller in width but unmistakably more ornate, with an entirely golden roof at the very top. A massive courtyard that stretched out in front of the palace had nearly 100 Frozen Fist Monks training relentlessly over a mosaic-tiled moon. Ven quickly noted that every third move sounded in a unified battle cry. Their standard-issue uniform included flexible white canvas wrappings around their feet and legs, secured together by criss-crossed leather strapping. A loose blue tabard hung down to their knees that was held tight by a single white sash of equal length. The attire was completely sleeveless showing off the lifetime of training and hard work that sculpted their bodies. A snowflake pattern was embroidered into their blue-grey gradient kimonos while a uniquely coloured undershirt was visible from the collar hugging tightly up to the base of their chins.

The grand staircase leading into the palace was guarded by two gigantic animated tiger statues that watched the trio's every step. A sense of wonder and terror struck the Kyst simultaneously for he had never seen such grandiosity before. Upon climbing over 200 wide set steps to enter the palace, Ven found once again, that he was the centre of attention as many of the Snow Elves had never met their distant Kyst elf cousins before. He nodded with respect to as many as he could, and all reciprocated in kind; with many placing their fist over their heart and bowing. Ven felt an unusual sense of equality and kinship as he proceeded. He wondered if all elves of Litore were not as competitive and solitary as his people.

The interior of the palace stole his breath away as much as the rest of the city did. After pushing through two silk curtains, they found themselves in the court of Grand Master Zenair. The King and Grand Master stood tall from his throne, which was little more than just a large pillow on an elegant dais. He was dressed similarly to the Frozen Fist, with loose hanging robes of blue and white. He wore a humble crown of jade and was adorned in several bamboo bracelets with precious gems in the shape of beads around his wrists, ankles, and neck. His skin was the colour of ice atop a lake and he had a head of thick white hair and a large but tidy beard to match. A wide smile crossed his lips as he saw the trio enter.

"Welcome, welcome. It is good to see you again Captain Sindrum Silver of the Scorn Guard," Zenair said while grabbing the captain's hand and kissing it gently. "Who is this refined specimen you travel by?" Zenair asked while directing his gaze upon Ven. The Kyst was so caught off-guard by the king's attitude he choked on his words, saying nothing.

"This is 'The Mighty Ven Devar' of the Great Northern Rainforest," Sindrum answered in Ven's stead.

"Amazing, it's been exactly 176 years since I had the pleasure of meeting one of our distant cousins from the north." Grand Master Zenair said as he too kissed Ven's hand.

"The honour is all mine, Your Grace," Ven finally managed to say. "Your kin and kind have been most welcoming since our recent arrival." The Kyst finished by returning a kiss on The King's hand.

Zenair turned to Sindrum and Zaskee with a coy look on his face. "I like him."

"You're not the only one, it would seem," Sindrum replied, which warranted a skeptical look from Ven.

"Please captain, regale me as to why you've made this most daring journey, unaccompanied by the usual goods and garrison?" Zenair said as he returned to his throne.

"You know the hearty people of Shadow Scorn were once your own and have endured much over the centuries. Most often at the hands of the Sesara zealots. We now find ourselves under a siege, the likes of which we have little hope in thwarting. To make things worse, we find ourselves in a civil dispute, as our renowned King Arwr passed the day prior to our departure." It was at that point that Sindrum did something most uncharacteristic, and got to his hands and knees in a plea. "Oh great Grand Master Zenair, never have my people sought help such as this. I beg, for the very survival of Shadow Scorn, that you return with us to put an end to this unjust siege."

Ven noted the look of shock on Master Zaskee's face quickly transform into sheer rage. He then turned his attention back to the famously proactive king, who was surprisingly staring at Ven.

"And what of you?" Grand Master Zenair asked. Ven's heart skipped a beat at the king's blatant dismissal of Sindrum.

"What he said," Ven hesitated in response, trying to turn the attention back on the vulnerable Scorn.

Zenair chuckled at Ven's awkwardness. "Why are you here beside the Scorn, clearly this is not your fight."

Ven dropped his head, completely unsure of what to say or do. "My story is one that we do not have time for your highness. However, I am bound to Princess Scáth by honour and promise," Ven answered hoping that would be enough to stay the topic, much to his disappointment it was not.

"Quite a promise to travel all this way, no?" The king queried once more.

"You have no idea," the Kyst chuckled lightly in reply. Zenair moved his glare back upon Sindrum who remained face down on hands and knees.

"Rise, captain. Long have the Snow Elves and Shadow Scorn peoples called each other allies. The fabled Frozen Fist will depart on the morning one day hence. Zaskee, ready the troops and I will see to our guest's immediate comforts."

The general bowed in agreement and sprung out of the court to prepare for war.

Ch11- War

4,099 Scorn Guard remained. Between the scouts, their first night raid, and the catapults that had originally softened the city, 17 ShadowScorn warriors had perished in what would soon be known as the 'Siege of Shadow.' After successfully repelling Renrit's first frontal assault, Aelis stood atop the great wall of ShadowScorn to see their new advance, once more with siege weapons in tow. She cursed the Renrit zealots for they were clearly forcing her hand. It was clear that they did not want to decimate the City of Shadow for that would leave them without a trophy. What they did want was open scale warfare where their numbers would simply prove stronger. Aelis knew the city would not survive many more bombardments and so she was left once again to devise a way out of this predicament. She sent one of her underlings to sound the palace bell that would send everyone into shelter. She knew too, that after thwarting their attack two days prior, the soldiers would not approach the wall to be met with more burning oil. Not that she had enough oil left for such a manoeuvre again. The labour and precise alchemical process required to create such oil would take far too long to rely on heavily.

"Archers! Braziers!" Aelis commanded down the wall. Her orders were relayed three more times by separate Scorn Guard. Within five minutes, nearly a thousand archers and half that amount of braziers, filled with the last of their oil, were positioned atop the wall. It was mid-day now and a rolling cloud cover had stormed in, occasionally bursting with detail as forked lightning scattered within, followed by earth trembling thunder. A mighty wind kicked up and the Scorn knew by the direction of their banners blowing madly that it was in their favour. The children of Aceia looked down over the land they called home, at the 12,000 trespassers with a healthy shock of concern. There were nearly a dozen great catapults lining their ranks, so the commander picked her targets. As for the 12,000 soldiers, Aelis knew most were not born and bred to be warriors like the Scorn Guard. Perhaps half that number of renrit soldiers were actually trained and held rank. The other half would be conscripted or most likely volunteer farmers, smithies, and labourers of the sort. Aelis knew in her heart if they could turn the tide of war in their favour, that many of said soldiers would turn tail and run back for the warmth of their homes.

"What are their war machines made of?" Aelis yelled to the 1,000 Longbow Archers standing on either side of her.

"WOOD!" They boomed back.

"What do we have?" She yelled in reply, goading her guards on.

"FIRE!" Their collective voices rang louder than the almost continuous thunder now.

"I want 100 Archers per catapult!" Aelis then drew her famed long sword 'Silent Death' from the scabbard on her back and held it over their enemies. Her soldiers understood and all dipped their arrowheads into the burning oil.

"Burn," she whispered to herself as she dropped the sword back down to her side, and a thousand flaming arrows shot forth from the city wall to blanket the Renrit siege weapons. Their fearless leader repeated this gesture a handful of times and less than a minute later, 10,000 oil-soaked arrows had rained down upon their attackers. The Commander of ShadowScorn watched as every last one of the war machines caught fire and collapsed. She couldn't be sure but estimated nearly a thousand of those arrows were blown asunder but not wasted, as the Renrit troops stood so thickly it was nearly impossible not to hit someone.

"She's brilliant," Agan Dusk unknowingly voiced. Scáth looked at him with a whimsical smirk he did not perceive. They were accompanied by Athvar and Faenla who were also unable to look away from the astonishing and terrifying display of war from Scáth's balcony. They could hear the unmistakable whistling of arrows accompanied by roars of thunder. The fire-lit arrows shining light upon the dark and rolling sky, only to be momentarily silhouetted against a flash of lightning.

The princess had never admired her dearest and oldest friend Aelis as much as she did right now. In the 60 years of life they had shared together, Aelis had fought, served, and now commanded in almost two dozen wars. Her determination and success was driven by the necessity of survival. Their enemies were only ever driven by greed, delusion, or zealotry.

"They must retreat," Athvar said with no tone of satisfaction or fascination at the scene before him. When the sound of a bellowing lur echoed out from the Renrit army, Agan pulled away from the balcony rail to leave.

"They are just getting started," the half-orc stated in a dire attitude before quietly exiting. Faenla similarly left to follow the fighter to the battlefield. The Scorn and gnome remained, frozen in terror by what they clearly saw crest the hill from the Renrit encampment. With every great step, the sound of a clinking chain could be heard as two anklets connected to a collar were attached to a 15-metre tall Mountain Giant. It was surrounded by nearly 80 spear-men and a wizard occasionally prodding it forward with arcane zaps.

"How?" Scáth spoke aloud but sought no answer and received none.

"Never in all my travels have I seen such a sight," Athvar said in disbelief. They strained the length of their vision to see the Giant dragging a boulder behind him. It was larger than any building in ShadowScorn, aside from the palace. Scáth instinctively reached out to place a comforting hand on Faenla's strong shoulder but found only air. At the same time, she sensed an unnerving presence enter her room.

"Athvar, someone has joined us," she whispered while slowly drawing her scimitar from under the folds in her robes; the same one given to her by Ven. The ever-wise and skilled gnome pulled a poison-tipped dagger from under his shirt and turned inwards to face the room. The group hadn't lit anything as they came up here to view the battle, and even though he could see pretty well in the darkness, for gnomes were a burrowing people, Athvar couldn't spot anyone. Suddenly, Scáth and a familiar Scorn Ruffian's face were momentarily illuminated by the sparks from their blades parrying.

"Help," Scáth said confidently, now fending off two Scorn attackers,

"Anytime, now."

Not understanding why he could only see Scáth without light, Athvar grunted in frustration before springing towards the fully prepped hearth. He heard the whoosh of steel overhead and leaped into a roll, dragging his dagger across the hearth, showering the fireplace in sparks. The whole chamber illuminated in a soft yellow to reveal five that Scorn ruffians had entered. The gnome gulped audibly before deftly avoiding another attack.

Aelis stood atop the wall and for the first time in her life as a commander, didn't know what to do.

"LOOSE!" She screamed at her archers and they readily complied, all aware of their target. The Mountain Giant saw the wall of arrows and effortlessly hoisted the colossal chunk of land up in front of him. Every arrow that would have struck the giant rebounded off or shattered against the boulder. As he neared the army they all broke formation to make way.

Aelis unknowingly took a step back in horror. She steeled herself and moved forward to the edge once more, to survey her options. Now, the entire Renrit Army was hollering in victory as they watched the impossibly huge giant gain ground. It stopped 40-metres away from the city gates, all the while deflecting arrows and missiles and not reacting to any of those that did find their mark.

Agan and Faenla were still unaware of the threat that lurked just outside the wall when they began climbing the stairs to Aelis. They both threw themselves to the ground as the main gates were blown asunder and a boulder skipped across the street, crushing nearly three squads of Scorn Guard and destroying the entire warehouse district. The pair changed their course towards the main gate and as Agan popped his head around the corner to see what had created such devastation, he quickly pulled back and looked at Faenla with hesitation.

"Mountain Giant," he said in possibly the squeakiest voice he had ever used. Faenla shot his ears up in surprise at the remark. The massive wolf also had a look around at what used to be the iradinium gate, saw the giant running towards them, and took several steps back before letting out a nasally whine. Agan ran towards the regiments that had suffered greatly from the rolling boulder and helped reorganize a strong defensive position.

"Pole-arm's out front!" Agan demanded and the Scorn Guard were happy to follow his lead. The Scorn, however, did not require much instruction as they formed three lines of semi-circles around the entrance.

Faenla darted up a staircase that brought him just above the entrance and waited to pounce. The giant emerged into the city with dozens of arrows protruding from its back, as angry and ready for a fight as ever.

"Now!" Agan yelled and the line of spear-men and women stuck the ankles of the giant repeatedly. It kicked out hard and sent a large chunk of the line scattering into the city. Faenla leaped from the overhang directly onto the Mountain Giant's neck, biting down hard and relentlessly raking with his mighty claws. The wolf could barely get its jaw around a small portion of the neck but it was enough to cause the giant to start panicking.

"Again!" shouted the half-orc and the next line of Scorn Guard stuck the giant as many times as they could. It didn't take long before the giant gripped Faenla by the rump and threw him into the attacking Scorn line. It let out a battle cry and the exhalation felt like the wind from a hurricane. Agan, never one to cower in fear, seized the chance to hurl his double-bearded axe, lodging itself deep into the Giant's jaw. It bellowed in agony, before reaching out and scooping a literal handful of Scorn Guard and popping them like berries in his hand. Several screams of terror continued to ring as they watched their comrades die a most gruesome death. This only spurred on the Scorn Guard and soon, a small female unit known throughout the city as the 'Ghosts of Aceia' came forth and began shadow-stepping all over the giant. Not every Scorn had the ability to shadow-step and only this group of women had this level of dexterity and precision. Clad in fine leather armour and cowls that rested below their eyes, they dealt devastating, coordinated attacks on the giant. One was grasped after just emerging from her shadow-step and was thrown aside. She would have splattered against a wall if not for two other ghosts shadow-stepping into pirouettes to catch their friend mid-flight, breaking her momentum. Just then, Agan heard the familiar howl of Faenla, running towards him. The veteran fighter crouched and grabbed a Scorn shield from the ground. Faenla leaped, landed atop the shield, and the mystically strong half-orc sprung upwards, sending the great wolf soaring to bite hard under the Giant's jugular.

Scáth ducked as one blade swung left to right over her head. She spun on her heel to avoid a long sword jabbing at her midriff. She held her scimitar out firmly as she spun, slicing the knees of one ruffian. She came out of the spin and kicked him in the back, which sent the ruffian tumbling into the other. Athvar had slid between the legs of one attacker, dragging his poison blade down one thigh. The Scorn man hit the ground fast asleep before the gnome even came to a stop. Athvar just managed to parry one slice of a short sword but not before he saw Scáth take a devastating slash across her back. Scáth yelped in pain and lurched forward, leaving an open strike to end her life. Athvar threw his dagger into the spine of the Scorn about to murder the one he vowed to protect. The ruffian fell down hard, not asleep but dead. Now defenceless, the other Scorn kicked Athvar directly into the fireplace and a crack was heard as his head connected against stone. The gnome didn't scream in pain as the fire nipped at his flesh, but the flames had barely taken hold and the majority of them were put out as he crashed into the logs.

Seeing this, Scáth quickly rushed to intercept the one who had just punted her friend. She feared the worst as Athvar wasn't moving to get out of the fire. The ruffian turned and quickly slashed at her, however, Scáth used a technique taught to her by Agan where she parried, increasing and changing her attacker's momentum to stab at an adjacent enemy. She did so with great success as the sword slashed right across the neck of the secondary attacker. After striking his own ally down, the ruffian growled in anger and punched Scáth squarely in the face. She recoiled back into the waiting arms of the other Scorn, formally sent off balance but now recovered.

"Athvar!" She screamed for her companion to get up and out of the still smouldering hearth. The gnome had barely come to consciousness from connecting the crown of his head against the charred stone, but when he did awake he panicked and scrambled out. The gnome fell on his arse and was unwittingly picked up by his throat, grappled by the ruffian who had just struck Scáth. Athvar went from clutching his burnt eyes to attempting to break the pressure on his throat. The ruffian held out Athvar to the restrained princess and gave her a purely evil glare. In the blink of an eye, the resounding crack of Athvar's neck rang out. He let out a last wheeze of air and then hung limply, for Athvar the Undusted was no more.

Aelis had completely lost her footing at the impact of the boulder smashing through her gates and she tumbled over the parapet. She threw out her arm as she went over, but not before one of her trusted captains shadow-stepped herself to Aelis, belly down, grabbing the commander's wrist. From there the captain known as Theena Whisp hoisted Aelis back up. Aelis looked over the edge to see her warriors, led by Agan Dusk, attacking the giant now inside.

"What now commander?" Theena asked in a surprisingly calm voice. Aelis turned back over the battlefield to see one Renrit legion marching on the city.

"Keep up the volleys. Grab 50 Archers to watch the entrance and fire on my signal." Aelis nodded with trust to Theena before sprinting down to the battlefield.

Faenla's nearly 220-kilograms seemed inconsequential to the Mountain Giant, however, his fangs ripping the stone-like skin to shreds wasn't. In the time it took the Giant to pull Faenla off its throat, which tore a huge chunk of flesh away in the process, two Scorn Ghosts had dexterously climbed atop the giant's head and plunged their long knives into both his eyes. Faenla was dropped onto the ground and immediately went to biting at his ankles while the ghosts and pole-arms continued to stick the giant without mercy. Soon, it fell back with a great thud, fortuitously filling a large portion of the blown-out portcullis.

Aelis shadow-stepped from the top to midway down the wall, drew her long sword and waved it in the direction of the temple. It notified Torvic to deploy his priests and the remaining Scorn Guard to the wall. The Arch Priest did as instructed and so went 90 Priests of Aceia and another 200 Scorn Guard. Torvic Gloom was right behind them when he suddenly paused, slightly tilting his head towards the upper palace.

Scáth let out a scream filled with anguish, without understanding how, the ruffian holding onto Scáth's biceps lost his hold on her. The princess wasted no time in jumping on him, driving the Scorn onto his back. She used her weight and momentum to drive her thumbs deep into his eye sockets. From there, she grabbed his dagger and lunged at the one who had just killed her friend. The fear in his dead-grey eyes was palpable as she came at him with a manic routine of slices and thrusts. He countered one swing with his sword and then grabbed her weapon arm. He swung across her throat and the courageous Scáth had no defence, it was over, she knew it. But then, her entire neck simply ceased to be., It had turned into the shadow that surrounded the princess. As the blade passed through without doing harm, her skin and flesh reformed and a look of sheer rage consumed the princess. She stuck her dagger deep into his clavicle and watched the life drain from his face. She instinctively ducked as she heard the sound of steel cutting air. The sword from the last Scorn ruffian soared overhead and she sliced open his belly, then kicked his feet out from under him and put her dagger to his throat.

"Tell me who sent you and I stay your death."

The ruffian, however, wasn't given the chance to speak when the voice that Scáth knew was responsible for all this, was heard.

"You already tortured Snik into giving me up, why go through the trouble of asking him?" Oren asked in a tone far too playful. Scáth connected the jewelled pommel of the dagger into the ruffian's temple before standing up to regard the Administrator, who had just entered the room. "Now that I think of it, more importantly, why haven't you already had the Scorn Guard arrest me?" Oren asked with a true sense of wonderment.

"Because everyone knows that the spine of Oren the Administrator is too frail to be behind all of this," the princess shot back with malice. "I know it is Katia who killed my Pa and had me stolen."

"That hurts a little, princess. Oh well, I'm sure I will get over it." As Oren spoke, five more Scorn ruffians entered her chamber. Scáth stood up straight and gripped her dagger, refusing to give up without a fight. Oren took several steps toward the princess, holding a small knife in his hand.

"I hope my twisted and unforgiving mother shows you the same fate as my pa when she grows tired of you," Scáth said solemnly but with strong conviction.

"You always were a mouthy brat." He was now almost face to face with Scáth. "A shame to kill such a beautiful thing though," He said, reaching out to caress her face, but was interrupted by the sound of five Scorn choking and gasping for air behind him. His eyes widened and he turned to see them all on their knees clawing at their own throats for air, and Torvic Gloom standing in the doorway.

Scáth kicked him in the back of the knee and drove her elbow into the crown of his head. Oren fell limply to the cobblestone and so did the newly arrived ruffians.

"Princess?" Torvic said weakly as he watched her rush over to a small figure with his neck bone protruding out from his skin. Scáth quickly rolled Athvar into her lap. With the gnome utterly lifeless, she began slightly rocking back and forth and singing the old-gnomish hymn he had sung many times over, throughout their journey together. Tears streaked down her cheeks but her voice did not waver. Torvic came and knelt beside the Princess of Shadow and placed a comforting hand on her shoulder. He understood that his divine power would be useless here, so instead, he offered the only thing he could, the comfort of a friend.

Aelis was now standing in front of her thousands of Scorn Guard at the main gate. They watched through the small gap left in the portcullis as the arrows above reigned down on the now sprinting Renrit soldiers. The Scorn steeled their nerves as the Renrits made ground even through the thick hail arrow. A great lightning bolt lit up the clouds and a heavy rain began its descent. The sound of thick drops hitting the decadent Scorn armour sounded like music to the warriors; a cadence and rhythm to fall into. The commander looked to Captain Theena with her 50 Archers all aimed at the entrance.

"Hold!" She commanded her now agitated warriors as the Renrit soldiers began funnelling towards them. As soon as the first score emerged into the city, Aelis dropped 'Silent Death' to her side and the archers above dropped every single soldier until the cobblestone ran thick with their blood. Eventually, the archers had to break off and turn their attention to the larger battlefield once more. Aelis smiled as the Renrit soldiers kept the frontal assault coming through the only entrance.

Agan watched from behind her and was stunned once more at her efficiency in battle. Thousands of Renrit were now dead, and aside from the giant, they had barely wet their blades. As another thick wave of soldiers was about to enter the wall, she held her long sword up once more.

"Ready!" She yelled, and in unison, every Scorn Guard grunted as they slid into battle stances. Agan spun the blackglass handle of his axe and Faenla gave a great howl.

"Darkness!" Aelis commanded and several priests cast a spell of utter darkness to engulf the portcullis. Utter darkness that of course the Scorn had no problem seeing through.

"Spears!" Aelis shouted and a volley of spears flew into the gloom, each and everyone finding its mark. After a moment of silence, and no more soldiers emerging through the black-out, Aelis spotted a large humanoid standing just outside the wall. She couldn't tell what it was doing or how it had been standing there for so long without being hit. Suddenly, a great pillar of flame burst forth, filling the entire cullis and burning away the darkness spell. The whole area filled with smoke and through that smoke charged a red Dragon-Blood Paladin with a well-armed and armoured troop behind him. With blinding speed and accuracy he slammed the chest plate of Aelis with his war maul, sending her soaring into several Ghosts of Aceia. It was all-out warfare as the two armies clashed at the main gate. The Dragon-Blood was bashing through entire lines of Scorn Guard with an ease akin to a smithy working an anvil. Several ghosts attempted to cut the Paladin down using their unparalleled coordination and speed, but every strike met with his impressive armour. It took the paladin little time to understand their routines and he eventually cracked the skull of two ghosts as they exited a shadow-step. Faenla jumped and bit the arm clean off of a soldier about to plummet their weapon into a staggering Aelis. The battlefield was clearly marked by Agan Dusk and the red Dragon-Blood, their equal heights standing several heads above the rest. As the paladin was about to drop his maul onto another ghost, Agan tackled him from the side and the two went into a barrel roll. They both came up, staring each other down.

"Traitor," the paladin growled, with smoke pouring from his draconic nostrils. Agan's face screwed up in confusion. This was the Dragon-Blood he was met with during the night raid. At that time there was a flicker of recognition in the half-orc but he hadn't been able to figure out where or how he knew the paladin. He lunged at his foe, chopping down with his axe. The paladin held his maul across his chest to catch the axe, bringing them close together as they struggled to break the lock. They both slid their weapons to the side and their pommels struck each other in the head. Agan was dazed by the mutual strike and heard the world around him go quiet as a loud ringing consumed him. In the blink of an eye, he was flooded with images of the previous 10-years. Being captured near the end of the 'War of a Thousand Dragons' by Sesaran soldiers helping the Dwarves of Silver Rock. Being held in a dungeon for years of mental torment and conditioning. Killing, assassinating, all for the church of Sesara. The name Macer O'Donnell sounded in his head, like the echoing cry of a memory brought to life. Then, being sent out to recover a ShadowScorn girl outside of Renrit.

"Scáth," the half-orc said with genuine horror. The name brought him back to the present as he knew he needed to find Scáth and protect her from the battle he understood to be lost as they were quickly being overwhelmed. He was brought up from his knees by Aelis.

"Agan!" She shouted right in his face, yet it sounded distant to the fighter. He turned to regard the Dragon-Blood Paladin that he remembered now to be Ragow, someone he had travelled from Serenstrom to Renrit with. Agan was in disbelief and thought perhaps he was seeing things as the wolf had done what he could not. Faenla had the paladin down on the ground as he was viciously whipping his powerful head back and forth while clamped on Ragow's throat. The Dragon-Blood went limp and Faenla rushed off in aid of other Scorn Guard. The half-orc heard Aelis clearly now but disregarded what she had been saying.

"We need to pull back,"

"What do you think I've been saying!" She yelled over the tumult of the battlefield and motioned to one of her Ghosts to sound the bell that would alarm the citizens to fall back to the Royal Palace. The Ghost of Aceia sprinted shortly before becoming one with the shadow, and not a moment later a secondary bell of a significantly different pitch was heard throughout the city.

"Dump the Braziers!" Aelis commanded Captain Theena who began to kick over the burning braziers of oil over the entrance to the city, thus blocking further entry for what she hoped would be enough time to finish their retreat back to the palace. The fight had begun to overflow into several of the streets in the city but the Scorn made quick work of those trapped inside with them.

Ch12 - Sesara

Ivan the Revered stood at the bow of The Horizons Edge as Port Ozos came into view; an unsightly seaside town at best, filled with rogues and renegades seeking ships to lay low on, or to make a quick escape on, across the Boundless Ocean. Much of the black-market trading happened here as opposed to Port Noga, the largest port on the east that also connected Litore to Serenstrom.

"Look Ifan, even some of the crew are concerned about yer chosen path. Everything about ye suggests yar a capable man. However, one does not wander into the Spire Lakes without wishing to dance with death." Captain Tsuni tried to cover up her growing soft spot for Ivan as opposition to his ideas.

"Even some of the crew?" Ivan said with an amused brow. Tsuni looked away, feigning frustration.

"Normally we don't give a care about our passengers but yee've been kind and given us all fair advice. We just don't want to see ye fall victim to the mindless gangsters who rule the Spires."

"I've done a lot of bad and stood by to a lot worse. Any fate I'm met with is well deserved. But, it does my worn-out heart good to see you all offering your care, even just to another passenger." Ivan finished with a sly grin and wink.

Tsuni blew a heavy sigh. "How long do ye think you'll be exactly? Perhaps the crew and I could do some local work and see yar safely returned to Serenstrom."

"A cycle. Two tops ," Ivan answered hopefully. Tsuni nodded, accepting that as a reasonable time to wait for what she could consider a friend.

"Stop off at the 'Snorting Stead' and tell em Captain Tsuni sent ya. It won't be free but they'll make sure to give ye the finest horse they got." Ivan nodded graciously and Captain Tsuni went to shouting orders at the crew to begin bringing them into port.

Before mid-day, the Horizons Edge was moored and Ivan Fjell was making his way briskly but confidently through the seaside town of Ozos. In the first fifteen minutes of walking through the sewage-stained, rocky streets, he had seen one bar brawl overflowing out the front door, three people getting mugged; the first and last carried out by the same robber, and one gnome being chased by three brigands wielding crude blunt weapons, and several pick-pockets. None of which slowed Ivan's pace by any measure. He was familiar with many of the backwater, lawless towns of Litore and knew even more how to remain inconspicuous. He saw the large wooden stable with 'Snorting Stead' painted brazenly on the front.

Suddenly, the sound of a woman and several crying children from down an unusually lit alley caught his attention. Ivan's heavy plate boots came to a grinding halt as he peered down the slim space between weakly constructed buildings. He cursed himself for even pausing to consider going down there, before eventually walking closer to the faint cries. The older-middle aged paladin saw a small crowd of people coming and going, and a single human standing on a box, rattling off numbers. They had all congregated around three small, rusty rod-iron cages. Inside was an ivory dragon-blood child, no more than eight years of age. The next contained a ShadowScorn girl, perhaps in her mid-teens. The third cage contained what Ivan could only guess was a river nymph, for he had only read of them in texts.

The paladin was pulled from his disgust by the man and obvious captor of these free-folk. He was short and fat with enough warts growing on his greasy face, to make any sentient creature recoil. He was adorned in very expensive foreign jewellery and by now, Ivan had spotted the four brutish guards scattered throughout the alley protecting him and the assets.

"You look like a man who could make use of some exotic goods." Ivan turned to the slaver with a fiery look. "How much?"

The slaver flashed his yellow rotted teeth with a sickening grin. "15,000 gold pieces for the Dragon-boy or river freak. 30,000 for the Scorn girl."

Ivan reached into a sack behind his large cloak and pulled forth a ruby-encrusted crown made entirely of gold. He also grabbed several precious gems and a sizable sack of coin.

"Deliver their cages to the 'Horizons Edge.' If any one of them is harmed or doesn't make it, you won't be so pleased to see me again," Ivan said threateningly before tossing the repulsive man the sizable hoard. He then looked to the Scorn girl. She wore tattered and soiled rags, no doubt the same clothes she was abducted in on the far side of the world. Ivan tossed a small leather pouch into the cage and cast a spell of telepathy.

"I'm a friend of King Arwr. Give that pouch to Captain Tsuni and she will take good care of you three until I return. Then we can find you all a way home." Ivan's voice rang clear in the girl's mind and her eyes widened at the calming remark of her king, and finding a friend so far away from home. He gave her a reassuring smile before leaving the alley.

It was early evening by the time Ivan was galloping out of Port Ozos on a truly remarkable stallion. He made the first leg of the journey in stunning time and would reach the base of the Spire Lakes far sooner than expected. From there, he knew he would have to navigate through the multi-kilometre tall mountains that shot forth from the ground like great spikes. Seldom were they ever more than a kilometre or two in width, and they were often dressed in trees and flora that seemed to defy gravity by clinging to the sides of the great spires. Vines that could stretch hundreds of metres, hung swaying in the wind or connecting one spire to another. He had a general sense of where his destination was, atop one of the thousands of the towering rocks near the western lakes. He would have to find safe passage around the treacherous paths below, all the while avoiding patrols of telekinetic gangsters known as the 'Fires of Fel.' A ruthless group that Ivan had dealings with in the past. They had built mighty bridges that spanned the lakes using their innate mental powers, subsequently holding hefty tolls for all those crossing, lest you wish your destiny to be found at the bottom of one of those lakes.

It was dusk now and Ivan pulled off the great road to join one of the many large caravans that had stopped for the evening. They were common along all the Great Roads in Litore; escorting goods, traveller's and pretty much anything needing transport. There were a dozen large, canvas covered wagons in a circular formation with a roaring bonfire in the middle. Ivan guessed about 60 people sat in the centre feasting, drinking, and sharing stories. He was halted by the perimeter of hired guards that encircled the camp, often paid impressive coin to protect the caravans from one destination to another.

"Fine evening, friend," Ivan said jovially while approaching one guard. A young human man dressed in rugged scale mail and a sword so old and well-used, it appeared multi-generational.

"Indeed. Looking to find shelter for the night?" The young man asked. Ivan nodded in response.

"You'll find the Road Master in the green tent." The young man pointed to a tent that was guarded by two others. Ivan instantly recognized the tent and carriage-wheel emblem, and made a well-educated guess as to who this Road Master was. Without another word, the revered paladin turned, mounted his horse and trotted down the road for another half-hour. Ivan had an extensive history on the Great Roads of Litore and was known by many Road Masters, some favourably and many not so much. In his younger days, Ivan had followed the fanaticism of his Macers with blinding loyalty. In fact, it wasn't until his defeat at the hands of Scorn King Arwr, that he began to see Sesara's teachings for how they were originally intended. Old age and worldly experience brought much to light, not least of which was the tyrannical rule the faith of his church was forcing upon Litore.

When the sun finally dipped below the horizon and the moons of Litore stole the night, he ventured behind a tall mass of bushes and made an impromptu camp. He kept his horse close and weapon closer. No fire was lit as the varied horrors that lingered in the night were always attracted to sources of light, knowing a good meal of flesh could be found close by. Ivan fell asleep soon after settling down. He was jolted awake by a singular scream echoing through the night. Then its all too abrupt end. He thought it came from the direction of the caravan that he had stopped at previously, but surely it could not be them. Ivan closed his eyes again determined to stay put, reassuring himself it was too late to be of any use. Moreover, it was likely those in trouble were bandits roaming the edges of the road looking for innocents to prey on. For the monsters that lingered, humanoid and not, used the cover of night to do their dark work.

The next time Ivan opened his eyes was to the first rays of sunshine spilling over the trees. The sounds of songbirds filled the air and he could tell that spring was beginning anew. With a rejuvenated sense of life and hope, Ivan climbed onto the saddle of his horse and continued his journey. It was ten minutes into riding that a familiar sense of discomfort shivered through his body; a particular sense that one could only gain from a life time of combat. Around the very next bend in the road, he saw the first severed limb. A forearm, and a small one at that. As he followed the trail of blood he found another arm belonging to someone else, a leg, and a limbless torso. In the middle of the dirt road were two partially devoured horses and an upturned cart. Ivan dismounted, pulling his shield off the saddle and drawing his great sword. Inspecting the remains, he discerned his worst fear, a human family of four.

He cursed himself for not following the scream when he had heard it. He understood there was likely little he could have done but he had broken a promise to himself, never ignore someone in need of help. A basic tenet of his faith and he knowingly disregarded it. Ivan spent most of that morning atoning the best he could, and gave them a proper burial. Several travellers and caravans passed by as the paladin cleared the road and dug the holes. Not a single person stopped to offer help or inquire about what had happened.

With his fine stead and the snow melt already on the way, the paladin made it to the Spire Lakes in far quicker time than anticipated. The terrain around the Spires was mostly jagged, uneven shale. Huge boulders and broken chunks of land lay awkwardly, the result of spires collapsing in prior years. Surely, many had fallen and crumbled during the Quake of Harazune, drastically altering the look of the land. Ivan spent the rest of that day walking his horse as far as he could before finding a safe shelter under a trio of large boulders that formed a sort of cave. He then collected enough food and water for his horse to stay tied up for a few days. He scouted several entry points to begin the climb up the area he figured would give him the best view of the western spires. Deciding on a location, he returned to his camp and found a deep rest.

He woke before the suns rise and found himself at the base of his chosen spire, as daylight began to fill the sky. He pulled a vial of dark purple liquid out from his satchel and gulped it down hungrily. He took a deep breath as the magic coursed through his old bones and weary muscles. It was a potion of strength that would grant him inhuman power for a half-day. Ivan reached up to grab the sandy-white stone and began his climb. After an hour of climbing a sheer rock face, he found some reprieve on a ledge with several small trees sprouting out the side. Looking down, he knew to be at least a hundred meters up and felt a sense of youth and adventure fill his soul. Looking up, he saw rushing clouds and vines that ascended a great distance before disappearing into the fluffy whiteness. He shrugged and reached out for a thick vine hanging beside him. After giving it a few good tugs he began a much speedier climb up. After nearly two hours of hoisting himself up he was in such thick cloud cover that he could not see the rock face in front of him. Pausing momentarily to catch his breath, his whole body and the vine dropped twenty centimetres before bouncing slightly under the tension. A look of sheer terror came across his face. He still could not see through the clouds but knew whatever this vine was attached too was starting to give way. He began to furiously climb, every so often his heart skipping a beat as the vine gave way a little more. In the blink of an eye, he emerged through the top layer of clouds to see an old, rotted tree, bent far over the rock face, barely supporting his weight.

Ivan watched as the few stubborn remaining roots of the tree started to tear away from the spire. Out of options, he swung his weight over to the rock face, swiping at it with his toes before the momentum pulled him back down. Not close enough, he knew. He swung again, building momentum but freeing the tree more with each swing. On the last one, the tree gave way and Ivan slammed hard into the rock, just barely getting a firm hand-hold. He hugged the stone tightly as the tree fell behind him, giving a great whoosh as it went by, plummeting to the ground. After steeling his nerves, he looked up and thought he could see the summit of this spire.

With the end in sight, he continued to hoist himself up until he eventually dragged himself over and onto a plateau of thick grass and strong ash tree leaves that danced in the wind. He lifted himself upright and took in the jaw-dropping view before him. Hundreds of colossal spires like he had just climbed scattered the landscape with glistening lakes between each and every one. After taking some time to survey his surroundings, he spotted his destination, a small wooden shack camouflaged by the lush flora. Best of all, it was only two spires over. Ivan called upon his faith to fill him with a sense of weightlessness. He took a long-running start and leaped off the edge of his spire in the direction of the shack. He landed a dozen or so metres below the summit of the next spire and had to climb up again. Then, casting the spell once more, he leaped out, feeling as free as a bird.

He landed firmly on the summit and brushed himself off before confidently heading towards the shack. Dropping his tattered travelling cloak and sword to the ground, he halted in his tracks as the front door slowly creaked open. Ivan immediately dropped to one knee and lowered his head in reverence.

An impossibly tall and thin alien walked out of the shack. Their skin was a starlight blue and its eyes long and wide. The pupils were that of swirling galaxies, and the nose was seamless against its oval face. It stood proudly and was adorned in otherworldly gear, with strong rugged shaped armour made from composites, not of Litore.

"Ivan the Revered. It is an honour to meet you." It spoke in the common tongue of Litore and with a slight reverb to its words. Ivan looked up, before quickly looking back down.

"The honour is mine, oh powerful Adjudicator. I bring word of a human who

fouls your edicts," Ivan continued, never raising his gaze. "The Leader of the Sesaran faith. Charles O'Donnell. I fear why Sesara has not struck him down herself for his sacrilegious ways, so I sought out the wisest council in our world."

"She is dead," the alien answered flatly.

The words left Ivan in confusion. "Who is dead?"

"Sesara, the goddess of life and sustenance, exists no more."

Ivan stood in defiance at the claim. That would be impossible, he cast several spells that day alone, granted to him by the divine power of Sesara.

"You lie," Ivan retorted incredulously.

"Why would I? You were there the day Aceia killed her and turned your armies away. You have spent half a lifetime denying the truth you've always known. So you believe in a religion that has no deity. Yet, the prayers of your followers fuel your magics, even though she is not there to receive it. She is gone, Ivan Fjell." The alien spoke completely devoid of any emotional attachment to the situation. Ivan's entire spiritual world began to crumble around him. Of course this all-knowing creature whose sole mission was to Litore's future was not lying to him. The paladin simply fell to his knees in shock with heavy streams of tears streaking his face. He did not know what to think let alone what to say next.

"The gods of old are dying. Soon none will remain but their children." The alien delivered the news to him as if it was doing him a favour. Ivan felt those words echoing in his mind, as he tried to decipher the meaning of 'children.' After a moment of silence from both individuals, this Adjudicator, which was one of a few inhabiting Litore, did their duty.

"A Negater will be dispatched this very night to erase Charles O'Donnell. What you do next is up to you, Ivan the Revered." With a brilliant flash of light, Ivan awoke in the darkness of night inside the temporary camp he had set up. His horse stirring at his abrupt appearance.

Ch13 - Evil Deeds, Good Reasons

Ven Devar, for one of the few times in his life, was riding atop a horse. To his immediate left was Grand Master Zenair, listening with eager elven ears, to the tale of his fascinating journey to ShadowScorn beside Princess Scáth. Behind them, also on steeds was Captain Sindrum and Master Zaskee leading 8,000 Frozen Fist Monks across the dried and earth cracked land between Litore Lake and Starlight Lake. It was an estimated eight-day march from The Crescent City to The City of Shadow and five of those would be across what was now a barren wasteland. The land they travelled across was wide and open, fostering a harsh wind, yet, the promise of springtime could be smelled on the breeze. Many of the bigger fissures leaked hot toxic fumes from the Underworld, that the marching army avoided at all costs. It amazed the mighty hunter to see the number of shipwrecks that littered the dried-up lake bed. They remained behind like bones of a carcass, often tattered and shredded hauls with bent masts, marking the once sturdy barques and schooners like gravestones. No doubt scavengers and looters had picked each and every wreckage clean after the lake had dried up, but it left Ven to wonder what stories could be found by inspecting any of the wrecks with a closer eye.

"Impressive is it not?" Zenair said while stroking his bushy white beard.

"I must admit, everything since leaving the confines of the rainforest has stricken my sense of what I thought possible. Sindrum tells me this was caused by dwarves in the west?" He inquired of the enlightened king.

"The Dwarves of Silver Rock devised war machines deep below the open air of Litore, in an effort to bring down their long rivals of Rhogar. Dwarves are among the greatest engineers in all the known worlds, but often lack foresight or truly anything that lingers beyond their crooked noses. The earthquake they caused had a ripple effect across every square kilometre of Litore. The Rhogarian's atop their mountains were privy to little more than an increased amount of avalanches. Yet, a chain reaction broke out causing innumerable quakes, tsunamis, and environmental catastrophes." Zenair suddenly stopped his recount and Ven could tell it brought great pain out of the elf. "Let us just say, your kin are most fortunate to be so favoured by Āina and Kaia. Many, many souls were wrought low and never recovered from the Quake of Harazune."

As if to accentuate the point of Grand Master Zenair, Ven noticed something not too far off in the distance. It grew exponentially in size but never moved. As the army kept its pace and direction, the hunter soon realized it to be a collection of bones, the size of which was unlike anything he had ever seen before.

"Gargantuan Water Dragons used to call Litore lake home. Benevolent creatures as likely to save a drowning crew of merchant's as they were to bestow forgotten knowledge on those deemed worthy," Zenair answered Ven's gaze with a heavy heart.

"Do these creatures still exist?" Ven asked with a self-surprised sense of worry.

"I do not know, although I suspect if any species could escape such a fate as extinction, the omniscient Water Dragons could. I even heard tell of ocean living Water Dragons," he offered with a hopeful attitude, and if nothing else recognizing the sense of loss that Ven felt. "You are different, aren't you Ven Devar."

The Kyst eyed the king most curiously. "I keep hearing that and never know if I am to feel insulted or complimented."

The king laughed with good intent. "Surely there is no reason to disrespect you. However, the other Kyst and elves of Litore do not fit your particular moral description. Do they?"

Of course, Ven was impressed with Zenair's astute observation, for he had never felt a sense of belonging among those elves that he lived beside.

"It is true, I find little comfort or kinship in my fellow Kyst.

Although I live by and for the most part agree with their tenets in life."

"Of course you do, which is why you're so favoured," Zenair replied in agreement. "From your tale, you find a great sense of familial ties to the gnome, half-orc and wolf you travel beside. Why do you think that is?"

Ven looked at Zenair in his icy eyes before shrugging halfheartedly.

"You are different, like them," Zenair said with a smile before looking back over the wasteland before them. "Not which of least is that sword strapped to your back. Where did you come by it?"

"I fell into a forgotten temple of my people. A blood-thirsty Vampire who took over the place nearly had my life, but in the end I think this sword protected me from its infectious bite." Ven drew the magnificent sword from its scabbard and handed it to the Grand Master. Zenair let go of his reins and inspected the artifact closely. Ven noticed the Snow Elf mutter a few words of magical detection over the weapon. The engraved vines and embossed runes along the blade-face glowed a faint green.

"The Sword of Hunters Protection," he whispered to himself as if not believing it. Ven watched with reverence as the sagely king made his connection with the weapon.

"You are correct. This sword did protect you, any wound you suffer may be lessened and redirected upon the foe who delivered it. However, that is only the beginning of this artifact's power. It is rumoured that Āina himself crafted this weapon for the Kyst in the First Age." The king threw it up in the air and as it did a number of imperceptible spins, he caught it again with a single finger resting on the blade tip in perfect balance. No doubt, Ven knew this was not a magical property but something the Grand Master Monk did to test the sword's balance and weight. "You will never find a short-sword like this again, I assure you." He handed it back to Ven who admired the now still lightly glowing runes and vines across the blade face before sheathing it.

In the distance was a massive ridge with a slight incline which Ven knew to be the edge of the lake bed. Several hours later they crested that ridge and could look upon Glass Mountain for the first time since departing for Moon Mountain. As the sun was setting, it made their destination appear as a prize, back-lit by the golden clouds of dusk.

They broke to make camp which did not consist of much more than eating dried meat and a large bundle of vegetables, before falling asleep wherever looked most comfortable. The Snow Elves could not be bothered by the cold and the Monks of the Frozen Fist were so disciplined, they could get a full night's rest standing up if need be.

Since leaving The Crescent City we have marched two days for every one night of rest. Tonight I find slumber in the trees, on a thick branch with my back planted firmly against the red bark. I watch these cousin elves of mine with a degree of envy. Their very level of camaraderie and emotional attachment for one another is something seldom shared between the Kyst. It's not that my kin cannot love or care deeply for one another, its that their long held tradition of looking in the past prevents them from living in the moment. Being too enamoured with the teachings long handed down from generation to generation has left them with a fear of not exceeding those expectations or veering away. Only an unreasonable man would argue that the Kyst are not one of the most grounded races on Litore, both spiritually and physically. But I know first hand that they lack the empathy and compassion for each other that fuels a unified and prosperous people. I think of Prince Rexous as being the clearest example of this. His inability to look past the obvious and view me as an ally rather than an adversary, was the only thing preventing him from being a greater warrior and elf than I. The ShadowScorn for example, are unjustly hated and persecuted without mercy, and are still a wealthy and fruitful nation. Through relying almost exclusively on each other after their mysterious transformations, they have managed to manifest a culture born from the many varied races of hopeful miners that re-settled there. In all the hundreds of pocket settlements in the Great Northern Rainforest alone, there are less than a handful of settlements that boast more than 5,000 Kyst. Yet, from what I saw in the ancient temple of my people, a civilization of thrice that number could have comfortably lived there. And that is nothing to speak of the other infrastructures that could have surrounded what I stumbled into. The images of the prophecy carved into the great hall of that temple burns in my mind like a persistent ember. I had never thought of the Kyst as divided before, but why would I? The life Silva offered me was the extent of my worldly experiences and so I could know no different. The sages often say that you must step back from any given circumstance or dilemma, to see and understand it better. I have seen what strength in unified numbers can do, and the kinship that my fellow elves of Litore show for one another, and so I see too the potential of exactly what the Kyst lack.

* * *

152

Sindrum and I have spoken little to one another since marching beside the Frozen Fist. Our goals, although he claims are separate, remain the same. Get to ShadowScorn in time with a force formidable enough to beat the armies of Serenstrom. My every waking moment is plagued with the anxiety of failing once more in protecting those whom I care for most.

-Ven Devar

With night overtaking the land and a successful retreat of all citizens to the palace, the Renrit army set a secondary encampment outside the city wall. They fortified their position inside and around the gate to make sure they could hold it. The palace was designed to support the cities populace for such retreats and this was hardly the first time it had done so. It was built strategically against Glass Mountain and thus had a large infrastructure to shelter the masses.

Agan had remained at the entrance to help seal the grand doorway after all were safely inside. Faenla went to immediately search for Scáth. The massive wolf nimbly weaved through the panicked citizens before making his way to the upper palace and Scáth's chambers. He gave a derisive snort as he entered to find it empty, aside from several dead Scorn men. He was about to bound away when a familiar scent caught his finely tuned nose. He padded through the pools of blood, leaving large paw prints as he went. He stopped near the hearth as he sniffed about a small puddle of blood and recognized it to be Athvars. He followed the scent with ease, leading him all the way back down to the dungeons.

Torvic had cast a spell of influence over Oren after slapping him awake from Scáth's blow to the head; a spell that made the Administrator all too happy to walk himself into a prison cell. From there, Torvic led Scáth through the magical safeguards and into the morgue where she laid Athvar to rest. The princess held her gnome companion tight before planting a soft, mournful kiss on his forehead.

"Thank you, sweet Athvar," she whispered as tears streamed down her face. Scáth could not have foreseen, nor ever would have guessed, the toll returning back home would take from her. Most people simply would have broken, but Scáth's true power was in perseverance. Very few in all the world could have suffered as much as her, and remained so strong willed. She understood now that she would gladly give her life, instead of losing another single loved one. She was interrupted from mourning by the murmurs of a frantic Arch Priest. She watched through watery eyes as Torvic rushed from stone slab to stone slab as if he had misplaced something, or rather someone.

"Torvic? What is it?"

"No, no, no. It is not possible," he muttered worriedly before eventually stopping and hanging his head in defeat. "He's gone."

"Who is gone?" Scáth asked, standing up and having no idea what he could be meaning.

"The Kyst Prince. Rexous' body is gone," Torvic answered in disbelief, just as a resounding thud gently rocked the palace structure.

"The doors sealed, which means they have made it into the city," Scáth said, walking up to a completely baffled Torvic. "This mystery will reveal itself in time. For now, we must see to our people."

Faenla stopped momentarily in front of the cell that held Oren, fully remembering this Scorn had once tried to sneak into Ven's room while he was recovering. Oren rolled his eyes at seeing the annoying wolf. Faenla snarled at the Scorn before continuing after Athvar's scent. He quickly bumped into the chest of Scáth emerging from an impenetrably dark corridor.

"Faen!" Scáth shouted happily as she buried her face into his thick, comforting fur. However, the wolf backed away and bared his teeth at the princess, who reeked of Athvar. A terrified looked came across Scáth but so too did the pain of losing Athvar. Faenla sensed this and dropped his body to the floor, burying his face in his paws and giving a low whimper. Torvic, once again surprised by the wolf's level of cognition, left the pair for a private moment and walked to Oren's cell.

"When the Queen finds out I've been put in here, there will be retribution," the shamed and dishevelled Scorn threatened.

"She knows, I assure you she does not care. Katia used you for her own gain like she did with everyone around her."

"Liar," the petulant Oren shouted. Torvic shrugged with disinterest, no longer caring for what his former associate had to say.

"What is wrong with you?" Aelis Andula asked the half-orc. Agan, once again, did not hear the commander. He was lost in a jumble of memories that were cascading back to him like a springtime waterfall. He was pulled from the overwhelming flood of memories by a soft hand caressing the back of his neck.

"Agan?" Aelis asked with a vulnerability he had not seen from the strong and stoic Scorn elf. Her skin seemed impossibly delicate for such a fierce warrior, it was a light grey, not the most common tone among her people. He was lost once again in her iridescent silver eyes that seemed as though they promised safety. Before he knew it, he found themselves just centimetres apart from locking lips.

"Commander!" The shout echoed throughout the foyer of the palace as hundreds of Scorn Guard hustled around them. Aelis lowered her head in disappointment before regarding her underling.

"Commander, there you are!" A breathless Captain Theena shouted, rushing towards them.

"Captain?" Aelis asked impatiently.

"The Administrator, he's been imprisoned. Scáth and Torvic request you both immediately."

Agan and Aelis shared a knowing look before beckoning Theena to lead them on.

Queen Katia watched the same battle unfold from her balcony as Scáth and Athvar had. A knowing grin crossed her face as she watched the Mountain Giant effortlessly obliterate the city gates.

"I see the Renrits took your advice, my Queen," Oren said emerging from the darkness behind her.

"Soon we can make the City of Shadow anew. Free from the besieging prejudice and hate of the world," Katia replied never turning her gaze from the battle before her.

"Then your plan is going accordingly?" He asked sheepishly. Now Katia did turn to regard Oren.

"That depends. You failed once before in ridding me of Scáth. We both know what will befall you if you fail me again." She placed a menacing glare on her pet puppet before turning back over the city. Oren bowed low before quietly exiting her chambers. He entered the hall and was met by 10 ruffians, surely enough Scorn to deal with the princess and any protectors. Queen Katia gripped the polished stone railing of her balcony as she watched the Renrit's pour into the city. She had been planning this day for the past three decades.

Her love for Arwr started out as a genuine and fulfilling romance. A relationship that made the Scorn citizens proud and confident in their monarchs. Katia had never known happiness like when she gave birth to her first child, Scarnin. It wasn't until some 30 years later that Katia understood the ShadowScorn would never stop being unjustly prosecuted. The Scorn as a race, had manifested almost overnight, and nearly 900 years later, the people of Litore still looked at them like some feature at a circus. From a young age, Katia had wanted to change the world's perspective of the ShadowScorn for the better. She had done everything in her power as a single child, parented by the only one she had left, a drunken father, to get her attendance with Prince Arwr and forge her own destiny. From there, the obvious had become blinding, as her now sixth decade as Queen had seen over 40 wars from the balcony she now stood on. Each and every war surrounded her like a cage, growing ever smaller.

After the birth of Scáth things had seemed promising, as more distant and nobles houses and cities began to trade with the City of Shadow. Eventually, a siege led by none other than 'Ivan the Revered' had them in an almost identical situation they were in now. King Arwr had led a desperate counter strike to break the Sesara army and through means widely unknown, he had even managed to end the war entirely. It had cost them a great deal though; Prince Scarnin was killed and the ShadowScorn population was decimated. Although she never openly admitted it, she had lost her favourite child that day. From then on, Katia and Arwr never saw eye to eye on anything again. He returned as a man who had witnessed the death of his own child. And though he never talked about it, had witnessed something truly divine. He remained a father to commend, for Scáth, but became a detached monarch and an even poorer husband. The loneliness and bitterness festered in Katia all the while, as each year brought new attacks and sieges without end. A life trapped inside, hunted without mercy to be met with fates unimaginable if they left the safety of their walls.

She vowed to never let another Scorn parent lose their child the way she had done. Katia had spent the next several decades devising a solution to the never-ending problem that was their existence, until the resentment, depression, loss, and torment had driven her to the cruel and slippery course that she walked now.

"Queen Katia, we are in full lock down." A large retinue of Scorn Guard now stood outside the Queen's chambers. She nodded in recognition but remained silent.

A significant amount of time had passed but Katia had not flinched a muscle. She was oblivious to the passage of time as she now watched the Renrit's quickly put out the flame blocking their entrance into the city, and their subsequent fortification of the gate.

"Ahem," came a weary feminine voice. Katia turned back to her chamber entrance to see a beaten and bloody Ghost of Aceia.

"Yes?" Katia prodded.

"I've been told to inform you that the cities Administrator has been imprisoned for treason. He was caught making an attempt on Princess Scáth's life. I assure you your daughter is safe and healthy," the Ghost said with a sense of optimism. It was obvious she was afraid to deliver the shocking and betraying news to her queen.

"Thank you for relaying this to me," Katia said in a tone she thought would be natural for the scenario. Of course, she was filled with sheer rage at giving Oren a second chance..

"If you wish, I could escort you to see her?" The Ghost asked.

"That won't be necessary, thank you."

"Scáth!" Agan and Aelis shouted in unison as they spotted the princess in the shelter, attending to many of the scared and wounded citizens, alongside Torvic. Aelis and Scáth threw themselves into one another, holding each other tightly. Agan attempted to give Torvic a nod of gratitude but the half-orc noticed the priest would not look him in the eye. So too did Agan go to give Faenla a rub between the ears when the wolf nipped at his fingers and bounded out of the shelter back into the main palace. Agan furrowed his brow at the odd treatment he was receiving and looked back to Scáth and Aelis.

"It's not your fault love, you've done everything right."

Agan keenly heard Aelis speaking in a soothing tone to a disgruntled Scáth. It dawned on the fierce fighter that his little gnome companion was not around. He walked up to the Scorn elves he had come to so admire.

"Where is the little man?" He asked of Scáth but she did not look at him. He asked again in a more forceful manner that had many of the surrounding Scorn looking at him with worry. Scáth hung her head and shook it. Aelis grabbed the brawny half-orc by the arm to pull him out of the shelter. Much to her shock, for she was larger and stronger than most Scorn men and women, his arm didn't even budge as she forcefully tugged. Agan ripped his arm away with ease and took a large step towards Scáth, his glowering yellow eyes staring down upon her. She met his fearful gaze with her own unyielding stare.

"Tell me," he demanded through gritted teeth.

"He's dead!" Scáth screamed in his face. All around them turned to witness the open confrontation. Agan's face didn't flex a single emotion over the next few seconds, before he quietly left the chamber.

Torvic watched the encounter and the ensuing Scáth stomping out of the shelter with Aelis hot on her trail. Torvic instructed one of his priests to have the soup brought out and distributed among the citizens before also following after the princess and commander.

The Arch Priest followed them into the Council Hall. He found the two Scorn standing still in front of the windows over-looking the Renrit soldiers fortifying their hard-earned ground.

"How many times did we watch our father's standing right here, staring down at a similar fate?" Aelis asked a fearfully quiet Scáth. The princess nodded. Torvic too remembered a similar scene as he had interrupted their fathers from a close moment shared between friends. So this time, he held back and allowed their two daughters time to reflect.

"I thought the world of them both. Your Pa, so brave and strong-willed. My

da used to tell me all the time how King Arwr filled him with such hope and courage," Aelis said while wrapping her arm around Scáth, who smiled at the kind memory.

"He used to say there never was a better tactician or friend than your Da," Scáth said, eliciting a tear from her oldest friend.

"I miss them both," Aelis whispered under a rarely heard sniffle. "Perhaps Aceia wills our reunion sooner than we expected."

Faenla was slowly and aimlessly walking through the winding and criss-crossing corridors of the palace. In a tired state, the wolf picked up the scent of his dearest companion, Ven Devar. Faenla began tracking the scent in an obviously excited mindset, quickly picking up his pace. Soon, he pawed open a door and peered in to see the empty chamber Ven had been recovering in. He lowered his coastal-blue eyes to the floor before turning back the way he had come. In search of Scáth, he was hit by an overwhelming pang of loneliness for his new pack. Before he had even made it out of the hall, he heard an all too familiar sound, but not one he had heard since leaving the coast. The undeniably annoying but unique sound of a SeaRaven, and one he had gotten to recognize in his time with the coastal elf. Faenla shot his ears up trying to locate where the sound had originated before bounding off. After hearing it once more, he found himself at the base of the spiral staircase. The cawing of the SeaRaven grew in frequency and the ever-agile wolf found himself in the bell tower on the very highest turret in the city. As Faenla crested the last stair, he saw the bird flutter away from the stone rail that surrounded the open summit. The SeaRaven flew over the city and towards Starlight lake. Amid seeing the bird leave and now being away from Ven for over 12 days, Faenla let out a series of long mournful howls. It blanketed the Renrit soldiers and skipped off the mountain to echo out over the highlands.

Ven was nearing the end of a Kyst meditation that would grant him a significant stay of rest. It was a skill that all Kyst practised since children, over-riding their bodies need for rejuvenation and allowing them to go several days without sleep. He sat peacefully high above the army, tucked against a tree when his eyes sprung open. The howl of Faenla rang through his head as clear as any thought ever had. Ven understood from an early time that his connection with animals was strong, but his connection with Faenla was something entirely different. He effortlessly and with pure grace leaped from branch to branch till he reached the camp of the Frozen Fist.

To his surprise, he was met with the open eyes of Sindrum and Grand Master Zenair.

"What is it?" Sindrum's words were the first for Ven since their dispute.

"We need to leave, now."

Ch14 - Out of Time

With the start of the sun's streak across the sky, came the next wave of Renrit soldiers. An echoing thud sounded rhythmically throughout the whole palace. Those discomforting bangs promised death and the end of all Scorn as the Renrits attempted to break their last line of defence. Agan came to the council hall in search of Scáth and found her alongside Faenla. He paused momentarily, wishing the wolf hadn't been there but he pressed forward anyway.

"Lady Scáth."

She turned to regard her friend with a smile. "I'm sorry, Agan. I shouldn't have shouted at you," she offered apologetically, but Agan held his hands up.

"No need, I know when I deserve it. I remember-," His words jumbled up in his throat for a moment. "-everything before the Morass Prairie." He seemed shameful, and not relieved as Scáth would have expected.

"That's wonderful!" Scáth gave an excited look. Yet, the half-orc just shook his head.

"You know not who took you from your home, but do you remember who caged you?" Agan asked sternly. A slight look of fear crossed the Scorn Princess' face. It was a difficult memory and she didn't particularly wish to think about it in this ultimate time of crisis.

"No." Scáth spoke with a tone meant to end the discussion. "You remember no one? Saw no one?" Agan pressed. "The tail of a red

Dragon-Blood, that's it," Scáth answered with irritation.

Agan had difficulty spitting the words out. "I was there, well my body was, not my mind, that, that was theirs. We picked you up outside Renrit and were to bring you back to the Sesara Cathedral in Serenstrom." Agan hung his head with a new shame unequivocal to anything in his past. Scáth took several shocked steps back in disbelief and Faenla protectively stood in front of her. Her eyes began to water and another thud shook the palace. She turned to look out the window as the Renrits were actively swinging a battering ram against the great doors.

"You're one of them?" She asked, her voice ailing.

A surprised look came over Agan. "No. Never. They used me like they use everyone."

"Yet you willingly escorted a kidnapped woman across thousands of kilometres-"

"-I wasn't in my right mind Scáth. I haven't been since my time in Rhogar. But you, Ven, and Athvar freed me from that mental prison of delusion and lies. I owe you my life."

Scáth looked from Agan to Faenla who was now taking a far less defensive stance. She wasn't sure if it was the inability to lose another person close to her or perhaps Faenla's innate understanding of the situation.

"Thank you for being honest, it'll be nice to die knowing the truth," Scáth said facing the window and with serious defeat evident about her.

"You're not going to die, Lady Scáth. If it's the last thing I do, you will not die here."

"We failed Agan. Aelis knows it, Torvic knows it, the people openly speak that I am to blame. Best case scenario Ven and Sindrum are two days away. We're out of time."

Agan took several steps closer to Scáth and peered out the window to view the army. "Ven Devar has gone to the end of his world twice now, whether he admits it or not, solely for you. He's a virtuous kid but a kid nonetheless. Wherever he is right now is born from his love for you. He simply does not know how to fail you." Agan gave Scáth a soft pat on her shoulder before exiting the council hall. Somewhere inside the princess, she wished all this would come to a swift end at the wrong side of a blade. She didn't think that she could handle anything else, for the last several months had brought mostly pain and loss. She thought back to those adventures and memories she had shared with Ven. The many close calls they had barely escaped.

Then she saw the Renrit's carting a large metallic object towards the doors. They disappeared out of view and reappeared after a few seconds, running to a safe distance. Scáth looked as straight down as she could before a massive explosion went off. The whole palace shook and a burst of fire, then smoke, poured from the doors. She placed a hand on the hilt of her scimitar and ran toward the entry with Faenla at her side.

"What was that?" Aelis asked as a great burst of light showed through the seams of the doors. She noted too that they were ever so slightly bent inwards.

"A bomb," Agan answered dryly. Aelis, Torvic and several others turned to regard the half-orc. "It's like capping the end of a cannon and lighting a fuse, but forget the ball and just fill it to the brim with black powder."

"What do we do?" Torvic asked the Commander. She just looked to Agan, for once out of ideas.

"You won't have a front door after a couple more of those, so we bide our time or face them head-on." Agan made it abundantly clear that there weren't many, if any, other options. He gave Aelis a nod and a look of absolute

trust in her to make the right decision. Scáth and Faenla came skidding around a great pillar in the foyer towards the amassed forces.

"What was that?" Scáth asked while catching her breath.

"The inevitable," Agan answered.

"It's the princess' fault, hand her over!" One Scorn Guard shouted and many more around her yelled in agreement. Scáth nearly fainted at hearing those words from her people.

"We're doomed without our king!"

"Listen to reason Commander Aelis, offer her up. Perhaps it'll buy us enough time for the Snow Elves to arrive." Soon half the troops were calling to surrender or to hand Scáth over as a hostage. Even Scáth contemplated surrendering herself if it meant the rest could have a better chance.

"Maybe they're right," she suggested to Aelis and Torvic. "I bring death wherever I go. Let me do this for the good of our people."

"Take that back right now," Aelis glowered at Scáth, before shouting at her subordinates. "I ought to put my blade to every one of your necks for uttering such treasonous vile! You spit on the honour of every Scorn who has fallen in battle against those wicked folk!" The commander shook with rage. Agan moved closer to the princess and so too did Faenla, standing tall behind her. Scáth quickly understood that surrendering herself would gain them nothing, for the church of Sesara was not here for hostages. So, she interlocked her fingers with Aelis and gave her dearest and oldest friend a loving look.

"Commander Aelis is right, to surrender now would be to surrender all those heroic acts of ShadowScorn past. I was betrayed by the very Scorn I swore to serve. Yet, I survived the annihilation of an entire city, travelled thousands of kilometres across treacherous lands just to serve you once more. I will not stop, I will not be thwarted by those who dare to scare us, to enslave us. I know this is the first siege that hasn't been led by a fearsome Scorn King, but I will fight for you, beside you, just as they have! Do not forget the words of our Alfather, 'Only in darkness is one truly revealed.' We must rise against evil, never surrender to it!"

After a long uncomfortable silence, Scáth felt silly and considered her speech had missed the mark.

"All hail the Scorn Queen!" The first guard to offer the princess up, shouted, before all in the great foyer chanted it. The sound of a thousand suits of amour rang out as every Scorn Guard took a knee and bowed to Scáth ShadowScorn, the first Scorn Queen. Scáth watched with a sense of pride she had never known, bolstered by Agan and Aelis also taking a knee. The moment was cut short however, as another explosion rang out and the great iradinium doors shook.

"Commander?" Scáth asked Aelis, alluding to Agan's prior ultimatum.

"These doors have never been breached and personally I'd like to keep it that way," Aelis answered in grim determination. Another deafening bang was heard and the doors tried to break free of the barricades and restraints.

"Torvic, have the priests take positions above. I want you to use every trick in the book to give us combat advantage as you see it. Agan, Scáth, Faenla, you know how to work as a unit, take the Ghosts and make sure this fight stays in the foyer." Aelis was loud and precise with her directions, so everyone quickly got into position, except for Agan. He remained there, never taking his eyes off the stunning commander. He took a large but slow step towards her.

"What are you doing?" She asked in that vulnerable voice he only heard when she spoke to him.

"I'm not going to die without having kissed the most terrifying and cunning woman I've ever known." He spoke quietly but with strong resonance.

"This is not the end."

"Perhaps, but-" Agan was cut off by Aelis forcefully bringing their lips together in a kiss that promised a lifetime of love and support.

"Don't let this be the end," Aelis said before shoving the half-orc back. He grinned widely and ran to fortify his position. The commander was joined by Captain Theena who had a rye grin.

"What?" Aelis shot her way.

"Nice to see ya soft on someone, commander. Too bad we're all going to die or be enslaved, but ya know." Aelis and Theena looked at each other before sharing a laugh.

"Get two capable Shadow-walkers to open the doors," Aelis instructed and Theena sent two Scorn Guard to ready the doors.

"Shields!" Aelis shouted and her command echoed throughout the blackglass foyer. A unified grunt emitted from the Scorn Guard and a bang of shields being planted to the ground. "It's time we send these Renrit's running once and for all! Kill or be killed and feel Aceia's cold touch once more!"

The Scorn Guard took up a battle cry as the doors quickly opened. A squad of Renrit's were awkwardly caught attempting to carry another bomb up the steps to the doors. Torvic saw this from the upper balcony that encircled the entire foyer as the mass of soldiers then began to charge inside. He quickly shot a bolt lightning at the bomb, charring nearly 30 soldiers and wounding dozens more in the massive explosion. It wasn't long before the first line of Scorn Guard were arm to arm, pushing with all their might against the pressing Renrit's. Hundreds upon hundreds of soldiers pushing and trampling each other to break the ShadowScorn's shield wall. Eventually, the second, third and fourth Scorn lines were supporting the first in holding a strong line of shields.

"One, two, push!" Aelis shouted with all her ferocity as every Scorn Guard pushed, forcing the whole Renrit line back a metre. Just enough distance to launch a volley of javelins, and the second line of pole-arm's to land vicious strikes into the bellies and throats of their enemies. This went on for an extended while, decimating the Scorn's strength and straining their resilience, but annihilating the soldiers before them. They could counter their exhaustion by having the first line of Scorn shadow-step to the very back and let the next line take the brunt of the forwarding assault. They did this a number of times in fact, but had to give up precious ground with each line's retreat. It was equally detrimental to the ranks of the Renrit army and perhaps because of the literal mob attempting to be the first ones to ever break into the Scorn palace. It took a familiar Dragon-Blood Paladin far too long to reach the front ranks and make a difference. Of course, he eventually did this by soaring in, propelled by his wings and hurling a ball of radiant light no bigger than an apple into the third rank of Scorn. That ball of light that went greatly unnoticed by all except Torvic, began to grow exponentially.

The Arch Priest quickly dropped a globe of darkness but it was too late as a great explosion of radiant energy went off, blinding all in the room. The Renrit's, including Agan who had spent much time among the Sesaran ranks, got over this effect far quicker than the Scorn Guard or anyone who had not suffered from it before. The half-orc closed his eyes, counted to five, and opened them to see the Renrit army pouring in like a swarm of insects.

"Shields! Priests, cover us!" Agan gave the command, as he watched the Scorn Guard being slaughtered and struggling to react in time. He rushed into battle. "Cover us!" He yelled at the top of his lungs. Eventually, random clusters of darkness appeared all around them, giving the Scorn a chance to recover. Agan cut a wide line through the enemies until he made it to Aelis and re-orientated her. She immediately went to shouting her commands, getting them back into a coordinated army, but it was all-out warfare in the foyer now.

Great streaks of energy burst from the balcony from priests shocking or incinerating entire groups of soldiers. It didn't take long for a wide swath around the fearsome Agan Dusk to be created. He made combat appear as though he himself had invented the concept. He weaved throughout and parried his enemies with such precision and omniscience, all around him fell with a single swing of his double-bearded axe. He was soon confronted with the impossible, the paladin who had just dropped the light was Ragow. The very Dragon-Blood he travelled with prior, and fought against at the city wall, and subsequently saw his throat be torn out by none other than Faenla.

"You're supposed to be dead!" Agan shouted, trying to get his only equal on this battlefields, attention. The paladin saw Agan and charged the fighter. He took a deep breath and Agan knew what that meant. He dropped to one knee and picked up a shield just as the Dragon-Blood breathed a flame so hot it felt like came from a true Red Dragon. Agan threw the shield that was glowing hot to the ground and leaped at his foe.

Scáth and Faenla found themselves hard at work. It was an undeniable truth now that the Royal Palace of ShadowScorn, after nearly nine centuries of safety, had finally been invaded. There were plenty of Renrit soldiers looking to wreak havoc throughout the palace and most likely start slaughtering citizens in hiding. Faenla jumped on one group, fully grasping the head of a soldier in his powerful jaw. The huge wolf landed and whipped his neck so forcefully that the soldier's body tore clean off with the head still in Faenla's fangs. All the while, the headless body flew into three other soldiers, knocking them down.

Scáth and a handful of Ghosts weaved among each other in a flurry of deadly strikes. Taking each and every Renrit zealot down with uncanny coordination. Scáth was amazed at how quickly she fell into a routine with the Ghosts, something she had to credit to Ven and Agan's training. Yet, for all this success, Scáth knew it would not be enough. The blackglass floors ran deep with blood and even though the Scorn Guard were superior warriors, the Renrit's still outnumbered them two to one. She surveyed the battle to see Aelis surrounded by soldiers but never missing a step. Agan was locked in a powerful series of strikes and parries against Ragow the Paladin, the two anticipating each other's next move with familiarity. Torvic was so drained that he was leaning against the rail, as his casting took longer and became weaker with every magical spell uttered. Faenla, with the heart of a true apex predator, was gaining a lot of attention for his destructive wave of mutilated and limbless victims was gaining notice.

The entire Frozen Fist army was in a full run now, as the leaders, on horseback, led the way in a slight gallop. Ven and Sindrum's unease was palpable and the wise Grand Master Zenair watched the Kyst closely.

"Devar!" He shouted from further behind as the Kyst was unconsciously getting his horse to go faster and faster. Ven looked back to see that he had created a gap but was relieved too, to see the king wave him and Sindrum on. "We'll be right behind you!"

Ven looked to the Scorn Captain who gave him a resolute and confident nod.

"Hyah!" Sindrum shouted, and his horse alongside Vens began an all out sprint, closing the final kilometres to the City of Shadow. As Sindrum and Ven made great haste through the sparse trees and the sound of hooves thudded against solid ground, the captain looked to Ven and wished for the Kyst to understand.

"Listen, before we face whatever is waiting for us, I need you to know something. I've made my regret clear. All I want and have ever wanted is what's best for the ShadowScorn race."

Ven didn't turn his head to regard the Scorn. "You act like I wasn't there when you died for them. I know what your intent is, it's everyone else you should worry about convincing."

Sindrum was surprised at the level of understanding the Kyst was now showing.

"I don't know why I haven't said this earlier, but, thank you. For everything you've done and continue to do."

Ven turned, regarding the Scorn, and gave a knowing nod of appreciation. The hunter hadn't necessarily forgiven Sindrum for what he had done to his beloved Scáth but he did admire the captain's willingness to undergo what they had gone through. Most importantly, Ven knew the mind of a warrior and it needed to be clear and straight for ultimate efficiency. Considering they were heading into a war unlike he had ever experienced before, forgiveness felt like the right thing.

The pair broke through the woods and reared their mounts as they took in the first glance of the city since their departure. Sindrum felt as though he might keel over inshock. Ven was filled with unrelenting frustration as they watched Renrit soldiers freely coming and going through the city gates.

"We're too late," Sindrum said faintly in disbelief. Ven didn't know what to do, the Frozen Fist was maybe twenty minutes behind them but he had an itching sense of familiarity.

"No, Faenla is still in there. If he's alive then so are the others." "How do you know?" Sindrum questioned with obvious skepticism.

"I can feel him." Then, Ven felt another familiar spirit around him, but not one he had felt since leaving the coast. "Bird?" he mouthed, looking to the sky in search of what he thought he felt. They both ducked as the SeaRaven swooped between them just over their heads and gave a loud screech. "I don't believe it," Ven said with a chuckle. Sindrum looked at Ven with even more questions but knew it was better not to ask. The SeaRaven flew along the edge of the woods towards the eastern end of the city and mountain.

"Come on," Ven said as he directed his horse to follow. Sindrum wasn't about to stand idly by after everything he had been through, and was quickly beside the Kyst. They followed the flight path that the bird took and managed to make it to where the city wall abutted the mountain undetected. The SeaRaven flew up to, and perched on, a small jut in the mountain face.

"Fancy a climb?" Ven asked with a sarcastic smirk. Sindrum rolled his eyes at the elf and moved in front of him to grab a firm hold and begin the ascent. Ven was impressed with the Scorn's strength and climbing prowess. Of course, Ven had spent his entire life climbing the tallest trees in the world and found this jagged rock face to be a breeze. They eventually made it to the top of the wall and slowly peered over.. They spotted a handful of scouts near the centre of the parapet but it was otherwise unoccupied. Hoisting themselves over the edge, they were relieved to see the Renrit's had only occupied the gate and not the whole city, yet he felt a deep pain when they saw the level of destruction that the city had suffered from siege weaponry. Sindrum led them down the nearest staircase and the pair made their descent with expert stealth.

"Where is everyone?" The hunter asked after quickly noticing all the buildings and homes to be void of any life.

"If the city is breached all citizens are to retreat into the palace."

Ven said nothing else, feeling slightly stupid for asking what now felt obvious.

"Sit tight," Sindrum instructed as they were in the middle of traversing a series of thin alley ways. Ven did just that and the Scorn quickly made his way to the top of a three-story-tall stone and timber-built house. The Kyst suddenly dropped low behind a half-rotted barrel as three patrolling invaders walked by.

"We've got a problem," Sindrum whispered from behind Ven. The elf jumped in utter surprise, knocking over the barrel in the process.

"What in the actual Underworld, Sindrum!" He shouted in a hushed voice. "How about a tap on the shoulder first."

"Shh," Sindrum pressed his index finger to his lips. Ven rolled his eyes as he got over the initial shock of being caught off guard. He still wasn't used to how impossibly quiet and stealthy the ShadowScorn people inherently were.

"They're flooding into the palace as we speak."

"How do we get insi-" Ven was interrupted by a patrolman.

"Hey, who's back there? Show yourself, now!"

Sindrum gave the Kyst a very unimpressed look.

"Yes, yes, my fault," he replied as he was already knocking an arrow for each invader. Ven noted that the bow string he had taken from the sunken Kyst ruin began to hum with pent up energy. Looking over his shoulder, he marked his targets now entering the alley. He stood abruptly with a twist and loosed his arrows with deadly precision. Each guard hit the cobblestone without a single guttural noise; the arrows moved so fast that they were imperceptible and excavated great holes in the men.

"Wow," Sindrum exhaled in disbelief. Ven ignored the flattery as he always did when it was about his skill at killing.

"So, how do we get inside?" Ven asked as if picking up right where he left off.

"The Scorn Guard have many ways in for just this occasion. Please be quiet." "Well don't spook me."

As they got closer to the palace they could hear the clear sounds of battle through the many broken stained-glass windows. On the east side of the palace, 40 strides from the Guard Hall archery range, Sindrum placed both palms on the stone-mortar wall. After a moment of searching high and low his hand finally dipped on a particular stone. He pressed firmly and as the stone slid back into the wall, each stone around it periodically began to depress and recede until a small doorway was present.

Agan took the razor-thin tip of Ragow's blade across his face while deftly leaning out of the way. It cut a large gash from his left temple, down his cheek to his chin. Before Agan could flex his core to straighten himself, the Dragon-Blood kicked his knee sending him to land hard against the blackglass floor. The fighter immediately swung his powerful legs out and tripped the paladin. The half-orc sprang atop his foe with his axe coming down hard. Ragow held his great sword across his chest, with the blade barely scratching his fine gauntlet and caught the axe. Agan gave a menacing growl and his yellow eyes gleamed with hatred. It became a pure contest of strength as their muscles bulged and strained. Agan leaned his whole formidable weight down on his axe, forcing Ragow's blade downwards just centimetres from slicing his own neck open. The Dragon-Blood took a deep breath, generating waves of heat but Agan had seen enough of that trick and drove his forehead into the snout of the dragon-blood. A clear crack was heard as Agan broke the large jaw of his enemy and subsequently gave the necessary force to drive Ragow's sword down. It cleanly separated the paladin's head from his body. Agan gave a great exhale and looked up, unsure how long he had actually been caught in the mortal melee with his former acquaintance. He saw everyone he cared about in the room stuck in the fight of their lives, as now thousands of Renrit soldiers and Scorn Guard lay dead or dying around them. And still, for every one Renrit that fell, two more took their place. Determined to meet a warrior's death in battle defending what he believed in, he charged back into the fray.

Scáth could not believe the scene before her. Never had she fought in a battle like this and never had she experienced the horrors of her dead citizens in such brutal reality. The smell of entrails and evacuated bowels bit at her nostrils, the screams of those horribly maimed filled her ears, and the constant splattering of her enemy's blood stung her eyes and assailed her tongue. Her lungs heaved to keep up with the demand of combat and her muscles ached with each jolt of a blade parry or retraction of her scimitar from enemy flesh. She counted at least half a dozen times where she should have been dead but the unparalleled skill of the Ghosts of Aceia had her back. They were now being seriously contested in holding the back line. In the briefest of respites, Scáth turned at the howl of Faenla. The ever-vigorous and spirited wolf had no less than eight soldiers on top of him now, pinning him to the ground.

"Faen!" She shouted with a fearful intensity that shocked even herself. She moved quickly to her animal companion's side but was halted once more by the endless barrage of enemies. She fought hard and continued to see Faenla's predicament worsen. The wolf gave a great yelp of pain as he was stuck in the shoulder with a dagger then in the hip by a maul. He barred his teeth and nipped all around but found no purchase of flesh.

"Faenla!" Scáth screamed again, tears clearing lines of white skin through red and black blood. She let out a wail as she suffered a deep slash across her ribs and just barely got her weapon up in time to deflect her attacker's death stroke. A large man who was clearly a lifelong soldier in the Sesaran faith had just finished cutting down a row of Scorn Guard before turning his eyes on the wolf and the eight of his men pinning the beast down. He walked over to them and raised his well-used sword above Faenla. Scáth screamed for anyone to help but her cries went unnoticed, or at least anyone who heard was unable to aid. The giant soldier fell his sword with all his might down at the wolf. Mid-stroke, he was launched onto his back as an arrow struck his chest, carving a fist sized hole through his sternum.

"Ven!" Scáth yelled in celebration so loud that Agan, Torvic, and Aelis looked in his direction. The Mighty Ven Devar sent a hail of arrows into the Renrit's holding his dearest companion down. He jumped down from the balcony to land in front of Faenla with a wide smile at seeing his best friend, arriving in just the nick of time. Faenla gave a great howl of elation that echoed around in the foyer, encouraging his allies, yet distilling fear into the hearts of the besiegers. Ven drew his ancient short-sword and trident as the two apex predators leaped back into the battle. They quickly cut a path to Scáth and the Ghosts, and upon reaching them the Scorn Queen threw herself at Ven.

"We did it, Scáth," he said with his face buried in her thick black

hair, eternally misting away. She squeezed him tighter and all in the
room stopped as the Crescent Lur of Moon Mountain sounded clearly.

Ch15 - Justice

The monks of the Frozen Fist stood in blocks of 50, eagerly awaiting their leader's command. Each and every one of the Snow Elves wore bracers of blackglass and iradinium, forged and given to them by the Scorn. It was just one of the many trades and perks the two cities had gained in their alliance over the years. All 8,000 of the monks simultaneously crossed their arms, then began rhythmically banging their bracers together. The impossibly durable combination of blackglass and iradinium chimed like that of the hardest rainfall, in the most threatening of hurricanes. Grand Master Zenair and General Zaskee stood in the front of the formidable army. The general cracked her neck from side to side before she gave the king a look that begged for permission to join the fun.

"Go ahead, dear," Zenair waved his hand at the broken gate and the Renrit soldiers who were now too excited by their breaching of the palace to have fully mobilized themselves into a proper defence. General Zaskee sprang forward and half the army took up behind her. They hit the Renrit troops like a tsunami. By the time the invaders were able to form a suitable defence against these masters of melee, the Frozen Fist had breached their weak impromptu fortification and were inside the city without even deploying the other half of their forces. General Zaskee led the assault without mercy, as was evident when she vaulted over a wooden barricade, kicking a soldier in the process, which broke his neck and forced the crown of head to connect with the top of his back. She landed on another soldier, wrapping her legs around his neck and used her momentum to throw him to the ground. The move, performed with such grace, ended with her on top and delivering a punch, shattering his nose and sending bone into his brain. She rolled forward to avoid the swing of a blood stained sword and leaped like a panther onto her next prey.

The ShadowScorn in the foyer were much quicker to react to the sound of their rescue and resume the battle against the now flanked army of Sesara. So too were they reinvigorated by the return of their legendary Captain Sindrum. He made his entrance slightly after the Kyst, with his forearm buckler and war pick already in use. Suddenly, the entire tone of the battle changed as the Renrits began pushing back out of the palace to regroup with their masses. It wasn't long before the Mighty Ven Devar and the 'Agora' Agan Dusk were leading the rally with unmatched skill and prowess in battle. Though all three sides boasted legendary warriors, it truly seemed like none could match the Kyst or half-orc. Faenla, Commander Aelis, and Captain Sindrum were right behind the duo as they maliciously fought and clawed their way back into the City of Shadow proper. From the stoops of the grand entry, they saw the unmistakable uniform and visage of the Snow Elves pitched in full battle against the bulk of the remaining forces.

"You look surprised to see me!" Ven shouted to Agan as he parried a sword thrust and countered by plunging his trident into the out-matched soldier.

Agan chuckled to himself. "Never had a doubt you'd return, elf!" He replied while burying his axe into the collar of another unfortunate soldier. "Just wasn't sure if you'd be in time is all," he added quietly. There were only 1,000 or so Scorn Guard left but they fought with a fire burning inside them unlike ever before. The ground being made by both sides seemed too good to be true, but eventually, the Frozen Fist and Scorn Guard were halted by the remaining two Generals of Sesara.

"If it isn't Agan the Defiler himself. Switched sides again have we?" A tall elf with golden yellow hair and sun-kissed skin emerged through the remaining ranks of Sesara troops. Ven instantly recognized him as a Solsta Elf but very unlike his kin it would seem. He wore gold and white scale mail and carried a mace that hummed with pent up energy. Ven, however, quickly turned to view Agan, confused as to how these two apparently knew each other. Before

Agan could respond, however, he was struck in the chest by the mace and an explosion of light radiated from the hit, sending the half-orc flying back into a crowd of Scorn Guard. The Solsta Elf then turned his gaze to Ven.

"You must be the Kyst I've heard so much about, aren't you're supposed to be dead?"

Ven screwed up his face for nothing this elf had said thus far made any sense to him.

"Shouldn't you be retreating to whatever psychotic hole you crawled out of? You are beaten, take your remaining troops and never return," Ven stated loudly and with finality.

His opponent laughed in his face. "Look around you outsider. This fight has been going on for far longer than any living person here. We've never been closer to fulfilling the edicts of our goddess. If not this time, then the next siege or the next after that. We will not stop till Aceia has felt Sesara's wrath." He spoke with such conviction that Ven was left truly believing the Sesaran faith would not stop. He was overwhelmed with anger that left a heavy pressure in his chest. He spun 'Hunter's Protection' that still glowed a forest green and lunged towards his foe.

By now the second half of the Frozen Fist had been sent forward at the lead of their fearless king and Grand Master. It didn't take long for them to reach the inside of the city where the battle had spread throughout. Many fires had burst to life and were beginning to fill the streets with smoke, which had elicited Grand Master Zenair to strike with his force. Zenair had estimated their forces barely outnumbered that of the remaining Renrit Army and by the looks of the Scorn guard emerging from the palace, a heavy toll had already been extracted. General Zaskee ducked and weaved through the countless enemies, occasionally using her bracer to deflect a strike too close for comfort. As she went, she delivered devastating blows to pressure points, that crippled her foes. In the midst of her dance through enemy lines, she was struck bodily by a kite shield with the symbol of Sesara etched in fine detail. The third and final General of the Sesara Army was a tall and heroic-looking human female.

"You should have stayed on your mountain where you were safe," the general spat as she wound up to deliver the death blow with her shield into the spine of Zaskee. Grand Master Zenair jumped nearly four metres in the air, clearing several lines of soldiers to land a knee against the kite shield, sending the general stumbling backwards.

"We thought this would be more fun, darling." Zenair gave a rye grin in his usual flamboyant attitude. The general planted her feet firmly and placed her rapier through a small hole in the centre of her shield. She approached him with a confidence that bordered arrogance. She thrust her rapier through the small hole of her shield straight at the chest of the king. Zenair sidestepped and grabbed the blade by one hand before she could retract it. With a strength that beguiled his slim, dexterous elven form, he squeezed and broke the blade in two with his bare hand. Even more amazing was the general looked to the king's hand expecting it to be fully sliced from gripping the blade, yet not a single crease of blood was drawn. She took a step back in shock before clasping her hands together and forming a blade of pure radiant energy.

"Impressive trick," Zenair admitted, never stopping his slow walk towards her. She took several precise and swift swings at the Grand Master but he nimbly avoided each one, feeling the hot energy of the whirring blade as he did. Even though this general of the formidable army was far more skilled than almost any in this war, Zenair Aradithas was the famed 'Master of Ice,' Head of the Frozen Fist Monastery and a legendary monk. With seeming ease he grabbed her forearm that was projecting the radiant blade and squeezed with a twist. He then hit her in the chest with an open palm sending her flying backward several metres, to land hard against the stone.

"Prove you know right from wrong and surrender," the king demanded while walking towards the general who was staggering back to her feet.

"If we surrender now, my Macer will have me killed. I'm dead either way," she retorted bluntly. Zenair placed his right index finger on her forehead and his left hand where her neck met her shoulder. He squeezed with his left and pushed with the right, doing so with such speed the human had no idea what was happening. In the next instant, she was paralyzed and falling to the ground before fading into unconsciousness.

Ven had been stuck in a series of strikes and parries for some time, against the Solsta Elf. He quickly found his opponent to be to swift and unerring. By now, Ven had figured that Agan would not be rejoining this fight. He was either occupied or even possibly knocked out of the fight entirely from the divine blast of energy. The Kyst Hunter wasn't about to let that mace unleash the same blast on him so he took a defensive stance in the fight. Staying on the back foot allowed him to understand the stamina of his foe and also attempt to exploit any potential mistakes the Solsta General made. He managed a light and small cut across the neck of his foe with his short-sword, and felt the tingle run up his arm and fill him with a small burst of energy, recharging his muscles. Similarly he saw the Solsta Elf experience a draining shudder coarse through his body.

Ven remembered Grand Master Zenair said this sword was highly magical and it had saved his life against the Vampire and Mountain Lion. Still, he had never imagined it could drain his enemies of stamina and replenish his own. The ability to maintain your energy in an open battlefield or mortal melee was often the difference between life and death. However, the Solsta Elf was infuriated by the almost necrotic-like energy that washed through him and headbutted Ven, cracking his nose, spurting blood profusely. Though the Solsta Elf didn't have time to notice his nose too was now bleeding, he struck Ven in the chest with his mace, creating another explosion of light. This time, the Solsta Elf had just as much damage deflected on him from the blast as the two warriors were thrown apart an equal distance.

The Kyst landed against a score of Renrit Soldiers who mercilessly began kicking and slashing at Ven. The hunter was quick to get his reinforced bracers and greaves up, to deflect most of the attacks. The short-sword also did a great deal to help but it wasn't five heartbeats before the great and mythical wolf body-slammed a trio of them off of Ven. The wolf quickly tore any other attackers near his companion to mutilated shreds. Faenla was quick to Ven's side, helping him get back to his feet after the devastating shock of the blast and brutal beating. Commander Aelis was standing over an unconscious Agan, protecting him at all costs. Scáth was quick to witness the second explosion and even quicker to head in the direction of the Solsta General. She was accompanied by the remainder of the Ghosts of Aceia and the princess had figured out by now that Aelis had secretly instructed the Ghosts not to leave Scáth's side. Flanked by the fiercest warriors in the city, she confidently strode towards the now recovered general. Perhaps, she would have thought twice about approaching if she had seen the many cuts and bruises on his face seemingly close and disappear with divine healing. Nevertheless, she moved closer with scimitar in hand and on a plan she did not fully understand. Yet, she had witnessed this general incapacitate the two greatest warriors she had ever known and knew she had to at least try.

"Please princess, go inside your palace with the other civilians where you belong," he taunted, clearly under estimating her. Scáth didn't slow and kept a steady breath about her. The cleric readied his spiked mace for an easy kill, and devastating blow to Scorn society. She was in range and he swung for Scáth's face. The Scorn Queen focused on the shadow within her and to the shock and confusion of the general, his mace passed right through her as she momentarily dematerialized. As Scáth reformed she had already slid her scimitar into his heart. She looked him in the eyes and all he could muster was the chuckle of someone in disbelief. A few short ragged breaths later he fell to the ground in a bloody heap.

Shouts and cheers erupted around her as the Scorn Guard celebrated their queen felling such a formidable foe. The battle quickly became a rout as the Renrit ranks soon crumbled with ever mounting pressure and loss of leadership. They finally surrounded the remainder of their attackers who were now barely 500 strong. In the end it was a catastrophic loss for the folk of Renrit and the church of Sesara. There were more bodies to scatter the streets than there was bare cobblestone from the gates to the palace. The soldiers dropped their weapons and locked their fingers behind their necks, and for a short moment that felt like a lifetime, there was silence. All who remained were left with an eerie and empty feeling inside.

Ven and Scáth had gone to the side of Aelis and a now barely aware Agan. Soon, they were met by Grand Master Zenair and Captain Sindrum. The Snow Elf bowed low to Scáth specifically.

"My deepest condolences, Your Grace. For all that has befallen you."

"Thank you, Grand Master. We are forever in your debt, and shall never forget what you have done for us." Scáth spoke as a confident leader would, before also dipping into a low bow.

Grand Master Zenair then pointed to Ven and Sindrum. "These two are solely responsible for getting us here in time, and have confided to me that perhaps there is trouble with the succession of your father?"

He questioned quietly, leaning toward Scáth. She understood his worry to stem from the sincere friendship and admiration Arwr and Zenair held for each other. However, Scáth only nodded in response as the crowd around them was growing, turning to watch the two leaders of the nations speak.

Katia watched as the Frozen Fist monks washed over the Renrit army with devastating effect; her decades worth of planning washed away. She sighed despondently before feebly lowering herself into a plush chair next to a roaring hearth. Katia knew that there was a score of Scorn Guard standing watch outside her door and sensed several more had arrived since the battle ended. She had a strong feeling that if prompted, those outside her door would not let her leave. She sat there effortlessly spinning the wedding ring on her finger. It spun so freely as she had lost a significant amount of her weight over the previous few months of delirium. Now though, Katia was remembering better times that felt like a different life. She hesitantly took the ring off and placed it on the stone ledge above the hearth next to an identical one, belonging to her late husband. She had never taken her wedding ring off and that simple act caused a moment of weeping for the first time since losing Scarnin. She didn't lift her hands away from the ornate blackglass rings for a significant while, as the heat from the fire offered the comfort of a hot blanket. Eventually, she was pulled from her sorrow when the door creaked open. Scáth entered boldly, shortly after Grand Master Zenair walked in and placed his back against the door upon closing it.

"Daughter," the queen said with a sensitivity Scáth had not expected.

"Katia," she replied coldly after the unusual gesture from her mother. "Will you tell me why?"

"They'll never stop attacking us. We'll never be treated as equals unless it is under their terms," she answered, almost pleading for Scáth to understand.

"That is not true."

"It is the only truth!" she erupted. "The whole world sees us as abominations. My way could have ended the bloodshed you look upon. No more of our children being stolen." As the words left her mouth, Katia looked to the floor, ashamed, and Scáth laid a heavy stare upon her.

"It would have only taken a different form. The personal destruction of your family by your hand taught me much and fortunately showed me a world outside our own. A whole band of citizens, each from a different race brought me home because they knew it was the right thing to do. If you didn't view them as only outsiders then you would know them as allies from all corners of Litore." Scáth scolded her stubborn mother who rolled her eyes in denial of the clear treachery.

"So you become queen, what of me?" Katia retorted with immaturity and obvious cynicism. At that point, Zenair took a step further into the room.

"I'm sorry to be seeing you like this, Katia. I would offer my condolences for Arwr but fear it would fall on deaf ears. It has been agreed that you and a small contingent of Sesara soldiers will be held in the prison of my city." He was stern but diplomatic with his delivery.

"I misjudged your willingness. I don't make the same mistake twice." Katia glared hatefully at the Snow Elf. He seemed taken aback at the idle threat but smirking, he coyly replied.

"I do hope not, for both our sake."

Scáth then stepped in front of her mother once more.

"Queen Scáth." Katia scoffed in jest at the very words. Scáth leaned in close,

gripping the armrests of Katia's chair.

"Know it is with a heavy heart that I now mourn for both my parents and lament the person you once were." Scáth never yielded with her water-brimmed eyes. As the first tear streaked down her cheek she threw herself back and made for the door. She paused as her hand clasped the knob. "No, I won't be their queen. I believe this fine city deserves a better royal family."

The former Princess of ShadowScorn swung the door open to reveal several Ghosts of Aceia in the hallway, before storming away. Katia sat there dumbfounded, lost in a cloud of delusion. The elite force of Scorn women entered, bearing impressive shackles for the former queen. Zenair lifted his head as it had remained low through most of this encounter.

"I hope you don't mind the cold," he offered with a wink before he too left the chamber.

Ch16 - Redemption

The Snow Elves went about corralling the remainder of the Renrit army and separating the Sesara troops from the ordinary folk who had joined for pay and food. In doing so, it became clear that 90 soldiers and nearly 400 relatively untrained civilians were left. General Zaskee and a legion of her monks escorted the 400 folk, who had freely taken up arms against the Scorn people, from off their kingdom's land. After a half-day march, Master Zaskee instructed her warriors to unbind the prisoners of war.

"Listen well! Go back whence you came. By royal decree of Moon Mountain and the sovereign people of ShadowScorn. If any of you are to be found in their kingdoms, you will be executed on sight." General Zaskee was firm and truly frightening in her warning. The groans and grumbles of battle-weary prisoners rubbing their freed wrists echoed out. They were left with nothing but a base layer of clothing to complete their multi-cycle trek back home.

Ven remained on the front steps of the royal palace, applying salves and bandages to Agan and Faenla's wounds. Aelis was coordinating the retrieval of the dead for proper burial rites. Soon, the scared but relieved citizens began trickling out of the palace and into their once again ravaged city.

"It's good to see you again, Ven." Agan placed a hand on his friend's shoulder. It was offered with a kindness that surprised Ven but warmed his heart.

"As am I, good friend. It would appear we have a wealth of tales to exchange." Faenla interrupted Ven with a chortle as if that was an understatement. "Tell me, where has our ever-wise and tiny companion so smartly hidden himself?" Ven was eager to see his gnome mentor after their success. A slight wheezy whine issued from Faen's snout and Agan's posture visibly drooped. A familiar feeling overcame Ven. "Well?" He insisted.

"That attempt made on my life, that spurred you into action. Well, it turns out the cities Administrator was behind it while Katia pulled the strings. His effort was far greater when he made an attempt on Scáth's life." Agan forced out the words that stuck in his throat like dry food. "She fought valiantly, as did Athvar, alas he finally met a fight he could not win." Agan could barely look at the Kyst's piercing green eyes and Ven's next words crushed him.

"Where were you two?" He uttered accusingly. Agan was devastated at the loss of Athvar for the gnome had truly helped his inner turmoil during the amnesia. But, he knew Athvar's death was not on his shoulders and wasn't about to let Ven blame him.

"Don't be so quick to rest blame. There were more days of battle than respite while you were gone. I mourn the death of our companion as much as anyone but I will not let you put his death on me." Agan spoke as if to a child which surprisingly resonated with Ven. He had regretted the words as soon as he spoke them and didn't really want to blame Faenla or Agan. The coastal elf sighed heavily, tied a knot in the wrap he had applied on the half-orc, and sauntered into the palace.

Agan sighed with great sorrow before he motioned with his chin for the wolf to follow Ven. Many gracious eyes and gestures were put upon the Kyst saviour as he walked through the palace halls. Again, he was the hero but had never felt further from it. He was caught off guard when a large and furry head nuzzled under his arm as he walked. He stopped to give Faenla a long and firm hug, generating the strength for what came next.

The two hunters, whose bond grew stronger with each passing day, made their way down the spiral staircase. They stopped to get out of the way several times as Scorn Guard carrying empty stretchers made their way back up. Soon, they entered the dungeon which was packed with Scorn, all of whom carried stretchers or were shoving prisoners into cells. Ven immediately noted Oren huddled in the corner of one cell looking severely dishevelled. He did not approach, as Ven did not trust himself to contain his anger. The pair continued towards the morgue when Ven noted the magical wards of darkness and protection were lifted. Upon entering, he witnessed many ShadowScorn already occupying the seemingly innumerable amount of stone slabs. It took him little time to spot Athvar's small frame laying atop a table, so very still.

Ven reached for the scruff of Faenla's neck for strength and the mighty wolf was right beside him to offer it. They walked over to the table, where Ven sat on the stool left from Scáth's visit. His breath was visible, and Athvar's now blue body was nipped by frost. Faenla curled up into a tight ball beside Ven to combat the cold as the Kyst placed his nimble fingers on the gnomes stiff hand.

"I am so sorry I was not there, dear Athvar. You deserved better than this. I wish I had told you in person that you taught me to live a happier and fuller life. That it is okay to make mistakes so long as you learn from them. Though you stood barely above knee height, you were the father figure I needed." Ven's eye's streamed with tears and his voice gave way. "I lament the short time we had and the lessons you could not impart. Yet, I take heart knowing the after-life will be a brighter place with you in it. Until we meet again beyond the Evar Spring Glade." Ven continued to sob as he rested his head beside Athvars.

Several hours had passed when he finally lifted his head from the table, apparently having fallen asleep at some point in his mourning. The morgue was filled with cries of the living and the silence of the dead.

"War robs us of more than life."

Ven turned toward the voice, seeing Commander Aelis sitting beside a mutilated Arch Priest Torvic Gloom. She gently stroked her fingers across his forehead, as if soothing herself while holding one of his hands. Ven did not openly lament the death of Torvic but he felt another insurmountable pang of loss at the sight.

"It darkens our heart with every ounce of blood spilled. It steals from our soul that which makes us beautiful." Aelis spoke with such calm and clarity it unnerved Ven. "And at the root of it all, sprouts temporary peace rooted in everlasting hate."

"I was told if it were not for you, the efforts of Sindrum and I would have been for nothing. I understand what little reprieve that offers you now, but you saved your entire race from that ignorance and hatred. So, from one regretful born killer to another, you are not alone in this guilt you carry." Ven wished he was not so young so perhaps he could offer words that would better comfort Aelis. Yet, where he thought he was alone in feelings towards hating his talent as a warrior, he found some comfort knowing he was not. And hoped that Aelis might as well. As Ven arose to leave and felt the cold stiffness leaving his muscles, Aelis offered one last piece of advice.

"Don't wait to be honest with Scáth. Given who we are, time is not an ally."

Ven nodded just once, understanding and agreeing with the wisdom. He spent some time searching for Scáth before spotting Sindrum, who was waiting uncomfortably to enter the Great Hall. Ven watched curiously for a moment and it appeared to him as though the Scorn Captain was mustering the courage for something. Once the captain entered, Ven went to the entrance and looked in as Sindrum walked up to Scáth who was seated alone at the counsellor's table. The Kyst leaned his right shoulder on the entrance and focused his acute hearing on the interaction.

"Queen Scáth? May I have a word?" Sindrum asked while lowering his head and dropping to one knee. She turned in her chair to face him.

"So long as you don't call me that," she said without humour. "The ShadowScorn and I are in your debt, Captain."

"I have a confession, then you should decide if that is true," Sindrum stated, still looking to the blackglass, glossy, translucent floor. Scáth felt a wave of heat hit her as she was already flushed with too many emotions.

"Speak."

"I was the one who took you from your room that night. I handed you off in Renrit." Sindrum confessed and an air of silent dread filled the room.

"Look at me," Scáth demanded through gritted teeth as this really wasn't a surprise to her. Sindrum looked up at her with shame on his face. "Tell me why."

"I wanted change, I didn't know in what shape or form but I felt as though the Scorn people needed something your father wasn't giving them. The confused mind is easily twisted by the confident one. Ven showed me the truth and I do not deny I was wrong. We agreed I would submit to whatever punishment you, decided fit the crime." After speaking true, Sindrum hung his head once more, awaiting judgment.

Ven saw from the entrance Scáth's chest heaved with anxiety and frustration.

"I understand," she said in a lighter tone than Sindrum expected so he shot his glance back at her.

"You do?"

"Share with me, what was it Ven showed you?"

"Believe me or don't, that is your choice, but I died on the shores of Starlight Lake. Ven thought I still lived and carried my body for a time through wintery woods. I assume your father sang of the Evar Spring Glade when you were a child?"

Scáth wore a predictably skeptical face as she slowly nodded in response.

"It's real. The Caretaker gave me a second chance and healed Ven's grievous wounds." Sindrum said, fearing she would not believe him. Yet, Scáth smiled with relief, finally having an answer to her dilemma, which only unsettled an already concerned Sindrum.

"You have a wife, do you not?"

The question baffled Sindrum and made the eavesdropping Ven shift uncomfortably.

"I do, Your Grace. Though she did not know of my crimes, I beg she not be brought into this."

"Is she a kind and firm woman?" Scáth persisted.

"The fairest. She's only ever bettered me as Scorn," he answered reverently, as a warm smile creased his lips at the thought of his beloved, Em.

"Good," Scáth said with a now weightless conscience. "She will make a fine queen and of you, a finer king."

Sindrum felt his heart skip several beats and Ven smiled in approval. "You jest, Your Grace," the captain said hanging his head low again.

"No. I've seen the outside world and know I can do real good out there, inflict true change. I lost my family to power and greed, I would not tempt destiny and subject myself to a similar fate. And truthfully,

I have lost the stomach for it." Sindrum looked up at Scáth in true awe. "You, on the other hand, died for your people and were given a second chance at life. I would be denying both our fates if I did not relinquish my place to you."

Sindrum, still kneeling, was paralyzed with shock. "I know not what to say."

Scáth offered her hand for him to take.

"Congratulations are in order, my friend!" A now entering Ven Devar declared.

"The people will still need to approve, of course," Scáth added in reminder.

"Of course," Sindrum wholeheartedly agreed. Ven clasped Sindrum's shoulder and gave a firm nod of approval.

"Go to your wife, you've earned the rest. I will make the announcement tomorrow." Sindrum took a step back and bowed low to both before exiting. Scáth and Ven remained in the silence, finally alone.

"You never cease to amaze me. Few have the wisdom to see what you do and fewer still the will to act on it," Ven said honestly and with great admiration. Scáth took comfort knowing Ven agreed with her decision to forgo her birthright. Although, something inside told her he would have been supportive either way, which only strengthened her feelings for him.

She took his hand. "I'm sorry I acted the way I did before you left. There was so much going on but I never meant to push you away."

Ven's storm-coloured cheeks blushed at her reminder of his ill-timed kiss. "Do not apologize, I should not have been so brash. It was unfair of me to assume you wanted-" Ven was interrupted by Scáth's firm grasp on his hand and her lips passionately locking with his. The sudden shock quickly dissipated and he wrapped his arms around her as they held that single kiss for the happiest moment in either of their lives. They slowly left the kiss only to be lost in one another's gaze. Her dark swirling iris, like the heart of a hurricane, back-lit by a soft white. His opalescent green eyes ever appeared as emerald jewels of love and hope to her.

The following afternoon, Scáth had all the ShadowScorn meet in the old town square. The crowd of amassed citizens standing where they had not so long ago prayed for their princess to return home, were now devastated when Scáth announced she would be renouncing her birthright. However, the dismay was brief as she declared a feast for all would be held in the hall that night for the celebration of a new monarch, in the form of their saviour, Captain Sindrum Silver. To all in the crowd, it felt like a natural succession, especially from one who had risked his own life on countless occasions for the city. It filled Scáth with a sense of pride and optimism for the future of her people. And lifted an impossibly heavy, lifelong burden off her shoulders. For the first time in her life, she was truly free to do as she desired. That evening saw the coronation of King Sindrum and Queen Em Silver, accompanied by unrelenting applause and celebrations for their new beginning. A great feast was thrown for all, in large part on resources Moon Mountain had carted over. Hundreds of tables were brought into the great hall, which truly amazed Ven Devar, as he had never seen something so large and grand, for all in the city did actually fit inside. The melodies and vocals of great bards echoed throughout the hall to a soothing effect. Few barrels of ale or casks of wine went undrained throughout the entire palace that night. At one end of the hall sat the royal table, with King Sindum and Queen Em at the centre. Aelis and Agan found comfort beside each other, as did Ven and Scáth. So too did Grand Master Zenair and General Zaskee join them at the table.

The companions swapped many tales, although most interests were put on the journey Ven and Sindrum had endured. They expressed the journey to be the most gruelling that either had experienced before, and detailed the many dangers they had encountered throughout. Ven took the time to pass around his newly acquired short-sword that saved his life against the Vampire occupying the ancient ruins of his kin. The whole table hung onto Ven's every word, most of all Sindrum, who to this moment hadn't gotten a full recounting of Ven's disappearance in the blizzard. Grand Master Zenair even spoke of older stories between himself and King Arwr, explaining how an unlikely relationship blossomed from dire times.

"I must admit, I leave on the morrow's dawn. My esteemed daughter, Zaskee will remain behind with half our forces to continue aid however possible. It has been an honour to serve alongside you all, and I hope our two cities continue to grow ever closer," King Zenair Aradithas wished, raising his glass in toast. All at the table joined in raising the drinks, to which all in the hall gave cheers to their leaders.

"What will the Mighty Ven Devar do next?" Queried King Sindrum with the respect and interest of a true friend.

"I'll return the remains of Athvar and Rexous back to the Great Northern Rainforest for the burials they deserve," Ven replied hopefully.

It suddenly dawned on Scáth and Aelis simultaneously as they quickly met eyes. They had both been told separately, by a rather incoherent Torvic Gloom, that the body of Rexous was missing.

"Is that all?" Zenair eyed Ven, betraying that he knew more about the Kyst than Ven thought. He averted his gaze from everyone at the table and answered bashfully.

"I may have a small kingdom awaiting my return. Although, I am no ruler and never will be. A far wiser and fairer Kyst, Ilthanis Veldove looks after what is left of my people in my stead. Along with the heartfelt folk of Athvar's kin."

"It is a great and honourable quest then!" Sindrum shouted, raising his glass once more and the Scorn well-rehearsed, reciprocated with a roar. As everyone drank, Ven made eye contact with the Grand Master, and received a very enthusiastic and approving nod. Ven returned the nod with a smile.

"And what will 'Agan, the Nation-less Knight' do next?" Sindrum addressed the half-orc in a liquor filled vigour. Aelis couldn't suppress an abrupt laugh.

"The Nation-less Knight?" She replied, sniffling back the ale she had snorted up in a chuckle. Agan, also taken aback, furrowed a brow at the Scorn King.

"Your reputation for fighting in the wars of other races has officially preceded you, Master Agan," Grand Master Zenair explained. Ven and Scáth found no shortage of good natured humour in this and the Kyst mocked a curtsy on Agan's behalf.

"First off, I'm no knight. I do think it fitting I remain with Ven until Athvar's remains see a restful burial." Agan looked at Aelis, hoping to garner her honest reaction. She just smiled and leaned against his broad shoulder.

"Ever will the heroes from the Siege of Shadow be honoured guests in our city!" Sindrum shouted, springing up to his feet. Not for the last time that night, every glass and tankard shot up in the air, spilling sweet wine and foamy ale hither and yon in merriment and celebration.

The next morning saw the group standing outside the destroyed gate of the city entrance. A dozen masons, and half that many carpenters and smithies worked busily around the clock to restore the gate and surrounding stone. Ven watched as Scáth approached Katia, their exchange was brief and appeared somewhat amicable. After seeing Grand Master Zenair off properly, along with the other prisoners and half the Frozen Fist army, Ven spoke to Sindrum.

"Are Athvar and Rexous prepped for travel? I've been gone too long as it currently stands."

Sindrum cleared his throat, gathering his thoughts before answering. "Athvar's remain's are ready, however, the priests are having trouble locating the body of Rexous. I am sure it's a misunderstanding with all the current confusion. I will alert you as soon as he has been located."

"Actually," Scáth interjected sorrowfully. "Before you returned, Torvic began acting strangely and mentioned the Kyst was gone. At the time I hadn't known what it meant and I did not get the chance to speak with him again." She bit off her words, as the loss was still too fresh for her. Ven took a step back from everyone, for some reason feeling a sense of betrayal.

"What am I suppose to do with that information?" The ill-mannered elf snapped. It was obvious to at least Scáth that he was simmering with anger. All felt the uncomfortable air settle when Scáth then placed a delicate hand on his arm and a firm look toward his eyes. Ven looked away in frustration, reluctantly understanding.

"Forgive me," he said before walking off with Faenla close behind. Ven was headed to the warehouse district, as he was set to grab horses and a wagon full of provisions for the journey back. Scáth watched him go with concern evident about her.

"Even after all this." Agan faintly motioned to the city of shadow in ruins. "His trials and tribulations are just beginning," The fighter stated for the benefit of all, but also as a reminder to Scáth of the precarious situation that Ven was returning to.

"Come along." Aelis wrapped an arm around Scáth. "We must aid the king in appointing a new Arch Priest and Administrator," she teased with sarcastic excitement, which had Scáth in a giggle.

"Can you believe that!" Ven exclaimed to Faenla as the pair strode through the recovering streets. The wolf, ever intelligent, snorted in agreement, just wanting to make Ven feel better rather than expressing an opinion. "Just gone! Surely he was dead, so Āina and Kaia know he didn't just walk out of there. Torvic had the morgue sealed tight with magical glyphs and wards preventing this very thing. Just up and gone!" Ven, refusing to look at the situation calmly, might have noticed that they were being tailed. The pair stopped to view the massive boulder that was used to demolish the cities entrance, for it now lay deeply embedded into a three-story building. A handful of masons stood around it, scratching their heads, at a loss for a solution that would cause minimal destruction to the remaining structure.

"Wow," Ven said in disbelief at the sheer size of it. Faenla bobbed his head in knowing agreement. Then, an elderly Scorn man stepped out behind them.

"Morning!" The high-pitched and excited voice had the pair shudder uncomfortably. They both turned to regard the Scorn. He was short for a human and was permanently hunched over; from a life in the mines, Ven guessed. His teeth were sparsely scattered throughout his mouth and his eyes were bloodshot with veins of shadow.

"Morning," Ven replied respectfully. The elderly Scorn left a long silence as he looked the hunter up and down. "Excuse us, we have a great many things to attend too," Ven continued politely before turning around to leave. He was met by the elderly man standing directly in front of him again. His eyes shot wide at the sudden appearance.

"You know not what awaits you, Ven Devar." The Kyst's expression quickly turned to a dower one. "Your return will mean the death of so many and the ruin of much more. They are better off without you." The Scorn peered deeply into Ven's eyes, who shook his head in frustration.

"Leave me be." He bared his teeth threateningly. This time Ven pushed past the Scorn with ease.

"Return and he dies," said the elderly man with sinister delight. Ven stopped in his tracks, turning to confront him.

"Who dies?" But the Scorn only smirked before fading from sight. Ven looked to Faenla.

"What is happening around here?" He muttered frustratingly, before hanging his head with a mountain of self-doubt looming over him. He was still reeling from the fact that he had killed Rexous; someone he had an extremely complicated but meaningful relationship with. It plagued his every waking thought and now this unusual encounter filled Ven with the want to give up. Still tilted in defeat, he shook his head, his long green locks flowing wildly like the anger boiling within. He pulled his long and wide hood up, barring anyone the chance to communicate with him and continued on with his task.

Ch17 - Claw Canyon

Claw Canyon sat a few days from Silva in the Great Northern Rainforest, and was currently enjoying the niceties of what home life could offer. Out of the 16 month calendar, winter was the only time that the Kintar berserkers and raiders were not battling. Although it rarely snowed in the rainforest, and when it did it never stuck around long, the Kintar took this time to recuperate. The weather conditions were poor. Rain often wouldn't cease for many cycles at a time and dense fog made life difficult. It was a time to reconnect with loved ones and share stories of their years glory. While celebrating every night at the opportunity to die in battle still before them. The Kintar of all ages and gender lived solely to impress and honour the God of Battle, Lokor. These elves, once akin to the Kyst, now sought meaning in the act of combat. It was their way of praying to the one they so idolized, and they found no greater honour than to give one's life in battle.

This winter was like any other. As the height of the third month neared, another cloudy morning hung above the large settlement of Claw Canyon. The Kintar were very intelligent; geniuses in the art of warfare. Their intellect transcended into their architecture, not to be outdone by the brazen Kyst in their tall trees, as they had built great homes up and down the jagged cliffs and walls of Claw Canyon. Timber homes clung to the blackened, wet, mossy rock, like fungi to a trunk. Long bridges strung between buildings, supported by thick rope, swayed in the howling wind.

A Kintar Berserker in his second century of life stood in the centre where the bridge swung the most, with his scarred hands gripping firmly onto the rope handrail. A fog given dew glistened against his mahogany red skin. Tribal tattoos covered him from his bald head to his bare toes. Furs from a bisonbear adorned just enough of his skin to keep the wet chill off his bones. A broadsword made from the serrated bone of a Timber Dragon was strapped across his back.

"They are not coming back, Njor," a strong voice sounded out, and Njor opened his eyes for the first time in hours. He did not, however, give Rinya the satisfaction of looking at them. Njor's grip tightened on the coarse rope in his grasp.

"Leave me," Njor retorted, answering in his guttural native tongue of Kintish. Rinya sidled up next to Njor and rested their left elbow on the rope, so they could still face the sulking Kintar.

"Bed a new lass, make a new daughter. For Lokor's sake, do something, anything, and spare us all this melancholy." Rinya both teased and begged simultaneously. He did rest his dark stare upon Rinya now. Njor SwordSplinter had been away later than most of the Kintar raiders, as he and a small troop had been hired out at great cost to attack Kyst settlements with Ven Devar. During that time, Njor's spouse and daughter had left Claw Canyon, in particular, to get away from him. In truth, many Kintar were beginning to look for other options in showing their respect to Lokor. More and more were questioning the way in which so many innocents had to die, just so they could prove themselves to their deity. Many of the other Kintar tribes that had spread to other rainforests in Litore, had already moved on from their old ways. Some might say that the Kintar of the Great Northern Rainforest were the last of their kind, rooted so deeply in their traditions and origins.

So, when Njor had discovered that his family had left him in search of a safer and more peaceful existence, he had spent the next several winter months in a hazy intoxicated stupor. He had still been drunk the night before when he first gripped the rope. Nearly half a day later, he found himself cold, sober, and irritated by his fellow berserker, Rinya.

"Not all of us can find comfort in the arms of a different person every night." Njor looked deadpan into Rinya's eyes.

"If your misses, well rather ex-misses, has proven anything, it's that your arms aren't that comforting." Rinya delivered the insult without missing a beat. Njor took a deep breath and sighed heavily.

"Are you here only to piss me off?"

Rinya chuckled. "Chief Warsmith requests you."

Njor looked back through the foggy chasm. "We'll need a drink first."

Less than an hour later, Njor SwordSplinter and Rinya WitBlade were standing before Chief Warsmith, Skerra Stinjara. 'Warsmith' was an honorific title bestowed upon the great leaders and tacticians of Kintar society. The Chief Warsmiths were so highly regarded, they would often be elevated into a role that would see them act as a ruler over tribes. Skerra was a burly Kintar female, with great vein bulging muscles and a mind that not only looked upon the present with clarity, but the future with careful foresight. Njor had found himself in this position before, and knew Skerra would never speak first.

"Chief Warsmith, what can I assist you with?" Njor offered with the bow of an adherent. When he looked up, he noticeably saw a pulsing vein in Skerra's neck. He furrowed his brow in worry.

"You organized a band of berserkers near the autumn equinox?" She queried angrily. Njor was caught off-guard, for this particular contract was not to be spoken of once completed, for this exact reason.

"Yes, Chief Warsmith. Nor for the first time, Chief Warsmith," he quickly answered.

"How many other times had you sworn your berserker's to secrecy?" Rinya looked to the floor, so as not to give away that they in fact had been privy to those prior secret jobs in great detail.

"None, I assure you." Njor responded, hesitantly.

"Lie to me again, Njor, and I peel the skin from your flesh and watch you feast on it. I have allowed your not-so-secret mercenary contracts to go unpunished because we once battled side-by-side. And to be fair, keeping our berserkers busy stays them from getting in trouble here." Njor listened, accepting her words.

"When we had finally rid ourselves of Silva, we did so with tact and a calculated risk of a return assault. But when you laid waste to the entire coast, under the behest of Uthul, your actions put the lives of every Kintar in the north at risk. You've been reckless in recent years which has only increased in frequency. Now you remain in a drunken haze and a burden to all at the news of your wife and child's departure." Skerra ended on a scolding note.

"Forgive me," Njor said dejectedly.

"My point exactly! 'Forgive me' is not in the vocabulary of Njor SwordSplinter, or our people. What has soured your spirit?" She asked, now out of concern for a friend. Njor remained quiet for a long moment.

"The world outside is changing unlike ever before. We can all feel it. Are we not one of the few tribes who cling to the old ways? Perhaps, I believed I could prove Torva wrong or make her proud anew. If I could show my true heart to Lokor, he would grant what I seek. I see now, I only sealed my fate through the actions I took to change it. So do what you will with me, Chief Warsmith." He firmly held his gaze on Skerra but with palpable loss in his eyes.

Skerra turned her vision to Rinya, who had remained with their eyes on the floor, until a long silence filled the room and they felt eyes resting upon them. So Rinya looked back up to meet the eye line of Skerra.

"You have battled long with Njor SwordSplinter and are among his few true friends, what say you to his fate?" Skerra asked Rinya. Rinya looked to Njor, who in return gave a small nod.

"I would, Chief Warsmith, throw him to the Sunken Swamp. He will either die in battle as all Kintar should or live to fight another day, proving Lokor's favour of him still." Rinya suggested with some degree of difficulty.

"With as little respect as possible, take your redemption trial and shove it up your arse. I've survived it once, I will not go again." Njor spat vehemently.

"Then you will kneel in front of Rinya right now and she will remove your pathetic head from your sad shoulders, and Lokor can banish your soul to the Underworld in shame," Skerra threatened. It surprised the Warsmith and Rinya both to see Njor contemplating his choice for as long as he did.

"Let us be done with it."

An hour later, Skerra, Rinya, and Njor had walked through the Great Northern Rainforest, east. They came to a large clearing where a 100-metre wide sinkhole dropped 20 or so metres into the earth. It formed a soggy and decaying patch of forest with brown scum layered pools of water. There were two caves in the sunken rock wall, enshrouded by vines and root systems that then spread out across the base of the swamp. One of the larger pools of muck in the centre was rumoured to be an underwater tunnel to the Underworld.

"Has anyone heard what calls the Sunken Swamp home these days?" Njor asked, hoping to gain some level of intelligence before entering the natural arena. Given its strategic placement and level of security with the caves, the swamp became a popular place for monsters and the sort to dwell, often fighting each other, and always leaving the strongest to call it home.

"I heard a bisonbear wandered in from the plains and fell in," Rinya said, looking over the edge down into the swamp with no sort of envy for Njor. "No, an Oni ate that beast months ago. My guess is that a demonic spirit still resides in one of the caves," Skerra said, mimicking Rinya's actions. Njor simply grunted in frustration before clasping arms with Rinya, and locking foreheads in a way to say good-bye to each other.

"Enjoy the show, Chief Warsmith." Before she could reply, Njor grabbed a vine and began his descent. When he reached the bottom, he wiggled his toes through his sandals to feel the cold coil of moss and roots. He unsheathed his bone-white sword, made from the horn of a Timber dragon. It was denser than any metal and could be sharpened to a razor thin edge without losing durability. It was with this sword that Njor had earned his last name, as all Kintar did, after having earned it.

Njor circled the perimeter with both hands on his broadsword. After no movement was detected, he cupped one hand to the side of his mouth and made the bellow of Bulk Elk. This was a trick Kintar often leveraged into ambushing Kyst Hunters. When this call lured nothing from the caves, he dropped his readied battle stance. He could not see this from his low vantage point, but a long line of vines and roots had begun worming their way through the swamp towards him.

The berserker looked back up to Skerra and Rinya, shrugging his shoulders. As he did so, an amalgamation of debris and vines took form from the earth. Lifted by the knees to a standing position was a humanoid shape, just a few paces behind Njor. When he saw Rinya shaking her head doubtfully, he realized something was behind him. Too late. Roots and vines sprung around his feet and quickly climbed up his legs. He barely managed to rip one foot free but was quickly grappled by the humanoid shaped monster. Njor was left wide stanced and arms restrained at his sides as this thing began to pull him down into the swamp.

Being the berserker he was, he began grunting and roaring like a raging bear. He breathed heavily and his muscles surged with adrenaline. Thinking of his lost wife and daughter, he roared and burst free of the restraining vines. Pieces of earth exploded like shrapnel from his sheer burst of power, as he deftly spun and sliced what remained of the monster, in half. Four more of what he now knew to be dryads, glided seamlessly across the swamp towards him, as if one with the ground. He ducked as one of them shot forth a long vine meant to skewer him. Unfortunately, he dodged right into another that pierced through his shoulder. The formidable Kintar roared in pain and grabbed the vine, yanking as hard as he could, pulling the dryad toward him. He met it by cleanly lopping its head off. Njor deftly side-stepped to avoid another stinger and wasted no time in rushing the dryad. He ducked low as a rotten log was thrown at him and then fell into a roll. The berserker came out of the dive already mid swing and sliced the dryad in half. The remaining two sent a volley of stingers at him. Already tired of being nimble, Njor started cutting the stringers in half, mid-flight. Favouring strength over dexterity, however, he was struck several times by their lightning quick vines. He hurled his broadsword, end over end, toward one dryad. It raised its tree-like arms to catch the blade with dozens of roots stretching out in aid. The blade never lost momentum as it split the dryad down the middle.

The last dryad fell into, and became one with the swamp again. Njor had a hand axe strapped to his waist, but instead he kept his hands free, watching the ground around him intently. His breath came in great gulps and his eyes were blood-shot with pure intensity. He spotted the dryad moving around him, attempting to get behind the berserker. Watching carefully, he jumped in a spin and came down, driving his forearm into the ground. As he stood up he gave a great grunt and ripped the dryad out of the roots and vines. He lifted it above his head and yanked in opposite directions. The dryads head popped from its shoulders and one leg ripped away from its hip. Njor threw the limbs down and roared once more like a great bisonbear.

The steam of anger released was visible against the cold, damp evening air.

Njor retrieved his great sword. "Where are the rest of you?" He quietly said to himself through heaving breaths. After hearing an unfamiliar disturbance in the northern cave, he turned his attention there. Completely looking the wrong way, a vine as fast as lightning and easily the width of a small trunk, shot out and wrapped itself around Njor, pulling him into the dark cave as quickly as it emerged. Rinya and Skerra both immediately took a step forward in response. As Njor's echoing yell faded, a great bellow was heard. There was silence for a long moment before his yell returned and he fired like a cannon out of the cave mouth. He was ejected with such force, his body skipped across the large pond in the middle, like a stone. Vines emerged from the cave like tentacles clinging to the sunken swamp. Great thunderous steps boomed from within. Njor rubbed his bruised head and slowly got back to his feet. Rinya couldn't be sure, but it looked as though Njor was waving them away. Another decibel defying roar sounded from the cave mouth, and Rinya and Skerra, who had both taken that previous step forward, now took a step back.

From within the cave emerged a massive scaled snout with what looked like half the forest hanging off it, and row upon row of jagged teeth. Great vibrant, piercing green eyes opened, offering a terrifying visage against the dark cave mouth.

"I see you, SwordSplinter, come to kill me with that which you stole all those years ago?" An almost snake-like voice resounded around the sunken swamp.

"If this is where I had known you'd been hiding, I would have come a long time ago." Njor answered defiantly. The beast emerged in its full fury. A Timber Dragon, with one horn on its head ridge missing. It spread its massive wings and stood on four powerful legs, with spear-like claws. The dragon blended seamlessly with its forest environment as the living forest grew on, and between, its green and brown scales.

"Lokor has forsaken me now," Njor mumbled to himself, getting back into his fighting stance.

The Timber Dragon's chest expanded and exhaled a huge cloud of spores throughout the whole swamp. From it, hundreds of pockets of fungi began to immediately grow on anything decaying. Njor recoiled in pain as the wave of spores washed over him, and the few cuts and stinger wounds he had received instantly began to grow mould, and decay his flesh. He roared with all the might he could and charged at the dragon. The great behemoth smirked its wicked grin and hundreds of vines shot from the ground. One skewered straight through Njor's foot but he did not cease his charge. The dragon reared to land his fore claw on the Kintar but Njor proved the faster. He slashed his sword across the claw, with the dragons very own bone. The dragon screeched from the gash along its front right claw and flew upward, the wind knocking the berserker over. The dragon did a mid-flight somersault and brought its long bark-like tail crashing down onto the prone Njor. He felt like a tree had just landed on him as the air was crushed from his lungs. Njor weakly rolled onto his back, as the dragon stood over him.

"The smell of rot, like a garnish on your flesh," the dragon snarled while lowering its head to devour Njor. The berserker called to Lokor one last time, to fill his spirit and fuel his bones with rage. As the Timber Dragon opened its giant jaw, Njor buried his hand axe between two of its teeth, sending it deep into the jaw. The dragon roared and reared up, with Njor still hanging on. The behemoth went to grasp the berserker with its wounded claw, but Njor acted first. He dropped the several metres and let his falling momentum, with his sword in hand, sever the other side of the giant clawed hand. As Njor landed on the ground, so too did the dragon's right forehand. The Greatwyrm spun like a cyclone and nailed Njor with his tail, before beating its powerful wings and taking to the tree canopy. The berserker was sent flying halfway across the swamp, before colliding with the unforgiving wall of densely twisted roots. He hit the ground, barely conscious, but enough to realize that most of his ribs were cracked and broken.. He found himself unable to move from the position of being on all fours. When he breathed, it was ragged, and a wet wheeze followed.

"There can be no doubt, Lokor favours him still," Rinya said to Skerra. The Chief Warsmith was awe struck, less than few ever lived to tangle with a dragon. Let alone twice with the same one. They both quickly made their way down and over to Njor. They quickly spotted that one of his lower right ribs had shattered and emerged from his back. It stuck out nearly a hand's width, but neither Kintar slowed in their march. Skerra placed her hands on both of Njor's shoulders, lifting his torso upright.

"Something feels wrong," Njor said weakly, trying to look over his shoulder to see why Rinya was inspecting his back. "I can hardly breathe." "We've gotta kill the fungi infesting your wounds. I've never actually seen a Timber Dragon's breath in action." Skerra spoke to keep Njor distracted as she lit a torch. She quickly looked to Rinya, who was about to pull out the remaining dozen centimetres of Njor's rib. Skerra gently hovered the torch over one of the pincer wounds that was now infected. "This will hurt." Skerra nodded to Rinya as she plunged the torch into his wound, and they tore out the rib. A shock of pain was visible in Njor's eyes before he abruptly passed out. Rinya let the unconscious berserker slump against them and Skerra took advantage as she burned out the rest of the festering spores in his wounds. They sewed him up and wrapped a bandage tightly around his torso. Once that was done, Rinya slapped his face several times. Njor came too, followed by a pained whine. "Ow," Njor said while taking a deep breath now that his lungs were unimpeded.

"Let's get you back and put a tankard in your hand." Rinya slapped their comrade hard in the back supportively, but aware it would hurt. Njor grunted, trying to act as though the simple gesture didn't want to make him vomit.

Day had turned to night by the time the trio sauntered back into Claw Canyon and a heavy curtain of rain fell upon the world. Rinya and Skerra were not surprised when Njor refused aid, even though he was walking with a bad limp. They paused on one of the many rope bridges that connected the buildings on both sides of the canyon. The rain had a way of filling the void in the canyon with a mesmerizing mist.

"It's quiet," Rinya noted suspiciously. All in the canyon seemed normal to Njor but he knew he had hit his head pretty hard.

"The patrols haven't returned," Skerra stated. understood how their Warsmith knew it, but they believed her completely. The Kintar were taught to be warriors from the time they could walk. Merciless training, and exposure to brutality from a young age, meant they grew up quick. From the time they could read and speak, they were taught the intricacies and finer points of battle strategy. This dedication to war and their reverence of Lokor, created Litore's most cunning and savage combatants. So, when a Kintar tumbled off the cliff edge above them, silenced by a single arrow to his chest, they watched as he fell out of sight into the mist below. Immediately, all three of them sounded the Kintar roar, yet only a few heart beats later were they halted with shock. A giant portal formed in the sky, that's edges held the appearance of torn fabric, and from it, fell a massive rotting cedar tree. It landed barely 30 metres up the canyon, and tore a whole row of homes from their anchors. Njor gripped the rope as the sight of it stunned him. The group watched as a second portal opened on the other side of the canyon and dropped a similar rotting tree. It too taking out a large sect of homes.

Njor looked to Skerra and Rinya who might have just for the first time in their lives, been left in shock.

"Get everyone out!" he shouted forcefully. Skerra looked to him, then to Rinya and quickly dashed across the bridge. As she neared the other side, Njor watched helplessly as an arrow whistled effortlessly into the neck of his Warsmith. Rinya gave a horrified roar at the sight of their beloved comrade murdered so abruptly. Njor spun his head and saw a single Kyst Hunter standing on the lip of the canyon. He stared at her, instantly noting her impressive armour and weapons. She did not draw another arrow, but stared back at him.

Rinya ran and dived beside Skerra, it was quickly apparent she was gone. Rinya looked back to the hunter standing dominantly above them, with a snarl. They saw more and more portals opening, destroying the whole of Claw Canyon's remarkable settlement. Soon, the Kintar warriors, berserkers and the few regular folk that weren't fighters, were using the carved out stairwells to surface in great numbers. Rinya was off to join them in haste, while Njor was held still by the stare of this peculiar Kyst. He first thought it to be Ven Devar who he had followed in the early winter, but soon understood this one to be female. As falling trees destroyed the world around him, he began to see Kintar being forced back and over the cliff edge. He listened to the screams and roars of kin plummeting to their death.

"Fight me!" Njor roared with sheer contempt. The hunter smirked and replaced her bow. She deftly climbed and leaped down to the beginning of the bridge that Njor was on. The rain had yet to cease, and small streams of water trickled between the wood planks. The Kyst walked confidently and drew back her hood while removing a sai from her hip. The hunter was none other than Eevie Hara, sister of deceased Qiri, and general to Vakar's new army. Her amber skin glistened in the moisture and her hazelnut eyes spoke only of murderous intent.

"You burned Silva to the ground." She never slowed her pace while she spoke.

"It was my genuine pleasure," Njor snarled sickly.

"I think I know what you mean," Eevie answered as another tree destroyed a row of buildings. She deftly jabbed the berserker in the upper shoulder before spinning low and dragging her tri-pointed dagger across his thigh. The pain only fuelled Njor's body and he responded by kicking the nimble Kyst. Eevie was thrown back a few paces but rolled with her momentum until she was back on her feet. She looked at Njor who was fuming now, his veins popping and his entire body tense with rage. Eevie hated berserkers more than any foe, but she knew who this Kintar was.

"Do you even remember him?" She spat rabidly.

"Do you remember all the vermin you've killed?" Njor replied in a rage while unsheathing his bone sword. He charged at the intruder, who threw a knife at him and found her mark in his other shoulder. Njor didn't slow and drove his hilt into her almost awaiting nose. She landed on her back and he swung down at her, hewing several boards in the bridge in two. Harra grabbed the side of the rope and rolled over the edge of the bridge to avoid his strike. She used her momentum and grip to swing herself up and through the bottom of the hole that Njor had just made, and planted her foot right under his chin. Njor stumbled back several steps and Eevie landed confidently in front of him. His eyes felt like they would pop from his head, for he saw only red.

He threw a hail of swings at her and she expertly dodged every single one. Wherever his sword aimed, she inexplicably shifted around it. His muscles did not tire though. He could swing his broadsword maliciously for hours. Eevie, well practised in her craft, found the opportune time to slice Njor's wrist deeply, as she dodged one sloppy strike. Njor barely felt the wound, but purposefully exposed his midriff for an attack. Eevie, hungry for this kill, took the bait. Njor deftly snapped out a free hand and caught the hunter by her fragile elven neck. Fury consumed her face as she strained her neck muscles against his iron grip. Njor was going to savour the imminent crack and vibration of her spine breaking. However, if the berserker had not been in the sheer frenzy he was, he may have felt the numbness consuming his hand and arm. Eevie smiled at him as there was barely any pressure on her neck now, for Njor's wrist was pouring blood. He looked at her and swung his sword with his good arm. She however, pierced her sai straight through his other forearm, and simultaneously drove her twin sai into his heart. He looked at her as if she had just revealed the answer to all his problems. She spun with lightning speed and kicked the berserker who had killed her brother off the bridge.

Njor felt a sense of weightlessness as he fell hundreds of metres to his ultimate demise. Thousands of Kintar fell around him, as an ambush of Kyst Hunters and Sages awaited for those exiting the canyon to the surface. He watched the bridge above disappear into the mist and all around him fell silent. He heard the sweet sound of clashing steel and felt the pride he had known when he had become a berserker. His final seconds of consciousness was the laughter of his wife and daughter echoing in his mind. Njor SwordSplinter hit the rocky basin below, the impact too sudden and powerful to be registered in his mind before blackness consumed him.

Several hours later, the canyon floor was littered with Kintar men, women, and children. Shrapnel of what their homes and lives used to be sat in heaps as the rain formed a small stream of watered down blood in an otherwise dried up basin. A single form walked up the valley to where the settlement had crashed. A larger than life human, clad in sparse leather armour, with a shield in one hand and spear in the other. His eyes glowed a blood red and his step carried an impossible weight behind it. His very presence brought a certain divinity to it, albeit diminished. This godly warrior was none-other than Lokor himself and he paused over the very dead and broken body of Njor SwordSplinter. Lokor knelt down beside the Kintar and placed his shield and spear on the ground. Even on one knee, he was still taller than any humanoid on Litore. Lokor gripped Njor's cold and stiff hand, the very act of which sealed the cut on his wrist. The glow around Lokor began to fade and the colour in Njor returned. Lokor gave a low sigh as his corporeal form faded from existence and into Njor. A moment later, the Kintar Berserker sprang up with a gasp.

Ch18 - The Beginning of the End

Vengeful-looking storm clouds rolled over Serenstrom to fully enshroud the pearlescent city. A warm rain flooded from the sky, extinguishing torches and forming fast running streams down the streets, to eventually pour out over the sea wall. Shutters clattered violently and doors were blown asunder, creating a cacophonous symphony, orchestrated by howling winds. A dense and heavy fog settled, making visibility past your hand impossible. A bolt of red lightning struck the highest structure in Serenstrom, the centre spire of the holy church. A wisp of smoke coiled off the polished stone and there remained a humanoid. He wore synthetic materials as an agile layer of armour over thick canvas clothing. A rigid but sleek helmet hid his face, save for two angular lenses where his eyes would be. They gave off a dim crimson glow as he analyzed his surroundings. He appeared from the lightning bolt on one knee and slowly stood to find himself on a small veranda. Peering in through glass doors he saw the darkened council chamber. Pulling on the pine doors, he made his way across the room with the silence of an owl. He walked up a staircase on the opposite side of the room with precise, calculated steps.

Soon, he found himself looking into the bed chambers of his target, Charles O'Donnell. The Macer slept peacefully in his silken sheets, lulled to sleep by the rhythmic sounds of the storm. Large stained-glass windows lined this circular room, the images distorted by the streaks of trickling rain. The room appeared slightly different through the lenses of the helmet, as it was designed to see through magical illusions and give the wearer perfect clarity in darkness. Creeping quietly, the humanoid held a crystal vial in his hand. As he loomed over the sleeping Macer, he slowly uncorked it and poured the radiant liquid into the snoring mouth of Charles. The Macer and everything he was adorned in, slowly and peacefully vanished from existence. He stood upright and placed a gloved finger to where his ear would be on the helmet and said with a distorted voice.

"The target has been erased."

The room suddenly filled with laughter of a maniacal nature, and he dropped his hand to his side where a weapon was strapped to his hip. The room turned upside down, sending the humanoid falling, only to connect against a hard surface in a dimension known on Litore, as the Void. A haunting and bellowing voice surrounded him.

"My, my, I must be special to warrant a visit from a 'Negator,' the voice of Macer O'Donnell echoed mockingly.

"What is this?" The negator asked, looking around slowly, hoping to discover his whereabouts and some means of escape. And yet, from everything his helmet told him, there was nothing false about his predicament.

"Your science is sorely outmatched by my divine sorcery. You and the Keepers still have much to understand about Litore." The voice faded wistfully, leaving the negator alone in a realm of greyness with waist height smoke swirling eternally.

Back in the bed-chamber of the Macer, all was normal as Charles stood at his foot board with a pensive but smug expression. He had achieved the impossible, for he had successfully defeated an agent of the Keepers; the 'protectors' of Litore, although that was a self-proclaimed title. He knew too that this would not be the end of their attempts against his life, which provided a great many bitter realities, but proved as well that Ivan's sudden disappearance was no coincidence in the connection to this visit. Now, his plans for unifying Litore under the edicts of Sesara would have to be fast-tracked.

He would start by taming a small section of the Magma Isles. This could be achieved with relative ease through the military might of the church and its immeasurable wealth. There, mostly Merchant vessels and Pirates sailed the seas; both excellent sources for spreading the word. The islands themselves were filled mostly by tribal folk, which the Macer was confident he could bend to his will through gifts and an iron fist. From there he could more easily populate and sway the central third of Litore, which had almost completely avoided the presence of the church of Sesara thus far. He too was owed a favour by the newly crowned King of Kyst, and could assure that the 'Guardian Elves' of the north would stay out of his way. The Kintar were cunning and intelligent creatures who relished battle with a god-given fervour. They could easily be bought with the promise of raids and tidy sums of gems and jewels. Whenever a town or Lordship refuted the good word of Sesara, Kintar raids could be issued with zero affiliation to the church or the Macer. For now, he crawled back into bed, confident on a good nights rest.

Aunna Morningthorne had just left a council meeting wherein it was decreed that Ivan the Revered was a traitor to the state. The news hadn't surprised her after the last conversation with her former mentor. A paladin named Runa Ringnir was appointed as Arch Paladin to the church and was granted a seat on the council. This, however, did surprise Aunna. For there were many more qualified and experienced paladin's to appoint before Runa. Ivan had spoken to Aunna before about Runa's potential to be a prized student if it were not for her obsession with strength, and at times, cruel nature. Given her own former training as a paladin before moving to Ifan's teachings as a Cleric, Aunna was perturbed by the fact that the Macer didn't ask her opinion.

Aunna shuddered when she heard Runa shouting after her. The oafish paladin came lumbering through the hall, brazenly bumping past many priests in the process.

"I just wanted to say, I know you and Ivan have always shared familial feelings for one another. I hope my replacing him does not pit us against one another." Runa offered genuinely. Yet, Aunna could tell this was meant more than an optimistic extension of goodwill but as a warning.

"Of course not Runa, congratulations are in order," Aunna said kindly, but with distinct distance. She half curtsied before abruptly walking away. Aunna then felt the firm hand of Runa clamp her wrist.

"You know I have ambitions, don't you?" Runa asked. Aunna stared back disinterested. "I thought a woman like you might know how to get in the Macer's favour." A lewd smile crossed her lips. Aunna easily tore her arm free of Runa. The Paladin was shocked with the power in which she did so.

"If arse kissing is your plan, speak with Igon. The Fjell brothers raised me, and we do not garner favour unless it's done with honour," Aunna scolded with a clear undercurrent of superiority.

"That got one killed and the other exiled. What do you think lies in wait for you?" Runa bowed low with a smirk and walked down the hall. Aunna watched Runa depart, containing her anger, before she continued to her tower.

She walked up her turret and the spiral staircase within. The walls, not unlike Ivan's, were lined with oil paintings. They were not of her victories and feats, rather, vividly detailed portraits of the most beautiful places she had travelled. There were vista's from the Kingdom of Elemental warriors in Elemenzin, the snowy mountain peaks of Rhogar, the jaw dropping crystal clear waters and sandy white beaches of the Magma Isles, and the fragrant and sun kissed fields of rolling lavender in Iridawnia. Each one she had painted herself, each one a memory of peacefulness immortalized on canvas.

She entered her chamber that was scattered with gifts and relics from the many countries across Litore. On her patio was a magically heated pool that had a stream of water perpetually being drawn into it from the sky. Aunna stopped dead in her tracks when she noticed a resplendent woman seated on the edge of the pool, skimming her hand across the surface of the steamy water. She couldn't see the woman's face but she was clearly outlined by a shimmering aura.

"At the dawn of the First Age, the first words I spoke were of peace and love between all races." Aunna felt the diadem on her head, a holy symbol to Sesara, tingle with warmth. "When man, elf, dwarf, and dragon-blood saw to the near and total decimation of each other, I wept for 11 days and 11 nights. My tears washed across the land to extinguish all flames. Man had twisted their belief into justifying war. Elves had forgotten the blood they sprang from and succumbed to pettiness. Dwarves had forsaken the eternal bond of kinship for the lust of gold and gems. Dragon-Bloods remained little else than children to the god of death."

Aunna couldn't tell if she was stuck in a dream or if it was some cruel joke of the Trickster god, Zeries. She had stepped her way around to face the woman who she was certain now was Sesara. For no dream nor trick could feel this wholesome.

"Why do you tell me this?" Aunna asked as if in prayer, with her voice slightly quivering.

"At the dawn of the Second Age, the first words I spoke were of the preservation of life and all things light. Man is fickle and quick to forget. Elves left the races in search of solitude and recovering lost tradition. Dwarves found the value of kinship once more but at the cost of respect for others. Dragon-Bloods ceased their murderous ways, but refused to better the world outside their own."

The Cleric of Sesara clearly saw the tears streaking across the divine cheeks of her deity. "Sesara, why do you weep?" Aunna asked with the frailty of a child comforting a crying mother.

"The dawn of a new age is upon you, an age without gods. First, you must weather the end of this era. I tell you this now as your mother, so you may ignite the next age with the wisdom to start a new era built upon peace." The tears never lessened. Aunna saw them filling her pool and generating ripples of pure radiance pulsating throughout. She was not surprised to hear the end of age was upon them, for she knew well that all things come to an end.

"An age without gods? How is that possible?"

"I am already dead, daughter. Soon the others will follow and that will be the end. You must rise up and lead the survivors into a time of peace and life."

Aunna nearly fainted at the words. "How can you be dead and before me at the same time?"

"Because you are my offspring. The seed inside your mother was planted by my will. So long as you live, a piece of me lives with you. Heed my words daughter, Charles O'Donell mustn't see the first sun rise on the new age. Find the others of your kind, or risk the end of Litore forever." As those words seemingly echoed out, Sesara laid a nourishing smile on Aunna before fading from sight.

Ivan returned his mount in Port Ozos with a fine tip to the stable hand. He made his way directly to the docks in search of Captain Tsuni and her ship, The Horizons Edge. An unforgiving storm from the north struck the city with a torrential downpour. It wasn't all too uncommon for storms like this to hit during the transition of winter to spring, but Ivan felt that something was unique about this storm. The violent winds and rain kept most folk indoors, which was a relief to the road-weary traveller as he wished to avoid any more detours.

Upon arriving at the docks, he easily spotted Tsuni's barque. Walking down the slip he heard the familiar voices and song reverberating through the Horizon's hull. Only a few crew remained topside to brave the storm, but found cover under tarps. They were elated to see Ivan's return and greeted him as such. One of the children he had rescued from the slave trader, the young river-nymph, was top-deck, enjoying the rain and briny wind. His faint and smooth scales twinkled in the torchlight and glistened in the rain. Ivan approached the boy and knelt beside him.

"Where is your home, child?" He asked with a heartwarming smile. The boy looked up to the crew mate beside him for approval. She appeared the perfect age to be a mother of a lad this old and gave the smile of approval he was looking for.

"Too long ago to remember," he sheepishly answered as the woman put an arm around his small shoulder. Ivan felt a rush of sadness strike him before cracking a smile for the boy.

"Well, let us see what we can do about that." Ivan stood and addressed the sailor. "Is Captain Tsuni aboard?"

She simply nodded in the direction of the captain's cabin before taking the river-nymph to join in the festivities below deck.

A single knock on the balsa wood door was met with Tsuni's irritated reply. "Knock again and I'll shoot ya, just enter damn it."

Ivan entered and heard the door hit a bottle that rolled across the floor to clatter against what was probably another bottle. The captain was sitting on the edge of her bed, half-dressed, looking like she had just drunk every tavern in the port dry, with a flint-lock pistol draped across one thigh. Even more amusing to Ivan was the particularly rugged and handsome man fully nude, passed out on the bed beside her.

"Thank Kaia it's you and we can leave this cesspool." She slapped her boy toy on the arse and not so subtly told him to get off her boat. All the while Ivan stood to the side chuckling and reminiscing of his younger days.

"Diverting times while I was away I see," he said, amused. She tucked her fiery red hair into her large floppy hat and drained the last quart of another bottle of rum before belching in reply.

"My ship isn't a daycare, Ifan." He bowed apologetically. "You were successful then?"

"I believe so. Although there were unforeseen revelations along the way." Ivan trailed off, lost in thought about what the member of the Keepers had said regarding Sesara.

"Which was?" Tsuni asked with growing interest.

"Apparently, Sesara is dead," he answered, not entirely sure if he believed it himself. She glanced a curious and skeptical expression at him.

"Are gods not immortal?"

Ivan halfheartedly agreed. "It's been known to happen. Usually, a god killing another god."

"Perhaps that is why the world has lost all decency," she said, throwing her empty bottle to the floor.

"Perhaps,"

"Well you can't be expecting to take those kids back to Serenstrom with you," she scolded.

"The river lad seems to fit in nicely. No doubt he would be invaluable to your ship and given a better chance at a life as a crew mate?" Ivan posited the question for Tsuni's consideration.

"Maybe," she answered dryly. "What of the other two?"

Ivan thought about it for a moment. It was likely the Dragon-blood could be reunited with his family, surely he was old enough to remember a place whence he came.

"The Dragon-bloods often pay kindness in kind. If we return him home, they may see the Scorn girl escorted home. No doubt she has seen it worse than any of them," Ivan said shamefully, knowing full well the ShadowScorn have always attracted the highest bidders of the worst kind.

"Before I blindly accept any more of your seemingly endless coin, why in the Underworld do you have so much of it? The greatest pirates I've met only dream of the riches you possess." Tsuni asked as the question that had been burning inside her since those kids had arrived.

"You've seen the armour I wear and the sword I carry. Either one of which could buy your ship and crew for life. Ifan was my brother, I am Ivan Fjell. Some call me, 'The Revered.' My spoils are born of bloodshed and the misguided idealism of my youth." Ivan lowered his head as if the weight of his ghosts forced him to do so. Captain Tsuni grabbed his salt and pepper beard and forced his worn out eyes to meet hers.

"I'd be a hypocrite if I didn't admit every one of us on my ship has had a complicated past. Yaana, our Master-at-Arms with the mean streak in her, used to be a devout follower in your church. She informed me who you were before we left Port Serenstrom."

For the first time Ivan could remember, he went flush red with embarrassment.

"Lets just say we have an understanding, Ivan." She turned to put on her red leather jerkin. She looked over her shoulder to see Ivan lost in thought, muttering Yaana's name under his breath. "She said you wouldn't remember her," Tsuni voiced with a slight look of disgust. Ivan looked to her, clearly asking for a reminder.

"When four of your priests had mercilessly beat her, two had finished with her by the time you caught them. Yaana refused your help and fled to the docks where destiny brought her to me." She passed to let Ivan settle in his returning memory. "Not a day in the past 10 years has gone by where she isn't reminded of what happened to her. It's amazing what privilege can do for memory," she spat venomously at Ivan.

Ivan sat there stunned in his shame, as the event slowly returned to him. "I had them hung for what they did. All of them," Ivan said defensively.

"Good for you," she replied sharply before leaving and slamming her cabin door.

Through a translucent orb set atop a stone-carved pillar was the image of Ven Devar arriving with 8,000 of Litore's greatest monks to save the City of Shadow. Vakar was stunned at Ven's ability to raise such a force and now understood why he had done so. This artifact of scrying that was mysteriously revealed to Vakar came into his possession after Ven was halfway through his journey. He watched in true awe at the hunters' increased prowess in battle. Vakar was very familiar with Ven's capabilities as a warrior and so he understood that these previous months on the road had honed all of his skills into perfect harmony. He scoffed dispassionately at the tender moment shared between Scáth and Ven, and was relieved to hear a polite knock at the door.

"Enter."

The door opened to reveal the Hunter Eevie with a large and brooding human paladin behind her. He was adorned in heavy expensive-looking plate mail and wore an expression of disinterest. Vakar waved them in and four more priests of Sesara entered with the still cold remains of Rexous.

"You're late," Vakar snapped at the Paladin.

"It cost a great deal to get him here as quickly as we did. Be thankful the Macer did this for you at all," the paladin replied dryly.

"Place him there," Vakar pointed to a large table made from a single slab of rich cedar. The priests placed the corpse down with a cold thud before briskly leaving the room.

"Good luck with whatever this is," the paladin offered with a concise level of condescension before he too left the room.

Vakar was so preoccupied at his alchemy table that he did not notice his sister-in-law still standing there.

"What are you doing?" She asked, evidently disappointed. When she received no response, her voice raised alarmingly. "Answer me."

"What does it look like?" He asked rhetorically, never lifting his true attention from his work.

"I've expressed my unmitigated disapproval of what you're doing, so you know that is not my meaning."

"I'm busy, Eevie. State your words clearly or leave." His harsh tone hurt the hunter.

"You're slipping. You spend hours intently staring into an empty space. You care little for the goings-on in the rainforest. I took revenge on Qiri's killer, which only further soured your mood. You show no interest in the final reconstruction of Silva. So I ask you, one, last, time. What are you doing?" Her voice was unyielding but inside she was desperate for him to open up. Eevie acutely saw Vakar's change in disposition after the death of her brother and his lover, Qiri. He was as focused and decisive as ever but lacked compassion and empathy. Vakar barely turned to answer her.

"I'm working," he answered. Her heart sank to the floor and she turned to leave, pausing a moment with the door ajar.

"What will Qiri think when you tear his dear friend Rexous away from his peaceful and well-deserved afterlife." Her words were finalized by the abrupt slamming of the wooden door. Vakar sighed heavily as he looked over his shoulder at the shut door. His gaze naturally fell over the slightly blued corpse of Rexous.

"Let us just get on with it," he spoke reluctantly to himself. Over the next several minutes he recited a series of words, locking the correct phrasing and inflection in his mind. The words came from a particularly old and dusty leather-bound journal. He had taken it from the 'Library of the Ancients' which was located in the oldest Kyst settlement in the north, River Luvium. He then lifted a small and stout crystal decanter that had been curing for nearly three cycles. A thick tar-like liquid floated atop black wisping tendrils of smoke. Walking over to Rexous, he recited an incantation from the book and held the decanter with one hand on the glass and one hand atop the cork. The wound in the chest of Rexous still appeared fresh but had burst blood vessels sprouting across his flesh. He uncorked the bottle and poured its contents into the wound and it quickly solidified. Vakar placed his hands on the temples of Rexous and recited the chant even louder with increasing speed.

The wound began to burn and smoke as the liquid in his chest boiled. Rexous, eyes still shut with rigor mortis, began screaming as only a zombie could. The unnatural bellow unsettled Vakar, yet with each passing scream, it sounded more and more like Rexous, as his soul was torn from the afterlife and stitched back together in his mortal vessel. His eyes shot open, turning from a dead, glazed-over grey to his normal cherry red. The former Prince of Silva was writhing so violently that Vakar had to take several steps back. After one particularly nasty convulsion, he fell off the cedar slab but caught himself on his hands and knees. He was making horrid choking noises as he desperately fought to refill his lungs with air. Vakar watched on in amazement, hoping to discover the extent of his success in the resurrection. True resurrection was long ago abandoned for it was seldom without terrible and unwanted effects on the re-born.

Rexous slowly looked up to see Vakar standing over him a few paces away. "You did this," his voice coarse, he growled frighteningly before lunging. His lunge was weak from atrophy but he still collided hard against a shimmering wall that Vakar had conjured between them. He hit the floor just as hard and lay there, unconscious once more.

"You're the only one who can bring an end to this," Vakar said, while hoisting him up and placing Rexous back on the table.

Ch19 - Hidden Roads

A slim cart carrying supplies and a small coffin tucked neatly in the middle was being driven by Agan Dusk. Ven rode atop a tame brown gelding with white spots on his face while Scáth sat comfortably on a sheer black steed. The Lady Scorn wore her PumaSheep cloak as gifted to her by Ven. She was covered in thick but flexible leather armour gifted to her from Commander Aelis. Customarily of late, she had a Scimitar strapped to her hip and one new addition, in the form of a hand crossbow. Her hair was pulled back at the top to form a long ponytail in the back. The side of her hair still flowed past her shoulders and misted away into the ethereal shadow around her. Her self-confidence had skyrocketed and an eagerness to finally explore the world had consumed her.

They were several days west of ShadowScorn now and were just leaving the spongy grass, rocky terrain, and rolling hills of the surrounding highlands. No roads were built around the City of Shadow for obvious reasons, so the travel had been slow going thus far.

"And there is no way I can convince you two to go back through the Morass Prairie? Guaranteed excitement and still the quickest option," Ven asked enthusiastically.

"Never will I set foot in that twisted scape again," Agan answered resolutely, and not for the first time.

Ven rolled his eyes. "Big baby," he said, before turning his gaze to Scáth. She looked at him with an understanding smile.

"Sorry, lover boy but it takes being possessed by a Bog Witch to understand," she happily agreed with Agan. Ven gave a great sigh and noticed that Agan was smiling at him slyly. The half-orc was well aware of Ven's rebellious side, the one who resented the station his people put on him and their social construct as a whole. So, it tickled Agan to see the way that Ven was forever awe-struck with Scáth and the way she so acutely handled him as no one else could.

"I do prefer my travel route though," Agan added. "Don't forget I've travelled Litore far longer than either of you."

"How could we, you never fail to remind us. Yet, you've spent little time in this corner of Litore. Don't feel too bad for not knowing the entire northeast is filled with wild monsters, unforgiving folk, and deadlier waters," Ven replied mockingly.

"Ven," Scáth chimed in sternly.

"Oh no, he's fine Scáth. The teenage elf thinks he's funny and I can handle a joke," Agan said lightheartedly.

"Teenager?!" Ven shouted with a furrowed brow.

Agan gave Ven a rye grin as he reached his great arm to slap the rump of the coastal elf's horse. Still a novice equestrian, Ven fell right off the back when the horse reared up. The Kyst grunted on impact and shivered as the defrosting mud and ice filled his armour and underclothes. Agan laughed harder than he had in years and Scáth couldn't suppress a chuckle, though she tried to hide it. However, when Faenla came sauntering back from his patrol and started licking the mud off Ven, they all shared in the laughter. He got up and cleaned himself off with the welcomed help of Faenla, before re-mounting.

"Well giggles, your plan by far is the most nonsensical. Let's just strut right on by Renrit, because there's no hard feelings there. Then travel through Iridawnia, only the most populated country on the continent where you surely won't be recognized." Ven finished his sarcastic rant glaring at Scáth. She, however, returned an entertained and amused smile his way.

"We cant go through the Morass and we can't go by boat. Since we're on the topic of remembering, don't forget this route was greatly endorsed by Grand Master Zenair. He assured me that if we stick to the base of the Skydore Mountains and cross through Gauntlet Ridge, we'll be in the rainforest before you know it," Scáth explained confidently. Ven honestly had no argument, but Agan began to question her.

"Just how does Grand Master Zenair know of this secret passage across the infamously impassable Skydore Mountains?"

Ven perked up at his companion's fine observation. Even he had heard of how that mountain range was said to be uncrossable, making Iridawnia one of the most secure nations in the world. Scáth shifted uncomfortably in her saddle and sighed quietly.

"This is for no one's ears but ours, understand?" She asked the boys rigidly. They both nodded with interest. "Zenair spoke of a great colony of reclusive Snow Elves that inhabit those mountains. In the earliest days of Iridawnia and the formation of the Dawn City, Leonis Skydore discovered the elves while looking for passages into his Kingdom that could be exploited by warring nations. The elves struck a bargain. They would bar any possible route through their mountains into Iridawnia, if Skydore promised to let them live as they always had and to keep their existence a complete secret. To this very day, few in all the world know of them." Scáth was showing a great deal of reverence towards the wishes of those elves. Ven was utterly amazed by the story but Agan scoffed in protest.

"Elves," he said disparagingly.

Ven shot him a dirty look. "You're half-elf in case you forgot. Perhaps it's time you start embracing less of your inner orc."

Agan focused his yellow orbs at Ven menacingly, but frankly, little Agan did could deter or intimidate Ven.

"Perhaps, he's right Agan," Scáth said peacefully, as her lineage was also elven. The half-orc turned his gaze to Scáth but his look was more of inner turmoil. He grunted and spurred his horse-drawn cart onward for some quiet. Scáth and Ven fell in beside each other a couple of dozen meters behind the cart.

Ven stared intently at the coffin for a long while, before Scáth interrupted the silence "You're not alone in this mourning."

Ven nodded solemnly. "Just wish I knew how to express it."

Scáth thought about that for a moment before grabbing his hand. "You don't have to express it. We all know how close you two became. Process your feelings however you best see fit," she said with a smile and squeezed Ven's hand. He attempted a smile but it quickly faded. He passed her the reins to his horse.

"Tie him up to the cart? Looks like we'll be in the woods soon so I'll run patrol with Faen."

Scáth gave him an approving nod before the Kyst rolled off the back of his horse and disappeared into the thickets.

The next several days saw little excitement. Agan began leading them northwest to give a wide range between themselves and the great trading city of Renrit. They knew it was possible that they'd pass a large number of prisoners that had been freed, and it could quickly become an ugly scene if they caught sight of each other; the party would have a few hundred angry and bitter prisoners of war chasing them. This route would bring them to Golden River nearing the north eastern tip of the Skydore Mountains.

A few kilometres south of Golden River and a hundred or so kilometres from the Skydore Range, the party of travellers stumbled by a Dwarven encampment. They had been following a sparsely used trail through weeping willow trees and thick knee-high grass.

"What is this?" Scáth asked Agan, as they travelled on their mounts, seeing a decently large base. Agan looked around the scene, trying to discern all he could. They were startled to hear a dense voice with a heavy brogue speak up behind them.

"Yar trespassin."

They turned to see a dwarf with geometric tattoos across what little skin was visible. A large brown braided beard hung past his round belly, and a dented and beaten iron helm lay atop his crown. When neither Scáth nor Agan replied, they heard another voice, this time coming from the camp.

"Lookin like rival prospectors be tryin' ta rob us," said an almost identical looking dwarf, yet this one sported a bald pate and a nasty looking mace on his hip. Five other dwarves came out from various tents and spots around the camp. Agan was quickly overcome with scenes of horror and waves of hot rage as times from the 'War of a thousand Dragons' flashed clearly in his mind. Scáth recognized his trauma but was reluctant to draw attention to herself. With her hood pulled low, she spoke calmly.

"Our mistake. We merely stumbled upon you and shall depart immediately," she said, while trying to get her horse and the cart back in motion. However, the dwarf with the mace was quick to block their way.

"Yee can't be interruptin' our day and on yer way without payin a fee," he said menacingly, while stroking the neighing courser Scáth was on. All the while, the dwarf was obviously trying to get a clear look under her hood. Agan noted that the dwarves were slowly but surely closing the distance on them, while one sneakily headed off, no doubt to alarm the rest of their troop. Agan knew too that these dwarves surely were mining the river for gold, but a cart full of goods and three fine horses could be a big score at the low cost of having to kill two lost travellers.

"There is no need for a show," Scáth said while tossing a hefty sack of coin at the dwarf. "That will be sufficient, now move aside if you will," she added in faint hope, whilst hiding her disgust. Scáth's face screwed up when all the dwarves laughed at her as if she had just performed some great jest.

"I'd be sayin all us here should like to see what be under that cloak, first. Hate to be thinkin' we was missin' somethin more profitable." The dwarves smiled grotesquely, revealing their rotted yellow teeth but also the fact they were privy to Scáth's heritage. The ladies words jumbled in her throat and she found herself flustered in confusion as to her next move.

Faenla and Ven were in the middle of stalking a large stag. They were barely a kilometre from the cart when the two hunters stopped what they were doing and fixed their ears in the direction of their companions.

"The cart stopped," Ven said to Faenla, not entirely sure if he should be concerned or not. They made eye contact and by the feeling Faenla gave Ven, they turned and sprinted back towards their allies.

Agan leaped down from the cart with a resounding thud. At that, several of the dwarves drew concealed weapons but Agan walked up to the leader, who was still stroking the snout of Scáth's horse.

"Move." Agan was fully twice the height of this dwarf and loomed over him. They stared at each other for a long while.

"Agan, don't," Scáth warned quietly as she watched on. She knew they were severely outnumbered and liked their odds even less without Ven and Faenla.

"Did she just say, Agan?" The dwarf smiled knowingly, for few dwarves in all the land didn't know the name Agan Dusk and his infamy against the Silver Dwarves. In a swift motion, his impossibly muscular forearm grabbed his mace to crack Agan's hip. The half-orc was the quicker though and caught the dwarf by the wrist, squeezing so tightly he dropped his weapon. Agan then used his other hand to grip the bearded leader by the throat, hoisting the 120 kilogram dwarf up with one arm to eye level. The dwarf miners jumped into action, Agan seized the opportunity to hurl the leader into a charging dwarf with a great grin on his face.

"From the Rhogarians!" Agan shouted, as the two dwarves toppled over each other into a contorted heap of limbs and hair. Scáth drew her small crossbow off her hip and fired it into the neck of the closest dwarf. She then hopped down from the cart, with her Scimitar drawn, to parry a miner swinging a large pickaxe. She drove their weapons downwards and shot her foot into the nose of the stout miner. His nose already bent from a lifetime of brawling, cracked once more and spouted streams of blood. The dwarf laughed, with the stench of ale on his hot breath. Her eyes widened in shock and she sidestepped a great swing, his axe splintering several planks on the side of the cart with ease.

Agan was without his weapon by choice, he had spent over two years fighting against the invading dwarves and cherished every neck he could break with his bare hands. The two dwarves who had collided with each other were back up in a frenzy. One threw several small hammers at Agan, most of which the brutish half-orc dodged, save the last one that caught him in the cheek. In the split second it took Agan to recover from the blow, the other dwarf had charged him, striking the half-orc as the bull of a dwarf rammed his helm into Agan's gut. He fell to his knees and then took an iron-helmeted head butt, knocking him to the ground, where the two dwarves relentlessly kicked him, laughing heartily all the while.

Scáth was overwhelmed, parrying and deftly dodging the swings and strikes of one persistent dwarf. Each and every swing could lay her low with a single strike for the strength of dwarves was truly legendary. The miner eventually swung for her, hoping to demobilize the Scorn, yet she jumped into a sidelong pirouette, thrusting her scimitar into his eye. She landed on one knee with her other leg out to the side for balance. It was something that she had picked up from the Ghosts of Aceia and she executed the manoeuvre flawlessly. The miner in front of her was now screaming in agony, trying to put his flopping eyeball back into its socket. Scáth suffered a major blow to her back from a war hammer that a miner striking Agan had thrown at her, leaving her winded and writhing on the ground.

With both Agan and Scáth defeated, dazed, and confused, the dwarves lined up the killing blows. With weapons held high, a projectile soared through the air from an unknown origin. It didn't have the whistle of an arrow or bolt but sounded like an angry wasp buzzing by your ear. A small dart stuck into the neck of the dwarf about to drop his mace into Scáth's skull. The veins of the dwarf bulged black as a necrotic poison coursed through his veins. His skin began to burst from exploding blood vessels, and bile drew from his lips and eyes before he fell over, dead. The remaining dwarves were stunned in horror. In the shock of it all, a woman hoisted herself over one side of the wagon and jumped on the dwarf standing over Scáth. This woman had long platinum hair that flowed wildly as she drove her hand-and-a-half sword into the heart of the miner. She wore a deep orange scarf that extended past her strategically placed plate mail, where padded leather armour filled in the gaps. Her gauntlets were embossed with a delicate gold, and the knuckles were made of spiked silver.

Agan seized the moment as well, grabbing the one dwarf standing over him by the thigh and shin, then bending his leg forwards so his toes were touching his hip. The dwarf fell in a scream so violent, he now made no sound. He grabbed the pickaxe of the dwarf that he had just mutilated and drove it into the miners chest.

Scáth and the newcomer made eye contact for a moment. The Scorn saw the woman's blood-red eyes and was mesmerized by the intensity on her face. The woman cocked her head at the sight of Scáth, for seeing a Shadow Scorn was a memorable first for most. Agan went to protectively stand over Scáth, who was suffering several broken ribs.

"Who are you?" he demanded.

She looked at the half-orc before turning to where the one dwarf had run off to alarm his allies.

"More are coming," she said quietly to see eight more dwarves emerging through the hanging vines of the willows. The woman got into a defensive stance, with both hands holding her thin straight blade, perfectly still, at a 45-degree angle in front of her.

"You need to get up Scáth," Agan said determinedly. Scáth

attempted to but immediately moaned in pain before falling back down.

"My ribs are broken," she responded in a painful panic. Agan grunted and hoisted Scáth into the cart.

"Use your crossbow," he snapped, before turning to face the oncoming dwarves.

As the hand-axes began flying at them, a familiar and haunting howl filled the air. Faenla soared over one of the tents to take down four dwarves, with his massive form. Ven lined up his arrows through the dancing branches and leaves of the willow. A twang was heard and the arrows soared through the trees, seamlessly severing branches as they found their marks into three unfortunate dwarven skulls. The newcomer and Agan made swift work of the final two, who were left with no choice but to earn a death in battle. Ven completely ignored everything to rush beside the injured Scáth. After reassuring him it was just a few cracked ribs, they turned their full attention to the intense and terrifying newcomer. She was currently searching the camp and the fallen dwarves. Her eyes had turned from her battle red to a brilliant silver that complimented her platinum hair. Her lips were coloured a dark red, much as her eyes had appeared in battle. Agan noticed that her fingernails were impossibly sharp, shaped like claws and made entirely of silver.

"I thank you for coming to our aid," Ven said with great appreciation and a humbled bow.

"I didn't," she answered with little interest.

"Oh, really?" Agan questioned skeptically.

"Yes, really," she answered dryly. "These dwarves have been causing a stir in Iridawnia for some time. I was hired to end their harassing of passer-byes and other prospectors." She looked to Agan and Scáth. "If you hadn't gotten in over your heads, far less life would have been so brutally spilled."

Agan scoffed at that. "They attacked us. What kind of a Bounty Hunter cries over spilt blood?"

"Why are you asking me?" She responded with as much condescension as she could muster.

"Then what are you?" Ven asked, attempting to save the situation.

"I'm a blood-seeker. I collect Monsters. Terrors of the night, slave traders and wicked folk alike. I, with the rest of my guild, strive to rid evil from this world."

The black eye shadow around her silver orbs and the quiet allure of her voice forced everyone to hang on to her every word. For all intents and purposes, she was human but was clearly touched or changed in some way. It wasn't just her unnatural eyes, but the way she perceived her surroundings, using every sense she had. Ven noted her eyes change and her ears twitch much like his did when focusing on sound.

"It is an honour to meet you then. I am Ven Devar of the Great Northern Rainforest."

She eyed him for a long while as if trying to place this Kyst Elf.

"I am Onstera Dentoress, of the Sanguis Quaesitor Guild," she said while walking towards Scáth and staring at her curiously. The Scorns' eyes appeared entranced by her approach which had Ven furrowing a brow. He would have stepped in between the two but Faenla had already done so. Onstera, wary of the gigantic wolf watching over the Scorn, stood beside the cart and slowly grabbed Scáth's chin. Ven and Agan both put their hands to their weapon hilts, ready for anything the newcomer might attempt. The two seemed almost opposite of each other, Scáth's hair so black it absorbed all light and Onstera's rich platinum hair reflected it. The way Scáth's skin ever so slightly changed from a pastoral grey to a porcelain white contrasted Onstera's olive skin tone under the dirt of the road and the blood of her enemies. In what was a brief exchange, Onstera broke her gaze, grabbing a small vial from her pouch and handing it to Scáth.

"For the pain," she offered softly before turning back to Ven and Agan. "I wish I could say it was a pleasure, but alas, it rarely is," she said disappointedly, before simply walking off with the sufficient evidence needed to collect her pay. After a moment of silence, the sounds of a distant river flowing and the whistling chit-chat of songbirds returned.

"That is not ideal," Agan said, finally breaking the tension. Scáth nodded, but Ven, still relatively new to the greater world, perked up in confusion.

"She helped and left without want. What isn't ideal about that?"

"The Sanguis Quaesitor's use to take a great interest in the Scorn during our earliest days," Scáth answered. When Ven looked at her with worry, she reassured him. "They haven't for hundreds of years.

Once we proved ourselves peaceful."

"One of the bloodiest battles I lost while fighting for the Rhogarians was when the Silver Dwarves hired out an entire guild of those freaks."

That information and her display against the dwarves was enough to convince Ven of the threat she may present but was not about to follow and confront her. With that, the group continued towards the mountains. Ven and Faenla took extra caution to patrol a smaller region around them instead of going out a greater distance.

The next afternoon saw a dreary wet spring afternoon as Scáth lay comfortably among their bedrolls in the cart. She had spent hours that day staring into Athvar's black glass opaque coffin, replaying the many brushes with death she had endured over the past year. The repercussions of her actions caused fear and took root in her mind, as the little body inside the coffin sounded with a thud with each dip or rock in the trail. Her chest began to heave and her breath became ragged. She was suddenly torn from the world of fear she found herself consumed by, as the firm grasp of Agan's hand rested on her shoulder.

"I know it feels easier to keep it bottled inside, believe me, it's better to get off your chest," he said with an understanding comfort not normally akin to his attitude.

"I almost died yesterday. We both did, and not for the first time in recent memory," she burst before properly recollecting her thoughts. "I always survive to fight another day because of you, Ven, Faenla, and-." She choked on Athvar's name. "Or some completely random act of luck like a Quaesitor leaping in at the last second. I was wrong in agreeing to this, I lived inside high walls my whole life for a reason. I don't belong out here."

Agan listened with an eager empathetic ear and allowed Scáth a long time to add any thoughts before he was reminded of a chapter in his life from long ago.

"You know, the Shadow Scorn do make their way across Litore from time to time. You're not even the first one I've travelled with." Agan let that hang in the air to garner Scáth's reaction, which was understandably doubtful. "It's true. She was a fierce, cunning, and skilful assassin. Although her real talents lay in that of espionage.

Never was there someone to match her in stealth or missions successfully completed. You could send her into a heavily armed fortress and sit back with a hearty whisky as she would extract or terminate a target with ease nearly every time." Agan continued to tell Scáth of this Scorns exploits and the successful life she had carved out for herself in a world that saw her only as a payday.

"I should like to meet her one day. What is her name?" She asked excitedly.

"Kithalyn Whisp. The last I saw of her was in the mines where the dwarves triggered the first Quake of Harazune. Perhaps if the fates allow, our paths will cross again. Not all stories of Scorn being sold end in tragedy, although it is an undeniable horror. Some are sold to wealthy families and trained to legendary status. Your people offer a unique skill set that none in this world can match, Scáth. Always remember you hold every advantage over those who wish to do you harm."

Scáth rested her head back and took a deep breath of relief. She was eternally thankful to have such dear companions, and felt the sense of excitement she had to be on the road, settle back over her.

Gauntlet Ridge

I am back to the whirlwinds of thoughts and emotions running through my mind and body, clouding my judgment and blooming doubt with every step closer I take to Sanctuary Island. Faenla offers me an anchor to it all, and for that I am grateful. Yet, it was Athvar who understood how to decode the jumble of feelings inside. I had hoped the guilt of his fall would wash away with the time spent back in nature embracing his lessons, but it lingers like an inescapable chill. I had gotten carried away the prior cycle and as a result, Scáth and Agan would have both met their untimely end at the hands of those filthy miners. This too weighs heavily on my conscience as it would have been no one's fault but my own for not being there. I understand I could never live with myself if I lost Scáth and so I must be, I will be, better. I will never underestimate my surroundings or the folk who populate Litore again. My return to the rainforest has plagued me every day since I left for the City of Shadow. Now I am on the road once more, I know there is nothing to fear. I will return to my fellow Kyst a more gracious and thankful elf, for they are the ones who made me who I am. To be anything less, I know now is to spit in the efforts of all those who came before me. I will do my best to repair the damage done between Vakar and I, and hopefully, all will respect my choice to give the mantle of monarch to a Kyst better suited for the task. Though I can now say I have travelled the land of Iridawnia, I can't speak much to it. We have stuck to the base of the Skydore Mountains where few settlements exist and the land is relatively barren. Agan went out one night to collect information regarding the distance left to Gauntlet Ridge and found out from a local source that it was only another day east. With any luck, we will be through the pass and across the Great Road within the next eight day cycle. Scáth remains confident that Gauntlet Ridge will be the break we've been needing, yet Faenla's unease grows stronger the nearer we get.

-Ven Devar

The group sat around a warm crackling fire as gusting winds and a heavy fog rolled down off the mountains. Ven and Scáth were resting their backs against Faenla who was curled with his large head resting atop the Scorn's lap. Agan sat on an old log, poking at the fire while savouring a wine skin given to him by Aelis. The night was dark as the low cloud cover obscured the otherwise gleaming moons.

"Have either of you noticed we've picked up a tail?" Ven asked nonchalantly. Scáth looked at him confused and Agan shook his head, which surprised the Kyst. "For a few days now. I'd venture to guess it's Onstera."

"What do we do?" Scáth inquired, genuinely interested in what the right play was.

"Let her make the first move, we will be ready," Agan answered confidently. Ven nodded, knowing Agan had most likely been through this scenario many times.

That night, as all but Ven rested peacefully, he heard a familiar sound emanating from deep in the sparse forest opposite the mountain line; several skin-crawling moans from the hideous monsters known as Siphons. Their wails, each unique and somewhat resembling the voice of the person they were before becoming the monster, were enough to frighten any but the most courageous. Siphons roamed all of Litore and normally in packs. For that reason, Ven was familiar with them and knew too that the current screeches and moans of these horrors were the last they would ever make. One by one the shrills grew in frequency and abundance then soon died out, leaving the evening wind to fill his ears. Ven took this as confirmation that the person tracking them was in fact the blood-seeker, Onstera Dentoress. Only someone from her guild could be equipped and prepared to defeat a horde of Siphons single-handed.

The night passed without disturbance and the group was at Gauntlet Ridge the following evening. A few fluffy clouds hung above, painted gold by the sun beginning its descent. After much debate about where the ridge actually started among the thousands of kilometres of mountains, Scáth found the frozen waterfall Zenair had described to her as the entrance. Surrounded by high walls that encircled the falls like hugging arms, a thick, white sheet of ice replaced the flowing water. A beautiful sight to behold but one that filled her companions with doubt. They all instantly recognized the lack of a basin and saw a seemingly bottomless hole the water fed into.

"You said our cart could go through the pass. It cannot climb waterfalls, frozen or liquid." Agan placed a lack-lustre gaze upon Scáth.

"Ha ha," she replied, rolling her eyes. "Ven, use the wood you and Faenla collected to build a fire on the left side of the fall, please."

Ven looked to Faenla who dropped a large bundle of firewood next to the frozen wall of ice. The coastal elf quickly doused the large stack of wood with oil to help it start, and soon a roaring flame lit up the tiny valley they were in. After nearly an hour had passed, a large enough hole had melted through the ice to reveal an extensive passageway. One also in fact, wide enough to drive a small cart through. Scáth winked at Agan in superiority, which brought a smile to his normally rigid lips.

The hunter was the first one in the natural cavern to survey its interior. It was dreadfully frozen inside, almost as if cold air was perpetually pumped through to keep the falls still. The circular tunnel was slick with a sparkling blue layer of ice. With the hopes of finding the other exit to make camp in warmer air, the group proceeded on. After two hours of walking their horses, and no end in sight, they gave up to make camp. It was roughly five metres in diameter and resembled a lava tube, however, Ven could tell by the scarring on the wall, that something organic had burrowed it. The group built a small fire and hunkered down next to each other. Faenla offered great warmth and acted as a large barrier from the rushing wind. Agan, still as always, slept off to the side and decided to take watch. While Ven and Scáth slept peacefully against Faenla, Agan felt a sudden pressure building inside his head. He vividly remembered such discomforts from those years serving in the frozen tundra of Rhogar, but before he knew it, the fighter was clutching his temples with each hand in a battle of wills.

"Ven," he blurted through agonizing breaths. Ven was easily woken, always on alert after his lesson with the dwarves, and saw Agan struggling on the ground. The Kyst jumped up, shoving Scáth and Faenla as he went.

"What's the matter?" Ven asked, checking him over for anything obviously out of the ordinary. When Agan made almost what sounded like a snore before toppling over, he looked back to see that Scáth and Faenla were sprawled out, deeply unconscious. Ven felt the hood by his neck move as the thick hide of the PumaSheep caught a dart. He rolled back into the centre of the tunnel and drew his faintly green glowing short-sword. He plucked the dart from his hood and smelled it, quickly identifying it as a sleep potion.

"I know it's you Onstera. Reveal yourself!" Ven roared angrily, his voice echoing down the tunnel. From a large ice stalagmite, stepped out Onstera holding a small crossbow. Her eyes had lost the silver and were pure blood red again. She replaced the ranged weapon in her hand and reached behind her black cloak to grab her decorated hand-and-a-half sword.

"What do you want?" he demanded while using his free hand to grab a dagger from off his chest piece.

"Your atonement. I found some interesting information on you after the dwarf miners. You laid waste to your own people and forest with the Kintar." Onstera tutted at Ven in great insult.

"What?" He spat incredulously. "I did no such thing," Ven said, raising his sword out to chest level.

"Oh there's no denying this one, it happened. You already told me who you were and survivors of the attacks, all blame the 'Mighty Ven Devar." Onstera pointed her sword at Ven in reciprocation but kept both hands on it, ready to strike. Instead, she clicked a button on the hilt. Ven heard a spring release as a small bolt discharged down the length of Onstera's blade. He reacted only in time due to his incredible hearing and caught the bolt in front of his face. The Kyst angrily threw the bolt to the ground, splitting his daggers and throwing them. She ducked and spun on one foot, deftly letting the daggers soar past her. Ven immediately recognized the rehearsed practice of this adversary and they clashed swords just as she came out of her spin. She was tall for a human at 183 cm, making them almost equal in height. Ven couldn't believe the sheer strength in her agile form as she pushed their swords apart with ease. She came at the hunter with a flawless attack routine, most of which were too powerful for Ven to parry so he was forced into a dance around her whirling blade. Much to Onstera's frustration, wherever she sent her blade, this elf effortlessly seemed to avoid it.

He noted its matte complexion from the silver it was made of, as it cut off a lock of his green hair. He then performed a series of back handsprings as Onstera lunged from one knee to the other, pushing him back with relentless aggression. His creative combat style came to aid as he stuck one leg out mid-spring, connecting his foot squarely under her chin to send his foe flat on her back. He landed in a low defensive crouch to see her slowly sitting up.

"I did nothing wrong. I'm a returning monarch to the Kyst people. Consider this your last warning," Ven said while slowly standing tall. He grabbed his trident and lowered it to his side as the last of the handle elongated, transforming his close-combat trident into the typical and deadly two-handed polearm.

She laughed at him which made his blood boil. "Of course you are. And I'm the Queen of all Sanguis Quaesitors," she retorted mockingly before dexterously getting back to her feet. Ven Devar wasted little time and sprang into action, creating an impossible to breach barrier with his spinning trident. He only ever broke the twirling to land a jab or slice against her with his sword. Cutting several small gashes across her body, he spun the trident staff around his back and used the momentum to deliver a heavy strike. It knocked her sword out of her grip, but while Ven was regaining control of the trident she grabbed it. Before it left his grip, however, she yanked hard and it spun into Ven's thigh, drawing a thick line of blood. He stumbled backward, focusing through the pain and readied his ancient weapon. He expected her to also have a similar wound for the magic in his sword was thirsty, yet she did not. He quickly scoured his fluttering mind for an answer. Perhaps she was warded against such magic he thought.

She smiled coyly at him before they lunged at each other at the same time. She thrust the trident at Ven but he ducked, grabbing the hilt and pressing the small button to elongate or shorten the weapon. It abruptly sprang together, dropping from her hand, as she wasn't expecting it. Ven shoved her hard against the wall as his sword tip rested in the deep of her neck. Drawing the smallest trickle of blood down her chest. He wasted little time on his surprise at the flat red shade of her blood.

"You've lost."

"Seems a tad definitive."

"I need only flinch to end your life," Ven threatened. Onstera smirked, somehow undercutting Ven's severity. "Here's what is going to happen. I will explain my journey to you. Then you're going to understand why these claims against me are false. You'll explain to me why they've been levied against me and who the accuser is. Understood?"

Onstera stared blankly for a moment before begrudgingly nodding. Ven explained the destruction of Silva, the journey to the City of Shadow, the Siege, and given the companions he travelled beside and the coffin in their cart, Onstera was left with little doubt.

"The King of Kyst in the Great Northern Rainforest decreed it so. Ven Devar is a betrayer and had slaughtered dozens of villages without mercy. And did so, beside a hoard of Kintar," Onstera explained as she confidently recalled the information she was given by a guild outpost. Ven thought back to the side of Glass Mountain when Rexous had said the Northern Rainforest considered him a traitor. He thought it to be some final moment of anger spewing from Rex, but what Onstera had just explained made perfect sense to him now.

"What's this new king's name?" Ven asked with disgust but a clear guess as to the answer.

Onstera thought for a brief moment. "Vakar, something," unclear if she had forgotten his last name or if one wasn't given. Ven sighed heavily and swiftly withdrew his blade from her olive-coloured neck and sheathed it.

"That vengeful bastard," Ven said under his breath in utter disbelief.

"You know him?" Dentoress asked with a faint curiosity now that things were coming to light for her.

"Mhmm, when I left to return Scáth home he was angry and confused, misplacing the loss of our home and loved ones on me. Travelling to ShadowScorn was the only real option I had, but I do regret how my decision impacted so many. They needed me and I left them," Ven answered shamefully. "I presume you magically put my friends to sleep? Which is why I got the dart."

She chuckled in acceptance. "Mind magic doesn't work on Kyst. It is a temporary thing, you could wake them even now, most likely."

"They teach you well in your guild. The brutish one would likely fell your head from your body if I woke him now," Ven said with only a hint of sarcasm, as he thought it to be a real possibility.

"And what of the pretty one? She seems even-tempered," Onstera remarked, with keen interest, while staring at the sleeping Scáth which had Ven feeling defensive.

"She is the wisest and most courageous of us," Ven answered.

"You set out to deliver her home, so why does she travel back to where it all began?"

"She believes it to be the right thing to do, and truthfully yearns for the life of adventure and freedom you and I have."

"Then perhaps I can be of assistance going forward with your quest," the member of the infamous guild offered.

"Do you always so readily flip sides like that of a coin?" Ven said accusingly.

"As I said before, we aren't just specialized warriors who slay monsters that lurk in dark woods and under bridges. There are more monsters among men and humanoids alike than that of roaming beasts wishing to suck out your eyes, heart, and liver for sup."

"I admit your skill pool would be an asset, but the others must agree to your joining. If even one of them, the wolf included, doesn't want you, you turn around and never bother us again. Clear on that?" Ven laid down his terms without err.

"Clear on that," Onstera agreed with a smirk, this time appreciating Ven's transparency. Ven approached Scáth first and gently shook her awake, as she took a moment to regain her surroundings Ven placed his forehead on Faenla's brow, who promptly woke up to immediately bare his long and terrifying fangs at Onstera.

"Wake up Agan would you?" He asked Scáth quietly and took up a stance slightly in front of the strange woman. Scáth had to slap the side of Agan's face a few times for Agan was harder to wake. The half-orc looked around before settling his glare on the newcomer, then slowly unclipped his axe and began to stand up.

"Wait a minute big guy. She was only here for me, but that didn't work out did it?" Ven glanced at Onstera with a glint in his eye.

She rolled her eyes. "No, it did not. Your elf here explained the situation and I believe I can help you moving forward."

"Only if you three unanimously agree," Ven quickly added. Scáth and Agan spent a tense moment gauging each other's thoughts while Faenla padded slowly over to Onstera. The massive wolf sniffed her up and down before stopping and making direct eye contact. Faen finally gave a derisive snort and licked her hand before sitting proudly beside Ven. The Kyst wrapped his arm around the furry wolf's thick mane and watched patiently as the others made their decision.

"I, at the very least, owe you my thanks. I fear what would have happened if our paths did not cross, perhaps fate wills our cooperation," Scáth offered with a small smile before wincing from her still very tender ribs. Onstera nodded once and with great depth as she kept her eyes and smile on the Scorn. Agan was now fully standing but had placed his trusty axe back on his hip.

"Ever made your way as far west as Rhogar?" He questioned.

"Not by a long shot," she quickly answered.

"Good. Ven pulled me from years of a living nightmare. I owe him much, so if you even move to harm him or the others, I will end you without hesitation."

"You people are so severe, I like it," she responded with mirth.

"I've lost the appetite for sleep, lets get out of this tunnel," Agan grumbled in a surly manner.

"You were only a kilometre and a half from the exit," Onstera said nonchalantly. All four of the travellers laid heavy stares on her for this pass through the mountains was assured to be unknown by all but a few in the world.

She just shrugged innocently. "Our whole code is built on knowing the unknown. Worry not, we respect the secretive nature of these things and keep it so." Agan rolled his eyes with grandeur, and continued up the tunnel.

A half hour later the group spotted a distant light and were soon back under the pale sky of early dawn. They were flanked on both sides by huge and looming rock walls coated in glinting ice. Their only route was barely a few meters wide and undulated like a snake, leaving them blind to whatever lay ahead. After a short distance, Scáth climbed over some of their gear and began tossing through a pile of mismatched items at the back of the cart. After several frustrating moments, she pulled a blue silky cloth out. Onstera, travelling at the rear watched with interest as the still-recovering Scorn attached the flag of the Crescent City to the back of the wagon.

The end of the first day saw the group miserably cold and only a third of the way across the pass. After they had stopped and made a small fire, Scáth went to grab dinner from their food supply, to find it all had frozen solid. Onstera had expected this and shot her a wink as she grabbed the food. This newcomer placed it in a large cooking pot and began concentrating. Ven and Scáth watched with keen intent as she held the pot on her fingertips and small flames burst to life in the palm of her hands. Agan, unimpressed rolled his eyes and put his meal over the open fire, laying a heavy stare on Onstera as he did.

"Do all in your guild know of the arcane?" Ven asked inquisitively. He was ever intrigued by other cultures but even more so by the vast amount of guilds spread across the land. He realized that the many guilds of Litore compared closely to that of the Hunters and Sages of the Kyst.

"Some more than others but we all know a little," she responded.

"Which is why you're unbothered by the cold?" He added. She only gave a small smile in reply.

"How many are in your guild?" Scáth asked next.

Onstera scoffed lightly in jest. "Changes every day given our occupational hazards."

The sound of Agan tearing off a large chunk of warmed-up jerky with his teeth caused a deliberate awkward moment of silence.

"Anyway, what's your plan for the Glacier Dragon?" Onstera asked the group with interest, expecting a great and cunning plan. All she got was the deadpan, indignant looks of the companions.

"What?" Scáth, Ven, and Agan asked in unison and with stark indignance.

"You can't seriously say your source for Gauntlet Pass failed to mention the Glacier Dragon?" Onstera asked concernedly. Ven and Agan looked to Scáth, who shrugged in disbelief, for Grand Master Zenair truly hadn't mentioned the Dragon that was known to guard the pass.

"We have to turn back now," Agan declared sternly. Ven looked at him with worry for he was well aware of Agan's part in the 'War of a Thousand Dragons'.

"We can't," Scáth replied.

"Excuse me?" Agan shot back frighteningly so, which caused a bit of stir from Ven. "Do you know why they call it the 'War of a Thousand Dragons' Princess? You will never comprehend the destruction a single Dragon can bring. We will die," he scolded in a tone that didn't sit well with anyone. Ven gave Agan a dark look for the disrespect he was showing Scáth, but the fighter paid no attention to it.

"Don't talk down to people when you want to make a point. We literally cannot, Half-Orc," Scáth said with equal disrespect, pointing Agan out for his arrogant words. "The waterfall has had a day and a half to refreeze that small hole we made. We'd have to burn the whole cart and everything in it just to break through."

Agan then pointed to Onstera. "She can burn through it."

Onstera chuckled. "Please, big boy. Warming our food and melting a multi metre-thick wall of ice are two different things. Even if I could summon the magic, the shadowy one is right. Forward is our only path," she said, giving Scáth a reassuring nod. Agan gave a bellowing growl of stubbornness before slumping back down.

"If that dragon finds us, this is all over," Agan said quietly, as if in lament, but making undeniable eye contact with Ven as he did. The Kyst's heart began to race but as he and Scáth were leaning against Faenla, the wolf placed his head on his lap to calm his emotions. Ven, thankful for the comfort, placed his gloved hand on Faenla and rhythmically stroked his fur.

By noon the following day, the second mountain that formed the line known as Gauntlet Ridge dipped into a huge valley on either side of the path. The vastness of the Skydore Mountain range stole their breath as a spectacular frigid ecosystem revealed itself. Rivers, trees, and grasslands scattered the landscape but existed in a state of being flash frozen; moments in time entombed as cases of smooth ice sculptures. As they looked down, they noted a half-kilometre drop to the icy basin. The edges of this thin bridge-like path they walked across, were lined with an ankle-height wall. Like the crest of a crashing wave frozen before being sucked back down.

"Everyone go slow, keep your mounts calm and look straight ahead," Ven instructed as he took the lead, climbing off his horse, ensuring the path did not appear weak anywhere in front of them, while also helping Agan keep control over the whinnying horse pulling the wagon. The wheels of the cart never seemed more than a handful of centimetres from the edge on either side. Onstera, although not showing it, was shocked by her actual fear for the likelihood of getting across alive. Just as they passed the 2/3 mark, a frigid tsunami of disturbed air hit them. Ven was blown back but quickly felt his cloak bitten by Faenla, stabilizing him. Agan, seated on the driver's bench, recognized this preternatural gust but was nearly thrown off his seat. The horse attached to the wagon had reared up and began kicking and thrashing until one hoof finally went over the edge.

The cart began sliding off the trail from the immense weight of the horse. Onstera's horse bucked her off and began galloping back the way they had come. It too, after a short distance, lost its balance on the slick pass, fumbling over the edge to tumble down to the valley floor. Onstera had landed hard on her back and gave a disgusting wheeze as the air was drained from her lungs. Agan grunted in denial as he tried to pull the draft horse back up the cliff but it was no good. He jumped to the ground trying to stop the cart from plunging to the bottom but the horse was still attached by the harness. He grunted with all his might as his feet were slowly skidding to the edge.

"Scáth, get out, now!" He shouted through gritted teeth.

Ven, just a short distance ahead, was back on his feet and surveying their situation. Just as he went to move in their direction, an earth-shaking tremor was felt behind him and the distinct sound of cracking ice under immense pressure rang out. He felt the coldest air in the known worlds enshroud his body as he stiffly turned.

A truly gigantic head with rigid plates of scales and dozens of horns, moved close to the hunter. The Dragon's soul-piercing white eyes were the size of Ven, and they stared at him wantingly. The Dragons diamond-hard scales shared the same slick blue texture as the ice that surrounded its natural habitat. Its massive jaws could swallow all of them, their horses, and the wagon in a single bite. Several rows of teeth resembled swords and sharper still than even the deadliest weapon he'd seen. Ven stood, somewhat paralyzed by his shock and the utter humility he felt at such a majestic, gargantuan creature. Faenla too, nearly cowed by the Dragon, backed up until he bumped into Ven.

The ShadowScorn, momentarily petrified by the sudden arrival of a real life Dragon, did everything she could to look away and listen to Agan. She had been dexterously climbing out of the tipping cart but was painfully pinned as Athvar's coffin had slid into her ankle. Agan could barely see over the cart now as his muscles strained under the weight of gravity sucking the wagon and horse off the path.

"I'm stuck!" She screamed for anyone to help her. Onstera had rolled onto her front, almost vomiting as she desperately tried to suck in air. Agan's brutish grunts stretched out into screams of agony, digging deeply to tap into any extra strength he could muster. The half-orc was not going to lose Athvar, no matter the cost. Ven was entirely entranced by the Glacier Dragon staring at him as his forked tongue slithered between his fangs. Scáth centred herself, and focused on the pressure against her ankle. Soon, she felt her foot dissipate into shadow and she quickly scurried up the cart to get out, now free. Faenla however, dashed behind the Kyst and pounced over the cart, biting Scáth's hood as the 250 kilogram wolf pulled her out the rest of the way with ease. They landed hard on the path and Faenla was quick to let go of Scáth but couldn't stop skidding in time. He dug his claws deep into the ice as his rear end and hind legs fell over the edge.

"Mid-day trespassers make the tastiest delicacies," the Dragons words slithered through barely open lips, projecting a booming voice via some powerful magic. It leaned forward, supporting itself on its 40-metre wingspan, like the arches of a bridge.

Onstera got to one knee and sent a short-sword spinning through the leather straps attaching the draft horse. The sword cut clean through the harness and Agan heaved with all his might to get the cart back on the path. The horse gave a horrifying whinny as it plummeted below.

Scáth wasted zero time in scurrying over to Faenla and tugged him up by the scruff of his neck. He kicked his powerful hind legs and found enough purchase with his claws to climb over the lip. He landed on top of Scáth before profusely licking her face in thanks.

"We... we are only humble travellers," Ven replied getting down to one knee, keeping his head down as he squeezed his eyes shut, trying to regain a measure of courage.

The Dragon's icy white and blue body stood up to its full 25-metres and took a deep breath. It blew a stream of cold air and precipitation behind them, quickly forming a tall wall of ice, blocking their route back.

"I witness five unusual creatures too far from where they belong, attempting to deceive the 'Great Watcher', the 'Frozen Death', 'bringer of the Darkened Age of Ice', Razilkinar-Ezardoon," the Dragon slammed its tail to the ground which had everyone stumbling on their feet from the impact.

"We are friends of the Snow Elves of Moon Mountain. We fly their banner even now," Ven said, lifting his hand toward the blue flag flapping in the wind, and then he bravely looked back to Razilkinar. The Dragon craned its long naturally plated neck around to the cart, looking not at the banner but at the group more closely. It paid little attention to Faenla but studied Scáth for some time, it then turned its truly frightening gaze at Onstera and bellowed threateningly towards her. She instinctively slipped her hand into a satchel, feeling around for a particular potion. However, the Dragon lost interest in her and sniffed the air all around the exhausted half-orc.

"The delicious stench of Dwarf blood. You reek of death, Agora," the Glacier Dragon lapped its tongue in the air around Agan.

"I fought for your kind in 'The War of a Thousand Dragons.' I am Agan Dusk, 'The Scaleless Dragon," the half-orc replied resolutely.

"So you are. You may watch as I devour your friends. If my hunger is satiated then you alone may leave." The Dragon flapped its icy wings, lifting it into the air which forced everyone to brace. It dove for Ven with its huge mouth agape, but instincts had replaced anything else the Kyst was feeling. He expertly rolled forward and drew his artifact short-sword. Before Ven realized it, the Dragon swiped its human-sized talon at him, slicing a deep gash down Ven's arm. The Dragon screeched in pain, which had everyone covering their ears. Ven was clutching the wound on his sword arm and noted a great slash down the hugely muscular shoulder of the Dragon, as bright blue blood poured freely. The Dragon, hovering with massive wings, roared in outrage. Before anyone else could react, a high-pitched horn echoed through the valleys, originating from their only exit.

"Pray our paths do not cross again!" Razilkinar-Ezerdoon hissed vehemently. As his titanic visage flew away, 50 or so Snow Elves lined the mountain in front of them. After Onstera and Scáth had stitched and bandaged the grievous wound that Ven had suffered, Agan hitched one of their two remaining horses up to the cart.

They continued down the trail until they were face to face with the leader of this troop. His hair and skin were snow white and his eyes, a dull blue. These Elves wore much more clothing and fine chain than their monk kin. They all carried ornate pikes for weaponry, each sporting a jagged blade of ice.

"Forgive us, word was just received from our kin of your passing. You may continue freely and safely." The leader addressed Onstera and Agan as Ven and Scáth recovered in the wagon.

"It is with our utmost appreciation that you grant us this," Onstera said graciously.

"Our dear friend Grand Master Zenair will be most pleased, thank you," Agan added. The Snow Elves all stepped aside at once and let the group travel on freely and without bother. Just as the leader promised, the next day and a half of travel through the mountains went smoothly, aside from the relentless cold in their bones. To their utter surprise, the exit was a clear road down into a springtime glade. Flowers bloomed and the grass seemed greener than ever. Animals grazed freely as bugs and insects returned with the warm air. Shortly after exiting the pass they heard a great rock slide behind them, undoubtedly filling in the exit, blocking the entrance, and keeping Gauntlet Pass a well-kept secret.

The Welcoming

Two cycles of uneventful, nearly peaceful travel passed the party by. Midway, they crossed the Great Road some distance west of the Morass Prairie. The land was soft and lush, teaming with life excited for spring's renewal. Streams cascading off the mountains behind them offered ample fishing, with many nights lulled to sleep by the gentle sound of water. Onstera and Ven put down a few Ferals and Siphons together while patrolling ahead of the wagon. Ven was grateful that the Quaesitor member had decided to travel with them. He had learned a great deal about the roaming monsters outside of his natural habitat and the most efficient way to put them down. He found her company to be filled with sass but in a playful way, albeit she lacked some social skills from the solitary life her people led. Scáth's ribs were still black and blue, but with the proper stretching and rest she had been afforded, she was back on her feet before they entered the Great Northern Rainforest.

When the trees that truly brushed the heavens came into view, and the definitive border where the forest met the grasslands, Ven and Faenla both paused. The group had stopped behind them and allotted the two natives some time alone to reflect. A looming omen of darkness hung above the forest; swirling clouds encapsulated the sky in a similar colour of hue to Ven's own skin tone. He wasn't a particularly religious elf, but when the clouds of a hurricane hung above his head, he couldn't help but wonder if Kaia, goddess of the sea, was responsible.

Ven looked on with heart-pounding hesitance, understanding what must be done but so desperately wanting to walk away forever. He was elated to be back in his former environment, the greenery soothing his soul. The bird song and chatter of animals sounded like a joyous welcome home. It was the duty to his people that truly cowed the courageous hunter. He wished, instead, that he was standing tall against the Glacier Dragon rather than having to confront the responsibility bestowed upon him by his former Queen.

The Kyst placed a tight grip of support on Faenla, who was at his side also reflecting on what it meant to be back. The wolf had lost his entire blood-line and pack in a Kintar ambush set for Ven. He felt a concrete grip as Scáth intertwined her fingers with his free hand.

"The Mighty Ven Devar has travelled halfway across the world and back. Seen Litore's highest peak, dined with royalty, fought in the 'Siege of Shadow,' Saved his friends from a mind-thieving witch, and stood tall against a great and ancient Ice Dragon. You can do this too, my love," Scáth whispered in his ear, as her head rested comfortably on his shoulder. Ven simply squeezed her hand tighter, it wasn't necessarily her kind words that filled him with courage but the fact he still so vividly remembered Scáth standing tall against horrible events, upon her return home.

"Let's set the horses loose and grab what we need from the cart. There are no roads from here." A heavy gust of wind kicked up as he finished speaking, and showed no sign of relenting soon.

Scáth and Onstera gathered the necessary supplies, leaving few items behind in the cart. The Scorn did ensure to fold her flag of Moon Mountain for safekeeping, tucking it into a satchel. Agan hoisted Athvar's coffin over his shoulder with relative ease. Ven strapped a large pack of food onto his back, before leading them into the forest. The Kyst and wolf took their first step back into the woodland realm, together.

Their journey would be five days before reaching the coastline to Sanctuary Island. During that time, Agan and Onstera were struck speechless in awe. The raw nature around them was stirring. Game, berries, fungi, and food of all kinds were plentiful; of course, any one of which could kill you with ease if you didn't know better. The trees around them were wider than the largest buildings they'd seen and stood as tall as mountains. When night fell, it was as if they had stepped into another plane of existence. Pools of water glimmered brightly, as if they were lit from the bed. Flora glowed every colour in the rainbow while birds and insects emanated bio-luminescence to fill the air with a wide array of fluttering colours. It left little doubt in the pair's mind as to how and why the Kyst race formed such a spiritual connection to their surroundings. Most of the time, Agan and Onstera had no idea where Ven was for his cloak and natural camouflage made him very difficult to spot, so they just followed Faenla and Scáth who never seemed to second guess where the Kyst was. The hurricane grew closer and in intensity each day, the trees swaying back and forth above them showered the group in rain.

On the morning of the third day, Ven was convinced that the forest was off its natural balance. It wasn't all too uncommon to go a few days without hearing the skin-crawling roar of a Kintar. Yet, after settling down for the winter, this was the time of year that they itched for battle the most. As the group traversed further, the animals grew sparse, leaving the coastal elf to realize that the majority of wildlife had been pushed to the forest borders. To make things worse, the previous night he had caught on to someone tailing them high above. He was expecting a patrol of hunters to reveal themselves and escort them back to the coast. Yet, the final words of Rexous continued to echo in his mind. Until now he truly did not want to believe Rex or Onstera. He was the hero of Silva, one of the greatest Kyst settlements in Litore. Almost everyone in the north knew of the Mighty Ven Devar and his feat against the Ice Demon Hoarfrost. Surely his name could not have been tainted such as either had suggested.

Ven and Faenla had stayed awake through the night, watching the swaying tree canopy. As the rest of the party woke up, they were displeased to see that the storm appeared to just be getting started. Even the wide and sturdy trees could blow over in the gale force winds, which Ven knew to be extremely dangerous. These trees were ancient and so it wasn't all too uncommon for their root systems to be rotted and collapse in storms such as this. As they collected their things and devoured their rations, Ven's face screwed up as he heard a faint but familiar voice carried on the wind. No one seemed to hear it, but Scáth noticed the concern present about him.

"What is it?" Scáth's question prompted Onstera and Agan to regard the hunter.

"Wait here," Ven instructed before jumping at the nearest tree and climbing with lightning speed. Onstera and Agan watched in awe at the dexterity and nimbleness of the elf, defying gravity. After a few moments of climbing, Ven entered the canopy line and wasted little time in snuffing out the Kyst following them. Walking to the end of one long branch he noticed a hunter crouching in front of him with his hood down, at the end of a separate tree-arm. Their cloaks billowed wildly and both struggled slightly to maintain their posture in the slick and forceful weather.

"You actually came back," The Kyst remarked as he stood up and slowly pulled his hood back.

"Ehan?" Ven said in surprise as he recalled the Kyst Hunter from Silva who had left the Bull Elk to die the day before the attack. The older and larger Kyst just gave a wicked smile as he looked over Ven's shoulder. Ven spun his head to see Rexous standing there, with a foot already flying into his back. He grunted and soared off the branch to hit the forest floor in certain death. He was ready though and managed to grab a branch on the way down and swing over to a wide tree arm. Down below, Faenla snarled viciously and the trio of warriors quickly spotted two dozen Kyst Hunters emerge out of hiding to surround them.

"Here we go," Agan mumbled as he put his hand to the blackglass and iradinium axe hanging. Onstera unsheathed her sword at the same time her eyes turned a pure blood red. She smiled when the hunters stepped back in hesitance, for building fear in their enemies was a Quesitor delight. Scáth felt the forest floors shift beneath her feet, and looked behind them to see roots erupting in explosions of soil.

"Spread out!" Yelled one of the Kyst Hunter's to her troop. Everyone on the forest floor scattered for their lives, as the falling tree shook the earth. It moaned as if in mourning during the descent, from bending and creaking timber.

Ehan and Rexous leaped onto the tree that Ven had gracefully swung too, strategically keeping him between them.

"You're alive?" Ven asked, tears brimming his eyes from a flurry of emotions.

"You're dearly beloved Vakar is to blame for that. My rest won't be returned until I've defeated you," Rexous spoke without any conviction. Ven's face grew visibly darker. "I told you on the side of that mountain, all in the north hate the 'Mighty Ven Devar.' Why didn't you just stay away?"

Ven looked behind his shoulder to see Ehan closing the gap, short-handled war scythe at the ready. Rexous too was moving in, with his traditional dirk in his right and Kyst Trident in his left. Ven breathed deeply as a strong gust of wind sprayed them with rain. He drew his gleaming artifact short-sword and twirled it, inviting them forth. Before a strike could be enacted, the falling tree burst through dozens of branches to strike their own with tremendous force. The slippery bark made it impossible for anyone to maintain their balance after the initial shock, and all three of them tumbled off. Rexous managed to dig his dirk into an adjacent tree and catch himself but Ven was thrown clear of any such opportunity. Ehan acted with cunning and hooked the round of his scythe over the branch before completely falling.

On the ground below, the adventurers were thrown asunder from the shock wave of the tree colliding with the ground. Onstera was up to her feet first and saw her plummeting companion.

"Above us!" she shouted for a lack of any other option. Faenla, however, had sensed Ven's descent and was timing his next move perfectly. The majestic wolf sprinted and sprang up one tree, leaping onto the newly fallen tree, then off again to catch Ven a full 15 metres from the ground. The wolf landed hard on his back as the two barrel-rolled back towards their allies.

By the time Faenla and Ven were on their feet, Rexous was already on the forest floor and entering the perimeter re-established by his hunters. Ven noted immediately that not all of these Kyst were from the same settlement but were adorned in uniformed armour, with matching cloaks and hoods sporting pointed brims.

As Rexous came into view, Agan and Scáth were both in disbelief. "You're dead," Scáth blurted in horror at the approaching Kyst.

"I was, and wish to be again. The King of Kyst won't let me die until Ven is brought before him," Rex replied dispassionately. As he got within reaching distance of Ven, Faenla bit the air around Rexous' outstretched hand. The wolf was met with an arrow but Faenla nimbly avoided it.

"Stop!" Ven screamed after hearing the arrow loose and Faenla barely avoiding death. "Just stop, Rexous. You've won. I will come with you, let them turn around."

Rexous put a hand up to stay his hunters and stood in front of Ven who was now on his hands and knees.

"We both know they'd never stop trying to rescue you. They die here, and 'The Mighty Ven Devar' meets whatever destiny has weaved for him. That is the only deal." Rexous spoke with a surprising amount of hate, given his previous indifference. Since his return from the afterlife, nothing had felt the way it used to, yet, this sudden burst of exhilaration at having his revenge, kick-started his emotions. Ven went to quickly pick up his short sword but was kneed in the face before his hand ever reached the hilt.

Agan, Onstera, and Scáth all lunged in anticipation, but so too did Rexous lift his hand. In expert rehearsal, every Kyst Hunter aimed their bows and pulled back on the string. The bow shafts creaking in anticipation of the release.

Two short whistles followed by a third longer one sounded, echoing through the air like bird song. Rexous and his hunters looked around for the origin but it was impossible to discern as the noise around them multiplied and quickly became a buzzing frenzy. Then, arrows soared from above, dropping several of the hunters surrounding the adventurers. In a heartbeat, it transformed into a bloody skirmish as unidentified Kyst adorned in random colours dropped from the trees and leaped from concealment to attack. Onstera and Agan joined the fray without hesitation, both fairing well after learning the ways of the Kyst Hunter from Ven. However, after engaging in combat, the outsiders were hard-pressed to match the dexterity and coordination of these coastal elves. Even Faenla, struggled attacking those who had learned so much from wolf packs.

Ven was quick to have his short-sword in hand, connecting his fist with the nose of Rexous. The former prince stumbled backwards and drew two small curved dirks. Ven quickly dove into a roll, throwing his split daggers as he went. Rexous had to use both dirks to deflect the daggers which left Ven time to draw and drag his razor-edged trident along the Rexous' calf.

"How are you here, alive?" Ven demanded to know as the skilled warriors were soon locked in a series of metal screeching parries.

"You left Vakar when he needed you most. Now we all suffer," Rexous said, as the two warriors shoved their blades apart.

Scáth gave a fierce uncharacteristic war cry as she drove her scimitar into the heart of an attacking elf.

"You trained her well. Just not well enough." Rexous threw a thin glass vial that shattered against Scáth, soaking her in its liquid. After the realization hit him, Ven's eyes went wide and Rex offered him a sinister smile.

"Don't do it," Ven pleaded.

"Ohn na eh," Rexous whispered a spell of recall in Old Elvish and Scáth disappeared in the blink of an eye. As Ven Devar watched his beloved vanish, his heart experienced a new height of pain and anxiety. He looked back to Rexous with fire in his eyes.

"Give her back," Ven demanded with hatred so dark and vile that Rexous wished for a moment he actually could. Rex quickly surveyed the skirmish around him and saw most of his hunters were dead or sorely pressed by the rebel Kyst and Ven's champion companions.

"Want her back? You know where to get her."

Ven let out a scream with a lifetime of rage behind it as he threw his trident at the neck of Rexous. Just a handful of centimetres from its mark, Rexous closed his eyes and blinked from existence much as Scáth had. There were over a dozen allies left and half that many uniformed Kyst. Everyone fighting alongside Ven stopped and watched in terror as he alone slaughtered the remaining Kyst with a display of efficiency unknown to any of them. But most frightening of all, was the sense of blind anger and revenge on display.

Just as he was about to plunge his sword into the chest of a Kyst on his back trying to claw away from this crazed hunter, Faenla bit Ven's bracer just hard enough to stop his killing blow. Ven nearly slashed his sword across Faenla's face when he felt the interruption. Faenla glared at Ven with those coastal blue eyes and snarled fiercely. He stared back at the wolf, tears streaming down his cheeks but still in complete rage. The mighty elf eventually collapsed to his knees and gave another scream of denial. He had lost Scáth to a stupid trick, one he and Vakar had created as children. In truth, it wasn't losing his love so soon after they had decided to be together that had him on his hands and knees screaming at the world. It was the fact he had done the unthinkable by not only verily slaughtering innocent Kyst elves, which was the very first blood of kin he had ever spilled, but also breaking a promise to himself that he would never kill out of anger or fear again. So, he sat there with his blood-soaked weapons laying in the dirt, weeping.

The half-orc walked over to Ven and Faenla. "We'll make this right. Now you must be strong, for Scáth," Agan put a hand on Ven's bobbing shoulders. After several deep breaths the Kyst wiped his face of blood and tears.

An unidentified elf wearing a dark brown cowl cautiously walked over and kicked the still crawling Kyst in the head, knocking him unconscious. She instructed a small group of her hunters to bind the sole survivor and bring him along. Turning to Ven, the Kyst hunter pulled down her cowl, revealing a coral sand coloured skin tone with hair and eyes to match. She then dipped into a great bow.

"I am Ina Enallea, lead Hunter of Shallow Bay. It is my great honour to meet

'The Mighty Ven Devar.' Though I do wish it were on brighter terms," She spoke as if meeting a lifelong hero, though in truth Ina was 150 years older than him. Ven was struck by some degree of shame and embarrassment.

"What is happening here?" He asked with pained frustration and confusion.

"It's my impression that your new ally here had already explained everything?" Ina motioned to Onstera who nodded back as if she had.

"How would you know that?" Ven snapped back.

"Well, we hired her to bring you to us of course. Your old friend has claimed the entire North for himself. Shallow Bay is one of the very last resistances left and surely we could not let you fall into his trap."

By now, Agan was glaring distrustfully at Onstera, and Ven contemplated doing the same. Faenla had let go of Ven and was trying lick at a nasty gash on his shoulder. Several of the Kyst following Ina aided the wolf with tender, expert care.

Ven looked to Agan for his thoughts, and saw the half-orc shaking his head unknowingly.

"Sorry, I'm going for the Scorn first," Ven said while wiping his blades clean. Then, he turned and brushed past Agan and Onstera to check on Faen.

"Ven," Onstera said as if speaking to a younger sibling. "I haven't been with your group long, but something tells me that Scáth would want you to be smart in her rescue."

Ven ignored her, but she clearly saw by the look on Agan's face that he agreed with her. So, she punched the fighter in the shoulder with a great deal of strength.

"She's right. Scáth would want us to be tactical and equipped in our effort to retrieve her. Let us grab a moment's rest and collect ourselves, Ven," Agan urged sensitively. Reluctant at first, Ven had felt Faenla's feelings supported the Shallowbay Kyst for now. He looked back to the elves he had slain so maliciously, burning the image of his massacre clearly in his mind. Truly, he never thought he would be capable of slaying his own people with such ease. Now that he had proved himself wrong, he was left disgusted with himself and felt perhaps that he was slipping down a darker path.

"Fine," he uttered reluctantly.

With that, the group quickly moved out in the direction of Shallow Bay which was only a day away. They kept up a good pace and walked through the night. Agan, Faenla, and Ven kept to the back and were exceptionally quiet as they went. Onstera was near the front conversing with Ina almost the entire way. Agan kept a close eye on Ven the whole day and feared rightfully so for his friend's well-being. Though Ven never openly complained about it, the half-orc was aware of the fears the Kyst had about returning. Agan had his own doubts about what their return would look like, but surely this had gone worse than either had expected.

"Hey," Agan prompted Ven. When he got no response he understood the elf wasn't about to talk, but that didn't matter to him. "Time offers us a great many things. Most importantly, reflection but also the chance to think on our next action. Sometimes we make the right decision and other times not so much. You've only ever done your best Ven, and so you'll see this made right." Ven said nothing and kept his pace, but did manage to find a brief second of reprieve in the encouragement, before it was consumed by hate once more.

The next morning, the group emerged from the tree line onto a rugged and rocky plateau just a metre above the crashing waves. After walking another hour, a great cliff arose beside them and offered shelter from those patrolling or hunting the forest.

"This is not Shallowbay," Ven said to Ina in anger.

"You would be correct. The Hunters and Sages of Shallowbay fled after Vakar's army occupied it. We took up these sea caves as a base of operations for now. I do hope that is okay with you?" Ina genuinely cared to ask.

Ven didn't see the point in asking whether he was okay with it or not. "Fine," he muttered in reply.

Ven and Faenla were afforded a small pocket cave off of a much larger one that housed at least a few hundred Kyst by his estimation. The rock wall that faced the ocean was filled with several dozen fist sized holes that had been carved by erosion over thousands of years. A literal keg of meat was brought in for Faenla and Ven was shocked to see a wooden tub was inside the cave, filled with hot water. By the level of accommodation, he figured that the Shallowbay Kyst had been forced out of their home sometime ago. Ven took his gear off and placed it on an armour stand. He promptly made his way into the tub, took a deep breath and fully submerged himself for as long as his extended breath allowed. He knew after his failure in losing Scáth, that he would not be sleeping this night and found as much rest as he could in meditation. Faenla flopped over onto a bisonbear-fur rug and belched with a full belly; all four legs shot in the air.

Wrapping himself in soft linens, Ven sat on a hay-filled mattress and fingered a plate of fresh berries and seasoned fish. After several hours of disassociation and staring at a mildew covered wall, he heard a soft knock on his sun-bleached wooden door. He shivered with anger as any disturbance was enough to set him off. Faenla sensed this and gave a snort while rolling onto his belly. The huge wolf lumbered over and pawed the door ajar.

The wolf met the eyes of Queen Saphier, who was in genuine surprise to see that the wolf had answered and the was Kyst seated on the bed.

"Your wolf answers the door?" She asked coyly.

"He belongs to no one," Ven replied dryly. Saphier chuckled at that and let herself in, past Faenla.

"My apologies for the intrusion, I simply couldn't sleep knowing the 'Mighty Ven Devar' was just down the hall." As she spoke, she studied the famed Armour of Silva, albeit with modifications and repairs, that the ShadowScorn had made. "It's not every day a queen gets to meet someone more famous than her."

Ven's shoulders slumped with a sigh before standing up. "Forgive me, I should have known. It is a privilege to meet you," he said, dipping into a courteous bow.

"I don't blame you, you were just a little thing then," she replied, running her finger along a silver line of iradinium on the chest piece. Ven understood what she was inferring but he truly did not remember ever making her acquaintance. "You're not such a little thing anymore, are you? No, quite an impressive specimen you turned into."

"I mean no insult, I just don't remember."

"I take no offence, it was a short visit brought on by your old mentor. Although the way he explained it, you were more like a son to him, were you not?" Saphier finally turned to meet Ven's powerful opalescent green eyes with her own that were the colour of jade.

"You knew Renic?" His stormy skin turned a shade darker.

"We grew up together in fact. Renic was not born of Silva, rather here in Shallow Bay. He answered a call to trade knowledge between their hunters and ours when you were found on that boat."

"Why did he never tell me?" He asked. By now Faenla had jumped up on Ven's bed as the fabric popped and hay burst out under the wolf's immense weight. Saphier had stopped beside a particularly large hole in the wall that faced the ocean.

"Renic Devar, like so many of us, did not see borders or communities as individuals from the whole. Our home is the Forest under Āina and on the Sea by Kaia. That's where he believed he came from," the queen explained with reverence for her old friend, and Ven could see how she might be the only person to miss Renic as much as he did. He joined her as they both looked out over the stormy ocean and pouring rain.

"When I entered the Great Northern Rainforest again after so many months, it did not feel as though I remembered it. What has Vakar done?"

"Near the time you left, a Kyst impersonating you with a hoard of Kintar laid waste to thousands of our folk, instilling a fear of death throughout the elves. Vakar offered peace and security during a time where there was only upheaval. After amassing an impressive number to his ranks, he began taking steps to imperialize the north. We were the last independent settlement big enough to defy him and when we dared, well let us say Vakar doesn't take 'no' for an answer."

Ven noted by the way she uncomfortably twitched that something severely unpleasant had occurred. He shook his head, wanting to deny that his dearest friend throughout his whole life was capable of such atrocities, but found the evidence indisputable.

"Now, all that had been in balance since our people's arrival at the dawn of the Second Age, has been thrown into chaos. His hunters work around the clock, decimating numbers and destroying fragile ecosystems. Sages practice increasingly dangerous magic. Feuds between old clans and new break out regularly, each and every one leading to more and more unjust outcomes. He led a military campaign into Claw Canyon over the winter, killing thousands of Kintar without mercy, dwindling their population to one he says 'can no longer threaten us.' We've lost the very bond to nature that made our people so unique." Saphier never stopped looking out over the ocean as her visage remained unyielding.

"I should never have left." Ven choked on the words, recognizing his failure.

"You're not responsible for another's actions. Though you may not wish to admit it, this was always in Vakar, buried somewhere within."

The two were silent for a long while, letting the brine filled breeze sweep through their hair. The hurricane had ceased somewhat, rejuvenating the smell of the sea and flora around them, and covering everything in a dew, highlighting nature's glory. A large flock of SeaRaven's flew across the water, save one that soared straight through the window between them, squawking all the while to land beside Faenla on the bed. The wolf shockingly nuzzled the tiny bird resting on his shoulder.

"Hahaha, hello again, Bird. Pardon the zoo I seemed to have attracted, Queen-" Ven looked with a smile to Queen Saphier only to see her utterly motionless. "-Saphier?" Ven asked, waving a hand in front of her. He heard the descent and inevitable landing of rain cease, the push and pull of the waves stop. He looked outside to see the whole world frozen in time, the air filled with droplets in mid-fall, birds held still in mid-flight. The only sound in all the world was that of Faenla and the SeaRaven. He slowly turned to view them on the bed, and yet what his eyes witnessed, his mind could not comprehend. Two, of what Ven could only guess were Kyst Elves, perhaps what the Kyst looked like at their creation, sat there holding hands. He instantly recognized their state of love for each other, and so too did flashes of ancient sculptures and paintings of Āina and Kaia appear in his mind. For this was truly them, sitting where the Wolf and Bird were just an instant ago. They both turned to regard Ven Devar with a familial smile.

Kaia in all her beauty spoke in such a tone that soothed Ven like the sound of rushing water. Āina's resonant and strong voice reminded him of branches and leaves rustled by the wind. They said together in perfect unison,

"Hello, son."